CUNNINGHAM SECURITY

OVERCOME

A.K. EVANS

Overcome

ISBN: 978-1-7328858-1-3

Editing & Proofreading
Ellie McLove, My Brother's Editor
www.mybrotherseditor.net

Cover Artist
cover artwork © Sarah Hansen, Okay Creations
www.okaycreations.com

Formatting
Stacey Blake at Champagne Book Design
www.champagnebookdesign.com

DEDICATION

To the women who have experienced any form of sexual assault.

Because you deserve better.

Because you own your body. Because the length of your skirt and the sway of your hips shouldn't be considered an invitation. Because you shouldn't have to be fearful. Because the only thing that should matter is if you said yes.

And because there are so many great men out there.

This book is dedicated to them as well.

The men who shouldn't be grouped with the bad apples. Men who are strong and powerful for loads of reasons that have nothing to do with having power or control over a woman. Men who will believe you. Men who will stand beside you. Men who will lift you up and encourage you. Not because you need them to, but because it's what you deserve.

PROLOGUE

Lexi

THIS HAD TO BE A MISTAKE.

Everything I had learned told me that this wasn't how it was supposed to be. It was supposed to look different. Sound different.

I had it wrong. If I ever told anyone, they'd tell me I was mistaken. But something was gnawing away at me inside telling me this wasn't right. It didn't feel good, and it wasn't what I wanted.

But where was the struggle? The blood? The bruises? The cries for help?

This is supposed to happen in an alley behind a dumpster. I'm supposed to be kicking and screaming and fighting.

But I'm not.

This doesn't happen in a dorm room. This doesn't happen in a bed. This doesn't happen with the guy you like.

But it is.

This must be a misunderstanding.

I wore a short skirt. I went on a few dates with him. I agreed to come back to his dorm room tonight. I cuddled up next to him. I leaned in to kiss him. I even enjoyed kissing him.

And in a matter of minutes, it all changed.

When the soft caresses and tender kisses turned into

rough and forceful restraint, the butterflies I felt in my belly disappeared and were replaced by paralyzing fear.

When he rolled me to my back and pinned me to the bed, I froze. I didn't fight. I didn't scream. I didn't try to get away. I only said no and asked him to stop.

The weight of his body hovered over mine.

I said no.

I sank deeper and deeper into the sheets.

But I liked him.

He gripped my wrists above my head.

I said no.

He forced my skirt up around my hips.

Maybe I had been asking for it dressed like this.

He pushed my panties to the side.

I said no.

He smiled through my growing opposition.

But I had flirted with him.

Then he raped me.

And I only said no.

I withdrew. I went somewhere else. Physically, I was still there, but my mind took me to a different place. Finals were coming up next week and I had a paper due in two days. I needed to get back to my dorm so I could finish proofreading that paper. I was always a good student and I focused on that as I lay there silenced and still in the bed of his dorm room.

Despite not wanting it to be there, my mind was suddenly back in the room with my body, and he was still on top of me.

I wanted to scream. It was there, at the back of my throat, but it wouldn't come out. The fear seeped into every part of me, but most especially, it silenced my voice. If I screamed, this might end up looking like an actual sexual assault.

It could be violent and bloody.

It could be worse.

My breath was caught in my throat. Perhaps it got stuck there simply to protect me.

But what about what my parents had told me?

Always stand up for yourself.

Before my parents dropped me off at college, my father gave me a lecture. "Don't go out alone at night. Make sure someone you trust always knows where you are and who you're with. Stay safe. And if someone ever tries to hurt you, you fight back."

I didn't heed his advice. I didn't fight back.

I didn't know for sure, but guessed that it couldn't have been more than twenty minutes later when my attacker finished. He rolled off me and fixed his clothes.

Feeling ashamed and embarrassed, I quickly got up off the bed without making eye contact and pulled my skirt back down.

It was over.

I needed to get out, so I moved toward the door.

But his voice stopped me as I wrapped my hand around the doorknob.

"Don't act like that isn't exactly what you wanted tonight."

That's when I knew.

Maybe I didn't run. Maybe I didn't fight. But just because I didn't fight, didn't mean that I gave my consent.

And just because I liked him doesn't mean it wasn't rape.

CHAPTER 1

Lexi

One hour later

I WALKED INTO THE TWENTY-FOUR-HOUR FREE CLINIC FORTY minutes from campus. The chance of seeing someone I knew was less likely here.

As I walked up to the reception desk, the woman behind the counter looked up at me. "Hi, can I help you?"

Did she really want to help me? Could she?

I swallowed down the emotions bubbling to the surface and barely squeaked out, "I…I'd like to be seen by a doctor."

"Sure. What's your name?

"Lexi Townsend."

She offered a friendly smile and asked, "And what brings you in today, Lexi?"

Could I say it?

I wasn't sure I knew what to call it. Rape seemed like the appropriate word, but I knew him. I liked him. I had been dating him.

"Um, can I…is there a female doctor on staff?"

Understanding washed over her and she moved into action. "Absolutely. Why don't you follow me back and you can complete the paperwork in the exam room?"

I really didn't want to follow anyone anywhere. I wanted

to leave. I wanted to climb in my bed and curl up under the covers. I never wanted to step out in public again. But he hadn't used a condom. Not being seen by a doctor wasn't an option.

"Do you have anyone you'd like me to call for you?" she asked gently, snapping me out of my thoughts.

My family.

I didn't tell her that. What would they think? How would they feel? I'd never bring this devastation on them.

I simply shook my head and decided to follow her into the room. It's not like she could make me feel any worse than I already did.

Once inside the exam room, she handed me a clipboard and said, "Take your time and complete this as best you can. I'm going to get the nurse who will come in and explain what the next steps are. Is there anything I can get you in the meantime?"

A do-over?

"No," I responded. "I just want to get out of here as soon as possible."

She gave me a gentle nod, walked to the door, and ended with, "Candace is the nurse. She'll be in to see you in just a few minutes."

"Thank you," I replied quietly.

Three and a half hours later, I was finally back in my car. I had been poked, prodded, and through a battery of questions, most of which I preferred to not answer. I had no intention of pressing charges or filing a report, but I was strongly encouraged to have the full SANE exam done in case I changed my mind.

While the nurse was incredibly patient and understanding throughout the process, it was the most humiliating experience of my life. The thought that I'd have to relive this nightmare again by filing a report made me sick to my stomach. And I couldn't even begin to think about the heartache my family would go through if they knew what happened.

I merely went to the free clinic to make sure I was physically okay. He hadn't worn a condom and while we'd been on a few dates, I didn't know him well enough to know his history. Before I left, I was given a referral to a therapist. I had no intention of ever mentioning this ordeal again, but I took the therapist's information and slipped it into my purse anyway.

It was just after one in the morning when I got back to my dorm room. I don't think I was ever more grateful for the fact that my roommate rarely spent any nights in our room. I needed to be alone.

Once I was there, I grabbed the items I needed and hurried to the showers where I found the silver lining… lockable shower stalls.

As the water warmed up, I removed my clothes. Stepping under the spray, I found myself continuing to turn the handle toward the hottest setting. No matter that my skin had turned bright red, the heat from the water surprisingly caused no pain. It did little to penetrate through to everything I felt inside.

Keep it together. Three exams. Three exams, a paper, and you're out of here. Just keep it together.

So, that's what I did.

I washed the filth from my body and I kept it together.

Four days later

"You're finished?"

I had just walked out of my last exam and called my mom.

"I'm finished," I answered.

"One year down, three more to go," she replied. She was so proud. "Logan and Luke drove up separately so we'd have more room to bring your stuff home until next semester. They left a few minutes before us, so they'll get there first. Dad and I are about twenty minutes away."

"Okay," I replied. "I'll see you soon."

I disconnected the call and walked back to my dorm. I couldn't wait to see my family. I'd been putting on a brave face for the last few days with the friends I'd made in my first year here, but my heart wasn't in it. I'm not sure if anyone could tell I wasn't myself or if they just assumed it was the stress of finals, but I didn't much care either way. I wasn't coming back.

Not quite ten minutes later, there was a knock on my door.

I looked out the peephole and was immediately overcome with emotion. My hands were shaking as I struggled to open the door. Once I accomplished that feat, I flung myself into Logan's arms and broke down.

"Hey," he comforted, his voice soft as he squeezed me tight. "What's going on, Lex?" He was truly concerned, but I couldn't find any words to give him the truth.

"How'd you get into the building?" I sobbed.

"Someone was walking out as we walked up to the door. They let us in," he answered.

Logan held on to me and shifted me back into the room. Luke stepped in behind him and closed the door. I continued to cry.

"Lexi," Luke called, the worry just as relevant in his voice. "What's wrong?"

I took in a few settling breaths and pulled away from Logan. Immediately, I regretted losing the comfort of his embrace. Trying to gather myself, I moved to Luke and hugged him as I lamented, "I'm sorry."

"It's okay. Are you alright?" Luke wondered.

After giving myself a few more seconds in the security of his arms, I answered, "I've just missed you guys so much. I hate it here."

This took them by surprise.

"What do you mean? You said you loved it here when you came home over the holiday break," Logan reminded me.

I needed to backtrack.

Shaking my head, I tried to cover it up. "I just mean that I hate being so far away from home. I miss you guys."

"It's only two hours away," Luke pointed out.

I didn't respond. Instead, I dropped my gaze to the ground, willing myself to keep it together. Finally, I spoke and told them what I needed.

"I want to change schools," I started. "I want to be closer to home."

Neither of my brothers had a chance to respond before we were interrupted by the ringing of my cell phone.

"Mom?" I answered.

"Hey, sweetie. We're here. Can you let us in?" she asked.

"Yeah," I answered. "Give me a minute."

I ended the call and shared, "Mom and Dad are here. I'll go let them in."

By the time I got down to the front door, I managed to compose myself. I greeted my parents with hugs before we walked back up to my room and dove into moving me back home for the summer.

Just over an hour after they all arrived, I left school knowing I'd never step foot on the campus again.

Eight weeks later

I was sitting in my car contemplating if this was the right choice.

I should have suspected I would end up here, but I didn't. Not necessarily because I thought it was bad, but because I didn't want to talk about it. I didn't want to relive it.

Not only that, it was going to serve as a bit of a blow to my pride that I even needed it. Wouldn't this just mean that I wasn't strong enough to take care of myself?

But something happened and I should have known it would eventually happen.

My mistake was believing I could push my rape and all the emotions it stirred up to the back of my mind where I could bury it without ever having it resurface.

With each day that passed, I kept pushing forward, remaining focused on what I had to do. If I kept myself busy, I wouldn't have to worry about the thoughts I knew could take over and completely break me.

I left school about two months ago and talked to my parents about transferring to a school closer to home. My parents lived in Rising Sun, Wyoming, and I settled on a school in the neighboring town of Windsor. They didn't think twice and immediately helped me make the arrangements. I also decided I didn't want to live on campus. I told my parents I'd prefer to get an apartment in Windsor that was off campus, but close enough that I wouldn't have to travel too far when the weather got bad. They were supportive of my choice, only after I explained that I wanted to have a quiet place to myself without the worry of a roommate. Being the person I was, they never suspected that I wanted to remove myself from any situation that involved constant interaction with people I didn't know. I'd always been outgoing, so the idea that I'd suddenly want to be secluded from others would never cross their minds.

I wanted to finish school.

I did not want to meet new people and make new friends.

People couldn't be trusted.

Of course, I began wondering if I could trust myself because I was making decisions believing I knew what was best for me.

And while I should have expected it, I was naive. Every night, I struggled to get a decent night's rest. At first, I had trouble falling asleep. Once I managed to get to sleep, I only got in a couple hours before I was woken by nightmares.

In those nightmares, I relived it.

My arms being pinned over my head. His body over mine. The smell of his cologne. And worst of all, him taking something that didn't belong to him, something I didn't want to give.

I needed to find a way to exhaust myself. I was so tired, but I couldn't sleep.

So, I had purchased a few small dumbbells on my own, but managed to convince my parents to let me take the elliptical from their house when I moved. Up until the point I'd asked them if I could take it, it had served mostly as a decorative piece in their finished basement or a place to hang a blanket. Since nobody was using it, my parents didn't require much convincing.

I'd been in my new apartment for three weeks now and hadn't had the elliptical moved yet. And every night since I moved into the apartment I'd experienced nightmares. When I was at my parents' house, I had them, but not like I was now.

I wasn't sure if it was because I was alone now, but I knew I couldn't go home. Being on edge all the time around my parents would be a surefire way to bring this hideous situation to light. I refused to do that to them and, instead, asked Logan and Luke if they'd move the elliptical for me.

Three hours ago, that's what they did. Only, while they were there, something happened.

Logan knocked on my bedroom door and told me they had just finished reassembling the elliptical in the spare bedroom. When I walked into the room, he went into the bathroom on the opposite side of the hall.

I was standing there with Luke talking to him when I felt someone come up behind me. From the time we were kids, my older brothers and I always joked around and spooked one another and our parents, so Logan didn't know he shouldn't have done something he'd done so many times before. He put his hands on my sides and made a noise to scare me.

I lost it.

I turned around so fast and lashed out at him.

"What the hell is wrong with you?!" I shouted, my arms coming out and pushing him away from me.

"Relax, Lex, it was just a joke."

"It's not a fucking joke, Logan," I shot back, my heart pounding so hard in my chest. "Grow the fuck up already!"

He stared at me in shock.

Never.

I'd never spoken to him like that before.

"Lexi, what's wrong?" Luke chimed in.

My gut twisted in despair. I lost my cool in front of them.

Shaking my head, I apologized, "I'm sorry. I'm fine. It's just been a long couple of weeks with switching schools, getting moved, and trying to find a part-time job."

My brothers gave me looks that told me they didn't necessarily believe I was giving them the truth.

"Are you sure?" Logan asked.

I nodded quickly and repeated, "I'm sorry, Logan. I shouldn't have said that."

He held my gaze a minute before he quickly brushed it off. "No harm done."

"Thanks again for bringing this here for me today," I told the both of them, waving my hand in the direction of the exercise equipment. "I really appreciate it."

"You're welcome," Luke replied. "You need anything else?"

I shook my head.

At that, Luke and Logan left. The second they walked out of my apartment, I fell to the floor and cried my eyes out. They were two of the four people in my life that I knew I could always trust and depend on to be there for me, and I'd just treated Logan like garbage.

Guilt consumed me more than it had over the last two months and I couldn't control it any longer. I cried for a long time, hating myself for everything I'd done. And for everything I didn't do.

When I'd gotten it all out, I grabbed my purse, my keys, and got in my car.

Now that I was parked here and had replayed the awful things in my head, I made my decision. I got out and walked into the building.

When I entered, I was greeted by two women. One was sitting at a reception desk, the other was standing beside it. They looked at me with friendly faces and both said, "Hi."

"Hi," I began. "I'm looking for Dr. Lane."

"That's me," the woman who was standing declared.

My eyes were pleading with hers when I stated, "I think I need your help."

CHAPTER 2

Lexi

Four years later

MY PHONE STARTED RINGING. I HAD JUST PULLED INTO A parking spot outside of the little café in downtown Windsor where I was scheduled to meet Elle for a brunch meeting in fifteen minutes.

It was early April, so the weather hadn't quite warmed up enough to feel like spring had arrived. The highs were in the low forties and since it was still only late morning, the current temperature was somewhere in the mid-to-high thirties. I left my car running with the heat on while I fished my phone out of my purse.

Looking down at the display I saw that it was Elle calling me.

"Hey, El. What's up?"

She sounded a bit flustered when she responded, "I'm sorry, Lex. I am just now leaving home, so I'm running behind. I should be there in about twenty minutes, though."

"Okay. I just got here; I'll run in and grab a seat. And probably a coffee, too. Do you want me to order you a cup of tea?"

"That'll be perfect. See you in a few."

I disconnected with Elle, turned off the car, and gathered up my things for our meeting before heading into the café.

Stepping inside, I found a small booth for two that was unoccupied. I claimed the booth and settled in on the side facing the front door so I could see Elle when she walked in.

After ordering my coffee and Elle's tea, I pulled out my laptop and my day planner to get my thoughts organized.

I worked as Elle's publicist. She was a musician and mostly performed at local venues. The two of us had grown close over the last few months. Not quite a year ago, Elle found herself in a bit of a situation that resulted not only in a near-death experience, but also left her with the need for a publicist. Our mutual friend and my former employer, Monroe, got us hooked up with each other, and the rest is history.

I graduated from college last year and, despite sending out multiple resumes for jobs in my field just before graduating, I hadn't had any luck finding a position. My brother, Luke, got a call from his best friend, Stone, telling him that his girlfriend was looking for a receptionist for her new dance studio. Monroe was Stone's girlfriend at the time. With no other job offers on the table, I jumped at the opportunity.

I still work with Monroe now, but no longer as her receptionist. She's got several dance instructors and a couple of receptionists working with her. I merely work with her on occasion when she's looking for advice on an event she wants to host. Once she got me hooked up with Elle, I decided to take a risk and try my hand at opening up my own agency. Of course, I was currently a one-woman show, but I was determined to prove myself.

Elle was my first big client. I was just happy that the two of us clicked immediately. It wasn't long before I was not only acting as her publicist, but took over the role of agent and manager as well. My years at college left a lot to be desired, but they gave me the foundation to successfully pursue this career. For Elle, I was everything wrapped up into one and I did it partly because I knew how, but mostly because I considered her to be my friend. And I had learned a long time ago that when you find someone who is a good person, you should hang on to them.

My other big client was Blackman Boards. Luke is a snowboarder and is sponsored by Blackman Boards. Just a few months ago, Luke and his two best friends competed in the Olympics. Luke won the gold medal in his discipline; I was so proud of him. Prior to the guys going out to Salt Lake City for the Olympics, I managed to use my skills to snag them a spot on a nationally televised morning talk show. When Wes, the owner of Blackman Boards and one of Luke's best friends, heard what I had done, he wanted to hire me.

As lucrative as the full-time position with Blackman Boards would have been, I stood firm in my decision to have my own agency. So, I politely declined the job offer, but Wes and I came to an agreement. When they needed a publicist, I'd be there.

I was flipping through my day planner to review my packed schedule for the upcoming week when I heard, "I'm so sorry, Lex."

I glanced up in the direction of the voice and saw Elle striding toward the booth.

"It's okay, Elle. I've been using the time to try and organize my thoughts on my upcoming week anyway," I responded as she settled herself into the seat across from me.

"Busy?"

I nodded, "Busiest week yet. But potentially a very promising one. After our meeting this morning, I've got an appointment to look at two office spaces. Tomorrow and Wednesday are full. Both days each have one more office showing and several meetings with current and potential clients. I'm hoping one of the office spaces will work well and I can make a decision on renting one of them by no later than Thursday because traveling all over Windsor and Rising Sun for meetings is rapidly losing its appeal."

"I've got to be honest," she started. "That sounds like zero fun. You know me; I hear the word schedule and it makes me shudder."

I let out a laugh and agreed, "It's a daunting week, but I'm up for the challenge. I like being busy anyway. It keeps my mind focused on productive things."

"Well, your determination is certainly paying off. I still can't believe you've only just graduated a year ago and you're already opening your own agency."

"And it's all thanks to you and your brother," I shared. "Between you and Wes sending referrals my way, I'll be busy for the next few months."

She grinned at me. "That's what happens when you're good at what you do."

I appreciated her positive praise. It felt good to know that people I knew and respected for their talent thought I was capable of handling some of their most important affairs.

Elle and I ordered our food and discussed some of the details for the meet and greet while we waited for the food to arrive. We managed to get through most of that by the time our food was set in front of us.

I was happy Elle had suggested the café because the coffee was some of the best I'd ever had and the food was right up there as well. It made me hope even more that I'd be able to find a location for my new office close by so that I'd be able to swing in each morning for a cup of coffee on the way to work.

We had just finished eating when we both heard, "Elle? Lexi?"

We turned our heads to the side of our booth and that's when I saw him.

Cruz Cunningham.

I met Cruz about a year ago when I started working at Monroe's studio. He worked for his brother's private investigation and security firm and they had been hired to update the security system in the studio. Cruz happened to be there when I went in for my interview. Monroe introduced us after the interview, but I didn't stick around long enough to chat.

He terrified me.

No, that's wrong. He didn't terrify me the way most men did. In fact, the reason he scared me was because, oddly enough, when I was around him I didn't feel the way I typically did around most men.

"Hey, Cruz," Elle greeted him, joyfully. Elle was dating one of Cruz's older brothers, Levi. Levi was the owner of Cunningham Security. "What are you doing here?"

"I just left the office. Heading out to do some fieldwork on a case, but wanted to stop and grab reinforcements," he answered as he jerked his head toward the counter. "I didn't expect to see the two of you here."

He might have been talking to the both of us then, but it was clear from the fact that he wouldn't take his eyes off me that he wanted me to give him an answer.

"Just having a meeting over brunch," I managed to get out.

The truth of the matter was that I had a bit of a problem with this whole Cruz situation and it made it difficult to be myself. I wasn't used to not feeling anxiety around men I didn't know well. For a very long time, the only men I could even think about being around were Logan, Luke, and my father. A couple months of therapy helped to reduce the uneasiness I felt around familiar faces and it had improved tenfold, but there was always some apprehension lingering.

This didn't mean that I didn't feel any nervousness around Cruz. It's just that what I felt wasn't consumed with dread. It was a butterflies-in-my-belly feeling. That reaction to him is what left me unsettled. This was mostly because the last time I had that feeling… well, it changed my life in a way I never thought possible.

"I figured that much considering the upcoming meet and greet Levi mentioned," he began. "I just thought you'd meet at Elle and Levi's place instead of coming all the way down here."

I didn't respond.

Instead, I stared up at him and drank in the sight of him. He had a head full of hair, its coloring a light shade of brown. It was a few weeks past the point of needing a cut because it began to curl around the back of his ears and at his neck. To be quite honest, I think it looked fantastic.

He had striking facial features. A set of blue eyes that reminded me of the color of a starry night sky. A strong jaw and a great set of lips. Cruz was physically fit, easily a requirement for the job he worked.

I was focusing on all of this and trying to figure out why I was suddenly noticing any man's appearance, let alone Cruz's, when Elle broke in and explained, "Lexi's looking at places for her new office after our meeting, so we decided to just meet here instead."

Cruz brought his gaze to mine and dazzled me with his smile. It was then I realized he had another great feature…perfect teeth.

Trying to snap myself out of it, I offered, "Downtown Windsor has all the best spots for real estate and some are reasonably priced. I'm looking to get something figured out before the end of this week."

"Nice," he started. "If you need any recommendations on locations, feel free to ask. I'm in this area a lot because of the firm."

Even if I did need help, I wouldn't ask him. No way. But I didn't think it'd be very nice of me to be rude when he was simply offering help, so I returned a friendly smile. "Thanks, Cruz, I appreciate that."

He gave me a nod before he concluded, "Alright, well, I've got to head out and get to work on this case."

"See you later," Elle chimed in.

"Bye," I offered with a wave of my hand.

I watched as Cruz walked over to the counter, paid, and left with his coffee and a bag.

When I brought my attention back to Elle, she was grinning from ear to ear.

"What's wrong with you?" I asked.

"You like him," she speculated.

Oh no. I couldn't deal with this.

"No I don't. I barely even know him."

She began nodding and insisted, "Yes, you do. From the minute you realized he was standing next to our booth until the second he walked out of here, your eyes never left him."

I shrugged my shoulders. There was no denying that Cruz was handsome; anyone could see that. I just wasn't sure how to break it to Elle that I wouldn't be going there.

Needless to say, I didn't have to figure out what to say because Elle went on. "And, just saying, he was not even remotely interested in the fact that I was sitting here. I think the feeling is mutual, Lex."

"It's not happening," I maintained. "And he already knows that."

Elle's brows drew together. "What? What does that mean?"

I took in a deep breath and let it out before I explained, "A couple months ago we were both at Luke's house. Nikki had just given me a makeover when Luke walked in and asked us to meet him downstairs. When we got there, he was standing there with Cruz. This was back when Luke had hired Cruz to investigate the situation with Nikki's father. I'm sure you recall that day because it was the only time I was ever late for a meeting with you. Remember?"

"Oh, that's right. But you never told me about something happening with you and Cruz."

"Nothing did happen with Cruz and me. I ended up leaving Luke's after I got off the phone with you, but Cruz left at the same time. He walked alongside me as we made our way to our cars. Before I got in my car and left, he asked me if I'd consider going out on a date with him."

"And you didn't say yes?!" she asked, clearly shocked.

I shook my head.

"Why not?" she pressed me further.

I looked around the café. It had a steady flow of customers, but nobody was looking in our direction. Elle and I weren't even on anyone's radar. I realized I wanted to share it with her.

"El," I began. "I have something I want to tell you."

Suddenly, she sat up a little straighter. She could hear the trepidation in my tone.

"Okay," she stated. There was so much caution in her voice.

I waited a moment before I spoke. I hadn't shared it with anyone besides my therapist.

"You know how close we've grown over the last few months, Elle. I know what you went through before you and I met and I believe you are someone I can share this with without any judgment."

"Of course. Anything at all. What's going on?"

I took in another deep breath. "I was raped four years ago."

Elle gasped.

I spoke quickly to help dissolve questions and concerns I'm sure she immediately had filtering through her mind. "I'm alright. Well, I'm getting there. It happened at the end of my freshman year in college."

"Oh, Lexi. I'm so sorry. I had no idea or I never would have just pushed you on the subject of Cruz."

"It's okay; you didn't know. But I'm not in a place where I'm comfortable pursuing a relationship yet. As much as I want to get there, I just don't think I'm ready yet. I thought I could deal with everything on my own. I switched schools as soon as I finished my freshman year. I only felt marginally better not being at the same school with my attacker, but it wasn't enough. I started seeing a therapist just before I started my sophomore year in school. It took me a long time to even talk about it with my doctor. Like I said, I'm getting there, but I have a lot of trust issues."

Elle's eyes were filled with tears.

"Apart from my therapist, you're the first person I've told."

"Lexi, love. I'm so, so sorry this happened to you," she lamented. "Thank you for telling me, because even though I don't know all the right things to say, I want to be there for you if you want to talk about it."

At her words, I felt a peace and warmth settle inside me. I wasn't sure what I expected the first time I told anyone, but I knew this felt good.

"Knowing you'll be there to listen is all I think I need. That and please don't tell anyone else. It's something I need to do in my own time. I dread telling my family because I'm pretty sure they won't take it well."

"Until you're ready to tell anyone else, Lexi, I'll be here to listen to you. And you can trust that everything will stay between the two of us. If you need me there when you do decide to tell your family or anyone else, you know you can count on me."

"I know. I wouldn't have told you if I didn't," I assured her. "Lately, I've been feeling the urge to talk about it. Unfortunately, I don't have the kind of time nor are we in a place right now that is conducive to having this type of conversation. I feel like I need to tell the whole story to someone, though."

"You tell me the time and place and I'll be there."

"Would tomorrow night around six-thirty or seven work for you? I'm going to see my therapist tonight, so tomorrow works better for me."

"No problem. Tomorrow works for me."

"I think I'm going to call Nikki, too."

"I think that's a great idea."

Before I could say anything else, my phone rang. I looked down at the display and saw that my brother, Logan, was calling.

"Hey, Logan. What's up?"

"I need to cancel my appointment with you for this afternoon."

That was odd.

"Is everything alright?"

"Yeah," he started. "I know you said you had a really tight schedule this week, so I'm giving up my appointment. One of my clients here at the shop needs your expertise on a project he's working on. It'll be huge for your career."

Logan still didn't know. He didn't know why I tried to stick to only female clients. Wes was really the only male client I had, but I didn't have the trust concerns with him. He was Elle's brother and I trusted him like I trusted Luke and Logan; I'd known him nearly my entire life.

"Um, well," I stammered, trying to think of a way out.

Logan cut in, "I'm not going anywhere else, so we can reschedule to meet on my stuff another time. I don't want you to miss out on this opportunity, Lex. You can still come here for the meeting. When I told him about what you do, he asked if I could arrange a meeting quickly. That's why I'm giving up my spot."

At least Logan had arranged for the meeting to take place at his shop. He would be there and it eased my concerns a bit. I'd just go to this meeting, explain how it wasn't going to work for me, and get out of it that way.

"Alright. I'll stop over as scheduled then."

There was no excitement in my voice.

"You're welcome, Lexi," Logan teased.

If only he knew.

"I'm sorry. Thanks, Logan. I appreciate the referral," I started. "I'm in a meeting right now, so I've got to go. I'll see you later."

I disconnected with my brother and looked to Elle. "Sorry about that."

"It's no problem at all," she remarked.

"Alright, so we're set with the meet and greet details on our end. You're going to have Levi get security squared away or, I guess I should say, Levi is probably already doing that without you having to ask."

Elle laughed before she confirmed, "Precisely."

"Great," I began. "I have to head out now to check out those two offices, but we're good for tomorrow night, right?"

Elle's face softened before she declared, "Of course. Let me know if you need anything between now and then."

"Will do," I replied as we both stood and grabbed our things.

The two of us walked outside together. Before she took off in the opposite direction toward her car, I called out to Elle.

"Yeah, Lex?"

"Thanks for listening."

She gave me a nod and a wink before taking off.

At that, I got in my car and took a deep breath. I had done it. I finally confided in someone about what happened and I was proud of myself.

One step at a time.

I was determined to get back all the pieces of myself that were taken from me. I just knew that some would be harder to find than others.

CHAPTER 3

Lexi

"HOW DID OFFICE HUNTING GO?"

I was back in Rising Sun at Logan's automotive shop.

"Very good, actually. I saw two places earlier this afternoon and the second one is nearly perfect. I still have a couple more locations to check out over the next two days, though, so I don't want to make any final decisions until then."

I paused a moment before I went on, "So, who is this client?"

"Grant Chambers. He's the senior VP of Logistics and Distribution for Glazier's Supply."

"Oh," I started. "He doesn't own the company, right?"

Logan shook his head. "No. He's the head of a new project the company is working on. The guy makes a lot of money and has been bringing his cars here for years to get performance work done on them. I have one of his cars here now and had to call him about something for that. We got to talking and he mentioned this new project he's in charge of seeing through. He didn't give me many details other than to explain that it was a nonprofit and they're hoping to get some charitable donations for it. I figured you'd probably be able to help."

I liked the fact that the guy was a longtime client of Logan's, but I was still uneasy about working with a man I didn't know. I didn't have an opportunity to respond to my brother or fret about the situation because one of his employees yelled out from across the shop, "Logan!"

We turned our heads toward his employee and that's when I also saw a man dressed in a suit walking toward us. It had to be him.

The man made his way over. Once he was standing in front of us, Logan made introductions.

"Lexi, this is Grant Chambers. Grant, this is my sister, Lexi."

Mr. Chambers held his hand out to me. I hesitated a moment, but realized Logan would know something was up if I didn't shake the man's hand. I lifted my hand, tensed the moment his hand touched mine, and quickly let go as I offered, "It's nice to meet you."

"I was just telling Lexi that the project you need help with is to find funding for a nonprofit."

Mr. Chambers nodded and confirmed, "Yes. I've been working on this the last few weeks. I've got the location locked down and a staff ready to go, but we want to get the public's help in continuing to provide funding for the nonprofit."

"Have you opened?"

"Not yet. It's been tough trying to balance work, this project, and home life. I've got two teenage daughters at home. My wife makes sure they get to practices, but I've got to be there for the cheerleading competitions for one and the basketball games for the other. Needless to say, I'm about a week behind and I can't delay opening much longer."

He was married and had two teenage daughters. This news instantly made me feel better.

"I can imagine how full your schedule must be, Mr.

Chambers. My schedule is pretty tight this week with appointments, but I do have time in the evenings open if there's a real need to push for this to be done quickly. I also have quite a bit of open space next week where I'd really be able to get a lot accomplished. Are you just looking for exposure for the nonprofit to gain donors? If so, that should be relatively easy to accomplish on a tight schedule. Of course we'll need to discuss details of the target audience. What did you say the organization was?"

"I didn't, but it's WAAR. And please, call me Grant."

What?

I scrunched up my nose and my brows furrowed. I had no idea what this was.

"I'm sorry… did you say war?" I asked, feeling sheepish.

Grant chuckled and clarified, "W-A-A-R. It's an acronym for Windsor Against Abuse and Rape. It's a rape crisis center where victims of sexual assault and abuse of any kind can seek refuge if needed along with access to the necessary services that'll help them through these traumatizing experiences."

I just managed to catch myself from audibly gasping.

"Mr. Chambers," I started before he cut me off.

"Grant."

I nodded and continued, "Grant. This sounds like a magnificent organization and I sincerely wish you all the best with it, but I'm not sure I'm going to be the best fit for you."

"Are you crazy, Lex?" Logan broke in.

I had almost forgotten he was standing there.

My eyes went to his and he continued, "I had no idea what the organization was when Grant and I spoke earlier today, but I think this is incredible. Can you imagine the number of people you'd be helping by using your talents to bring funding to the center?"

He had me there. I couldn't deny how incredibly

important it was that victims of sexual assault receive treatment to help them cope after suffering through such a heinous crime. I was seriously stuck.

I turned my attention back to Grant. "You're just looking for me to help promote the organization to gain donors to support your operations, correct?"

"Mostly. The truth is, we want the donations, but they'll mean nothing if the victims don't know we're there to help. We want to spread the word and let people know they have a local resource with highly skilled professionals accessible to them."

I was in a tough spot.

"Can you give me the night to think it over?" I asked. "I can take down your number now and give you a call tomorrow morning with my answer."

"Sure," he agreed.

I took down his number and just as he was about to walk out, he turned around and made one last-ditch effort to convince me. "I've always trusted Logan when it comes to recommendations he's made on my cars. When I told him about this, he insisted you were the right person for the job. I trust his judgment on this. I hope you'll take his words to heart. There are no words to describe what WAAR will mean to my wife and daughters. There's also no telling how many people you'll help in working with us on this. Please take the time to consider that before you make a final decision."

"I will."

At that, Grant left.

"You'd be foolish to pass up this opportunity, sidekick," Logan lectured from beside me.

That was the nickname Logan and Luke had dubbed me with after the three of us had successfully pranked our parents when we were younger. I demanded they allow me to be in on the fun, and when I delivered side bursting laughter on several occasions, they gave me the name. It stuck for all these years.

"I didn't say I was passing it up. I just want to think about it. You both said it yourselves. This is such an important cause; I think it needs to be handled properly."

"Even more reason you should oversee it. Have faith in yourself, Lex. You're a natural at this. I have no doubt you'll go above and beyond to make sure these victims get the help they need."

He was right. I would.

It was the kind of thing I was so passionate about, I'd even consider doing it pro bono. Not that I was able to do anything pro bono since I was really trying to get myself up and running. This was just that important that it would have felt wrong for me to profit from it.

"I appreciate the vote of confidence, Logan. I promise I won't consider it lightly."

Logan settled his hand on the top of my head and ruffled my hair. "Alright, I've got to get back to work. Let me know what you decide to do and don't hesitate to reach out to me if you need help with the new office… whether it's deciding on one or moving into one once you settle on it."

"Thanks, Logan."

"Anything for you, Lexi."

"This sounds like great progress."

I was sitting across from my therapist, Dr. Camille Lane. She was the woman solely responsible for helping me keep it together all these years. I knew the amount of work I had done personally was something to be proud of, but I couldn't diminish her role in all of it.

I had just told her about the first of two things I needed to share with her: that I'd finally told someone other than her about my rape.

"It is," I agreed. "I just can't seem to get over the feeling of relief I felt as soon as I told someone. And it blows my mind that I'm looking forward to sharing it with someone else. I didn't expect it would feel this way."

"What did you expect?" Dr. Lane asked.

I shrugged my shoulders before I answered, "Disappointment. Blame. Judgment."

"Why do you think that is?"

"I don't know. All these years I just thought that if I told someone they'd see it differently. I guess I always assumed that they'd think I should have fought back or that I could have avoided it."

Dr. Lane reiterated what she'd been telling me for years. "Your response to what you experienced is completely normal. In fact, an overwhelming number of individuals have the same reaction. Freezing is the most common response to trauma."

"I know, but now I feel guilty."

"About what?"

"It's been four years. I haven't trusted anyone to be there for me through this other than you. Part of me believes that I should have given them the opportunity to help me through it. Of course, the other part of me is terrified of disappointing them."

"While so many individuals can experience a similar version of sexual assault, the healing process is different for everyone. The truth is, you've found a way to help yourself heal. While there's no doubt that an extended support system can be beneficial, it's not something you need to rush yourself to have."

"Things are changing for me," I began. "My life is no longer school. I want to have a successful career doing what I love and I don't want to be hindered by this anymore."

"Do you believe that it's hindering your ability to be successful?"

"To a degree. My bigger concern is that people who love me want to see me do well, so they're offering their support by sending referrals my way."

Dr. Lane didn't respond. She gave me a minute to collect my thoughts before I went on to explain the second thing I needed to discuss with her.

"Logan gave up his meeting time with me today so that one of his clients could take his appointment slot. It was a man and I was initially very hesitant, but I couldn't just say no because Logan would know something was wrong. He'd be so disappointed."

"Disappointed?"

"That I didn't tell him. That I kept this to myself for so long. Mostly? That I didn't trust him with this. He's going to be devastated to know that he made things more uncomfortable for me."

"Do you blame him for putting you in those situations?"

I shook my head furiously. "Not at all. He doesn't know."

She let that settle in.

After it did, I dropped the news on her. "The client wants me to help with the opening of a rape crisis center."

It took her a second before she spoke. "Are you planning to accept the job?"

"Do you think I should?"

After giving me a knowing smile, she responded, "You know I can't give you that answer. You have to decide what is right for you."

I took in a deep breath. "I was really hoping you'd throw

me a bone here and tell me what to do. This organization is necessary. I wouldn't care if there were five others in the city; there can never be too much help for this. But this hits so close to home for me. I just don't know if I'm up to the challenge. To be honest, I never expected this and, going into this meeting, I thought the biggest hurdle was going to be coming up with a plausible excuse so that I wouldn't have to work with a man."

Dr. Lane broke it down for me. "Let's take it one hurdle at a time. Before you decide on what working for the center will mean for you personally, how do you feel about the fact that it'll require you to work with a man?"

"Initially it bothered me. A lot. He's a long-standing client of my brother's shop, so that helps a little bit. But it was what he said before he left the meeting that made me feel a bit more at ease."

"And what was that?" she wondered.

"Aside from reiterating how many people I could play a part in helping, he said that he couldn't begin to describe what the organization would mean to his wife and two teenage daughters. I can't help feeling like one of them might have experienced some form of sexual assault and he's doing this so he can feel like he's helping or making a difference. Deep down I know there are good people… good men in the world. It's just been very hard for me to not feel that anxiety around them. But hearing what was almost desperation in his voice made me believe that he is one of those good men."

Dr. Lane questioned me on the next part of the problem. "So, aside from how you feel about working with a man on this, how do you feel about the cause?"

"Of course I believe in it. I just don't know if being part of it will set me back."

"What role would you play?"

"Mostly just spreading the news about it. There are two parts to that, though. I'd need to try and solidify financial backers whose donations will help pay the operating costs so that the center will remain free to the victims. That's the easy part. I'd also have to get the word out to the victims. That's the hard part. The logistics of it are easy; the emotional part of it is what's difficult."

I paused a moment and thought about it. Dr. Lane left me to it.

"I want to do it," I finally declared. "I think I'll be fine as long as I do my job and stick to that."

That was the reality. I had plenty of valid concerns about taking on this project. Concerns so legitimate that, should anyone know the reason behind them, most people wouldn't blame me for declining to take on the job. But when I thought long and hard about it, I knew it wouldn't help me. I wanted to heal. I didn't want this awful incident that happened four years ago to continue to plague my life every day. I wanted to own my choices. I wanted to be the one in control of my decisions. This felt like my first real attempt to give myself that control.

So, I was going to take it.

I was going to grab hold of this opportunity to prove to myself how far I'd come. In the end, I knew I'd be successful because not only was I capable of it, but this cause was too important to me to allow it to be anything but a victory.

After talking a bit longer with Dr. Lane, I left and made my way home to my apartment.

I was still in the same apartment my parents had helped me with when I transferred schools. They'd supported me through college, but as soon as I graduated I wanted to take that burden from them. When Monroe offered me a steady job and I got a couple months of consistent income under my belt, I took over full responsibility of my living expenses.

I liked where I lived. My apartment wasn't a place I planned to live in forever, but I was happy here for the time being. The space had become familiar and it was my own.

I made myself a quick dinner and called Nikki. She'd been officially dating my brother Luke since last fall, though they'd hooked up with each other prior to that. Luke was head over heels in love with her, and it filled me with such happiness to see them finally together in a meaningful way.

"Hey, Lexi. What's up?" she answered after the third ring.

"Hi, Nikki," I greeted her. "Are you free tomorrow evening? I have something important I need to talk to you about."

"I think so. I have appointments at the salon until about five-thirty, but I'm free afterward. Is everything okay?"

"Yeah. I don't want to talk about it over the phone, so if you could hang tight until tomorrow around six-thirty to seven, I'd appreciate it."

"No problem, babe. Where are we meeting?" she asked.

"My place, if that's alright. Elle's going to be here, too."

"I'll be there," she announced.

"Thanks, Nik. Oh, by the way…I don't want you to lie to Luke about this, but I'd prefer if you not tell him that I've got something serious to talk to you about. Can you be discreet for the time being?"

Without hesitation, she responded, "Absolutely."

The two of us chatted for a bit before hanging up. Afterward, I moved to the spare room in the apartment where I had all my workout equipment stored.

After the rape, I had such a hard time sleeping. I found that if I worked out just before bed, it would help exhaust me so that I could get a few hours of rest. But then, several months after I started seeing Dr. Lane, I learned I no longer needed the elliptical. I'd grown so accustomed to exercising after a long day, though, that I didn't stop working out. It kept me in shape and made me feel refreshed, so I stuck with it.

I got in a forty-five-minute workout before calling it a night. Then I showered and got myself ready for bed. When I climbed into bed, I let the events of the day filter through my mind. I thought about everything I'd accomplished over the course of the last four years and let that settle in me. Just before I drifted off to sleep, I told myself how proud I was for not allowing myself to continue to be a victim and that in the morning I'd take the next steps to continue fighting for what I deserved.

CHAPTER 4

Lexi

IT WAS TWENTY-FIVE MINUTES BEFORE I WAS SCHEDULED TO BE AT A showing for another office space. Since it was close by and I had some time to kill, I decided to make a stop in Colvert's Café again for my daily dose of caffeine.

After I parked in the lot, I pulled out my phone and made the call I promised I would. It rang twice before I heard, "Hello?"

"Hi, Grant. This is Lexi Townsend."

I was met with silence, so I added, "I met with you yesterday at Logan's shop."

He was silent a moment longer before he responded, "Oh, yes. Good morning, Lexi. Excuse me for the momentary lapse in memory. I just got off the phone with another call and my mind was still on that conversation. Please tell me you are calling with good news."

"It's okay. I've certainly been preoccupied before, so I completely understand. And yes, the reason I'm calling is to give you good news. I'd definitely like to oversee the publicity for the WAAR project."

Grant audibly sighed.

"Thank you. You have no idea how much stress you are helping me avoid here."

I let out a small laugh and noted, "You're welcome, but I have to be honest. After having the opportunity to think on it, I'm just really looking forward to being part of something so important."

"Well, you're a lifesaver in my book. So, what do you need to get things going?"

"I'm thinking we should set up a meeting. Originally, I didn't think I'd have any time to get together this week, but one of my clients for Friday morning emailed me and said she needed to reschedule that appointment. I could squeeze you in then if you're free to meet."

"I'll make that work," he announced.

"Great. Can you meet at ten on Friday morning at Colvert's Café?"

To set myself at ease, I preemptively decided that it would be best to meet at a public place. Since this was going to be a new experience for me, I wanted to be in control of the location. Much to my relief, Grant agreed. Before we hung up, I gave him my email address and asked him to send over all information and details he had on the center. I wanted to go into our meeting with a full understanding of what had been decided on to this point.

After finishing my call, I turned off my car and made my way into the café. I stepped inside, placed my order, paid, and moved to the side to wait while the woman standing in line behind me gave her order.

As the barista called out my name, I lifted my hand to grab the cup of coffee while simultaneously glancing at the clock on the wall behind him. I had time to make it to my appointment, but it was likely I was just going to make it if I didn't hurry.

Once my coffee was securely in my hand, I turned quickly while looking down and instantly regretted it. I had collided with a hard body and all I felt was massive burning on the back of my hand, my wrist, down my arm, and at the base of my throat.

"Ow!" I shouted dropping the now mostly empty cup to the ground.

Of course, this was at the same time I heard, "Whoa. Are you okay?"

"It's burning," I rasped, as I hastily attempted to remove my jacket.

After I had my jacket off, I pushed back my coffee-soaked sleeve and saw the skin was bright red.

"Come with me," I heard.

That's when I looked up and saw that the hard body I had run into belonged to Cruz.

"I'm alright," I insisted, even though I was absolutely not alright.

"You're not," he countered. "And if you don't get this taken care of you could end up with some serious scarring."

As Cruz held on to my fingers, he looked over my head and yelled out an order, "Cool towels, now."

The pain from the coffee was too severe to ignore. If it hadn't been, I'm sure I would have been able to focus on the fact that for the first time in four years a man was touching me. I might have reacted differently to that touch if I didn't feel like the skin on my arm and the upper part of my chest was on fire.

I was fighting back tears threatening to fall when I felt a bit of relief on my arm. Cruz had wrapped cool towels around my hand and arm.

Sweet relief.

I closed my eyes and let out a breath. A tear spilled down my cheek.

"Lexi," Cruz called.

I opened my eyes.

His were watching the tear fall.

"Trust me," he pleaded when he brought his eyes back to me. They were full of concern and anguish. "We have to take care of this immediately to make sure you don't have burns that require medical attention. The office is within walking distance, right around the corner. Come with me so I can help you."

I was in so much pain that I couldn't think about anything other than doing what he said and going with him. And I wasn't the least bit terrified to go with him.

I slowly nodded my agreement.

One of the café employees had already come up and started cleaning the mess of coffee off the floor.

I apologized for the mess, but she apologized to me and was more concerned that I was alright.

At that, Cruz picked up my jacket and held my arm as he walked beside me out of the café. He walked with me around the corner to the Cunningham Security office.

We made it to the front door where he used the key pad and entered a code to unlock it. Cruz guided me through the quiet office space, down a wide hall with doors to private offices on both sides, until we reached what I assumed was a break room. There was a refrigerator, table with chairs, microwave, sink, and cabinets.

"Have a seat," he urged as he let go of my arm for the first time since he wrapped the towels around it.

I sat.

Then, I watched.

Cruz flipped open the doors on a couple cabinets searching for something. Finally, he located and pulled out a rectangular plastic food storage container. He turned on the sink and tested the water temperature before placing the container underneath the stream of water. Once it had reached a level that satisfied him, Cruz turned off the water and brought the container over to the table.

"Put your arm in here," he instructed as he gently wrapped his fingers around mine and lifted my arm.

The cool water immediately offered some relief to the burns.

"Are you okay?" Cruz asked as he sat in the chair in front of me.

I looked up at him and answered, "It feels better now. Thank you."

His eyes narrowed a bit as though he were trying to figure something out, but he wasn't looking at me. Well, he wasn't looking at my face.

I looked down to where his eyes were directed and realized I had my healthy arm up against my chest as my hand rubbed back and forth against the scarf resting there.

"Are you only burned on your arm?"

My body tensed as I lifted my head.

"No," I squeaked out.

"Let me see," he encouraged me.

My hand gripped my scarf a little tighter.

"I'm… I'm fine," I stammered.

"Lexi," he stated, a clear warning in his tone. "Let me see."

Slowly, with one hand, I removed the scarf from around my neck. I wore my scarf today specifically because I was wearing a scoop neckline, form-fitting top under my open front long-sleeved cardigan. Without the scarf, I felt exposed.

"Fuck," Cruz mumbled under his breath.

He stood and walked out of the room.

The second he was gone, I dipped my good hand in the water and brought it up to my chest. It did little to help with the pain.

Not quite a minute later, he walked back into the break room and came toward me carrying something.

He spoke gently, "Sit back in the chair a little."

His voice was comforting and I was in pain, so I did as he asked.

"I'm going to put this cool cloth on your chest. You okay with that?"

I needed relief and he was asking my permission, so I nodded.

Cruz carefully placed the cloth at the base of my throat and over my chest. Somehow, he did it without even touching me. What he gave me in that moment was something I couldn't quantify. I brought my free hand up to my chest and held the cloth in place as tears fell from my eyes.

"Fuck, Lexi. I'm so sorry."

Cruz sounded like he was in agony.

"For what?" I asked.

"For burning you."

"The coffee burned me, Cruz. You just happened to be there when it scorched my skin."

He shook his head and maintained his guilt, "No. I ran into you and caused you to spill the cup."

"I was rushing and wasn't watching where I was going. It was my fault."

He finally gave in and suggested, "Agree to disagree? Where were you going in such a hurry anyway?"

My meeting.

I forgot.

I immediately shot up out of the chair and blurted, "Oh no. I'm going to be late. I completely forgot about my appointment. I have to go."

"Wait. You can't go. You've got to let that arm sit in the water for at least another ten minutes."

"I can't. I have to meet my realtor so she can show me an office space and I need to be there in…" I trailed off looking for a clock. After seeing the time on the microwave, I looked back to Cruz and finished, "Three minutes."

"Where's the office space?"

"Down the road from Colvert's."

"Do you have your phone?"

"Yeah. Why?"

"Call your realtor and explain the situation. Tell her you're running a few minutes behind, but will be there shortly. If that works for her, you'll give yourself another five minutes in the water and let me put some aloe on your arm. The burn on your chest concerns me, though. You might need to take a quick trip to the ER."

I didn't have time for a trip to the emergency room. A trip to the ER is never quick.

Instead of arguing that point, I called my realtor. I explained the situation to her and she was more than willing to wait a few extra minutes for me so I sat back down and put my arm back in the container of water. Cruz picked up the cloth and walked over to the sink with it. After running it under the water and squeezing out the excess, he brought it back over and placed it back on me.

"Let me grab the first aid kit with the aloe. I'll be right back."

"Okay."

I had been sitting there alone for not quite a full minute when someone, who was not Cruz, walked in.

"Oh," he said as he realized I was sitting there. His brows drew together, but he continued to walk toward me. I sat up a little straighter.

Please come back Cruz.

The man asked, "You are?"

"Lexi," I answered quickly. My voice was hoarse.

"Elle's girl?"

Elle. He knew Elle.

"Yes. Elle and I are friends and I work with her."

His eyes dropped to my arm in the container and my hand holding the cloth over my chest before he asked, "Is everything okay?"

Cruz walked in before I could answer. "She was burned, Dom."

"How the hell did that happen?"

Dom.

He was the guy who had gotten to Elle just in time to save her from being killed by her stalker.

"Coffee," I confessed.

"Ah, I see," he started as he walked to the refrigerator and put something inside. "Cruz, I'm ready to rock when you are."

"Give me a few minutes to see to Lexi's burns and we'll head out."

"You've got it," he shot back as he walked out of the room.

"I'm sorry, Cruz. You've got work to do; you don't have to take care of me," I babbled.

Cruz had lifted my arm out of the water and was gently drying it off with a soft towel when he stopped and looked up at me with a cocked eyebrow.

"I hope you're joking," he grumbled.

"Back in the day I was known to pull a prank or two, but this is definitely not one of those times," I responded.

His face softened, but he said nothing before he went back to tending to my arm.

"Looks like second-degree burns on your arm and hand. I think you'll be okay with just some aloe, but I still think you should go see a doctor."

"As much as I think you might be right, I don't have the

time today to sit in an emergency room or urgent care center and wait hours to be seen. I have one appointment I'm already late for and I've got a full schedule for this afternoon. It's doubtful any place will be efficient enough to get me in and out over my lunch break."

I had no idea why I was being so chatty. It wasn't like me… at least, it hadn't been like me in a very long time.

After he finished applying the aloe to my arm, Cruz directed his attention to my chest. He brought his hands to the top corners of the cloth and pulled it away from my skin. Once it was exposed, Cruz maintained, "You've got to see a doctor, Lexi."

I looked down at my chest, but really didn't need to. It hurt. It hurt far worse than my arm.

"What time is your lunch break?" he asked.

"What?"

"Lunch. What time are you having lunch?"

"One."

He thought a moment and concluded, "Can you meet me back here then? My mom is a doctor. I can have her meet us here to look at the burns."

"Oh, Cruz. That's okay. I'm sure I'll be fine. I don't want to get your mom involved and inconvenience her."

"Please, Lex." There was nothing but desperation in his voice. "I feel awful about this. I'm not going to be able to sleep tonight thinking that you'd end up with scars that you'll have to live with the rest of your life because of me."

The weight of Cruz's words rocked me.

I swallowed hard and croaked, "Ok, I'll meet you back here at one."

"Good," he began as he put some aloe on his fingertips. "Let's get some aloe on you in the meantime."

Before I could react, Cruz's hand was at the base of my

throat where he began applying the aloe. I turned my head to the side and looked out the window.

He's only trying to help you. He's taking care of you.

My hands were balled in fists and my heart was pounding.

Cruz's fingers moved down to the top of my chest and applied the aloe there. His touch was delicate, but my insides were shaking. My breathing grew shallow and, despite how hard I tried, I couldn't stop the tears from falling.

"Lexi?"

I turned my head toward Cruz.

"Am I hurting you?"

I shook my head. "I think I'd prefer to do this part."

He pulled his hand away immediately and apologized. "I'm sorry. I wasn't trying to make you uncomfortable."

"It's just… it's really sensitive."

He dipped his chin and held the aloe out to me. Once I finished applying it, I stood and reiterated, "I better get going since I'm already late. Thanks for the aloe, Cruz."

"I'll walk you back to Colvert's."

"You don't have to do that," I stressed.

He sighed. "Sorry, but you aren't going to talk me out of this one. I can't send you out of here to walk to your car that's not in our parking lot. It's just not in me to do that."

He's such a good guy.

We walked out of the Cunningham Security office and back toward the coffee shop parking lot.

We walked in silence for a bit until, eventually, he spoke.

"Still not interested?"

"In what?"

He laughed. "Ouch. I might need the aloe when I get back to the office. Perhaps it works when one's ego has been burned."

Oops.

"I'm sorry."

And I was genuinely sorry.

He was a nice guy and I believed he was a good one at that, but it just wasn't in the cards for me. So, I simply told him that I was trying to focus on my career.

It was hard not to miss the disappointment on his face, but he respected what I said and accepted it. Seeing him do that affected me in ways I never imagined.

"Things are just really busy right now," I continued.

He gave me a nod of understanding and added, "Yeah, same here. We're working a couple of cases right now that have the whole team putting in a lot of hours."

"I'm not sure if that's a good or bad thing," I admitted.

"Come again?"

"Well, it's just that I think it's good that you're busy. Obviously, that means that you're good at what you do and you're catching bad guys. The downside of you being busy means that there are a lot of bad guys out there. That doesn't make me feel warm and fuzzy inside."

Cruz's face softened before he explained, "Not all of our cases involve the really bad guys."

I rolled my eyes. "There shouldn't be any if you ask me."

He chuckled, "Then I'd be out of a job."

"Point made."

We arrived back at the coffee shop parking lot, where I directed us to my car. When we were standing next to it, I turned to Cruz and said, "Thanks for walking me back here and for the aloe."

"You're welcome. I'll see you later, right?"

"One o'clock," I confirmed.

At that, Cruz opened my door for me and waited while I folded into the car.

"Stay safe," he urged just before he closed my door.

I smiled up at him as I started my car. It wasn't until I drove off that I saw Cruz move to head back to the office.

I continued to glance up in the rearview mirror and watch him walk away until he turned the corner out of sight. Then, I spent the next two minutes of my short drive trying to get myself together.

CHAPTER 5

Lexi

"I NEVER WOULD HAVE GUESSED YOU WANTED TO TALK TO US about Cruz tonight!" Nikki exclaimed. "I'm so excited."

I made it through my day and was back at home. Nikki and Elle had arrived not too long ago and I just finished filling them in on the coffee situation from this morning. Nikki was not yet aware of the real reason I asked her to come to my place tonight.

"Calm your jets, sis," I warned her. "It wasn't exactly my idea of fun to be burned by scorching hot coffee this morning and then needing to meet Cruz's mom this afternoon."

"You met his mom?" Elle asked.

"Yeah," I sighed. "Cruz was particularly concerned about the burns on my chest, but I explained how busy my day was today. He offered to have his mom meet me on her lunch break to check me out. I was in a lot of pain and didn't want to let the burns go untreated if they weren't just superficial, so I agreed."

And I was grateful that I did. Cruz's mom was a wonderful woman. She was incredibly professional and I felt at ease having her check out my burns. Thankfully, she didn't have any bad news to report. In fact, she beamed, "It's good to know my son listened to me when he was younger. Treating the burns the way he did right away helped tremendously."

Ultimately, she gave me some instructions on how to best care for the burns and gave me her number to contact her if I had any questions.

"Well, this all happened today and you called last night, so what's going on?" Nikki wondered.

I took in a deep breath and let it out before I shared, "Elle and I had a brunch meeting yesterday morning at Colvert's. Cruz stopped in."

"So this is about Cruz?"

I shrugged my shoulders. "It is and it isn't. Elle was just as excited yesterday morning at the prospect of something happening between Cruz and me as you are right now. I ended up sharing some information with her that I want to share with you."

"Okay."

Looking to Elle, I found a comforting face with encouraging eyes.

"Four years ago, back when I was in college, I was raped."

"Oh, babe. Are you okay?"

I offered a face that I hoped conveyed the truth. I wasn't a hundred percent, but I was getting there. "I'm working on it."

"I'm going to guess because you asked me not to mention anything to Luke that your family doesn't know. Please tell me you haven't been dealing with this on your own for the last four years."

"Shortly after it happened, I started seeing a therapist. Up until yesterday when I told Elle, my therapist was the only person who knew."

"I feel awful," Nikki went on. "I should have known. The signs were there months ago."

My head jerked back. "What do you mean?"

"At Thanksgiving when I first met the rest of your family. I remember your dad talking to you and I knew I recognized the look on your face. I had been talking about how I grew up right by the beach and you said something about wishing you could have lived close to the beach. That's when your dad stated how he was glad you didn't because you'd have been in a bikini all the time and that he'd always have to worry about you as a result. I saw the look on your face when he talked about how too many men think that what a woman wears is an invitation for them to do whatever they want. At the time I couldn't place it, but now I know. I've seen the same look before…on Emme."

Emme was Cruz's sister-in-law and one of Nikki's best friends. I never even considered the fact that Nikki would have been such a good person to talk to not only because I trusted her, but also because she had been there for Emme throughout her ordeal with her abusive ex-boyfriend.

"Please don't feel bad about not knowing, Nikki. I'm telling you now because I'm ready. I've done a lot of healing on my own over the last couple of years, but now I'm ready for the next step. It's different for everyone. For me, the next step is finding a way to trust and be vulnerable again because I don't want this controlling my life anymore."

I then went on to tell them what happened to me. I gave them details and explained how it happened. I knew it wasn't easy for them to hear, but it was oddly refreshing for me to get it out. I was surprised to get through it all without breaking down too badly.

"Lexi, love, you know we will both help you any way that we can. I don't want to be insensitive to your needs, so I need you to tell me what I can do."

"Thank you, Elle. I just need to know that if I'm having a particularly bad day that I've got someone I can call. Ever since it happened I had many times where I wanted to call someone just to talk, but I didn't have that. I only had my therapist because that's what I chose. I want that to change, but I don't want you to pity me."

"Are you kidding?" she started. "I admire you. That's something I've done since before I knew about this. Now that I know this, I admire you even more. I'm in awe of your strength and determination to not let it control your life. Gosh, I'm simply heartbroken and feel awful that I pushed you about Cruz. Knowing what you endured at the hands of someone you were interested in is just terrible."

"Well, that's one of the predicaments I'm in right now," I confessed. "It should come as no surprise that I've not been attracted or even remotely interested in guys over the last few years. Mostly, I find that I'm tense and nervous around them. I'm very untrusting and it's been the reason that I've made sure to only work with female clients. But Logan called me yesterday and said he had a client that needed my help. It was a man, but I couldn't turn it down or Logan would know that something was wrong."

"Do you want to tell them?" Nikki asked.

I thought on it a moment. I did. I wanted to tell my family, but I couldn't get over knowing that I'd completely devastate them when I did.

"I want to, but I'm worried about how they'll react."

Without any hesitation, Nikki insisted, "If you're worried that they won't believe you, Lexi, you're wrong."

I shook my head as I spoke. "It's not that. It's going to hit them hard and I don't want to bring that disappointment to them.

"Your family loves you. They'd never be disappointed in you," Elle chimed in. "Why would you think that?"

My worried gaze settled on my friends. Their faces mirrored my own.

When I answered, my voice was quiet. "I never fought back."

That did it. I'd gotten through telling them about what happened, but as soon as I took a minute to think about how my family would feel when they found out, I lost my composure. I broke down into tears and immediately felt Nikki engulf me in her arms. She held me tight while I cried and, since I hadn't had the comfort of a loving embrace during a breakdown like this for years, I took full advantage.

Between Nikki's fierce hold on me and Elle's soothing voice, I eventually calmed down.

"Whenever you're ready to tell them, we'll be there for you. If you want us there when you tell your family, all you need to do is ask," Elle offered.

"Thanks, girls. I need some time before I do that. Besides, my schedule is a bit crazy right now considering I took on this new client."

"Is this the guy Logan referred to you?" Nikki asked.

I nodded. "I thought the issue was going to be that it was a man that I'd be working with, but I never expected the project to be what set me on edge."

"What is it?"

"A rape crisis center."

"Lexi…" Nikki trailed off.

Before she had the opportunity to continue, I interjected, "I know, Nik. I initially turned it down, but Logan was standing there and told me I needed to think about how many people I could help by doing it. That right there is another reason I know he's going to be devastated when he finds out the truth. Aside from that, he's right. I've talked with my therapist about it and I've really taken the time to consider it. Ultimately, I think this will be good for me."

"You've got to do whatever it is that you feel is going to help you heal," Elle started. "I'm so proud of you. This is one hell of a way to fight back."

"That's how I see it, too. I know I didn't physically fight back then, but if I can help other people who experience sexual assault, it makes me feel like I'm finally fighting."

The girls agreed with me and, to give me a bit of a reprieve from all the heavy talk, we moved our conversation to the things going on in each of their lives. While they mixed in things unrelated to their love lives, they ultimately both made their way there.

Nikki went on and on about Luke, but thankfully spared me details about their sex life. I was happy for her and Luke, but there was no way a sister would want to hear any of that about her brother. Elle talked about Levi and where things were headed with the two of them. In both cases, I realized that each of them had experienced something heartbreaking. They had good men by their sides to see them through that heartache. Luke helped Nikki heal years afterward, while Levi was there for Elle throughout her entire ordeal.

Hearing them talk about their relationships was a double-edged sword for me. On one hand, I was overjoyed that they'd each managed to find a fulfilling relationship regardless of any obstacles they faced. But on the other side of it, it made me feel a bit despondent.

The fact that I was making strides in all areas of my life was evident. I had graduated from college at the top of my class. I was determined to have my own public relations agency and was already feeling successful with some of my current clientele. With the help of my therapist, I finally got to a place where I trusted enough in my own strength to share what I experienced. I also knew that even though telling members of my family would be devastating, I would ultimately get through it. For the first time since starting my career, I was taking on a male client that I didn't personally know. In doing that, I was also making progress in my own recovery by helping an organization find funding to be able to offer resources and support to women who were survivors of sexual assault.

Despite all that, there was that one thing that was now blazing in bright neon letters in the front of my mind.

A relationship.

A romantic relationship.

I hadn't considered the possibility of one in years because I wasn't ready and I certainly wasn't looking.

Now there was a complication. There was Cruz.

And something was so completely different for me now. I was stuck.

Being stuck and with two girls I trusted to see me through, I blurted, "I don't think I know how to have a romantic relationship."

"What?" Elle asked.

"I haven't dated anyone since the rape and I don't trust easily."

"Ok, we can handle this," Nikki started. "First, do you feel that you are ready to start dating?"

I shrugged my shoulders. "I'm not sure. I know that I don't want to be alone for the rest of my life."

"That's good. So, is there a reason you just came out with this now? Like, let's say, something that might have to do with Cruz?" she hinted her suspicion.

Visions of his handsome face popped into my head. His concerned looks and his gentle touch early today filtered through my mind. I felt a smile tugging at my lips.

"Oh yeah," Elle piped up. "Judging by that look, it definitely has something to do with Cruz."

"He scares me," I admitted.

"Cruz is not someone you should be afraid of, babe."

"Not like that. He scares me because I don't feel around

him the way I feel around other men I don't know. Typically, I'm overcome with such horrible anxiety that there's no room for anything else. But it's different with Cruz. It's like I'm stuck between feeling some uneasiness and being completely drawn to him. I've been wondering if that apprehension is a result of what I've been through or if it's typical girl-likes-boy jitters. I would have probably gone with the second option, but there was an incident today that makes me think it's more about the rape."

"What incident?"

I went on to tell them about how I felt when Cruz was tending to my burns. I explained how he asked my permission to put the cloth on me, but when he went to apply the aloe I nearly lost it.

"My guess is that it's a combination of both, Lexi," Nikki declared. "Obviously, I think it'd be normal to feel scared about what your first sexual experience would be following the rape. And I'm not just referring to the act of sex. Cruz touching your throat and the top of your chest, even if it was only to apply the aloe, when you haven't been touched by a man in years would make anyone fret. On the other hand, when you feel attracted to someone and they touch you, that's bound to cause all types of sensations and feelings. I'll spare you the details, but I remember what it was like the first time Luke touched me."

"Me, too...with Levi," Elle sighed dreamily. "Have you considered what you would want to see happen if you took the step to put yourself out there again?"

"Not completely," I said. "I do know that I'd need to go slow and that I'd like to develop a friendship first. I have to trust that person before I could ever take any steps."

"Do you think Cruz is someone you could trust?"

"I think he's someone I'd like to try and see if I could trust."

Big, bright smiles spread across their faces. Hearing this made them happy. I had to acknowledge it felt good to hear myself admit it. Even still, I was weary.

"Don't set yourselves up for heartbreak," I cautioned them. "I'm not sure this would even work out. I mean, I know Cruz expressed interest in me a couple months ago and again today, but this would be a long road. I don't know how it'll play out for me until I'm in it, but my guess is that it's not for the faint of heart."

"Lexi, you might not know the whole story about what happened to Emme, but Cruz was the one who found her in that basement. He took care of her until Zane got there. He's seen a lot, babe. I'm certain if he's interested in you, this isn't going to scare him away."

"One day at a time, love," Elle added. "The Cunningham boys have what it takes to weather any storm. Zane did it for Emme and Levi did it for me. After my situation was resolved, I needed us to just be a couple for a while. Levi didn't want me to move out, but he didn't fight me on it because he knew it was what I needed. I think it's safe to assume Cruz will be like his brothers when it comes to giving you what you need."

"I agree with Elle. Take it one day at a time and only offer what you can. I'm not telling you that you've got to share the rape story with him off the bat, but be clear about your intentions. If you only want to try and be friends, just tell him that. If and when it becomes more than that for you, only you will know what you'll need to share with him."

One day at a time. I could do that. It's what I had been doing for years now.

"I can do that," I announced proudly.

I made a mental note, not that I needed one, to discuss this newfound feeling with my therapist at my next meeting.

I didn't want to do anything that would reverse any of the progress I'd made.

With that, the girls and I shifted our conversation and spent the rest of the evening on much lighter topics.

When they left that night, I went to bed feeling the best I had in years. I didn't expect things would get better for me overnight, but I was optimistic. With my decision to fight back against my attacker reaffirmed, I fell asleep dreaming of a future that involved not just a promising and fulfilling career, but also a life filled with family, friends, and a companion with which to share it.

That companion might have looked a little like Cruz Cunningham.

CHAPTER 6

Cruz

"Send it over right away and I'll shuffle my caseload around to make this a priority."

"Appreciate it, Cruz."

"No problem, Detective. I'll call you when I've got something."

I disconnected the call and started rearranging my schedule. From a work standpoint, it had been a shit week.

Over the course of the last few weeks, we had been swamped at Cunningham Security. A lot of what we were dealing with were run-of-the-mill PI cases, but there were currently two larger cases that were far more serious in nature. Luckily, we had a large team of guys. This meant that we could spread out the smaller cases individually and work collectively on the larger ones.

Sometimes, our larger cases came from unlikely places, such as the Windsor Police Department. Like right now, I'd just gotten off the phone with Detective Baines of the WPD and he was hoping to bring us in on a case. It was going to be one of the larger ones. They'd been working the case for a few weeks and had been hitting dead ends. In fact, it was getting worse. It was a missing person's case, which isn't always something that gets slid across the desk of a private eye.

The truth of the matter is that our firm spends a lot of time investigating real estate or insurance fraud. There's also an overwhelmingly large amount of infidelity cases. Occasionally, we might have someone who is adopted looking for their biological parents, but rarely do we ever deal with a missing person's case.

In most instances when someone goes missing, it becomes a very labor-intensive job that requires a lot of man-hours. Most individuals rely on the police departments to find their loved one because the costs associated with hiring a private investigator quickly add up with the number of hours required to solve such a case.

So, at times like this, when the police department reaches out for help, we do our best to work with them. We've needed one or two favors from them over the years, and it's been nice to have a relatively healthy, positive working relationship with them.

"Such concentration before your stakeout."

I looked up from my desk to see Lorenzo standing in the doorway. I'd been working an insurance fraud case for the last couple of days.

I shook my head and answered, "No stakeout anymore. Just got off the phone with Baines. He's got a missing person's case he's sending over."

"High profile?"

"One of them is," I replied.

"One?" he questioned.

"Yeah," I confirmed. "I guess I should have said he's sending over multiple missing person's cases. They've got five disappearances in the last three weeks. The most recent is a wealthy family and they're putting a lot of pressure on the police department."

At that moment, my computer chimed indicating I'd

received an email. I looked at the sender of the email and announced, "This is it."

Lorenzo walked into my office and sat in the chair on the opposite side of my desk. I quickly opened the locked files using the password he'd given me over the phone and printed them.

Thirty minutes later, Lorenzo and I had scoured through the documents.

"I don't like the way this one feels, Cruz," he grumbled.

I was just as unsettled as he was. "You're not alone. Five women in the last three weeks. All are young, between the ages of eighteen and twenty-three. This is not going to be good."

"I'm not liking that look this early in the morning."

Lorenzo and I directed our attention to the door where Dom stood.

"What look?" Levi asked as he materialized beside Dom.

"A case from the WPD. Five young women have gone missing over the course of the last three weeks."

"Fuck," Levi muttered. He took a minute to think before he looked to Dom and jerked his head toward my office. "Get up to speed on this with them."

With a downward jerk of his chin, Dom agreed.

Levi addressed the three of us. "Send all of your case files for everything but this one over to me. I'll redistribute them to the rest of the guys. I want the three of you to focus solely on this one. Something tells me this isn't going to end well."

"You've got it, Levi," Lorenzo shot back before my brother moved from the doorway and toward his own office.

For the next two hours, Dom, Lorenzo, and I combed over every detail for each of the cases. When the three of us had sufficiently taken in all of it, I announced, "We've got to get a plan together quickly. I get the feeling it isn't going to be long before we've got more added to the mix."

"This is bullshit," Dom snapped. "A sex trafficking ring right in our back yards."

"You've got to stay focused, Dom," Lorenzo reminded him. "It pisses me off, but we can't let our emotions get the best of us. If you let that eat you up, you'll get distracted and another girl gets taken."

"Oh, I'm not distracted. I'm going to eat, sleep, and breathe this case until we find these motherfuckers."

I dropped my head and let out a laugh. There wasn't anything funny about this situation, but having someone like Dom working with us would only serve to motivate us more than we already were.

"We don't know for certain that it's a sex trafficking ring either. It could be a serial killer or someone simply kidnapping," Lorenzo added.

Dom gave Lorenzo a disbelieving look. "We've been doing this long enough. We don't get a lot of missing person's cases, but you know that everything in those files tells us exactly what this is."

Lorenzo dropped his gaze because he knew Dom was right. Maybe it seemed a bit presumptuous of us to automatically assume it was a sex trafficking ring, but as Dom said, the three of us had been doing this long enough to know the difference.

"Alright," I started. "How about you guys get your other cases over to Levi? I'm going to make a quick run to Colvert's to grab some coffee. When I get back, we'll come up with our game plan."

"Still holding out hope that you'll see her there again?" Dom joked.

He was referring to Lexi.

I didn't answer him, so he took the liberty to keep at me. "I already told you she's never going back there. The girl spilled hot coffee everywhere and burned herself. She's probably too embarrassed."

"She has no reason to be embarrassed; I'm the one who caused her to spill the coffee. For the record, though, I've been getting coffee from Colvert's for years. Don't make this about her."

Lorenzo started laughing before he chimed in, "You've been going there for years, but you always used to do it on your way in to the office. Now, you're going later every morning. That's all about her and you know it."

I didn't deny it. I did the only thing I could do.

I stood and informed them, "I'll be back in fifteen."

As I walked out of my office, leaving them behind, I heard Dom yell out, "It'll be longer than that if she shows up today."

Leaving the office and heading toward the café, I thought about what Dom and Lorenzo said. I knew there was a very real possibility that they were right. The truth was, I started going to get my coffee later and later because I was hoping to see her again.

After seeing her there with Elle at the beginning of the week, I took a chance the next day that she might stop in again. I was right, but that encounter was an utter disaster. It seemed that each time I was around her, luck was never on my side.

When I first met her months ago at the dance studio she had gotten a job at, she barely spoke two words to me before she ran out. In those few moments, though, there was no denying the fact that there was an attraction on both ends. Unfortunately, as luck would have it, Lexi was gone before I had an opportunity to do something about that attraction.

I saw her again a couple months ago when I was investigating a case for her brother, Luke. She happened to be at his house when I stopped by with some information on that case. That day, I learned a bit more about the kind of person she is. I'd just delivered life-changing news to Luke's girlfriend and Lexi stayed strong and supportive throughout it. I knew I wanted to learn more about her and not let another opportunity pass me by, so when she got up to leave I excused myself as well. However, once again, I was unsuccessful in my efforts. Even though I knew we both felt that mutual attraction, Lexi turned me down when I asked her out. She said she wasn't interested in a relationship and that she wanted to focus on her career.

My worst bout of luck with her happened only days ago when I bumped into her, sent coffee flying, and burned her. To know I was responsible for causing her pain like that gutted me. She tried to stay strong, but I knew the burns were bad. I could see her fighting against giving in to the pain she felt. Watching the tears leak from her eyes when it first happened was bad enough, but then it happened again when I tried to make it better. Putting aloe on her chest and seeing her cringe in pain overwhelmed me.

Even though I managed to talk Lexi into coming back to the office so I could have my mom check out her burns, I didn't get her number. Of course, in my line of work it was something I could easily get without her giving it to me, but I didn't want to be that guy. I didn't want to overstep boundaries and bulldoze my way into someone's life, especially when that person had already turned me down once. I wasn't against trying again to convince her to give me a shot, but I refused to be the guy who does what he wants without a care for anyone else's feelings.

As I approached the café, it started to hit me just how much I hoped Lexi would be there. I hadn't spoken to her since she came and had the burns checked out. More than anything else, I wanted to know that she was healing alright. She'd been on my mind for days and I was worried about her. Just before I walked in, I decided that if I didn't see Lexi today I'd reach out to Elle instead just to ease my mind a bit.

On that thought, I opened the door and stepped inside. It took less than five seconds for me to spot her. The relief I felt in seeing her beautiful face was short-lived because I immediately noticed she was not alone. She was sitting across from a man in a suit.

A wave of jealousy coursed through me.

It would seem my luck was getting worse and worse.

I knew it was likely that she was in a meeting with a client, but it didn't change the fact that I wanted to be the one sitting at that table with her. I chose not to go over to her on the off chance that I'd interrupt such a meeting.

Caught up in my assessment of the situation, I almost didn't notice when Lexi's eyes caught mine and she offered me a smile and a wave of her hand. I gave her a nod before she turned her attention back to the man she was sitting with and I moved ahead to place my order.

While I waited for my coffee and the breakfast sandwich I decided on at the last minute, I pulled my phone out of my pocket and looked through emails. I did it mostly to distract myself because the truth was that I was itching to go over and talk to Lexi. It was then I realized I shouldn't have ordered the sandwich. Coffee would have had me in and out. Now, I was stuck, tense and waiting.

The perusal of my emails was brought to a halt when I heard, "Um, Cruz?"

I looked up from my phone into those almond-shaped, chestnut-colored eyes. I felt my face instantly soften while my body relaxed at the sight of her standing in front of me.

"Hi, Lexi. I've been worried about you," I shared, not caring if it was too forthcoming. It was the truth. "How are the burns?"

"They're healing," she began as she held up her arm and slid her sleeve back. There was a bit of redness there, but it was much better than it had been a few days ago. "The first couple of days were pretty painful. I'm doing much better today, though."

"Your arm looks like it's healing well. How are your chest and throat?" I wondered.

She was wearing a shirt with a high neckline, so I couldn't see if it looked any less angry than it did on Tuesday. Lexi pressed her hand to the top of her chest and explained, "Not as great as my arm, but still better. The clothing irritates the burns, so I keep bandages on during the day. Your mom gave me some special bandages with medication in them that help heal the skin while keeping it hydrated. I think I'm going to make it through this without any scars, so I'm happy about that."

"That's good to hear. I'm glad you were here today. I've been coming in every day this week hoping I'd see you and could check in on you. If I had your number, I would have called."

Her face grew concerned. "Oh, I'm sorry. This is my first day back here since then. Thanks for thinking of me."

I glanced over at the table she had been sitting at when I arrived. The man she was with was gone.

"Work meeting?" I asked, jerking my head to the table while trying to keep my voice neutral. It was none of my business, but I had to know who that guy was.

"Yeah," she confirmed. "Grant's a referral from my brother, Logan. He's got an important project he needs my help on."

"That's good. So, business is doing well then?"

I knew I was making small talk and I didn't care. I wanted to know everything I could about her. The longer I asked questions and talked, the more time I'd have with her.

She answered with a nod of her head, but there was a questioning look in her eyes. It wasn't something I'd ever seen before, so I asked, "Is something wrong?"

"It's just...well," she stammered. "I've been thinking and it seems pretty obvious that you like Colvert's. I was wondering if maybe one morning you would like to meet me here for breakfast."

To say I was shocked would be an understatement. Perhaps my luck was turning around.

I wasn't going to pass up this opportunity, so I quickly recovered and suggested, "Sure. How about tomorrow morning?"

She jerked back a step and repeated, "Tomorrow?"

I shrugged my shoulders. "Sunday works, too."

"Tomorrow works," she concluded.

"Cruz!" I heard Bobby shout from behind the counter.

I turned toward him and saw him holding up my order. "Thanks, Bobby."

"See you Monday," he shot back.

"Tomorrow," I corrected him.

He cocked an eyebrow.

I wrapped an arm behind Lexi and settled my hand on her opposite shoulder. "I'm bringing a date for breakfast."

Bobby smirked and gave us a chin lift before he went back to business.

I looked down at Lexi and saw a bit of trepidation in her features. "Are you okay?"

She turned toward me while stepping out from my arm before she responded, "I don't want to give you any mixed signals. I know you expressed interest in me a couple months ago. I'm not sure if that's something you're still seeking, but I want to be honest. I'd just like to get to know you better without the pressure."

"I'd be lying if I said that getting to know you better is all I wanted. That said, I think it's a great place to start and see if there could be something more. No matter what, I don't want you to feel any pressure. We'll take it a day at a time."

She gasped.

"What's wrong?"

She shook her head, "Nothing, I just…it's nothing. So, what time should we meet tomorrow?"

"I'm an early riser, so I'm good whenever you are."

"Me too," she noted with a smile on her face. "How about nine?"

"Works for me."

With that, Lexi and I made our way outside.

"Are you parked in the lot?" I asked.

"Yeah, did you walk?"

"Yep."

I walked her to her car. I couldn't deny the fact that I had the news from the WPD in the back of my mind.

When we got to her car, she unlocked it and put her bags inside.

"I'll see you tomorrow morning," I promised when she turned back to me.

She nodded and folded into the driver's seat. Before I could close her door, she asked, "Did you want a ride to the office?"

I grinned at her and shook my head. "I'm good, but thanks. I could use the exercise."

Her eyes traveled the length of my body, but she didn't respond. I didn't mind being under the scrutiny of her intense gaze; it only helped me to feel like there was a possibility of more with her at some point.

Just as I was about to close her door, she called out, "Wait!"

"What's up?"

"I should give you my number in case anything comes up and you need to cancel."

I pulled out my phone again, hit a few buttons to get to the screen to add a new contact, and handed it to her. She put her number in. I saved it and slid the phone back in my pocket before I informed her, "Happy to have your number now, but I think you should know I have no intention of canceling tomorrow."

"You never know. Things come up," she stated innocently.

"Well, that won't be happening in this case," I assured her. "I'll text you when I get back to the office so you'll have my number. Don't use it to cancel on me."

She laughed.

It was the most beautiful thing I ever witnessed.

When she settled down, she looked up at me and promised, "I won't. See you tomorrow, Cruz."

"Looking forward to it, Lexi."

CHAPTER 7

Lexi

IT WAS FIVE MINUTES TILL NINE AND I WAS SUPPOSED TO MEET CRUZ in just a few minutes at Colvert's Café. After I left from our impromptu meeting yesterday, I spent the better part of the day thinking. I'm lying. I spent the entire day thinking about Cruz.

I had actually spent several days prior to yesterday thinking about Cruz. Following girls' night on Tuesday evening, when Nikki and Elle came over and allowed me to cry on their shoulders about everything I'd been through, it felt like I'd had a breakthrough. Finally speaking about it felt liberating.

I guess having been so quiet for so long about what I went through was stifling me in a way I never realized.

On Wednesday afternoon, I called Dr. Lane and scheduled an appointment with her for Thursday evening. I was grateful she had an opening and could fit me in quickly because the more I thought about it, the more I realized that I had some insecurities. It was one thing for me to resolve to my friends that I was going to take the next steps in healing myself, but I didn't want to risk having a setback.

I needed Dr. Lane to confirm that it was not wrong for me to move forward in this manner. I had a feeling I knew what she was going to say to me, but even still, I needed to be sure.

Sure enough, when I met with her on Thursday evening and explained that I had a newfound strength and determination to get back a part of my life that was taken, she supported me… in the way that therapists do. She never attempted to talk me out of it and truly made me believe that if I felt I was ready, then I needed to explore that. For more than three and a half years, she had been working with me to give me the tools I'd need when I was ready. Now that I was ready, I had to put those tools to use.

Even though I had already expected my appointment with her to go as it did, it still gave me a boost in confidence to push forward with my mission.

So, feeling positive about how things went with Dr. Lane, coupled with how I felt after seeing Cruz yesterday, I was convinced that this was the next step for me. Next would come telling my family, but I had to take this one day at a time.

Today was just one more day in my road to getting all the parts of myself back. One of those parts was the prankster in me. That decision was reaffirmed by Cruz's lighthearted nature yesterday.

He walked me to my car, joked with me, and I left feeling happy. My day was filled with such good vibes from that point forward.

I wanted that feeling to continue.

So, I woke up, got ready, drove to the café, and put my plan into action. I walked from the parking lot to the front door. I peeked inside and saw him sitting sideways at a booth. I stayed outside, pulled out my phone, and called him.

"Hello?" he answered after one ring.

"I'm so sorry," I started. "I have to cancel."

The tone of my voice was serious.

"Is everything alright?" he asked.

"No."

I watched as he sat up in the seat and his body went on alert. I almost felt bad, but thought it'd be worth trying to get a laugh out of him.

"What happened?"

"Nothing, per se. I just started getting cold feet. I was worried after you called it a date yesterday and then I thought about it all night. When I woke up this morning I realized that maybe it wasn't the best idea."

His shoulders visibly slumped. He was upset by this.

I didn't like seeing him like that.

Cruz rested his elbows on his thighs and looked down at the ground while he spoke, "Lexi, I told you yesterday that there was no pressure. I really just wanted to have the chance to get to know you better."

I opened the door and walked in.

"Promise?" I asked as soon as I was standing in front of him.

Cruz lifted his head, his face lit up, and he pulled his phone from his ear.

"Sorry," I giggled. "I couldn't help myself."

Cruz smirked as he stood and waited for me to sit. When we were both finally seated, he looked across the table at me and concluded, "Smartass."

"Did you really believe I wasn't coming?"

"Yeah. This was months in the making for me, so that wasn't cool at all."

"When I was younger, my brothers and I always played pranks on our parents and each other. I haven't joked around with anyone like that in years. To be honest, you should consider yourself lucky. That was pretty tame."

"I'll have to keep that in mind."

The two of us ordered our breakfast and quickly fell into an easy conversation.

Not even ten minutes into our conversation, my cell phone rang. I looked down and saw the number.

"I have to take this. I'm so sorry," I apologized to Cruz.

"It's ok," he insisted.

"Hello?"

"Hi, Lexi. It's Rachel. I'm sorry to call you so early on a Saturday, but you told me to let you know as soon as I heard back from the other agent."

"Yes, absolutely," I insisted. Rachel was my realtor and had submitted my offer for one of the office spaces I checked out this week. "What did they say?"

"Congratulations! The place is yours. I explained you had a sense of urgency with this and they were willing to accommodate that. You are welcome to move in as soon as we complete the rental agreement and get the payment for first and last month's rent plus the security deposit over to them."

"That's awesome. How soon can we meet to get that squared away?"

"In my line of work, I have so many clients that are not available to meet on the weekdays. As a result, I end up working on the weekends, which means if you'd like to meet up sometime this weekend I can try to squeeze you in. Do you have any time available?"

I didn't want to risk losing this office space, so I asked, "Can you do it this afternoon?"

"I can make that work. I have a lunchtime showing today, so I can meet you just before that. I'll get the paperwork prepared this morning, so all you'll need to do is sign and bring a check. Can you be at my office around twelve? That should give us enough time to take care of it all and still allow me to get to my showing on time."

"I'll be there. Thank you for getting this taken care of so quickly, Rachel. I'll see you later."

I disconnected the call and looked up at Cruz. "That was my realtor. I put an offer in on Thursday for the office I wanted and I got it," I beamed.

"Nice. Congratulations."

Our food arrived before I could thank him. We both took a few bites before he asked, "Where is it?"

I couldn't hide my excitement. "It's right down the road! It was the space I looked at on Tuesday after our run-in with the coffee." I told him about the exact location and the building I'd be moving into.

I watched as his face softened. "You'll be close by," he said, gently.

I'm not sure where I got the courage from, but I noted, "If this goes well this morning, maybe since we'll be so close we can meet up for the occasional friendly breakfast or lunch. That is, of course, if you aren't off fighting the bad guys."

He laughed and explained, "Well, I guess that'll depend on how soon you move into your new space."

"I'm signing the papers later today, so probably this coming week. Are you working on a case with bad guys right now?"

Cruz didn't answer right away and his mood changed from upbeat to serious. I didn't like the look and had a feeling I knew what it meant.

"Your silence tells me that I won't like the answer," I continued.

"It's better you don't know the details, but you're right. A case was slid across my desk yesterday and it's not a good one. When I'm working, it's the only case I'll be working on. What I don't like is the fact that I'm still unsure of just how many bad guys we're dealing with."

I took a deep swallow before I asked, "Do you ever get scared that something could happen to you?"

"I don't necessarily think about something bad happening to me. I know what I've got to do to keep myself safe in high-risk or dangerous situations. What does scare me is what can happen or what sometimes actually does happen to victims."

"What do you mean?" I wondered.

"The kind of case I'm working on now is the kind that has lots of innocent victims. What they endure can cause long-lasting effects. Most will live the rest of their lives suffering from having gone through such an ordeal."

I couldn't even begin to imagine what could be happening and I wasn't sure I wanted to know. All I could think at that moment was that it seemed Cruz and I were both on a path to do something that would help others.

"Well, I hope everything goes well for you with this case and you can get through it with the least amount of fallout. That said, you should know we've got something in common."

"We do?"

"Yes," I started. "Do you remember that meeting I was having here yesterday morning?"

He nodded.

"I can tell you about it since my job is to promote the organization anyway. They're going to be opening a rape crisis center here in Windsor."

"Really?" he questioned as he sat back in his seat.

I didn't know if he thought it was a good or a bad thing.

"Yes," I stated firmly, even though I knew I was feeling uneasy about what his thoughts on it were.

"When?"

"Two weeks," I began. "The location and the staff are all squared away. The name is WAAR and it stands for Windsor Against Abuse and Rape. Initial funding is being provided by the company Grant works for, but they want to secure donations to help with the ongoing operational costs. It's a good cause and one I'm certain people will donate to, so I feel good about taking on this project."

Without a moment of hesitation, Cruz insisted, "You should. If there is anything I can do to help, let me know."

There was a part of me that wanted to know more on how he felt about sexual assault, so I pressed him a bit. "I will, thanks. So, you agree it's a worthy cause?"

"Absolutely."

There was no doubt or reservation in his tone. He continued, "Unfortunately, the security firm has put me in a position where I've seen how frequently something so awful happens. I saw firsthand what it did to my sister-in-law, Emme. The devastation left behind for victims of sexual assault can be horrific. Having a resource available locally to help anyone in that situation is definitely a good thing and one I'd be proud to support."

I took in his words and felt an odd sense of security fall over me.

"I like to think of them as survivors, not victims."

Cruz took a moment before he agreed, "You're right. A lot of people who experience sexual assault don't see it that way. This crisis center will hopefully provide them with the tools they'll need to get past the devastation they feel and eventually see themselves as the survivors they are."

I offered Cruz a genuine smile before I took another bite of my food. After I chewed and swallowed, I pointed out, "Sorry. This conversation quickly took a turn into pretty heavy stuff for a breakfast..."

I trailed off because I wasn't sure what to call it.

Cruz finished a bite of his food before he reassured me, "It's okay. I've dealt with much worse at a far earlier hour. Besides, it might be heavy stuff, but it's positive."

I gave a gentle nod of my head.

Cruz went on, "And you don't have to put a label on this, Lexi. We're just friends having breakfast."

"Friends?" I repeated. I hadn't made any new friends that were males in nearly four years. I had acquaintances, like Levi, who I knew through their girlfriends. I certainly wouldn't consider them friends and, beyond that, males in my life were virtually nonexistent.

"Well, we're not enemies, are we?"

We weren't. And I didn't ever want us to be.

To top it off, I decided that I was ready to start fighting back. If I was going to make sure that I was successful, I knew this was going to be part of my healing and recovery. I needed friends. I needed to try to give someone an opportunity to allow me to trust them.

"Ok," I said softly. "Friends having breakfast."

Cruz and I spent the next hour being friends. Our conversation was much lighter than when it had started. In fact, I spent a good portion of our time together in fits of laughter. I couldn't remember the last time I had been so carefree and had so much fun.

As it turned out, I wasn't the only one who had hilarious stories of memories of their childhood to share. Cruz, the youngest of three boys, had his fair share of shenanigans to talk about. It was hysterical.

We finished our breakfast and got the check. Cruz didn't give me an opportunity to pull out my wallet because the minute the check was put in front of us, he picked it up.

"Don't even think about it," he warned.

"You don't have to pay for me, Cruz," I insisted.

He grinned before he responded, "I know, but I'm going to."

"But I invited you out for breakfast," I argued.

"Doesn't matter, Lex. I'm buying breakfast this morning and I don't want a fight from you about it."

I huffed out a sigh. "Fine, but I'm buying next time."

Cruz threw some bills on the table and perked up. "Next time?"

"Oh, well...I mean, I just thought we had a good time and could try getting together again. I had so much fun."

"I did, too. I'm happy to hear you enjoyed yourself. I'd definitely like to spend some time with you again soon."

Now it was my turn to perk up and smile. "Great. You've got my number now, so just reach out to me whenever you have a chance and we can set something up."

Cruz and I left Colvert's, where he insisted on walking me to my car. We made our way to the parking lot and he made sure it wasn't awkward by immediately offering, "If you need any help getting things set up in your new office, just let me know."

"Thanks, Cruz. I appreciate that," I started as we stopped beside my car. "And thanks for having breakfast with me this morning. I haven't laughed like that in a long time."

"Well, that's going to change then."

"I'm sorry?" I asked, not understanding what he was getting at.

"Someone that looks as beautiful as you do when you laugh should be doing it every day."

I felt myself grow somber. My gaze dropped to the ground and I explained, "Life has gotten in the way."

My body instinctively flinched when I felt Cruz's hand settle on the side of my face near my jaw. I felt his thumb swipe back and forth across my cheekbone. "Do you want to talk about it?" he wondered.

The nerves I felt started to dissipate and I surprised myself when I looked back up at him and replied, "We've had enough heavy stuff for one day. Maybe another time."

His face grew concerned, but he didn't push me. "Anytime, Lexi. I'll listen to you whenever you want to talk."

I gave Cruz a nod before I turned to get in my car. Once I was inside, Cruz closed my door and waited while I started the car and pulled out of the lot.

On my drive home I realized that somehow, in my battle to get all of the parts of me back, I managed to have the best day I'd had in ages. I never expected I'd feel as comfortable as I did at breakfast to the point I'd be able to laugh and really enjoy myself. And when the prospect of opening up to Cruz and telling him about my past presented itself, I didn't balk at it. Sure, I didn't share anything today, but I was a bit stunned to realize that I actually wanted to tell him about it.

It was like a light switch had gone off. The bricks that settled on my shoulders years ago slowly started lifting as I went through therapy. Earlier in the week when I told Elle and Nikki about my rape, I felt more bricks lifting. Suddenly, that urge to get it all out to the people who mattered in my life took over.

So, I accepted that I'd have moments that would make me sad. Moments when someone like Cruz would tell me that I should be laughing every day because I looked beautiful doing it and then I'd realize that someone else took that away from me. And while I accepted that fact, I also recognized that I didn't have to allow it to continue to be that way. I could get back what was taken and I could be happy again.

CHAPTER 8

Lexi

IT WAS ALREADY WEDNESDAY.

From the time I left Colvert's on Saturday morning after hanging with Cruz, the days flew by. Saturday afternoon, I met with Rachel and signed my lease. Afterward, I called Elle and told her about my morning with Cruz. She was so happy to hear it went well and I found I was thrilled to be able to share something positive with my friend.

That evening, after dinner, I got in a workout, showered, wrote in my journal, and climbed into bed. Just before I drifted off to sleep, I received a text from Cruz. He wanted to check in and make sure everything went well with finalizing the lease. To say I was happy that he had reached out was an understatement. I responded and let him know that all was good. Of course, he once again offered to help me with the move if I needed it. I thanked him again and explained that I'd certainly reach out if Luke and Logan were unavailable.

That night, I fell asleep feeling happier and more content than I had in such a long time.

On Sunday, I spent the better part of my morning going over my schedule for the week, planning and preparing for a few meetings I had, and packing up the things I'd be taking with me to my new office. I ordered some office furniture and made a call to my brothers. While the new furniture would be delivered to my office, I had a few heavy things at my apartment that I needed moved as well and would need their help. I managed to convince them to help, not that it required much convincing. The simple fact was that my brothers loved me and would drop anything they were doing to help me when I asked them. Of course, I never tried to take advantage of that and they knew it, which is likely the reason they always came through for me.

By the time Sunday evening rolled around, I worked out, journaled, and watched a movie. When I settled into bed that night, I had to be honest and admit that I was disappointed I hadn't heard anything from Cruz. I knew I had his number and could reach out to him, but something stopped me. I still had some nerves about pursuing something with him even though he made it clear that he was content to be friends and just get to know one another. Somehow, that knowledge made me a little sad and I had a feeling it was because I was beginning to realize that I wanted to try for more.

Monday was filled with work and a meeting. I spent all day working on the WAAR project campaign before I went to my meeting with Dr. Lane on Monday evening. The campaign was coming along nicely and I'd easily be able to get all of my thoughts finalized before I met with Grant on Thursday to propose my ideas and the approach I thought we should take to launch the center.

My session with Dr. Lane went well. I had two topics I wanted to discuss with her. The first was the fact that I was planning to tell my family about the rape. I thought they should know and I felt ready to do it. I just didn't know what reaction I'd get from them and that is what terrified me most. I explained that I had no doubt they'd believe me, but I wasn't sure I was prepared to help them cope with how it made them feel.

"You can't control their reaction," Dr. Lane insisted. "All you can do is tell them what you want to tell them and understand that they are entitled to feel however they feel about it. The same way that you needed to cope with what happened on your own terms will apply to them as well. It's not your job to fix it for them. You can only tell what you are comfortable telling. You should expect they might have questions, but you only have to answer what you want to answer."

"They're going to be devastated," I murmured.

"They love you, Lexi. That reaction is completely normal. Allow them to process it and deal with it in a way that they feel is best. And if you or any of them need to speak with someone about it afterward, I'm more than happy to help."

"Thank you, Dr. Lane. I have one other thing I want to discuss with you," I informed her.

"Sure."

"On Friday, I approached the guy I was telling you about last week. We ended up meeting for breakfast on Saturday morning."

"How did it go?"

My insides warmed and I answered, "Fantastic. It was the best day I've had in a really long time."

"Did you experience any anxiety or panic?"

I shook my head. "Nothing related to fear," I replied. "I went in determined to have a good time. I even joked with him when I first arrived. I haven't joked with anyone like that in years. The little anxiety that I did have could be best described as excitement more than anything else. I never felt fearful."

"That's great news," she remarked. "Is there something else you wanted to discuss regarding Saturday morning?"

"I think I like him," I blurted.

Dr. Lane didn't respond, but I knew she was happy to hear that.

"A few months ago, he expressed interest in dating me. I wasn't ready then, but I think I'd like to try now. He's a really nice guy. I know that my past is going to be an obstacle moving forward in a romantic relationship. I don't want to put him through all of that and have him deal with my baggage. And I know that I'm attracted to him enough that I want to try to pursue something, but I can't help wondering if he'll run as soon as he knows the truth."

"Lexi, we all have baggage. If the roles were reversed, do you think you'd feel burdened by him telling you about something that he experienced out of his control?"

"Never."

"Just as we discussed regarding telling your family, the same things apply here. You told two of your friends about what happened and trusted that they could handle what you had to say. And those conversations went well. Trust is an important factor here. You need to trust in yourself to know when the time is right. You also need to trust that you can make a good decision about who to give your trust to when you decide to share this part of your story with them. Once you do, you need to give them the opportunity to take it in while understanding that they may all have a different reaction. When it comes to a romantic relationship, I don't suggest trying to proceed without being forthcoming about what you've experienced. Ultimately, though, it's up to you to decide when, how much, and with whom you want to share that information."

"What if I tell Cruz and he decides not to stick around and try to see if there could be something more between us?"

"That might happen. You can't change how he'll react any more than he can change what happened to you. All you can do is prepare yourself for all the possible outcomes and hope that you'll end up experiencing the best of those. And if not, it doesn't mean you can't continue to try and trust others with it."

Dr. Lane gave me a lot to think about, so after a bit more discussion with her, I left and went home. I skipped journaling Monday night because I needed to take time to process my conversation with her. Despite a taxing workout that was a bit longer than usual, I found it difficult to sleep Monday night.

Tuesday was nearly identical to Monday, minus the therapy session. In place of therapy, I did end up with a phone call from Cruz just after dinner.

"Hello," I greeted him after two rings. I had been holding the phone in my hand after just one ring, but I didn't want to seem too eager.

"Hey, Lexi," he replied. "How's it going?"

"Good. It's been a productive couple of days, that's for sure. Catch any bad guys today?" I asked.

"I wish. One case with three guys dedicated solely to it and we've not yet caught a single bad guy. We've got a couple hours left, so I'm hopeful."

"You're still working for a couple more hours?"

"Bad guys don't take evenings off. Crime isn't a nine to five job," he pointed out.

That made sense. "I guess so. That totally sucks, though."

Cruz laughed. "Yeah, it does. But we haven't all been working every night. Last night, Lorenzo put in longer hours. Tomorrow, Dom will. Hopefully, we can make some progress and put an end to this one soon."

"I hope so. It makes me worry," I said before I even realize it.

"You're worried about me?"

The shock he felt at my admission was evident and I didn't know what to say.

I was silent so long, he called, "Lexi?"

"Yeah, I'm here."

"You got quiet."

I took a deep breath. "I'm sorry. That kind of slipped out before I could stop it," I started. To try and recover, I went on, "But the truth is, I'm worried for purely selfish reasons."

"Oh yeah? What are those reasons?"

"Well, for starters, you're easy to tease. Add to that the fact that you're the first person I've wanted to joke with in years and I'm not looking to give that up so easily."

"Princess, I'm easy to joke with because it's hard not to be happy around someone like you."

Princess.

"Princess?"

"Sorry. That kind of slipped out before I could stop it," he apologized, even though I had a feeling he really wasn't since he repeated the words I'd just spoken to him. "But back to the point I was going to make, I'd be crazy to not let you tease me. Anytime, anywhere, I'm up for you to tease me, Lex. To that end, I'm always careful when I'm working on a case with really bad guys."

There was no denying the sexual innuendo in Cruz's words. I didn't know what to say in response to that, so I didn't react to it at all.

"Be extra careful tonight," I advised. Then, to steer the conversation in a different direction, I continued, "Guess what?"

"What?"

"I am moving into my new office tomorrow," I beamed with excitement. "I can't wait to be in my very own professional office."

"Congratulations. Did you get your brothers to agree to help you?" he wondered.

"Yes. They are going to be helping me move everything. They kind of owe me," I teased.

"Really? What debts are they repaying?"

"Um, I'm only the best sister on the face of the planet. They're lucky to have me. I'm one of a kind, you know?"

Cruz didn't respond. I thought we got disconnected and was about to call his name to confirm when he spoke softly, "I don't doubt that you are."

Now we were both silent.

Finally, Cruz broke the silence and asked, "So, let's make a plan to celebrate."

"Celebrate?"

"Your new office. It's a huge accomplishment. Are you free this weekend?"

"Elle's meet and greet is on Sunday, so that's out."

"What about Saturday? We can go out to dinner."

"Okay. Dinner on Saturday," I agreed.

At that, Cruz explained he needed to get back to work. He wished me luck tomorrow and said he'd reach out later in the week once he figured out a place to go. I was looking forward to spending more time with him and couldn't wait for the weekend to arrive.

For the time being, I needed to set that aside and focus because I had a huge task in front of me today.

My brothers arrived at my apartment early this morning and loaded the things I needed into their two trucks. I didn't have a lot to move, so the two trucks were perfect and would only require a single trip.

After everything was loaded up, they followed behind me to my new office space. I had just stepped inside and was trying to figure out where to put everything while they carried all of my stuff in.

Four and a half hours later, long after the office furniture had been delivered, I ordered a pizza so the three of us could have lunch together. Luke and Logan managed to get my furniture moved and put where I finally decided I wanted it. They came close to losing their patience a few times because I had them put my desk in one spot and decided I didn't like it there and wanted it moved. I did the same with the couch and they let their displeasure with me be known. As was always the case, they quickly got over any grievances they had with me and I tried to keep that in mind when we finished our lunch.

"Need anything else moved, sidekick?" Logan asked as he stood from the couch.

Luke and Logan were both big guys, so I gave them the couch while I occupied the chair at my desk.

"No, I think I'm good now. Thanks for helping me today."

"So proud of you and everything you've accomplished, Lexi," Luke chimed in. "Sometimes I can't believe you've only been out of college for just a year with everything you've achieved in the last couple of months."

I let out an uneasy laugh and confessed, "This almost didn't happen."

"What do you mean?" he pressed.

It was now or never. Not technically, but I knew I needed to do this.

"I need to tell you guys something," I murmured, feeling the nerves and sadness wash over me. The sadness was all because I knew I was about to rip their worlds to shreds.

"Lex," Logan called. "What's wrong?"

I took in a deep breath and reminded them, "Do you remember how I switched schools after my freshman year of college?"

They both nodded. The confusion and anticipation in their faces was unmistakable.

"There was a reason I switched schools."

"Yeah, you said that you wanted to be closer to home. It didn't make much sense to any of us considering you moved closer, but didn't spend any more time at home," Luke pointed out.

"I did want to be closer to home, but there's a reason for that. That reason has less to do with actually being closer to home and more to do with me needing to leave where I was," I offered.

"What are you talking about?" Logan questioned me.

I felt my insides trembling and the tears welling up in my eyes. I took in a deep breath to try and calm myself, but it did little to help. I just needed to say it.

"The weekend before the spring semester ended, I was raped."

"Jesus Christ, Lexi, are you kidding?" Luke clipped.

I shook my head.

The air in the room changed. Thick with tension and fury didn't even begin to describe it.

I pushed past it and explained, "It was a guy that I knew. We went on a couple of dates. After one of them, he invited me back to his dorm room to watch a movie. I liked him and I never thought I had any reason to be fearful, so I went. We kissed and I enjoyed kissing him. He wanted more and I said no. I said no so many times, but he wouldn't accept that."

I stood there watching my brothers and the tension rolling off their bodies. I couldn't keep it in any longer and lost hold of the last bit of control I had. My body was overcome by sobs. In an instant, I felt Luke's strong, protective arms wrap around me. I cried in his chest as I heard Logan storm out and slam the door. I jumped at the sound, but Luke just held me tighter.

After a while, he apologized, "I'm so sorry I wasn't there to protect you. Fuck, Lex. I'm so sorry. Do Mom and Dad know?"

I shook my head.

"All this time you've kept this to yourself?"

"I've been seeing a therapist since about three weeks after I moved to my apartment years ago. She's local and she's been vital to my recovery."

"That's it? Just your therapist?"

"Up until a week ago, yes."

"You've carried this by yourself all this time? Lexi, we would have been there for you and done whatever we could to help you heal."

"I was afraid," I admitted.

"Of what?"

I looked to the door before bringing my eyes back to Luke. "That you guys would be angry or disappointed with me."

Luke shook his head, loosened his arms, and reassured me, "He's not disappointed with you, Lexi. He's about as angry as I am right now, but it's not directed at you. Give him a minute to calm down, he'll be back."

As if on cue, the front door opened and Logan walked in. There was nothing but pure anguish in his eyes. Nervous about what he was going to say, I pulled my bottom lip in between my teeth and chewed. Surprisingly, he said nothing.

That is, he said nothing until he walked over, engulfed me in his arms, and squeezed me tight. Then, he spoke and his voice was ragged, "Our sidekick. You've always been there for us, and the moment you needed us, we weren't there for you."

"You didn't know, Logan," I cried with my arms wrapped around his neck.

It took a bit, but when Logan loosened his hold on me, he stepped back, looked me in the eyes, and stated, "That's where you went."

"What?"

"You. The Lexi we grew up with. I thought it was just that you were growing up and being responsible, but that wasn't it. We should have known something wasn't right when you went from being the goofy prankster to the isolated introvert."

"I need your help now," I started before he cut me off.

"Anything, Lexi. Whatever you need," he insisted.

My eyes went back and forth between my big brothers. "I don't want to deny you your feelings because I know how important they are, but as soon as you can, I want you to let go of the guilt you have. I've carried it long enough for all of us; I don't want to see you go through it, too."

"Why didn't you tell us sooner?"

"I was embarrassed and I didn't want to be a burden. I didn't want to put my family through that kind of heartache."

Luke proclaimed, "Lexi, you have nothing to feel ashamed about. Someone took advantage of you. And you are our family, not a burden."

"I didn't fight back," I shared.

"What do you mean?"

I looked down at the ground and closed my eyes. When I opened them and looked at my brothers, I explained, "I didn't fight him when it happened. I laid there and thought about finals and the paper I had due for a class."

"Your mind did what it had to do to protect you and get you through it," Luke announced. "If you had fought physically, your attacker could have hurt you even worse."

"I know," I started. "I've been dealing with that guilt for years now and I understand it, but I just can't help hearing dad's voice telling me to always fight."

"Do you plan to tell them?"

I dipped my chin and answered, "They need to know and I want them to know. I just think I might need you guys there for me when I do."

"Of course, we will be," Luke affirmed. "You tell us when."

"Oh my God," Logan suddenly exclaimed.

"What?" Luke and I asked in unison.

"Lexi, I'm so sorry. Grant. The crisis center. I pushed you to do it."

I needed to calm his worries. "Logan, it's okay. I'm actually looking forward to doing it. It's my way to fight back. Knowing that I can help other women and girls that have been sexually assaulted is going to help me in my own healing. I was more concerned about working with a man. That's what had me so hesitant in the beginning. I have a meeting scheduled with him on Thursday and I know I have this office, but I am going to keep my meeting with him at Colvert's instead of here. I have such a hard time trusting men now. In fact, except for the two of you, Dad, Wes, Stone, Zane, and Cruz, I'm uneasy around men."

"Cruz?" Luke repeated.

I nodded.

"I've seen him around Windsor a few times now at meetings I've had at Colvert's. We had breakfast together on Saturday. We've texted back and forth and spoken on the phone a couple times since then. I don't know what it is, but I feel comfortable around him."

"Does he know, Lex?" Logan asked gently.

I shook my head. "No. Other than my therapist and the two of you, the only other people who know are Elle and Nikki."

"Nikki knew?" Luke gasped.

"Luke, don't be angry with her," I insisted. "I told her last week and asked her not to tell you. She respected my right to privacy and the fact that I wanted to be the one to tell you myself."

"I know it's got to be on your time frame, but if you think things are going to get serious between you two at any point, the sooner you tell him, the better," Logan encouraged me.

"I know, but I'm worried. I really like him and I like the fact that I feel like myself again when I'm around him. He's the first guy I've been interested in since the rape. What if I tell him and he decides he can't handle it?"

Luke walked over to me and wrapped his arm around my shoulders, "I can't speak for Cruz, but I'd like to think I know the kind of man he is. If he likes you, Lexi, this isn't going to make him walk away."

I leaned into him and whispered, "I hope you're right."

He squeezed my shoulders.

My brothers spent the next two hours with me. It was funny. Prior to me bringing this to their attention, they were ready to walk out the door, but as soon as they knew what happened, I became their priority. I appreciated them more than I'd ever be able to express.

When we finally left the office, Logan followed behind me to my apartment. I tried to tell him it wasn't necessary, but he insisted and asked that I respected he needed to do it for his own peace of mind. He'd been given a lot of information to digest and process, so I didn't argue with him.

When I got home, it hit me. Talking about what happened to me wasn't easy for those hearing it, but it was making me feel so much better to get it out. Sharing it with those I knew loved and cared about me made it easier to breathe. I hated that I brought the devastation to Luke and Logan; but in the end I knew they'd get through it and once we all came out the other side, we'd be even closer. My parents were next, but I had a couple of busy days ahead of me. I needed time to gather my thoughts before I went to them.

Just before bed, I sent a text to Cruz.

I'm all moved in. Operation Celebration is a go!!

He responded a minute later.

Happy to hear it. Out hoping to catch a bad guy, so I can't call. I'll reach out tomorrow.

Me: *Ok, be safe. Good night, Cruz.*

Cruz: *Night, princess.*

I didn't understand where the nickname came from, but it made me smile. I liked that Cruz's impression of me was a good one. I hoped as time went on he'd continue to only see the good or, at the very least, when bad stuff trickled in, the good would always outweigh it.

CHAPTER 9

Lexi

It was late Thursday morning and I was on my way back to my office. I had just met with Grant at Colvert's to discuss my plan for WAAR. Grant trusted my judgment and agreed to my proposal.

"This is all great, Lexi," he praised after I'd set everything out in front of him and explained it all. "I think this is going to do well and really get the center the funding we'll need to continue to provide crucial services to sexual assault victims."

"Thanks, Grant. If you want me to proceed with this, I can get started right away. We just need to get some paperwork signed first. I purposely left the rest of my day today and all day tomorrow free in hopes that you'd be happy with this and I could start pushing this out to potential donors immediately."

"I can't thank you enough for this. WAAR is going to help so many people. I don't even know how to tell you how much this will mean to my family if it's a success. I'm already beyond thankful that you've decided to come on board to help ensure that beyond getting funding we'll get the word out that there's a valuable resource out there for those who need it."

Grant was so excited about the opening of the rape crisis center and it made me proud to know I was going to be part of such a worthy cause. We spent the remainder of our meeting going over some additional details and completing the necessary paperwork.

WAAR would have medical professionals on staff to evaluate and treat those in emergency situations and there'd be several individuals on hand to accompany victims to the hospital if they needed to go. There would be counselors there to provide one-on-one therapy sessions to anyone who needed it for as long as they needed it. Nobody would need to worry about having insurance to cover the costs associated with any of the services they'd receive through the center. Qualified staff members would be on hand to help support any individual who wanted to report their abuse. The choice to report would remain with the victim, but if they chose to report it there would be someone there with them through the process. Someone who believed them.

One of the biggest fears that so many sexual assault survivors have is that nobody will believe them if they choose to report it. They blame themselves in many cases for what happened to them and that is another reason they choose to remain silent. Sadly, I knew this firsthand because I blamed myself for a long time.

The part of the center that I was most excited about was the group therapy sessions that would be offered. Not a single individual would be forced or required to be involved in the group therapy, but it would be offered for those that wanted it. I felt this was particularly important because, except for Dr. Lane, I was alone. I wasn't comfortable talking to my family or friends about it in the beginning because of my own shame and embarrassment. I liked to think if I had an easily accessible resource that would have allowed me to connect with women who went through something similar, I would have taken advantage of it. Dr. Lane had mentioned survivor groups to me, but there weren't any that were relatively close to where I lived.

The group therapy sessions would allow survivors to speak to the group and tell their story. They could share anything they wanted about what they experienced, how they felt, what their fears were, or anything else that helped them to cope. It got me thinking that it would be great for those who were further along in their recovery who wanted to help others to share their stories of healing and success so that those who felt hopeless would see that it does get better.

At the end of our meeting, I told Grant I'd head back to my office and I'd reach out to him tomorrow once I had everything in motion. We left Colvert's and I was now pulling into the lot outside my office.

I parked my car and was getting my things out of the backseat when I heard, "There you are."

I jumped and turned to see Cruz walking toward me. Seeing him there filled me with relief and I knew it was because I had worried about him from the moment he told me he was out trying to catch bad guys.

"Cruz," I called. "You scared me. What are you doing here?"

"Didn't mean to sneak up on you. I felt bad I couldn't call you last night and properly congratulate you, so I figured I'd stop by today and do it in person."

Well, that was sweet of him.

I closed my car door and hit the button to lock the doors before I looked back up at Cruz. I was thrown slightly off-kilter. I hadn't expected him to be here and now that he was I was surprised at how good it was to see him again.

"So, are you going to show me the place?"

I grinned up at him and said, "Sure. Follow me."

Cruz walked beside me as we made our way to my office.

I opened the door and we stepped inside. While Cruz closed the door behind us, I set my things down.

"This is it," I exclaimed as I held my arms out to the sides. "It's not much. I've got this common space, my private office, a bathroom, my necessary furniture, a few accent pieces that give it a little flare, and me."

"It's nice," Cruz stated as he looked around the space. I noticed he wasn't necessarily looking at the furniture and décor. He was looking at the walls, the ceiling, and the windows.

"I mean, I know it's nothing like the office you work in, but it's all I really need and I got it at an affordable price. The only downside is the shady business next door; I think they're running a meth lab out of there or something. It's definitely drug-related because there are way too many shifty characters going in and out all day."

Cruz stopped inspecting the place, spun around toward me, his body tense, and practically exploded, "What did you just say?"

I held his eyes a moment before I burst out laughing. Cruz visibly relaxed as I fought to get my hysterics under control. "You should have seen your face," I managed to get out through my laughter.

"That was not cool, Lexi. Joking about canceling a date is one thing, but joking about something like that where your safety is concerned is not funny."

I rolled my eyes and challenged, "Do you really think I'd move into a place where something like that was going on right next door?"

He shook his head in disbelief at me, but he was smirking so I knew he wasn't angry. He even mumbled under his breath, "Smartass." Then, he changed topics. "Late start this morning, then?"

"No, I actually had another meeting with Grant earlier at Colvert's."

His brows pulled together and he wondered, "If you've got this new office space now, why wouldn't you meet here?"

Check mate.

I wondered if I should tell him the real reason. It took me a minute, but I finally decided I wouldn't reveal everything. Instead, I'd give him something and see how he responded.

"I don't know Grant that well and I thought it would be better to meet in a public place where it's less likely something bad could happen."

"Considering he knows your brother, I'm guessing he wouldn't hurt you. That said, it's kind of a waste for you to have this space and not be able to use it. If you'd like, I can certainly get some surveillance equipment installed here."

"I appreciate that and I'm definitely interested, but I'm going to need to hold off. I just spent a ton of money on my rent and security deposit plus most of this furniture. I'm going to need some time to save up first."

"We can work something out for you," he started. "I'll get the equipment you need here figured out and I can come in and install it myself to save you some money. We can work out a payment plan for the equipment if you'd like. Don't take a chance with your safety."

"Really?" I asked. "You'd do that for me?"

"Lexi, I'd do a lot more than that for you."

I swallowed hard and tried to ignore the intention in his tone. To avoid it even more, I asked, "How would it help, though?"

"What do you mean?"

"Well, if I have a client come in for a meeting, it's not like having a security system here would do anything in the event they tried to attack me, right?"

Cruz nonchalantly answered, "We'll set up surveillance monitoring. I can install cameras that'll go to a live feed. We can monitor everything from the office."

"You guys do that?"

He nodded. "For some clients, we do."

"How does it work? Would someone be watching my office all the time? And what does that cost? It can't be cheap."

"You'd be able to turn the monitoring off if you ever wanted the privacy, but it would always be there for you to turn on whenever you felt it was needed. I personally think you should do it. I know it'd make me feel a lot better," he shared.

I asked again, "What do you think this will cost me?"

Cruz shrugged his shoulders and looked around the space. "I don't know. Let me get back to the office and look at your options. Are you going to be here for a while?"

I nodded and clarified, "The rest of the day. I got the go-ahead from Grant on my campaign proposal on the rape crisis center, so I'm going to be working on that for the next two days."

"Alright. I've got a stop to make after I leave here. When I'm done with that, I'm going to go to the office, figure out what I need, and then I'll be back. Does that work for you?"

"What about your case? Wait! Did you catch the bad guys last night?"

I watched as his expression went hard and he clenched his jaw. "No, we didn't. There was a development in the case, which is why I was working later last night, but we haven't gotten anyone yet."

"I'm sorry. Why don't you focus on that for now and we can figure out my stuff afterward?" I suggested.

Cruz took a few steps toward me and spoke softly, "I can't do that, Lexi."

There was something in his eyes I couldn't read. He looked distracted. "What is it, Cruz?"

"My case, Lexi. I didn't want to tell you about this, but I think you should know. And it's not like it hasn't been in the news. A week ago, I got word from the police department that five young women had gone missing over the course of the last three weeks. Last night, we got word that another woman went missing. We believe we've got a sex trafficking ring on our hands."

I gasped.

"Are you joking?" I asked.

I felt myself begin to panic.

Cruz shook his head and cautioned, "This isn't something I'd ever joke about. Given that these cases are local and you are very close to the age range of the women being targeted, I'd really like to make sure you've got round-the-clock surveillance here at your office. Not to mention that if your home doesn't have surveillance, it'd be a wise idea to have it there as well."

My eyes welled with tears as I thought about the women who were taken. I was raped once and it changed my life. I couldn't even begin to imagine what life would be like for these women.

"Are you going to get them back?" I rasped, my voice sounding nothing like my own.

"I promise I'm doing everything I can to make that happen. If I'm going to be able to focus on that, though, I can't be worrying about you the way that I have been for the last week."

I brought my hand up to cover my mouth, hoping I could stop myself from completely breaking down into tears. It was useless because at the same time Cruz lifted his hand to the side of my throat and slid his hand around the back of my neck. He pulled me toward him and as he did I didn't feel any anxiety about him touching me, but anxiety over the looming threat. As soon as my forehead hit his chest, I gripped his shirt in my hands and took deep breaths trying to calm myself down.

Cruz gently squeezed the back of my neck with one hand as the other ran up and down my back. "I'm sorry. I didn't tell you this to upset you, Lexi."

I needed to say something to him and reassure him that I was glad I knew what was going on, but I didn't want to leave the comfort of his arms where I felt safer than I had in years. Keeping my body pressed to his, I tilted my head back and revealed, "I'm grateful you told me."

He tightened his arms around me and asked, "Will you let me do what I've got to do to get you set up with security and surveillance here?"

I nodded.

"What about your home?"

I shook my head and advised, "I don't have anything there either."

"I'll go get what you need here and come back to install it. After, if you are okay with it, I'll follow you back to your place so I can check it out and see what you'll need there. Will you let me do that?"

Cruz.

In my apartment.

Other than my brothers and my father, no man had ever been there. But when Cruz asked to come there, I didn't have any doubts about it.

"Yes."

I felt his body relax before he asked, "If I let you go now and leave, are you going to be okay?"

I dropped my forehead to his chest again and took a deep

breath. Just as I was about to step back and pull away, I felt Cruz press his lips to the top of my head.

I didn't want that. I didn't want his lips kissing the top of my head. I wanted them kissing mine.

I kept my hands pressed to his chest and looked back up at him. His eyes were searching my face. I did the same until my gaze settled on his lips. I believed he was about to lean in to kiss me when my phone rang pulling us both out of the moment.

Reluctantly, I stepped out of Cruz's embrace and moved to get my phone. I looked down and saw that Nikki was calling. I would call her back.

"It's Nikki. I can call her back," I started as I walked back toward him. "Sorry about my meltdown a minute ago. I'm alright now and will be fine until you get back."

Cruz shook his head and said, "Don't worry about it. It's not exactly easy stuff for anyone to hear. I've been doing this for quite a few years now and these kinds of cases are still a tough pill for me to swallow. All we can do is work hard to make sure we get these women back quickly and safely and then get them the help they need."

"And now they'll have WAAR here to help them."

"That's right," he began. "Well, congratulations again on the place. I'm going to head out now, but I'll be back soon. If you need anything in the meantime, don't hesitate to call me."

"Thanks again, Cruz. I appreciate you taking the time to do this for me."

"You're welcome, Lexi. See you in a little bit."

At that, Cruz left my office. I waited a whole three seconds before I freaked out and ran back over to my phone. I needed Nikki's advice. So, I tapped on my screen and held the phone to my ear. When Nikki greeted me, I began to fret, "You aren't going to believe what almost just happened to me."

"What?" she shot back, slightly panicked.

"If you hadn't called, I would have kissed Cruz."

"Tell me everything," she ordered.

I did. I told her everything. I also told her that he was coming back to my office and that he'd be going to my apartment afterward. Nikki, as was always a seemingly effortless task for her, talked me through all my worries about what might happen with Cruz. I knew I was nowhere near ready to take any big steps, but there was that small piece of me that wanted the comfort of Cruz's kisses. It was the part of me that could still feel the one he pressed to my head moments ago, making me realize I wanted more from him.

And there was that part of my heart that hoped Cruz wanted to give that to me.

CHAPTER 10

Cruz

I walked into my brother's office feeling like I was carrying the weight of the world on my shoulders.

"Hey, Levi. You got a minute?"

"Sure, Cruz. What's up?"

I sat down in the chair on the opposite side of his desk and announced, "I just got back from visiting Detective Baines. The WPD got a report early this morning of another missing woman."

Levi sat up a little straighter and clarified, "This is in addition to the one who went missing last night?"

"Yeah."

"Fuck," he muttered.

"I'm going to get all of the information over to Dom and Lorenzo before I go, but I can't work on this case today."

Levi's brows pulled together. He knew something wasn't right because I never removed myself from a case like this. "What's going on?" he asked.

"It's Lexi."

My brother grinned at me. "Is it finally your turn?" he joked, knowing I'd given him and Zane a hard time when they started dating Elle and Emme.

I took a deep breath.

"I'd like for it to be, but she's not exactly interested right now and wants to focus on her career. That said, there's definitely an attraction on both ends."

"So, if it's not about that, what's happening with Lexi?"

"She just signed a lease on a new office space not far from here. I stopped over there this morning before I met with Baines. She doesn't have any security or surveillance there and actually scheduled a meeting with a client today at Colvert's because she doesn't like the idea of being in her office alone with someone she doesn't know well."

"You want to get her set up?"

I nodded and went on, "At her apartment, too. She's right in the age range of the women being taken. Add that to the fact that the case I just learned about this afternoon is one that occurred at the Windsor Mall, which isn't far from her office, and I'm not alright leaving her without any protection."

Levi didn't hesitate and ordered, "Get her squared away with everything she needs. She's Elle's friend and will soon be your girl. I don't want any money for anything; just get her covered. Make sure you update Lorenzo and Dom before you leave. I might bring another guy in on this case. It's growing too quickly."

"Agreed. Thanks, Levi."

I stood to leave, but he spoke again. "Just so you know, I've got to tell Zane. After you did everything you could to torment him when he got together with Emme, it's only fair he has the opportunity to do it to you in return."

"You can tell him what you want. There's nothing going on."

"Yeah, yeah. I'm sure there will be soon enough."

I shook my head and walked out. After getting the case files from my office I went to Dom's and found he and Lorenzo were both just about to leave.

"Headed out?" I asked.

"Yeah," Dom answered. "We're going to follow up on some of these cases and see if anything was missed that can help us."

"There's another one," I blurted, stopping them in their tracks.

"What?" Lorenzo asked.

"Reported early this morning. All of the details are in this file," I offered, handing the file over to him. "I'd check it out before you head out. It's the newest one, so we might have better luck. I'm out today, but let me know if you find anything worthwhile."

"Where are you going to be? This is your only case right now," Dom pointed out the obvious.

Here we go. I knew I wasn't going to hear the end of it.

"I've got to install security and surveillance at an office and apartment," I shared, thinking they might not question it.

I should have known better.

"Something tells me the security isn't for just anyone, is it?" Dom goaded me.

Dom and Lorenzo were both smirking at me, so I did the only thing I could. I narrowed my eyes and kept my mouth shut.

"Yep," Lorenzo started. "It's the girl…his burn victim."

"She's not my anything yet. Her new office has no security and she's blocks away from where the newest woman went missing. She's the same age as these women. I'm not taking any chances."

Dom walked over, held his hand out for the file, and replied, "Go take care of your girl. We'll handle this."

"Thanks," I began. "By the way, Levi might be adding someone else to the mix. Too many women are disappearing too quickly."

They nodded their understanding and walked back to the chairs to review the file. "Later, Cruz."

I made my way back to the supply room where we stored all of our surveillance and security equipment. I got what I knew I needed for Lexi's office and grabbed a few extra items for her apartment. I didn't know for sure what I'd need there, but with any luck I'd be able to get something set up with the extras I was bringing.

Once I loaded everything up in my truck, I took off toward her office.

On the drive over, I had to be honest with myself. There was no doubt that a physical attraction existed between Lexi and me since the first time we met. To this day, I knew that attraction was still present on both ends. What I didn't know was if that was all that there was for Lexi.

I knew I was intrigued by her in the few instances I had been around her, but then we met and had breakfast on Saturday morning. That did it for me. Talking to her, seeing her uninhibited for the first time since meeting her, and hearing her laugh for those few hours was all I needed. I knew there was something special about her and it was something I wanted in my life.

On every occasion I had been around her before we had our breakfast date, she'd always been so reserved. It was obvious she was being cautious, but it wasn't ever unfriendly or off-putting. Perhaps it was because of what I do for a living, but seeing that in her made me realize there was something more to her that she didn't let others see.

That is, she never showed it to me until Saturday morning when I sat at Colvert's waiting for her to arrive. The moment she called and told me that she needed to cancel, my stomach sank. When she stood in front of me seconds later proud of herself for making me believe she wasn't coming,

I knew I hadn't been wrong about her. She laughed through a good portion of our date, and from the moment we parted ways that morning I knew I wanted to be with her again. I craved her playfulness. Part of me wondered if I wanted more of her and her lighthearted nature around me simply because I had enough stuff in my life with work that was serious. Either way, it didn't matter what it was; all I knew for sure was that I wanted more of her. I fought the urge to call her every day because I didn't want to seem overeager. Thankfully, my case did a good job of occupying my mind and made it a little easier to resist the temptation to pick up the phone.

Seeing her again earlier today and almost instantly being reminded of that lively spirit did me in. Of course, I wasn't exactly thrilled that she nearly gave me a heart attack telling me she thought there was a meth lab next door to her office, but I was willing to deal with it if it meant hearing her laugh like she did.

I wasn't proud of myself for taking Lexi's carefree attitude away from her when I told her about the case I was working on, but I thought it was important she knew what was happening. Hearing that she was already being cautious by scheduling her meetings in public places made me feel a little better, but I didn't like that she didn't feel safe enough to do it in the space she was paying for.

What didn't sit well with me at all was the absolute shock and horror I saw on her face when I shared that there was likely a sex trafficking ring happening right under our noses. I expected she would be upset, but her reaction was so much more than I would have ever imagined. I did my best to comfort her and, luckily, she agreed to let me put the security measures in place for her.

I arrived back at Lexi's office, gathered up the equipment,

and walked to the entrance. I tapped on the door before opening it and walking in.

There she was, sitting at the desk in her office. The nice thing about the space was that she had her own separate area, but with the door to it open she could see out into the common room.

"You're back," she exclaimed as she looked up and saw me.

"I told you I would be," I responded.

There was a look of genuine happiness on her face. I couldn't deny that it made me feel good to see it.

As I walked into her private office, I confirmed, "Are you alright with me just doing what I think needs to be done or do you want me to go over all of it with you first?"

"I'll be honest," she replied. "It's not my forte, so you'll get just about the same result telling me about it as you would if you spoke to me in a foreign language. I trust your judgment, Cruz."

"Ok, I'm going to get to work then."

For the next couple hours, I worked on getting everything set up in Lexi's office. I got the security system with motion sensors covering the entire space as well as monitors on all of the doors and windows. I even added options so that she could have the place armed when she was inside working. The motion sensors would be disabled, but the exterior monitors would still be operational. I added cameras everywhere, excluding the bathroom, and called the Cunningham Security office to confirm that the feed was live and functioning.

When I finished, I walked back in to Lexi's office, where she was furiously typing away on her keyboard. She was so focused she didn't see me standing there, so I took full advantage and just watched her. Lexi was so beautiful, it would have been easy to watch her all day.

After giving myself some time to take her in, I cleared my throat. Lexi looked up at me and asked, "Are you finished already?"

"I'm not sure how long you expected it to take, but it's been a few hours already," I explained.

Lexi's eyes drifted to her computer and back to me before she responded, "Wow, I guess you're right. I was so caught up in my work, it didn't feel like that much time had passed."

"Are you able to take a break so I can show you how it all works?"

"Yes," she said as she stood. "I'm already so far ahead of where I expected to be today, so I'm good to leave after you show it to me."

I spent the next fifteen minutes explaining the entire system to Lexi. I gave her the security code, showed her where the cameras were, and demonstrated how to arm the office when she was inside and when she locked up in the evenings. I also made sure she knew how to turn the cameras off if she wanted or needed the privacy, but confirmed she could turn them on so they'd send the feed to the office. Finally, I ensured she was aware of the fact there were two important buttons on the keypad: one that would send an alert to the police station and another that would send an alert to our office.

"Do you need to go over it again or do you think you've got it?" I asked.

Lexi thought a minute before she declared, "I think I've got it."

"Okay. If you come in tomorrow and forget, just call me and I'll walk you through it without a problem."

"Thank you, Cruz. I really appreciate you doing this for me," she said.

"Don't mention it, Lexi. I wasn't kidding when I said it'll help me focus on the case a bit better if I know that you are safe no matter if you're working or if you're at home. Speaking of which, I'm ready to go whenever you are."

Lexi hesitated a moment, but after a few seconds passed, she finally spoke.

"Yes, I'm ready. Let me just grab my things."

I waited while Lexi packed up her stuff and walked to the front door with her key in her hand. She set the alarm on the office without any issues, locked the door, and walked out to her car.

Twenty minutes later, I was pulling into the lot at Lexi's apartment complex. I had to admit I felt a bit of relief at the fact that she didn't live in a bad area nor was her place too close to where any of the missing women were last seen.

Carrying the extra security equipment I brought from the office, I followed Lexi to the front door and into her apartment.

"If you want to set your stuff down, I can show you around," she offered.

I put everything down just inside the front door and urged, "Lead the way."

Lexi didn't move.

At least, she didn't move her feet. She did lift her arms out to the side as she shrugged her shoulders and stated, "This is my living room."

I didn't look around the room because I was too captivated by her. She was adorable without even trying and I didn't want to miss a moment of it.

She turned around to walk out of the living room. My eyes dropped to her ass that was covered by her black, form-fitting jeans. Lexi had a great ass.

Before she caught me staring, I started to walk and followed her out of the living room into her kitchen. It wasn't huge, but it had all the amenities you'd need. Just off her kitchen wasn't what I'd call a formal dining room; however, she made it her own and it would serve its purpose.

From there, Lexi took me down a short, narrow hall. She opened the door and pushed through.

When she spoke again, her voice was husky. It was the sexiest thing I'd ever heard. "This is my bedroom."

Once again, my eyes never left her face. What was different about this was that she was no longer the goofy Lexi she was out in her living room. The Lexi standing in front of me was sultry and seductive with just the sound of her voice and the look in her eyes.

I took two steps toward her and closed the distance between us. Then, I watched as her lips slowly parted.

"I like it," I admitted, though I wasn't necessarily referring to her bedroom.

She closed her mouth and swallowed. It was easy to feel the nervous energy coming from her.

I lifted my crooked finger to her chin and brought my thumb up to swipe across her bottom lip. Her body tensed.

"Lexi," I whispered.

"Hm," she responded.

"I know you said you just wanted to get to know one another, but I feel like there's more here. The look in your eyes tells me that you might feel the same."

"I do," she revealed, her voice trembling.

Relief coursed through me. "Can I please kiss you?"

Her eyes rounded. Then, she answered, "Yes."

I lowered my mouth and gently brushed my lips back and forth across hers, while my hand that had been at her chin moved to the side of her neck.

Just as I was about to kiss her, my phone rang and killed the moment.

Damn.

Lexi tensed up and took a step back.

I begrudgingly pulled my phone from my pocket and saw my brother's name on the display.

"Zane," I said into the phone as a way of greeting him.

"What's this I hear about you and Lexi?" he replied.

My eyes were focused on her. She looked a mix of frustrated, nervous, and something else I couldn't quite figure out.

"Now's not a good time," I warned. I was not having this conversation with him.

"Fuck, bro. Are you with her?"

Lexi managed to get herself together and mouthed that she was going to be out in the kitchen.

I nodded.

Once she stepped outside the room, I shared, "Yes, I am. And let me just say that you've got impeccable timing."

My brother laughed.

"Consider it payback for all the times you tormented me when it came to Emme."

I grunted in response. I had to be honest with myself. It was likely I deserved what I was about to get from both Zane and Levi. I never held back with my opinion when it came to their relationships and I certainly pushed their buttons, especially Zane's. I needed to prepare myself for the fact that he was probably going to give it back to me just as hard.

"Alright," he started. "I'll let you go for now then. Just a quick question, though. Does Luke know you've got a thing for his sister?"

"There's nothing going on. We're just friends," I insisted, even though I didn't necessarily believe what had just come out of my mouth.

"Famous last words," he shot back. "I recall the day I told you, Levi, Mom, and Dad that Emme was just a friend. Maybe nothing had happened between us at that point, but that didn't mean I hadn't already decided that I was going to find a way to change that."

"I've got to go," I replied, a bit frustrated.

He laughed and ended, "Have fun. Later, Cruz."

I disconnected the call and stood there staring out the window, thinking about what had happened just before my phone rang. I'd been dying to kiss Lexi and was mere seconds away from it happening. Maybe luck wasn't on my side anymore. Or perhaps I'd really done some awful things to my brothers that it was only fair I dealt with the same in return. Either way, I was now beyond frustrated and even feeling a bit remorseful for what I'd put them through.

Shaking my head, I turned and walked out of Lexi's bedroom back toward the kitchen.

When I stepped inside the kitchen, I found Lexi's back to me as she stood at her counter chopping something. I took a moment to check her out again because she was so incredibly sexy. It was a bad idea since it only served to make me more turned on.

I took a deep breath and tried to regain my control. After a futile attempt to tamp down some of my sexual frustration, I spoke. "Sorry about that," I apologized.

Lexi spun around with a butcher's knife in her hand pointed right at me.

I held my hands up and took two steps back even though I was already across the room from her.

She let out a breath and set the knife down on the counter. "I'm sorry, you scared me. I didn't hear you come back down the hall."

I gave her a minute to calm herself down. She finally did and went on, "I don't know how long you'll need to install what you brought, but I figured since it's getting late I could make dinner for the both of us. Do you like fajitas?"

"Works for me," I started, trying not to let my excitement show. The truth was, I wouldn't have cared if she was going to serve liver and onions; I would eat whatever she made just so I'd be able to spend more time with her. "I brought enough with me to get you set up with at least a basic security system tonight. I can get started on that now and then I'll want to come back as soon as you are free so that I can install a few extras I'd like you to have here."

"Sure. I know you've got a lot going on with your case, so I can try to work with your schedule. That said, my plan was to spend the entire day tomorrow working on the campaign for WAAR. I can do that from here if tomorrow works well for you."

"I can make that work. I'll try to be here first thing in the morning so I don't interrupt your day."

She nodded her agreement.

At that, she went about making dinner while I got to work on her security system. Roughly an hour later, Lexi found me in the middle of the installation and told me dinner was ready. I followed her back to the dining area, where she had set the table for two. Aside from the plates and utensils she set out for us, there was also a serving platter filled with chicken, peppers, and onions. She had guacamole, sour cream, salsa, and cheese set out in smaller dishes with a pile of warmed tortillas between our two plates.

"Looks amazing," I praised her.

And it did.

"Thanks. I'm sorry I don't have much to offer you in the way of drinks. I've got water or wine."

I chuckled. "Water is fine."

After grabbing drinks, Lexi and I sat to eat. As we each took a tortilla and began assembling our fajitas, Lexi wasted no time in diving into conversation.

"How's the installation coming along? Is there a lot of work left?"

"I've got about an hour left," I explained. "I'm not keeping you from anything, am I?"

She shook her head. "No, not at all. I didn't have anything planned for tonight other than doing some work. I'm a bit under the gun to get things squared away with the crisis center since there's just over a week left before it officially opens. Considering I was a bit busy before I took on this project, I've been putting in some long days. At least now I've got the office squared away. It's just one more thing to check off my ever-growing to-do list."

"You've garnered a lot of clients in a short amount of time then?" I asked as I held the fajita up to my mouth.

Lexi nodded and added, "Yeah, I guess so. Obviously, things started with Monroe and her dance studio. Since then I've added Elle and Wes as clients. I've got a few smaller businesses that I work with. One of my friends from college is planning to open her own yoga studio in Windsor as soon as she finds the perfect location, so I'm meeting with her next week to help her with that project. Obviously, I've also picked up Grant and the center. Needless to say, I've certainly got enough to keep me busy."

I felt bad not responding to what she said, but I felt compelled to share, "These fajitas are amazing, Lex. Where'd you learn to cook?"

"My mom taught me the basics," she responded. "I've picked up a few things on my own, though. I'm glad you like them. So, what about you?"

"What about me?"

"Well, you wondered if you were keeping me from anything by being here. I was just curious if I was keeping you from anything."

I sighed. "I'm pretty much married to work right now. It's been really busy over the last few months. Now, with this new case, I put in even more time than I usually do."

"Do you like working so much?" she wondered.

I shrugged my shoulders. "I like feeling useful and I like the challenge this career gives me. I give myself more free time when I'm working on things like real estate or insurance fraud cases. But with something like I'm working on now, I tend to overwork. I don't mind the extra time I put in, though, because it's necessary. The longer it takes to find these women, the longer their road to recovery will be. Some may not ever fully recover."

Lexi swallowed hard, set her fajita down on her plate, and sat back in her chair.

"Is everything okay?" I asked.

She looked down at her plate before she looked back at me and answered, "I feel awful, Cruz. You shouldn't be here with me right now; you should be doing whatever you've got to do to find those women."

"Lexi," I started, my voice soft. "I already told you that I haven't been able to fully focus on this case since I learned about it because I've been worrying about you. You fit the profile. I need to ease my concerns about your safety so I can focus on finding them. Even setting up the security and surveillance in your office and apartment won't make me not worry, but I'll rest a little easier knowing you've got some protection."

She held my eyes, but said nothing.

"Don't worry that I'm here and nothing's being done. Dom and Lorenzo have been busting their asses just as hard and they're working on the case as we speak. Before I came to your office earlier, Levi told me he was going to put another guy on the case so we can hopefully make more progress."

Finally, Lexi spoke. "Are you going to find them? Will you get those girls back?"

"We're doing everything we can to see that they're brought home as quickly as possible. I promise you that. We won't stop until we take down whoever is behind this."

Lexi seemed to accept my response and got back to eating. We finished dinner, moving our conversation to much lighter topics. It took her a minute to loosen up again, but Lexi was soon back to being her funny self.

After dinner, I attempted to help Lexi clean up, but she insisted I get back to work.

So, I did.

About an hour later, I had completed the installation on the system. I found Lexi, gave her the rundown on how this one worked, and gave her the code.

"Thank you for this, Cruz," she offered.

"You're welcome, Lexi. I'll stop back tomorrow morning around nine, if that works for you, to add the last few things to it."

"Nine o'clock is fine with me."

I nodded, took a few steps backward, and bent down by the couch, where I began packing up my tools.

When I stood and started moving toward the front door to leave, Lexi called, "Cruz?"

"Yeah?" I responded as I turned toward her.

She was shifting nervously back and forth on her feet and fidgeting with her hands. "May I hug you?" she finally got out.

For the life of me, I couldn't understand why she thought she needed to ask me that. I thought I made it rather clear how much I liked her. Instead of pointing that out, though, I dropped my tools and simply held one of my arms out to her. Lexi took two steps toward me and wrapped her arms around my waist. I brought my arms around her and held her tight.

"Thank you, Cruz. Thank you for doing this for me."

I squeezed her a little tighter in response and pressed a kiss to the top of her head. She tilted her head back and brought her eyes to mine. They stayed there only briefly before they dropped to my mouth. I let her gaze linger on my lips a bit before I asked, "What is it, Lexi?"

After her eyes searched my face, slightly frantic, she practically brought me to my knees when she shared, "I want you to kiss me, Cruz. I haven't been kissed in a very long time and I think I'd really like for you to be the one to do it."

She was looking up at me, her eyes hopeful. I was certain I'd die if I didn't kiss this girl. She didn't have to ask me twice.

With her beautiful body pressed up against me, I dropped my mouth to hers. The spark I felt the second my lips connected with her soft ones was something I knew I'd never forget. I brought my tongue out to tease her lips and she wasted not one second before she opened her mouth to let me in. My tongue explored her mouth while Lexi took the liberty to explore mine with hers.

She leaned further into me and I took her weight, all while keeping my mouth connected to hers.

We kissed for a long time, my arms keeping her tight against my body. Eventually, she pulled away. When she did, she buried her face in my chest. I found the reaction odd.

"Are you okay?" I asked.

I felt her take a deep breath before she pulled back and smiled up at me. "Yeah, I'm fabulous."

I loved it…that excited, happy look on her face.

I smiled back at her and said, "I should get going."

She nodded at me and dropped her hands from around my waist.

"I'll see you tomorrow morning," she reminded me.

"Nine in the morning," I repeated.

At that, I opened the door and urged, "Be sure to set the alarm after I leave."

"I will," she assured me.

I dipped my chin and closed the door behind me. I waited until I heard her lock the door before I walked away. Then, I got in my truck and replayed that kiss with Lexi in my head the entire ride home.

Nine o'clock couldn't come soon enough.

CHAPTER 11

Lexi

IT WAS EIGHT FIFTEEN THE NEXT MORNING WHEN MY PHONE RANG.

"Morning, Cruz," I answered.

"Hey, Lexi. Listen, I'm really sorry to do this, but I've got to cancel on you this morning," Cruz let me down gently.

"Is everything okay?" I worried.

"Something came up on the case and I've got to get it handled right away. I know you've got work to do and I didn't want you sitting around waiting for me. If you wanted to go to your office, you can. I'll still come by today if you're available later in the day. I don't know what time it'll be, but definitely not before early evening at best."

"Of course," I started. "Please do whatever you've got to do. I'll head to the office for a little bit today to get some work done, but I should be back here around five."

"Really sorry, Lex."

He sounded tortured.

"It's alright, Cruz. I'd prefer you take care of your case anyway. You've got me set up at the office and I'll be spending the day there today, so I'm good. Don't worry about me; just focus on what you've got to do."

I heard him let out a sigh. "Thanks for understanding. I'll see you tonight."

"Sounds good. I'll see you then."

I disconnected the call and felt a wave of disappointment wash over me. I barely slept last night because I spent so much time replaying my kiss with Cruz over and over in my head.

After what happened in my office earlier that day, I had mixed emotions. On one hand, I knew how badly I wanted to experience having him kiss me, but on the other I was nervous about the fact that I was finally feeling attracted to someone. I worried about what might happen if I gave into what I was suddenly feeling…what I wanted to delve deeper into.

Just before he left last night, I found the courage to ask for something I wanted.

His arms around me.

Oddly, I found a great sense of security there. I didn't necessarily understand it, but I didn't want to dwell on it either. It's not like I had been through sexual assault recovery before, so I didn't know what to expect. As Dr. Lane had expressed to me throughout the course of the years I'd been seeing her, everyone's road to healing is different. There was no instruction book on how to proceed. I had to start listening to my instincts and trust in myself. I had to believe in what I was feeling.

For me, it felt like it had been a long road already. Continuing to move ahead would certainly challenge me, but I knew I wanted to get to a place where I could rediscover my sexuality. I didn't want to live the rest of my life believing that kissing, hugging, touching, sex, and other intimate acts were bad. And the only way for me to know how I'd react in those situations was to put myself in them with someone I could trust. I knew, though, that to be fair to myself and him, I was going to have to be forthcoming with that person before it was too late.

So, I decided I wanted Cruz to kiss me. I had nerves about asking him, but they melted away the instant his lips touched mine. His kiss felt wonderful and I had to admit that the biggest reason I felt such disappointment with him not being able to come by this morning was that I wanted to experience that again with him.

But he had important work to do. I wanted him to do what he needed to help those girls and bring them home.

On these thoughts, I went about getting my things ready and left for my office.

As soon as I arrived, I dove into my work for the rape crisis center. It would be officially opening a week from Monday, and the closer we got to that day, the more determined I found myself. I wanted WAAR to be a success. The success I was searching for with it wouldn't be based on the amount of donations we brought in, though. In my opinion, the center's success could only be defined by the work it did for each survivor that walked through the doors.

Halfway through my day, I took a quick break to have some lunch. Afterward, I made calls confirming my appointments for next week. One of those calls was to Lennox, a girl I had been acquaintances with in high school, but managed to become friends with while I was in college. She didn't know about my rape. When I was in the spring semester of my sophomore year at my new school, we had a class together. I wasn't looking for friends while I was there, but we needed to do a group project and I gravitated toward her because she was someone familiar. We forged a friendship and have kept in touch since graduating. She was going to be opening her own yoga studio in Windsor and wanted my help, so we had scheduled a meeting for next week.

"Hello?" she answered after one ring.

"Hey, Leni. It's Lexi. I'm calling you from the phone in my new office," I began, realizing she probably didn't recognize my number. "I just wanted to confirm our meeting for Tuesday afternoon."

"You finally found an office?"

"Yeah. I looked at a few last week, put in an offer on this one, and officially moved in on Wednesday."

"That's awesome. Congratulations! I've got news of my own," she hinted.

"What's going on?"

"I found the perfect location for my yoga studio and I'm signing the lease on Monday," she shared.

"Oh, Leni, I'm so happy for you. Congrats to you, too!"

"Thanks," she started. "I'm so excited for our meeting on Tuesday, so consider me confirmed. I can't wait to start."

I suddenly heard a loud, blaring sound come through the phone.

"Oh shit," she cried. "That's the smoke alarm. I forgot about the food in the oven. I've got to go, Lex. Send me your new office address and I'll meet you there on Tuesday."

I laughed. "Sounds good. Don't set your place on fire!"

She disconnected the call and I sent her the address for my new office. After, I confirmed I had all the details finalized for Elle's meet and greet this weekend and sent her a quick text.

Me: ***Hey, El. Just wanted to let you know that I need to move our meeting tomorrow to the morning if possible.***

I got back to work and about five minutes later, she responded.

Elle: ***Sure. Is everything alright?***

Me: ***I have dinner plans with Cruz.***

Elle: ***WHAAAAAT!***

Me: ***He kissed me last night.***

Elle: ***Ack! I'm so excited. How was it?***

Me: ***Fabulous. Absolutely fabulous.***

Elle: ***Details tomorrow morning!!***

Me: okay. ***My place around 10. Does that work for you?***

Elle: ***I'll be there.***

I got back to work and before I knew it, I was packing up my things to head home. I grabbed what I needed for Elle's event on Sunday since I had no plans to head back to the office until Monday morning.

After securing the alarm at my office, I walked out to my car and made my way home. It was nearly five-thirty and I hadn't eaten since lunch. I checked that the sauce I pulled out of the freezer earlier that morning had thawed before I turned on the oven and went about making my turkey meatballs. Twenty-five minutes after I put them in the oven, they were finished. I wasn't typically a big pasta eater, but I decided to live a little today. I grabbed a bowl, filled it with pasta, put a few meatballs on top, and ate dinner.

Once I finished, I cleaned up the kitchen and decided to change into my workout clothes. I put on a pair of yoga pants, a sports bra, and a loose-fitting tee. It was approaching seven and I hadn't heard anything from Cruz. I didn't know what time to expect him, but figured it might be best to get my workout in now.

An hour later, just as I finished my workout and started walking to my bedroom to take a shower, I heard a knock at the door.

That would be just my luck. Cruz would show up now, when I smelled and was covered in a sheen of sweat.

I opened the door and, despite being overheated from my workout, felt my temperature skyrocket at the sight of Cruz.

"Hey," I greeted.

Cruz's eyes traveled the length of me before he replied, "Hey."

I stepped back to allow him to come inside and, after I closed the door, I continued to step back. I *did not* want Cruz smelling the grossness that was likely me in that moment.

"Sorry," I lamented once I had moved far enough away. "I

didn't know what time to expect you so I figured I'd get my workout in. I was just about to jump in the shower when you arrived."

His face did something and his expression changed, but I wasn't sure what it was or what it meant.

"I brought everything I need to get your security system finished up. I won't need to be in your bedroom, so you can go shower if you want. I'll just get to work."

I nodded and offered, "I don't know if you ate anything, but I have some leftover spaghetti and turkey meatballs if you'd like. I can heat them up quickly before I hop in the shower."

"I didn't eat," he shared. "I finished doing what I had to do and came right here to see you."

He didn't eat. And he came right over. Not to finish installing my security system, but to see me. I had to admit how good that felt.

With that, I turned and walked to the kitchen to heat up some food for Cruz. When it was ready, I walked back out to where he was in the living room, sorting through a bunch of equipment. As I gestured toward the dining area, I stated, "Food's ready. I set it on the table out there. I'll be back in a few minutes."

"Thanks, Lex."

I made my way to my bedroom, closed the door, and walked into the bathroom. I locked that door. I didn't think Cruz would go against what he said and follow me into my room, but habit made me lock the door.

Twenty-five minutes later, I had finished in the shower, dried my hair, and thrown on a pair of sweats and a T-shirt. I went back out to the living room and saw that Cruz was still working. I didn't want to interrupt him so I made my presence known and settled myself on the couch. No matter how hard

I tried to fight it, between the lack of sleep last night thinking about Cruz and the workout I had just put in, it didn't take long for me to give in to the exhaustion.

"Lexi?" I heard Cruz's gentle voice call.

My eyes shot open and I took in my surroundings. I was on the couch in my living room and Cruz was sitting on the edge of it next to me. I had fallen asleep with a man in my apartment!

I quickly scooted myself up and rested my back against the armrest.

"I'm sorry," I apologized.

"It's okay. I just finished up and didn't want to leave without letting you know. Plus, I didn't think you'd be comfortable sleeping here on the couch all night either."

Well, that was nice of him.

"Did you get everything squared away?" I asked.

"Yes. Everything is good to go. There aren't any new instructions for you, so you'll arm and disarm the system the way I showed you yesterday."

"Thank you. Now, will you see to it that a bill is sent to me or should I stop in to get an invoice?"

"Don't worry about it."

"Pardon?"

Cruz grinned at me and explained, "This one's on the house."

"What? Why?"

"I told Levi yesterday what I was doing and he said he didn't want any money for the equipment. He wanted you covered and told me to take whatever was needed to see to it that you were."

I was shocked. "He can't do that."

Cruz laughed. "He owns the company; I think he can."

I knew I'd see Levi this weekend at Elle's meet and greet event, so I would have to talk to him about it when I saw him. I figured it was best to talk to Cruz about his compensation.

"Ok, I'll talk to Levi about the equipment then. What about your labor?"

He didn't respond. That is to say, he didn't respond with words. Instead, he gave me a look that told me I was crazy to even mention his labor.

"I'm serious," I went on. "Between the time you've put in at my office and then here at my apartment, it's been a lot of hours. You need to be paid for your work."

"Lexi, I'd never accept a single penny to keep you safe."

I felt my belly flutter at his words.

"Are you sure?" I confirmed.

He brought his hand up to cup the side of my face. As his thumb stroked back and forth across my cheek, he answered softly, "Absolutely."

I liked the feel of his hand on my skin, so I tilted my head and leaned into his palm as I closed my eyes. Before I could open them, I felt his breath hit my lips as he whispered, "Can I kiss you again, Lexi?"

I really wanted to kiss him again so I nodded.

Cruz closed the distance between our lips and kissed me. The moment his mouth was on mine, my hands went to his hair and my body shifted so that my head was on the armrest of the couch. Without disconnecting his mouth from mine, Cruz managed to shift his body on the couch so that he was lying beside me. Suddenly, our bodies were pressed together, his front to mine, as we continued to kiss each other. Warmth spread through me.

For the first time in a very long time, I felt desire.

Desire for a man.

One that made me feel safe.

As our tongues continued to explore, I couldn't seem to control what I was feeling. Cruz separated his mouth from mine, only so he could nibble at my lip and kiss along my jaw. I let out a moan. That's when Cruz pressed his hand to my belly so that I'd fall to my back. He buried his face in my neck, shifting his body halfway onto mine, while my fingers ran through his hair. Cruz's hand that had been at my belly slid to my side. His lips were pressed to the skin at the side of my throat, his hand beginning to glide up the side of my body.

When his hand reached my underarm, his mouth moved from my neck back up along my jaw to my mouth again. His tongue dipped inside, tasting me again.

I was so consumed, so caught up in the lust I had for him, that by the time I realized what was happening, it was already too late. Cruz's hands had both continued to slide up the underside of my arms until my arms were pinned underneath his above my head. The heat that had been running through my body only seconds ago was doused immediately and I felt nothing but ice-cold terror.

Not again.

This couldn't happen again.

I panicked.

Even though his mouth was on mine, a muffled sound escaped me. I pressed as hard as I could against his arms. Cruz pulled his head back and that's when it came out.

"No!" I screamed. "No, no!"

He was frozen. I was freaked.

"Get off me!" I shouted as I began frantically trying to free my body.

In an instant, Cruz lifted his body off mine. I was free. I bolted up off the couch and moved to the middle of the room, free from the danger.

"Lexi?" I heard. "Honey, what's wrong?"

My head snapped in the direction of his voice and I saw Cruz standing a few feet away looking at me, terrified.

I couldn't say anything. I was trying to catch my breath and my heart was pounding so hard I could hear it in my ears.

"Are you okay?" he worried.

I shook my head because I couldn't find my voice. I began feeling dizzy and I knew my legs weren't going to hold me up much longer.

"Hold on to me, Lex," I heard Cruz order, his voice inches from me.

I didn't move.

"I'm not going to touch you, princess. Just wrap your arms around me wherever is comfortable for you and lean into me."

I couldn't hold myself up any more, so I wrapped my arms around his neck and pressed my cheek to his chest.

"Just breathe, honey. Nice and slow. Deep breaths."

I tried to regain control of my breathing. I wasn't having much luck.

"I'm going to lower us to the ground so you don't fall," he said, gently. "Keep holding on to me and slowly bend your legs. okay?"

I slid my cheek up and down on his chest.

Cruz carefully lowered us to the ground and he did it without putting a finger on me.

I was hanging on to Cruz, trying to calm myself and catch my breath. I wanted the warm comfort back, something Cruz always managed to give me whenever I was around him.

"Please…" I struggled to get out through my quick, shallow breaths. "Please hold me."

Cruz engulfed me in his arms and held on tight. There was no concept of time in that moment, but I knew that it wasn't until his arms were around me that I was able to start finding peace and security. I don't know how much time passed before I finally steadied my breathing and dropped my arms from around his neck. When I pulled away, I not only lost the comfort of his arms, but also fought against every urge to bury my face in my hands so I wouldn't have to face him. As embarrassed as I felt, I knew I couldn't stay quiet about what had just happened. Cruz deserved to know the truth and I wanted him to have it.

I lifted my head and looked at Cruz. There was nothing but genuine concern and worry on his face.

"I'm sorry," I croaked.

His face went soft. "Lexi, what just happened?"

"I should have told you sooner. They told me not to wait, but I was scared."

"Who?" he asked. "Told me what?"

I took in a deep breath and closed my eyes. After I let it out, I opened them and gave it to him. "My brothers. They told me the other day not to wait to tell you the truth."

I paused a moment before continuing, "Nearly four years ago, when I was at the end of my freshman year in college, I was raped."

The air around us became frighteningly thick with a mix of anger and tension. Nearly all of it was radiating from the man in front of me.

"I should have said something before," I repeated.

"Why didn't you?" he asked, his voice hoarse.

"I was scared."

"Of what?"

"You," I sighed.

"Lexi, I would never hurt you. Ever," he responded. I was certain I heard a bit of disappointment in his response.

I shook my head, upset that he misunderstood what I was saying. "I know that. Oddly enough, somehow, I know that."

I paused a minute.

Cruz left me to it. Then, I continued, "I like you a lot, Cruz. You are the first man I've been attracted to since it happened."

"What triggered your panic attack?"

My eyes filled with tears and my voice was shaky when I confessed, "My arms being pinned above my head."

A tear leaked from my eye. Cruz watched it fall.

"Lexi, I'm so sorry."

I nodded and agreed, "Me too."

"You don't apologize," he insisted. "Something awful happened to you. You did nothing wrong and you have nothing to be sorry for. I feel horrible for doing something that made this more uncomfortable for you."

He paused as his eyes darted back and forth, searching for something.

"Ah, Lex. The burns. This is why you broke down that day when I tried to put the aloe on you, isn't it?"

I nodded. "Other than the hugs and comfort I've received in the arms of my brothers or my dad, no other man has touched me since it happened. You were the first and I couldn't control my reaction."

"I assume they know?"

"Luke and Logan do. I told them on Wednesday. My parents don't know."

"Are you getting help?"

"I started seeing a therapist shortly after it happened. She's been vital to my recovery. Other than her, nobody else knew until last week when I told Elle and Nikki."

Cruz dropped his head, looking defeated. I didn't know what was going through his mind and I was too scared of what his answer might be if I asked. So, I stayed silent and let him collect his thoughts.

"Are you okay?" he asked when he lifted his gaze from his lap.

I wasn't sure how to answer that. I mean, physically I was. My heart and my mind were another story. I just had a panic attack after Cruz and I had been kissing on my couch. He witnessed it and I still didn't know how he felt about it. I responded with, "I guess that depends on you."

"Me?"

Could I tell him and not have him pity me? I guess I'd never know unless I said something.

"I should have told you, but I like you. And I was worried that if I told you what happened, you'd walk away from me. I don't want that to happen."

"I guess I've got some work to do," he stated firmly.

"What?"

"Warrior, if you think it's possible that I'm willing to walk out on you because of what you just told me, it's obvious to me that you don't know me the way I'd like you to. I've got to put in some work to make sure you know that I'm not the kind of man who'd ever walk out on a woman like you."

"A woman like me?" I repeated.

"Yes, a woman like you. One who is smart, talented, and determined. One who is beautiful and strong. In fact, she's so strong that she's not only experienced what she has in life and has come out the other side, but also knows what I do for a living and supports it all while encouraging me. A woman whose laughter is music to my ears, especially after a shitty day at work. Mostly though, you're a woman who, for the first time in years, has made my heart start beating again for something other than work. So, yeah, Lexi…I'd never walk out on a woman like you."

I made his heart start beating again?

"Cruz," I whispered because my heart was in my throat.

At that moment, he stood and held his hands out to me. I placed my hands in his and stood. As I stood there staring up at him, he confirmed, "I like you, Lexi. A lot. And I want to do whatever I've got to do to make sure we've got a fair shot at whatever we want to see happen between us. I want you to know that you can share any part of what you went through with me, and if that isn't something you want to share, that's okay too. If the two of us together is something you want to explore, you should know that I am more than ready and willing to explore it. And, more than anything else, I want you to know that there is zero pressure from me for things to go any faster than you are ready for or can handle."

"I want to try and see if there could be something between the two of us."

The smile that spread across his face was breathtaking.

With the difficult task out of the way and the adrenaline no longer pumping, I found myself feeling exhausted.

"Tired?" Cruz asked, as if reading my mind.

I nodded slowly.

"Are you going to be alright by yourself tonight?"

I wasn't sure. I didn't know how to communicate that to Cruz without making him feel some sort of obligation to me.

I didn't have to ponder it too long because he tugged my hand and started guiding me toward my bedroom.

Once inside, he instructed, "Get in your bed and try to sleep, Lexi. I'll stay here tonight out on the couch in case you need me."

"Really? You'd do that for me?"

"Will that make you feel better tonight? To know that I'm here just in case you need someone?"

"Yeah," I rasped, answering him honestly.

He leaned in, pressed a kiss to my forehead, and offered, "Good night, Lexi."

"Good night, Cruz."

At that, he turned and walked out of my room, closing the door behind him.

Twenty minutes later, cuddled under the blanket, I was no closer to sleep and I was craving the comfort of Cruz's arms around me. I threw back the blanket and walked out of the room. As I entered the living room, I caught his attention.

"Everything alright?" he asked.

I walked over by the couch and shook my head. "I can't sleep."

"Come here," he urged as he held his hand out to me.

I fell beside him on the couch and he quickly curled my body into his. He was on his back, my front was pressed to his side, and my cheek was resting in the crook of his shoulder. I took in his scent and my body melted into him. Cruz pulled the blanket off the back of the couch and draped it over us.

Minutes later, I was asleep.

CHAPTER 12

Lexi

I was incredibly warm wrapped in Cruz's protective embrace. I hadn't opened my eyes yet, but I knew exactly where I was. I wasn't too proud to admit that I might have purposely kept my eyes shut so that I wouldn't have to leave this spot.

Unfortunately, I had no idea what time it was and I had a meeting this morning. On that thought, I reluctantly opened my eyes and tilted my head back to look at Cruz. He was awake, looking down at me.

"Morning."

Something changed in Cruz's face before he returned, "Morning, Lexi. Sleep okay?"

"Yeah," I answered as I cuddled into him. "What about you?

"Never better."

I let the happiness I felt in hearing him admit that seep into my mind and heart. The truth was, Cruz wasn't small. He was easily six-one, maybe six-two. His body was lean and muscular and while he would have probably managed to do alright if he had been on the couch on his own, adding me to the equation made it a tight fit. Even still, he didn't seem to mind.

"Thank you for staying here for me last night, Cruz."

Although we were still on the couch, he managed to

shrug his shoulders and share with a bit of nonchalance, "You needed me."

"You could have run," I pointed out. "It would have probably been easier than what lies ahead for us."

"Maybe, but I think we'll be worth the effort. Besides, I've never been one who backs down from a challenge."

We'll be worth the effort.

I wanted that. I really wanted that.

"Hey," I called softly. "Any chance I can talk you into giving me a good morning kiss?"

"Lex…" he trailed off.

Instead of lowering his head to mine, he lifted me clean off the couch and positioned me on top of him.

I stared at him, but made no move. Neither did Cruz.

"I'm not kissing you, Lexi," he stated.

"Oh," I responded, feeling disappointed.

"You are going to kiss me."

I perked up. I dropped my lips to his and kissed him. Cruz kept one arm around my back while the other went to my hair. My tongue dipped inside his mouth, where it intertwined with his. It wasn't long before my moans filled the air around us and I felt Cruz harden between us. Surprisingly, at the feel of him, I grew more and more turned on and began rocking my hips over the length of him. Cruz growled. I wanted more. I wanted to feel pleasure.

"Cruz," I rasped, my voice ragged.

"What do you want, Lex?" he returned, his voice just as needy.

"I want to feel good."

His arm tightened around me. I rolled my hips. Cruz's eyes dropped to my mouth. I rolled my hips again.

His phone started ringing.

"Fuck," he muttered as he reached his arm up over his

head to the end table. He held the phone to his ear and answered, "Yeah?"

I started to move so that he could have privacy to take his call, but the second I did, Cruz's arm tightened around me. Three seconds after that, his entire body went alert.

"Did you say seventeen?" he asked the person on the other end of the line.

There was silence as he waited for a response.

"Right. I'm on my way."

A second later, I watched as Cruz dropped his phone back down to the table.

"I get the sneaking suspicion that you just got some really bad news," I blurted.

"Yeah, you'd be right."

I took in a deep breath and explained, "I think I'd rather not know what it is. I can imagine something bad enough and I'm not sure I want to know if it's worse than that."

Cruz kissed the top of my head. "Lexi, if I had known what you went through, I'm not sure I would have ever told you any of the details of my case. I would have just done what I needed to do to make sure you stayed safe. As it is, I'm pissed at myself for what I did last night."

"It wasn't your fault," I insisted.

Regret flashed in his eyes before he closed them.

I hated seeing that look on him. I knew, better than most, how easy it was to blame yourself for something that wasn't your fault. I didn't want Cruz carrying around that guilt.

"I'm all right now, Cruz," I insisted. "In fact, I'm better than all right."

I touched my lips to his again and we kissed. Unfortunately, all too soon, Cruz brought both of his hands up to frame either side of my face. He gently tugged my head back and looked tortured.

"Lexi, I'm sorry. I have to go to work."

I pulled my bottom lip in between my teeth before I responded, "Okay."

"Princess, you've got to know that if I hadn't gotten that call just now, I wouldn't be leaving you like this."

I nodded. "Are we still having dinner tonight?"

He grinned at me. "I'm not sure what would make you think that we wouldn't be having dinner tonight."

"I don't know. It's just that...well, we made those plans before last night happened," I stammered.

In one swift move, Cruz carefully got us both upright on the couch. Then, he stood and held his hand out to me. I placed mine in his and stood opposite him.

"I wish I had more time now to talk to you about this, but unfortunately, I don't. The quick and easy? First, last night I thought we decided together that we wanted to try and see if there could be something more between us. Canceling dinner isn't going to help us accomplish that. Also, we agreed to dinner before last night. We agreed to it to celebrate your accomplishment in your career and the move into your new office. What happened last night doesn't affect that. There are, however, some things that last night does affect. We'll discuss those tonight."

Some of it sounded promising; some of it sounded downright terrifying. I didn't want to dwell on the possible downsides to whatever it was that he wanted to discuss, so I offered him a simple nod of my head.

"It's going to be fine, warrior. I promise."

I had no reason to doubt him, so I accepted him at his word. "I'm looking forward to tonight, then."

"Good. Do you have anything planned for today?"

"I'm meeting up with Elle this morning to go over a few of the last-minute details for the meet and greet tomorrow.

Other than that, I'll just be here working until it's time to get ready for dinner," I noted.

"Ok," he started as he moved to pick up his bag with the equipment he brought to finish my security system. "I'll give you a call later today and let you know what time to be ready."

I followed Cruz over to the front door, where he stopped and turned back to me. "Sounds good," I replied.

"See you later, Lexi," he said as he leaned over and gave me a peck on the cheek. Then, he put his hand to the door knob and opened the door.

"Bye, Cruz."

After he left, I locked the door, set my alarm, and went in search of my phone. I scrolled through my contacts, found the person I was looking for, and tapped on the screen.

"Hey, Lexi. Everything still good for this morning?" Elle greeted me.

"Yes, but I was wondering if we could change the location. The time, too, if needed."

"Sure, what's going on?"

"Well, is Levi home?" I asked.

"Yeah, he's still here."

I gave myself a minute to consider what I was planning to do and realized it was the right decision for me. "I'd hate to inconvenience him if he's got things going on today, but would it be possible for him to hang around for a bit this morning so I can talk to him about something? I'd like you there as well."

"I'm sure that's fine. We'll be here, so come over whenever you want," she assured me.

"Thanks, El. I'll see you soon."

I disconnected the call and got myself ready. Thirty minutes later, I was on my way to Levi and Elle's place.

When I arrived, there was no denying the nervous tension in the air. That tension was coming from me and Elle. Not Levi. That man exuded confidence like he was being paid to do it. Though I guess, in a way, he kind of was.

It was that confidence that made it easy for him to open up the conversation. "Is everything alright? I'm guessing this might have to do with the security system Cruz installed?"

"Yes, everything is good with that. Well, other than the fact that Cruz told me I wouldn't be receiving an invoice. I really don't mind paying for the equipment," I remarked.

"It's not a concern for me, Lexi. Aside from the fact that I know there's something good brewing between you and Cruz, you've become an important part of Elle's life. She's had to deal with enough bad stuff over the last few months that I want to see to it that the good people who are in her life stay safe."

I tried to ignore the fact that he mentioned the situation with me and Cruz and focused on how much he loved Elle. Nevertheless, I didn't want him thinking I was trying to take advantage of my friendship with her.

"It's completely not necessary, but I do appreciate your generosity, Levi."

"No problem at all," he returned. "So, if that's not what you wanted to discuss, what's going on?"

I had to do it quick, like ripping off a bandage.

"I had a panic attack last night," I blurted.

Elle looked worried while Levi grew curious, so I quickly explained, "Cruz was at my place last night installing the additional pieces he needed for the security system. As you noted a minute ago, Levi, there's something brewing between me and Cruz. We kissed last night. A lot. I suddenly had a flashback to when I was in college and I lost it."

"Oh, Lex," Elle started. "Are you okay?"

I nodded. "I am now. It took a little bit, but Cruz managed to help me get through it. Of course, it was tough for him because he's the one who triggered the attack."

"I don't understand," Levi cut in. "What did he do?"

Uh oh. I suddenly realized maybe I should have thought this through a little bit better. It seemed to me that from the moment I told the first person that wasn't my therapist about the rape, I couldn't seem to stop. It was like a rippling effect. I told one person. That turned into two, then three. I couldn't stop myself from speaking out. I quickly realized that telling people was helping me cope, so that's not what bothered me now. What was a problem was that if I told Levi about this, I would end up telling him about my make-out session with his brother, something I'm not certain he would want to hear.

"Gosh," I hesitated. "This is awkward."

"Lexi, did Cruz do something to hurt you?" Levi asked, not a trace of humor in his tone.

I gasped. "Oh, no. Nothing like that at all. I'm sorry." I let out a sigh. "I'm just struggling with this because I know I want to gag whenever Nikki talks to me about things getting hot and heavy between her and Luke. I don't know if it's different for guys, but I would imagine that hearing about your brother's...encounters is not exactly on the top of your list."

"Can you tell me what you need to tell me and spare me the details?" he wondered.

"Right," I said. "Well, we were on the couch, kissing. Cruz's body was mostly on top of mine and he slid his hands up my arms. They were over my head. I panicked and started kicking and screaming at him to get off me."

At this point, Elle was now looking very nervous. Levi still looked confused.

I enlightened him. "I said earlier that I had a flashback to when I was in college. When I was in my freshman year, my attacker pinned my hands above my head when he raped me."

Levi dropped his head a minute and took a few deep breaths before he lifted it again and lamented, "I'm so sorry that happened to you, Lexi…both the rape and the flashback. I'd like to think I know my brother well enough to know he got off of you."

I nodded and added, "Yes, and he helped me through the panic attack. He even offered to stay the night on the couch in case I needed him. He's a great man."

A look of pride washed over Levi's face before he agreed, "He is." Then, he asked, "So, while I understand needing to talk about what happened to you to have a support system, I get the feeling this is about more than that."

"It is and it isn't," I began. "I spent a lot of years dealing with my rape on my own. I've only recently told the people I'm comfortable with. It's been very good for me to be able to do that. I really like Cruz and I want us to have a fighting chance at something special. That said, I know what I dumped on him last night is not an easy pill to swallow. I think he's the kind of person that will keep what I told him private. I realize, though, that if things progress with us the way we are both hoping they will, he might need to unload his feelings about it to someone he trusts. I was hoping you'd be able to be that person for him."

"It goes without asking," Levi declared. "He's my brother, Lexi. Of course, I'll be there for him and, whether things get where the two of you hope they do or not, you as well."

I blew out a breath and dropped my shoulders. More bricks were gone. "Thank you, Levi. I appreciate it; I didn't want him to have to hold this in."

Levi's face softened further before he shared, "You should

know, I hope this thing between you and Cruz goes where you both want it to go. If there's anything else I can do, don't hesitate to ask me."

"I won't."

With that, Levi made sure there was nothing else I needed to discuss before he gave Elle a proper goodbye and took off. Elle and I spent the next hour with me giving her the details of my night with Cruz. Then, we moved on to the details of her meet and greet.

Cruz

The bad news kept coming. It was one blow after another and it didn't matter if I was thinking about work or my personal life. The truth was that, until recently, my life consisted of working a lot. Now, I had a reason to devote more time to my personal life and the only case I was working on was taking up an insane amount of my personal time.

Standing up from my chair in the conference room, I announced, "We're up to ten women. Ten in a matter of weeks. Two of them were picked up on the same night. And the most recent one to go missing is a seventeen-year-old girl."

I looked around the room at the guys surrounding the table: Dom, Lorenzo, and Pierce. Every file on every missing woman was spread out across the length of the massive table. We were stuck.

"We've got to work harder. No, not harder. We need to work smarter. There has to be something we're overlooking. This is happening right under our noses and all we've got is a bunch of dead ends, no leads, and a list of missing women that keeps growing."

"Cruz," Lorenzo called to get my attention. "We've been over these files a million times and we've followed up on every lead that we did have. Even with nothing new, it's not like we've been sitting around waiting for the next one to fall into our laps."

"It's not enough," I went on, my frustration beginning to get the best of me. "We've got to do something different."

"You alright, bro?" Dom asked. "You know we all feel the same as you, but you're getting agitated over this beyond what any of us have ever seen from you. What's going on?"

"Nothing," I clipped. "That's precisely the problem. These guys are smart because they know where to hit. There's been no camera footage to tap into. I don't like thinking that these fucking guys are outsmarting us. There are ten women missing. Ten women who've been taken against their will and are likely being bought and sold by some sick bastards. That's happened and we're sitting here trying to figure out where the fuck to go next!"

All I felt was rage and, being so consumed with that as I ranted at my team, I never noticed Levi walk into the room.

"Cruz!" he yelled out.

I turned to look at him.

Levi's eyes went to the guys and he instructed, "Can you guys give us a minute?"

They got up and moved out of the room. Once they left, Levi closed the door and stared at me a beat before he asked, "Do you need to be off this case?"

"Don't have time right now, Levi. I've got to get to work."

"Let it out, Cruz."

"What?"

"Lexi came over this morning to meet with Elle to go over

some things before the event tomorrow. She told us what happened last night with the two of you."

The mere mention of what happened last night had me on the verge of another outburst. I hadn't even begun to process how I felt about what I'd learned. That said, I was taken aback at learning she'd shared with Levi.

"What exactly did she share with you?" I shot back.

"She told us about her panic attack. She also explained what brought that attack on. I know what happened to her in college, too."

I dropped my head to the ground and closed my eyes.

My Lexi.

My thoughts drifted to her. I thought about everything from the way she kissed, the sound of her laughter, and the feel of her sleeping beside me last night. I was so lost in my thoughts I never noticed Levi move closer to me until his hand was on my shoulder giving me a squeeze.

"She told me because she likes you, Cruz. She wants things to work and she knows that what you learned last night was some heavy stuff. Lexi wanted to make sure you had someone there to listen to you if you need to get out what you're feeling about it."

I let out a laugh, "And here I thought I did a good job of hiding how I really felt about it. Obviously, she saw right through that."

"I'm sure she didn't see everything that you feel about it because I've got to imagine your feelings are pretty close to what mine would be if I learned that happened to Elle. My feelings would not be nice and I'm convinced that would not make her feel all warm and fuzzy inside. The girl that was at my house this morning spoke about you and it was all warm and fuzzy."

"I want to kill the motherfucker that did that to her," I finally admitted.

"Figured as much," Levi replied. "And I'm guessing I'm right to assume you didn't tell her that."

"That would be an accurate assumption," I confirmed. "I knew the last thing that would help her after telling me about such a violent act would be hearing me tell her how I wanted to enact more violence. So, I thought it, but I didn't tell her how I felt."

"You need off this case?" he asked.

I shook my head. "As much as I want to be with her right now, I *need* to put this case to bed. And I know Lexi wants to see that it happens, too. She's terrified for these women."

Levi nodded at me and advised, "Understandably so. That said, you're going to need to keep these two situations separate, Cruz. Losing your cool with the team is not going to help you find these women. If you need to talk about it, find me and we'll deal with it."

"Thanks, Levi," I started. "I've got to get back to work."

He nodded and added, "I don't like the fact that the two of you have a long road ahead of you, but I think if you and Lexi can work through it together, it'll be good for the both of you. I know you have what it takes to help her beat back any lingering demons and, on the other side of it, I can already see that she's giving you something other than work to be passionate about again."

"Yeah," I agreed. "She is."

At that, I turned and walked out of the conference room. I found the rest of the team in Lorenzo's office. When I walked in, they directed their attention to me.

"Sorry about all that in the conference room earlier," I began. "I'm dealing with some of my own stuff and this case feels like it's eating me alive."

"It's all good," Dom insisted. "We all understand it, man. It's not exactly like we're happy about what's happening. We've just got to stay focused on what we need to do."

"To that end, I'm going to go back to the start of this

case," Pierce chimed in. "I didn't investigate the first few with you guys. I've looked over the cases again and I've got something I want to dig a little deeper into."

"Which is?"

"Jenkins."

"I'm sorry?"

"Frank Jenkins. He owned a business in town, but has since retired. He's well known among the locals and he's a regular at The Rusty Spur," Pierce clarified.

This offered little explanation, so I pressed, "What does this Frank Jenkins and the tavern have to do with this case?"

"Anything that's happening in town, this guy knows about it. Some of these women we're searching for were picked up close to the tavern; I'm hoping he might have something to offer us."

"What time are you heading out?" I asked.

"Lunchtime. He'll be there; he's always there."

I wasn't sure if this guy would be able to offer us anything useful, but it was worth a shot. "I'll ride along," I offered.

Pierce dipped his chin and we got back to work.

An hour later, we took off to The Rusty Spur.

CHAPTER 13

Cruz

"READY?"

That was me talking to Pierce. We had walked into The Rusty Spur roughly forty minutes ago. Frank Jenkins wasn't there when we arrived, but Pierce insisted he'd be showing up. We sat at a table, ordered food, and Jenkins walked in five minutes later.

He took a seat at the end of the bar and looked to the bartender, who confirmed, "The usual?"

Jenkins gave a nod while the bartender disappeared to the kitchen before coming out and setting a beer in front of him.

Pierce and I figured it was best to let the guy eat before we questioned him; so, after we finished our lunch, we waited.

Now that we had filled up and Jenkins had pushed his plate back on the bar, I was ready to see if he could offer us anything.

"Yeah," Pierce agreed. "Let's go."

I threw some bills down on the table and followed Pierce over to the bar. He sat on the stool closest to Jenkins on his right side. I sat next to Pierce.

"Hey Frank," Pierce greeted him.

His eyes narrowed in response, but not in anger. I believed he was taking a minute to figure out why he recognized Pierce.

"You're the investigator," he announced, finally remembering Pierce's familiar face. "Reynolds, right?"

"Sharp as a tack, Frank," Pierce praised him. "You got it in you to help me out again?"

"I don't like when bad stuff is happening in my town, so if there's something I can do to right any wrongs, you know I will."

Pierce filled him in. He explained the situation and with each word he spoke, Jenkins grew more and more agitated. He did not like what he was hearing. When Pierce finished, Jenkins asked, "How can I help?"

That's when I interrupted, "Hey, Frank. I'm Cruz Cunningham and I'm working with Pierce on this case."

He gave me a nod.

I continued as I slid the file over to him, "Have you seen any of these girls around here over the course of the last three or four weeks?"

He opened the folder and pulled out the sheet with all of the pictures of the missing women. His gaze shot to the seventeen-year-old girl that was reported missing last night. "She was here two nights ago. Pretty young thing…didn't belong in a place like this."

"Are you sure it was her?" I questioned him.

"Not a doubt in my mind," he confirmed. "She didn't know it, but when she walked out of here, I kept my distance and made sure she got to her car safely."

"And I assume that she did?" Pierce asked.

Jenkins nodded before looking back at the pictures. He moved his finger across them and added, "These two as well." He pointed to one of the photos and continued, "This one was here maybe a week and a half ago." Jenkins slid his finger across the page and went on, "She was here about two and a half weeks ago."

"You're certain?" Pierce pressed.

He gave us a look that told us he was certain before he concluded, "Faces like these are ones you don't forget. The moment those girls walked in here, there were eyes on them. They stood out not because they made their presence known, but because they were timid and beautiful."

"Were any of the eyes on them anyone that you'd be concerned about?" I asked.

He shrugged. "I try not to judge people, so I can't say for sure. Now that I know to be on the lookout for something out of the ordinary, you can rest assured I plan to pay better attention to what's happening here."

Pierce stood and pulled a card out of his pocket as he requested, "If you see or hear anything, you'll call me?"

"Will do," Jenkins confirmed as he took Pierce's card and tucked it into his pocket.

At that, I gestured to the bartender. She came over and I asked, "Is the owner here?"

She shook her head and offered, "No, but he'll be in later this evening. Was everything alright with your order?"

I stood next to Pierce and answered, "Everything was fine. Just business stuff. Someone will call or stop by later."

After Pierce and I thanked Jenkins for his time, we took off.

When we arrived back at the office, the two of us updated Dom and Lorenzo.

We finally had something. Three of the girls had been spotted at the same tavern in town and were taken shortly afterward. We couldn't say for sure with the first two women, but the seventeen-year-old had been seen there on Thursday and we received word early this morning that she'd been reported missing.

"These guys are being smart," Dom noted. "If this Jenkins

guy saw to it that she made it to her car safely, these guys are waiting until the women have left the area before they go after them."

"I'm going to get Michaels to check the security footage. Maybe we can see if there is anyone who follows her out of the lot," Lorenzo suggested.

"Good call," I remarked. "The owner of the tavern will be in later tonight. If Michaels is having any trouble getting that footage, we should follow up with the owner tonight. Perhaps we should also look at any of the footage from inside. We can see if there was anyone who paid extra attention to her. If we can nail down the dates that our other two women went missing, let's get that footage, too. Maybe we'll be able to narrow it down if we're seeing the same people."

Pierce added, "Keep in mind that the Spur has a lot of regulars. It's likely we're going to find a lot of guys who are there every night. We'll have to be thorough."

Lorenzo and Dom took off to Michaels' office, Pierce to his own, and I went to Levi's. I knocked on the door and went in.

"How's it going?" I asked as I walked in and sat in the chair on the opposite side of his desk.

"From the time you and I finished talking this morning in the conference room until about ten minutes ago, I've been handling the final details of security for Elle's event tomorrow."

"You've got enough guys on it?" I asked.

He nodded. "Locke and Tyson will be with me. Though, now that I'm thinking about it, I'm wondering if we should change things up."

"How so?"

"I'm guessing you are better equipped to answer that. How's Lexi with this kind of thing? Do you think she'd want you to be there?"

I let out a laugh and admitted, "I'd like to think she would want me there, but I'm not sure if it's necessary. She seems to be okay with public places. I'm going to be seeing her tonight, though; I can run it past her. Are you good with a last-minute change if it's needed?"

"Whatever the two of you need. Just let me know," he advised. Then, he went on, "Get anywhere on your case?"

"We did."

I went on to tell him about the meeting Pierce and I had with Jenkins and the confirmation that three of our missing women were seen at the tavern days prior to their disappearances. I also updated him on our plan moving forward.

"As much as I don't want another woman taken, I know that it's going to happen," he started. "It would be great if the next woman were to walk in there. If this guy is keeping his eye out and spotted these women the second they walked in, perhaps we can stop the next one before it's too late."

"Yeah," I agreed. "They aren't picking these women up at the tavern. They're finding them there and then they're taking them after the women leave the parking lot. I don't want these women to be traumatized any further than they have to be, but we'll have to make a judgment call in the moment if we can risk letting the woman get taken so we can follow them or if we need to jump in before that happens."

Levi shook his head. "This pisses me off. I know you guys will make the best decision. I just hate that this is a choice that even needs to be made."

"You and me both."

We sat in silence, letting the weight of the situation settle on our shoulders. Levi eventually broke the silence. "So, you're seeing Lexi tonight?"

"Earlier this week, we planned to have dinner to celebrate

her moving into her new office. Now, I'd like to think we've got a little more to celebrate."

"Happy for you, Cruz. I really hope it all works out for the two of you."

"Thanks, Levi. I should get going. I need to get home and shower. After unexpectedly staying at her place last night and getting the call this morning about another girl missing, I never went back to my place. I'm guessing any chance I'll have with Lexi will be shot to shit if I show up smelling terrible."

Levi laughed and joked, "I knew I smelled something!"

I rolled my eyes and stood. As I walked to the door, I confirmed, "I'll keep you posted on what the deal is for tomorrow."

"Later, Cruz."

I gave him a chin lift and walked out. As I walked to my truck, I pulled out my phone to call Lexi. I told her I'd be by around five thirty to pick her up for dinner. She said she'd be ready.

At that, I turned on my truck, went home, and used the next hour and a half to take a shower, get ready, make a reservation, and count down the minutes until I could drive over to Lexi's.

I'm not sure what I expected when I walked up to her door and knocked, but it certainly wasn't what stood before me.

Lexi was something else entirely; I couldn't get over how beautiful she was.

She was all dolled up in a pair of black pants and a top that fit every curve of her body perfectly. She had a scarf at her neck and a pair of heels on her feet. Even with the heels, she was still quite a few inches shorter than me.

But it was her face that did me in. Her sweet face and her gorgeous smile.

"Lexi," I started, finding it difficult to catch my breath. "You look so pretty."

Her smile widened. "Thank you. That's such a relief. It took me so long to figure out what to wear."

"Well, what you settled on is perfect."

Lexi took a step back and let me inside. "I'm ready to go. I just need to grab my purse and a light jacket."

"Take your time."

I waited at the door while Lexi grabbed her things. After we locked and secured her apartment, I reached for her hand and held it all the way to my truck.

Dinner was nice. Lexi and I had effortless conversation. I'm certain this was because she asked a lot of questions. I had no problems giving her answers to any of the questions she had either. It was my assumption that she needed that—to know she could ask questions and trust she'd get answers. And it wasn't as though she asked anything so deeply personal that I'd have a problem sharing. Even still, I knew I liked Lexi enough that she could have asked me anything and I'd give her an honest answer.

After dinner, we walked back out to the truck. I turned it on, reached my hand over to hers, and looked her in the eyes. "We need to talk."

"Okay," she replied.

"We're close to my place. I'd love to show you where it is, but want to make sure you're comfortable going there."

I felt her hand tense as she delayed in giving me an answer.

Nope. She wasn't ready.

"Sure," she answered hesitantly.

I was not going to take her to my place. I drove out of the lot and back to her place. When I pulled into the lot at her apartment, she questioned, "You live in the same apartment complex?"

"No."

"I don't understand."

I parked the truck, turned it off, and looked back at her. "Lexi, you tensed up the minute I asked about going back to my place. I'm not going to force you to go somewhere you aren't comfortable going. That's why we're here."

"Oh."

I allowed Lexi a minute to process that on her own as I stepped out and moved around to open her door. We held hands as we walked to the front door of the apartment.

Once we were inside, Lexi's uneasiness skyrocketed.

"Warrior, what's wrong?" I asked after we sat down on the couch.

"What you said this morning...I'm just nervous."

I began wracking my brain trying to remember what I said this morning that she'd be nervous about. I came up with nothing.

"I'm not following you, Lex."

"You said that we'd talk tonight about what things changed after everything that happened last night."

I sighed. "I also told you not to worry about it and that everything was going to be fine. Seeing you like this right now tells me you don't trust what I told you."

She sat silently, contemplating.

"I'm not sure I know how to do this right," she shared.

"Do what?"

"Be in a relationship and trust. I had one boyfriend throughout high school. We didn't start dating until I was in my junior year. We were together until a few months before graduation. He thought it would be best to break up since we were both heading off to different schools. I was upset initially, but quickly realized that it was high school love and not the real thing. I went to college and met people. I made friends, but didn't date. Until...until him. Then, I switched schools. I haven't been interested nor have I dated anyone since."

I needed to calm her fears. "We're good, Lexi."

"We are?"

"We just got back from dinner. There was no awkward silence or uneasiness in our conversation. When we had breakfast together last weekend, we spent nearly the entire time laughing our asses off. You said yourself that I was the first person that made you want to joke around in the last four years. Keep in mind, I told you that you're the reason I feel like my heart is finally beating again. We've got great chemistry, Lexi. Don't put this kind of pressure on yourself. We're good."

"Well, what about..." she trailed off as she directed her gaze everywhere but at me.

"Look at me," I urged.

When her eyes came to mine, I questioned her softly, "What about what?"

Her voice was barely a whisper when she answered, "Sex."

"That's what I wanted to talk to you about tonight," I replied.

Her body stiffened.

"I don't want to have sex with you."

Her eyes rounded. "You don't?" she asked, unable to hide her shock.

"No."

"Oh." She looked back down at her lap and I could see she was relieved, but maybe also a bit disappointed. I couldn't understand it.

"Maybe I should clarify," I started. "I want to have sex with you; I just don't want to have sex with you tonight."

Her hopeful eyes came back to mine.

"There's no rush," I assured her. "It takes as long as it takes for you to get to a place where you want that, too. I don't care how long it takes you either. Nothing, Lexi, nothing happens before you are ready for it. To that end, when you think you might be ready for any physical intimacy, I need you to tell me. If it's needed, I'll take the lead on everything else, but you are taking the lead on that."

Her eyes filled with tears. "I wanted to wear a dress tonight."

I shook my head, confused. "What?"

"When you picked me up tonight, you told me I looked pretty. I told you I spent entirely too long trying to decide what I should wear. I really wanted to wear a dress."

"So, why didn't you?"

"I can't," she rasped, closing her eyes. "I always wear pants, even when I'm home alone, sleeping in my bed. I was wearing a skirt that night. I haven't worn a dress, skirt, or shorts in four years. I wanted to do it tonight because they used to make me feel sexy and I want to feel like a woman again, but I didn't want you to think I was ready to have sex. And after years in therapy, I do know logically that what I wear shouldn't matter, but it doesn't change the fact that I still feel nervous about being in anything but pants."

My blood was boiling. I wasn't angry at her; I hated the bastard that thought he had a right to her body because of what she was wearing.

"Tomorrow, Lex," I quickly tamped down my anger and stated.

"What about tomorrow?"

"After Elle's event, I'm taking you out again. You should know now, I have no plans to have sex with you tomorrow either. What I plan to do is pick you up and take you out so we can have a good time with each other just like we did earlier tonight and just like we have every other time we've been together. When I pick you up, you'll be wearing whatever the hell you want to wear. Dress, skirt, shorts…hell, it could be a fucking bikini for all I care."

"A bikini?"

"Yes."

Her face scrunched up and she noted, "I think it's still too cold for a bikini."

I grinned at her, happy to hear her joking, but went on, "It's your body, Lexi. You can wear whatever you want to wear and nobody has a right to assume they can take anything from you."

"I know that. Logically, I know that, but it's still scary."

"You don't have any reason to be fearful with me, princess. I would never hurt you. And I'd never let anyone else hurt you. I have to believe on some level you trust me and you know I'd do whatever was necessary to protect you; otherwise, I don't think we'd be sitting here right now. We'll take baby steps. I'm taking you out tomorrow and you can wear whatever will make you feel good. You'll always be safe while you are with me. okay?"

I watched as Lexi's hands went to her throat. She began sliding her fingers over the fabric of the scarf tied at her neck and pulled the ends of it through one another. Then, she removed it completely from her body.

"I hate wearing them."

It took everything in me to not allow my eyes to drop to the exposed skin at her throat and the top of her chest. I was a man who was seriously attracted to her, but I felt like she had just taken a huge step forward. I wanted to see to it that she knew she could trust me and keep taking those steps.

Apparently, she wanted to take another step forward because she shifted on the couch and curled up next to me. With her body pressed into my side and her head lying in the crook of my shoulder, she said softly, "Thank you, Cruz."

I pressed a kiss to the top of her head before I responded, "It's really not necessary to thank me, but you're welcome, Lexi."

We stayed like that a long time without any words. Lexi eventually tipped her head back, looked up at me, and broke the silence.

"Cruz?"

"Yeah?"

She gave me a disappointed look and stated, "I just have one question."

"Shoot."

"Since sex is off the table, does that mean we can't kiss and touch?"

I laughed. "Where I'm from, kissing and touching is not the same thing as sex."

Her eyes began to sparkle.

"But we need some rules first," I declared.

"Rules?"

"Yes. I need to know that you know what to do if something isn't right for you. So, I think we need to come up with a safe word."

"A safe word? Like what they do in the BDSM community?" she asked, her body going tense again.

My face softened. "Yes, for the safety. I want you to know that no matter what we're doing, whether it's kissing and touching now or if it's sex later down the road, all you need to do is say one word if you aren't comfortable and it all stops. Immediately. One word will tell me that something is wrong. I need to know you feel safe and that we don't ignore the fact that something could happen that would cause you to have another panic attack. I don't want that for you and I think this could be a great way to see to it that it doesn't happen."

Lexi sat up straighter on the couch and stared at me. She

didn't say anything for a long time. I almost began to wonder if she was offended that I had suggested the use of a safe word, but at that moment she spoke up and approved, "I think that's a really great idea."

I grinned and asked, "So what's the word?"

"Hmm," she started as she tilted her head back and looked up at the wall behind the couch. "Well, I guess it should be something that'll really kill the mood, right?"

"It doesn't have to be. I'd just prefer it be unmistakable. So, it can simply be the word 'stop' or you can do something a little more creative like a color or a food. You could even say something completely off the wall if you feel like it needs to be."

She thought another moment before her eyes got big and she announced, "Cupcake."

"Cupcake it is."

The smile on her face grew to epic proportions before she questioned, "Can I kiss you now?"

"Yeah, Lex. You can kiss me...you can touch me, too."

Lexi leaned back in to me, pressed her hand to my chest, and tipped her lips up to mine. "I think I'd really like it if you'd do the same."

My mouth came down softly on hers. There was a bit of closed-mouth kissing before Lexi brought her tongue out to tease my lips. I opened my mouth and gave her access. As I savored the taste and feel of her velvety tongue and soft lips, Lexi's hand at my chest slid up to my neck and up to the back of my head. Her fingers ran through my hair as she moved her body from the couch and straddled my lap. My hands were immediately at her thighs, squeezing. Lexi moaned and began rolling her hips over me. I groaned into her mouth as my hands made their way from her thighs to her hips.

I tore my mouth from hers and growled, "Fuck, you're so sexy."

There was nothing but burning hot desire in her eyes as she continued to move herself over my length. One of my hands dropped from her hip and slid down over her ass. I squeezed it gently. She let out another moan and brought her mouth back to mine. Her hands moved from my hair to my shoulders and arms and back up again as we continued kissing. My hands were at her ass, hips, and thighs until I slid them up her back and into her hair.

Touching her made me a little bit anxious. I didn't want to do anything to upset her or bring her mind back to a terrible time in her life, but I also tried to keep in mind what she had said just a few minutes ago. She wanted to feel like a woman again and she wanted to feel sexy. I hoped in feeling my hands on her body after she asked me to touch her along with the kisses I gave her and the groans I let out that she was beginning to feel like the beautiful woman I saw every time I looked at her.

Framing her face with my hands, I broke the connection at our lips.

"Cruz," she breathed.

She was so beautiful. I already knew how gone I was for her, but hearing her say my name like that, full of need, I knew there was no turning back.

"You just keep getting better, Lex."

"Right back at ya," she responded.

Lexi dazzled me with a goofy grin just before she dropped her head and nuzzled her face in my neck. I wrapped my arms around her back and squeezed her tight.

"Thank you, Cruz."

"Kissing you is not something I need thanks for."

"I wasn't thanking you for that," she started. "I was thanking you for making me feel safe…for making me feel protected. I feel like I'm well on my way to getting all the missing pieces of myself back."

"Lexi..." I trailed off, too overwhelmed to know what to say.

"Don't say anything, Cruz. I don't want you to say anything. I just want to be here with you like this. Will you hold me and lay next to me on the couch for a bit? I enjoyed that last night."

I gave her a gentle squeeze before I shifted us on the couch. Then I held her close for a long time. I felt her warm breath as it hit the skin at my throat. It eventually evened out and I knew Lexi was asleep.

CHAPTER 14

Lexi

It was the Monday after I had experienced the best weekend of my entire life.

I had an incredible date with Cruz after which he made me feel safer than I had in years. Going into the date, I was nervous for a multitude of reasons. Obviously, I was experiencing first date jitters, but most of my anxiety was stemming from the words Cruz said to me before he left my apartment that morning. Even though he tried to reassure me that it would be fine, I still worried how he'd feel once he had a few hours to let the news I'd shared with him settle.

But I had worried for no reason because, just as Cruz said, it was all good. In fact, it was better than good. With each conversation we had, he proved to me that I wasn't wrong to put my trust in him. It was evident the moment we started our conversation that he had put some serious thought into what a relationship with me would look like. His suggestion to use a safe word in the event things were going too fast, too far, or even to a place that was scary gave me control that I didn't expect I could have again.

If that wasn't already enough, he did it again on Sunday.

I was up early on Sunday and spent the entire morning through the late afternoon with Elle at her event, which turned out to be a huge success. She hadn't had one since before her situation with her stalker ended, so I was happy how it all turned out for her.

By the time we packed everything up, I managed to walk through my door just after five thirty. I called Cruz, at his request, when I got back.

"Hey, Lex. How'd it go?"

"It was a total flop. We spent the entire day there and only had a handful of people show up," I replied. "Elle was pretty disappointed."

Silence for a beat before he questioned, "Really?"

I felt my lips twitch before I let out a giggle. "You make it so easy, Cruz. Do you really think I would be getting home just now, which is significantly later than the event was set to end, if it hadn't gone well? It went really well. Elle had a huge turnout and didn't want to turn anyone away."

"Smartass."

I heard the teasing tone of his voice and knew he wasn't mad. I didn't get a chance to tell him anything else because he asked, "How long?"

"For what?"

"Are you being a smartass again?"

"Um…no?"

"I can be ready to leave here in about five minutes. How long do you need before you're ready to go out tonight?"

"Forty-five minutes," I replied.

"Forty-five minutes?" he repeated.

"Is that too long?"

"Not at all," he started. "I'm just surprised you can get ready that quickly."

"Well I already know what I'm going to wear, so the biggest hurdle is out of the way," I noted.

"Can't wait to see you," he returned softly.

Before I had a chance to respond, Cruz disconnected the call.

As much as I wanted to dwell on his words, I didn't have time. I dropped my phone, hopped in the shower, and got ready.

For the first time in years, I put on a dress.

When I opened my door to Cruz, his head had been down. His heated gaze traveled from my feet, up my bare legs, over the curves of my hips and chest, and to my face.

And for the first time in years, I felt strong and proud.

Most of all, standing before Cruz, I felt safe wearing that dress.

I watched the muscle in his jaw working.

"You look so pretty, Lexi."

I felt pretty. With the way he stood there looking at me and the sound of his voice when he said those words, it would have been impossible not to feel pretty. Best of all, even though he had made it very clear he liked what he saw when he looked at me, I didn't feel like a piece of meat.

I smiled at him and pointed out, "You said the same thing last night when you picked me up."

"Did I?" he asked. "Maybe it's the truth."

"You are certainly beginning to make me feel like it is."

At that, we went out on our date and had an incredible time. As was typical, we spent the entire time laughing and it was never once awkward or forced. When he brought me home, Cruz walked me to the door.

"Do you want to come in for a while?" I asked.

Cruz stepped just inside the door and closed it, but answered, "We both have a long week ahead of us and you've had a very busy weekend. I probably shouldn't stay."

I put my hands to Cruz's chest and shared, "I had a really great time tonight, Cruz. Thank you for giving this to me."

"Happy to give it to you."

"Can I give you something now in return?"

I felt Cruz's fingertips dig in slightly at my hips before his hands moved around my waist and pulled me into his body.

"All I want is to know that you had a good time tonight," he began. "I don't expect nor do I want you to do anything for me in return."

Disappointed, I dropped my gaze from his and stared at his throat.

"Why do you look like I've just crushed all your hopes and dreams?" Cruz asked.

I shook my head, feeling frustrated.

Cruz squeezed me a little tighter. "Look at me, Lex."

I did as he asked.

Then, I felt the back of his knuckles brush along my cheek as he urged, "Tell me why you're sad."

"I feel pretty tonight," I started. "For the first time in a very long time, I feel sexy and confident. All I wanted to do was kiss you before you left."

I barely got the words out when Cruz's mouth came crashing down on mine. With his lips pressed to mine, I slid my hands up his chest and around his neck. As our mouths opened and our tongues began to taste each other, my body melted further into his. One of Cruz's arms stayed wrapped tight around the upper part of my back, but the other one... oh, the other one. It dipped lower and lower until it slid down over the curve of my ass.

I loved it, so I gave him a moan as encouragement.

He gave me a gentle squeeze.

I *really* loved that.

After a bit more squeezing, kissing, and moaning, Cruz tore his mouth from mine. His forehead resting on mine, we both fought to catch our breath.

Cruz did it arguably faster than me because he started speaking. "Don't keep it in, Lexi."

"What?"

Pulling his head back from mine, he instructed, "With me, you don't have to hide anything. Give in to what you feel, princess, no matter what it is. Scared, sexy, or anything in between. It doesn't matter what it is; if it's in me to see you through that, I will."

And of everything he did for me in the last few minutes, what he had just said was what I loved most.

"I feel like I'm dreaming, Cruz. Are you even real?"

"It's time to wake up, warrior. I'm as real as it gets."

Once those words slipped out of his mouth, he pressed a kiss to the tip of my nose and declared, "I'm going to head out now."

I let the disappointment of that wash over me for about two seconds before Cruz added, "I had a fantastic time tonight. And you were, by far, the most beautiful woman in the restaurant. Don't think I'm leaving because I don't like what I see. This wasn't about me and what I want. Tonight was about giving you what you needed…giving you what someone took from you. I hope you got that back."

Warmth spread through me. "I did, Cruz. I got that and so much more."

"Good night, Lexi."

"Good night."

So, with everything Cruz gave me for the last two days, I went to bed last night feeling happier than I could ever remember.

But thoughts of Cruz had to be pushed to the back of my mind…at least until tonight when I had my meeting with Dr. Lane. I didn't always see her weekly, but when I left her office last week knowing that I'd be going out on a date with Cruz this past weekend, I thought it was crucial to have the appointment scheduled.

For now, though, I needed to focus on work. It was the start of a new week and I had a lot of work to get done before the official opening of WAAR next Monday. I pushed the campaign out late last week and, with all the excitement of the weekend, hadn't had a chance to check up on it until now. I didn't have to work too hard to find out because as soon as I got to my office and opened my email I saw one that told me I was going to get an update.

Lexi, Call when you have a minute.

Grant's signature was attached to the bottom of the email.

I was nervous, but knew that if there were any issues, I'd handle them immediately. So, I picked up the phone and called Grant.

The phone rang twice before I heard, "Lexi, thanks for calling."

"It's no problem. I got your email. Is everything alright?"

There was no denying the excitement and relief in his voice. "Things are perfect. Over the weekend, we received thousands of dollars in donations for the center," he shared.

"That's incredible. I'm so happy to hear that."

"They're still coming in. Some donations were made anonymously, but there were also tons of high profile individuals who've put out a lot of money. These donations will help us ensure that WAAR can continue to be an ongoing, dependable resource for sexual assault victims. I wanted to personally thank you for your hard work on this. You have no idea what it means to me."

"I'm overjoyed at the news, Grant. This campaign being successful is, by far, one of my proudest accomplishments. I came in this morning ready to get to work on the second half of the equation. All those donations won't mean anything if the women who need the help don't know it's there. I've got a busy week ahead, but I'm motivated to see this through."

"We appreciate everything you've done, Lexi. If you need anything throughout the week, please don't hesitate to reach out to me. I'll be spending most of my time at the center finalizing all of the details, but I can be available if there's something you need."

"That sounds great," I responded. "I'll be in touch later this week to update you."

After disconnecting the call with Grant, I gave myself a minute to celebrate the success of the first part of the campaign. Then, I got down to business. The hours passed quickly as I worked. In fact, I was so consumed with what I wanted to get done, I worked while I ate lunch. I managed to get just about everything I needed done, but had to stop working when I realized the time. If I was going to make it to my appointment with Dr. Lane on time, I couldn't keep working. So, I shut everything down, locked up the office, and walked to my car.

Just over an hour later, I was sitting on the comfortable chair in Dr. Lane's office and I had just finished telling her about my panic attack from Friday night and the subsequent dates I had with Cruz.

"And now that it's been a few days since the panic attack, how are you feeling?"

"Very good, actually. It wasn't pretty that night, but he did an incredible job handling the situation. I'm finding that I'm becoming more and more attracted to him. I feel a lot of things for him that I haven't felt for anyone in a long time. And they're all good things. Most important of all is how he's handled me since I told him everything."

I paused a moment thinking about him and the safety he provided me while I sought to regain so much that was taken.

I continued, "Even though I haven't been attracted to anyone until Cruz, I think I've always known that I still wanted to find a way to heal. I don't want to be alone for the rest of my life. I've always worried what would happen when I'd finally be ready for that step and told the person I was with what happened. I have asked myself a million questions. Would that person even stick around? If they did, what would happen if I had a panic attack in the middle of it? What if I thought I was ready to take that big step with someone and then during it I realized I wanted to stop? Would they respect that? Would it happen all over again? Oddly enough, as awful as it was, I feel like having that panic attack on Friday was probably one of the greatest things that could have happened."

"How so?" Dr. Lane asked curiously.

"A lot of reasons, to be honest," I started. "Obviously, it was the perfect opportunity to bring up what happened to me. I knew I wanted to tell Cruz about it, but trying to figure out how I would do that gave me anxiety. More than that, though, his response to it has quelled so many fears that I've had. He has reassured me that there is no rush for physical intimacy and I believe him when he says that. Beyond that, he's very big on communication about everything, but the physical connection, in particular. He suggested using a safe word so that I knew I only had to say one word if I am feeling uncomfortable with anything and it stops, no questions asked. Just knowing I have that control now is empowering."

"I think the use of a safe word is an excellent idea. Outside of what happened on Friday, is there anything that has happened that's made you feel uneasy or hesitant?"

I shook my head. "No. Well, not really."

Dr. Lane's brows pulled together.

I went on to explain my conversation with Cruz about

wearing dresses and how he helped me accomplish something I really wanted to be able to do again.

"He's been wonderful," I gushed. "What he gave me when he promised a night with no expectations regardless of what I wore helped me in ways I can't even begin to describe. I know it's still going to take me some time to feel completely confident wearing whatever I want again, but I no longer have doubt about wearing what I'm comfortable in around him."

"It seems to me that Cruz is going to be a very positive part of your healing process," Dr. Lane pointed out.

A grin spread across my face. "I feel excited again. It's excitement over rediscovering a part of me that I thought I had permanently lost. I don't want to feel fearful about sex anymore and the communication I've had with Cruz has given me such a tremendous amount of confidence and security about exploring that with him."

And it did. I knew I was wholly responsible for my recovery, but certain aspects of it would be difficult to achieve without a willing partner. I was grateful that Cruz seemed to be a very willing participant and that he didn't appear to have any issues with allowing me to set the pace for the physical part of our relationship. He basically insisted that I would be the one to decide what happened and when. That power and control he handed over to me when he, as a partner in the relationship, didn't have to meant more to me that I could ever tell Dr. Lane or Cruz.

Dr. Lane and I wrapped up our session, but I didn't schedule another one. I told her I'd reach out when I needed to meet again.

At that, I left and went home. After eating a quick dinner and getting in a workout, I sat down to journal. I wrote a few words, but decided I wanted to do something I hadn't done in a long time.

Picking up my phone and scrolling through, I found Cruz's name and tapped on the screen.

"Hello?" he answered.

"Hi, Cruz."

"Is everything alright?" he asked.

I loved the concern he showed for me.

"Yeah."

"Oh, I'm surprised. You don't typically call me."

It made me happy to see that he recognized the effort I was making. "I know. I'm trying to work on doing that more. I really just called because I wanted to see how your day went if you had a few minutes to talk."

"For you?" he started. "Always."

And just like that, I'd gotten over another hurdle.

Cruz and I chatted for a long time. After, I got back to my journal for a bit before I climbed into my bed. Just before I fell asleep I realized that since Cruz came into my life I had spent more nights falling asleep happier than I had been in years. Warmth spread through me at that thought and I easily drifted off.

CHAPTER 15

Lexi

"I think it's time. I'm ready."

"Are you sure?" Cruz responded. "There's nothing wrong with waiting if you're still having concerns."

I shook my head, convinced I was making the right decision for myself and I was doing it on my own terms.

It was Thursday evening and I was cuddled up with Cruz on the couch at my apartment. I was on my back; he was on his side next to me with his head propped up in his hand. After I got home from work, I got in a quick workout, showered, and started dinner. Cruz showed up ten minutes later, helped me finish cooking, and we had dinner together.

While I had spoken to Cruz every day this week, tonight was the first night the two of us were seeing each other since Sunday.

It had been an incredibly busy week up to this point. Other than my meeting with Leni on Tuesday to talk about the grand opening of her yoga studio, which was still quite a few weeks away, my week was filled with work for WAAR. Beyond that, I had finally rescheduled my appointment with Logan and was set to meet with him tomorrow morning. After my meeting with Logan, I was going to be meeting with Grant at my office for one last update before the center opened on Monday.

"I appreciate you worrying about me and wanting to make sure I'm not rushing anything, but I'm sure," I began, bringing my attention back to my conversation with Cruz. "Knowing what I know now I realize I've already waited too long. Part of me wishes I would have done this sooner."

"Is there anything I can do to help you with this?" he asked.

I shrugged my shoulders and replied, "I'm not sure yet. Telling my parents about the rape is going to be difficult, but I want them to know. The problem is that I don't know how they'll react. I know they love me and they're going to be devastated. It hasn't been easy to tell anyone about this, so I have to face that hurdle along with trying to handle their reactions to it."

"You don't have to do it alone, Lexi. If you want me to be there to support you, I'm more than happy to do that for you."

I wasn't sure what I wanted. I knew I didn't want to do it on my own, but I also didn't want to overwhelm my parents. This was going to be hard enough on them as it was.

"I don't know what to do, Cruz," I answered honestly. "On one hand, I think it would help me tremendously to know that you, Logan, Luke, and Nikki were there when I tell them. On the other hand, I'm trying to put myself in my parents' shoes. I can't imagine the disappointment they are going to feel."

Cruz's arm curled around my shoulder a little tighter. "Why would they be disappointed with you?"

"Lots of reasons," I started. "I know they'll be disappointed that I didn't tell them sooner, that I didn't fight, and that I didn't report it."

"You didn't fight?" Cruz questioned me, clearly confused.

I shook my head and explained, "When it happened I didn't fight him. I let him do it."

"Did you say no, Lex?" he asked.

I nodded.

"You didn't let anyone do anything. He wanted power and control so he took what he did from you to get that. You aren't at fault and nobody can blame you for any part of it."

I sighed. "I wish I had tried harder to fight him and I wish I would have reported it. Those are my biggest regrets. It breaks my heart to even think about the disappointment I know I'm going to see in my parents' faces…especially my dad. I know I can't go back to change it and that my reaction is one that's extremely common. Even still, it doesn't change the fact that sometimes I wish I had done something more than I did."

Cruz's hand cupped the side of my face, where his thumb swiped back and forth across my cheek. "You said no. That's all it should have taken."

I closed my eyes as I dropped my head to the side toward him. "I know," I whispered.

"If you don't want to answer, it's fine, but can I ask why you didn't report it?"

"There's a lot of reasons for that, too," I shared, with a roll of my eyes.

The truth was that I not only knew that my parents would be disappointed, but that I was already disappointed with myself for my lack of action. I often wondered how many other women might have experienced what I did at the hands of my attacker because I remained silent.

I continued, "Shame, guilt, and responsibility, to name a few. It's taken me a lot of years to get to where I am now, to know that I shouldn't have ever felt any of those things. Hindsight makes me wish I could go back and do things differently. He could have done it to someone else after me and that's something I could have possibly prevented if I had reported him."

"You still can," Cruz enlightened me. "There's no pressure

and I'm not in any way saying that you have to do this, but if it's something you want to do, the state of Wyoming has no statute of limitations on it. It's not too late."

I didn't respond because I wasn't sure if it was something I wanted to do. Instead, I rolled to my side and slid my arm over Cruz's waist. I shifted my body as close as possible to his and felt his hand curl around the back of my neck and into my hair.

With my face inches from his throat, I quietly asked, "Will you be there with me when I tell my parents? I don't think I want to do it without you."

"Warrior, you name the time and place and I'd be honored to give you that," he said softly.

"I'll call them tomorrow and set something up for one of these upcoming weekends if that works for you," I declared.

"That works for me."

"I think I'm going to make sure Logan, Luke, and Nikki are there, too. I'd love to have Elle there as well, but I think that'll be pushing it for my parents."

Cruz's hand drifted from my hair down my back and around my waist. He squeezed me gently and insisted, "I'm good with whatever you decide."

At that, I shifted my head closer to him and pressed a kiss to the base of his throat. I felt his fingertips press deeper into the skin at my back.

"You know," I began as I peppered kisses along his neck. "I think I'm really beginning to like you a lot."

I felt the vibration of his laughter against my lips as they moved back to his throat.

"You've got to know the feeling is mutual," he returned.

I tipped my head back and looked up at him. When his eyes came to mine, I assured him with a goofy grin, "I do."

His mouth came down on mine. As our tongues began to

glide against one another, I realized I wanted to take the next step. I wanted more of Cruz. I slipped my hand under the hem of his shirt at his back and touched my fingertips to his skin there. He was so warm. My hand moved up to the middle of his back and out to the side before it slid back down his side to his waist.

He groaned into my mouth.

I needed more.

I pulled my head back, disconnecting our mouths, and stared up at him through hooded eyes. "I want more, Cruz. I'd like to feel your skin against mine."

The lust in his gaze was undeniable. His voice was thick with emotion when he ordered, "You've got to be clear, Lex. What exactly do you want?"

"Tops off," I answered. "Can we do that?"

"Anything you want, princess," he immediately replied as he lifted his torso from the couch and moved to lift his shirt over his head.

I watched with avid fascination.

Oh my.

Cruz.

He was so beautiful. I stared at his body and licked my lips.

Cruz was on his knees, his ass resting on his heels, as he straddled one of my thighs. I scooted back a bit toward the arm of the couch and sat up. Bringing my hands to Cruz's hips, I shifted so I was resting myself on my shins in front of him.

I wasted no time.

I leaned forward and pressed my lips to the middle of Cruz's chest. His hands that were holding the backs of my arms tightened momentarily before he dropped them to my hips. My mouth continued to move up his lean, muscled torso to his collarbones. I kissed along each side, feeling Cruz's grip around my waist tighten and pull me toward him. My hands were roaming over his naked upper body and Cruz was keeping his hands planted at my waist.

I didn't like it. It wasn't enough.

"Touch me, Cruz," I begged. "I want to feel your hands on my skin."

A low growl escaped from the back of his throat as his hands slowly went under the hem of my shirt. He didn't remove my shirt, but he was touching me, at my hips and my waist. I continued to kiss him, but craved more…much more than I think he was comfortable with knowing my past.

You are taking the lead on that.

I recalled Cruz's words and quickly decided I'd need to go after what I wanted. My hands left his body and went to the shirt I was wearing. After I pulled it over my head and tossed it aside, I stayed there in my lace-trimmed bra and gazed up at Cruz. I loved the way he was looking at me.

Like I was sexy, but sweet.

Like I was strong, but precious.

His look only served to make me more courageous.

My hands found his. I slid them up my sides until they were cupping the sides of my breasts.

"You are so pretty, Lexi," Cruz croaked. "So beautiful," he went on, his fingers squeezing gently.

"Kiss me," I pleaded.

He lowered his mouth to mine and kissed me. I kissed back because it was that good, but it wasn't what I wanted. I pulled back and said, "No."

Cruz immediately dropped his hands from my body and pulled back from me. "Are you okay?"

"I'm perfect, Cruz," I assured him.

He still looked concerned.

I eased that concern and explained, "I stopped because I didn't want you kissing me on my lips. I want your mouth on my body."

I just barely saw the heat in his eyes intensify before he dropped his head to my neck.

Yes!

My hands were fisting his hair. Cruz's mouth moved from my neck to the upper part of my chest. He kissed me there, slowly and very delicately. Taking his time, he lavished his attention in that same spot, not making a move to go further south.

"No scars." His voice was nothing but guttural relief.

It took me a second to understand, but then I realized what he was doing. He was kissing every spot where I had been burned, spots that weren't noticeable because he acted quickly and took care of me that day. I had no scars from Cruz and I had a feeling I never would.

"You took them away," I breathed. "You took care of me, Cruz."

At the sound of his name, Cruz changed. He became more desperate for me; he was hungrier.

I shifted my legs out from underneath me and fell to my back. Refusing to take his hands and his mouth from my body, Cruz came with me. There were no nerves or anxiety in that moment, only pure lust and desire. As he settled over my body, his mouth went lower, leaving a trail of kisses right over the top swells of my breasts. Relief splintered through my body as his mouth closed over my nipple, the delicate fabric of my bra the only thing separating us.

I moaned in relief at the sweet sensation.

Cruz's hand at my other breast squeezed before pulling the lace down and exposing my nipple. His lips moved across my chest and sucked the bared bud into his mouth.

"Cruz," I whimpered.

More sounds escaped him. They were the sexiest sounds I'd ever heard.

He exposed my other breast and flicked a single finger over the hardened peak several times before capturing it between his thumb and forefinger. It was magnificent.

A shrill sound filled the room and, quickly coming out of my lust-filled fog, I realized it was his phone.

"No," I panted. "Please, don't stop."

"Ignore it, Lex," he ordered.

So I ignored it.

Cruz kept at it, filling me with such want and need for more of him.

The ringing started again.

I tried to ignore it. Cruz couldn't.

He dropped his forehead to the space between my breasts and muttered, "Fuck."

When he lifted his head, he apologized, "I'm sorry, Lexi. I have to take it."

I gave him a quick nod, but said nothing otherwise. Cruz pulled his phone out and held it to his ear.

"Yeah?" There was no denying the irritation in his tone.

That is, it was irritation until I saw his face go alert. That's when I knew it was work and he'd need to leave. I brought my hands to my breasts and slid the lace cups back into place over them. Cruz watched me as he listened to the phone.

"I'll meet you there. I'm coming from Lexi's, so give me an extra five minutes," he responded to the person on the other end of the line.

He waited as the person spoke before he replied, "Yeah, me too."

Cruz disconnected the call and slid his phone back in his pocket. When he brought his eyes to mine, he looked tortured. It was like he couldn't bring himself to tell me he had to leave.

I made it easy for him.

"You have to go," I stated.

Disappointment wasn't even the correct word to describe the look on his face as he nodded. He hated having to leave as much as I hated the fact that he had to go. And that was a lot.

"Twice now," he started. "Twice I've left you like this. Christ, Lexi. I'm so sorry to do this to you…to us."

I was struggling with the idea of him leaving, but I knew he had an important job. I wanted him focused and didn't want to make him feel any worse than I could tell he already did.

I sat up in front of him and asked, "Are you going to catch a bad guy?"

"Based on the call I just received, I'm guessing I might do that while, quite possibly, also saving at least one girl from being abducted."

"Then go, Cruz," I demanded. "I'll be here when you're done saving the world."

He brought his hand to the side of my throat and allowed his thumb to move back and forth across the skin there. After giving himself a minute to look at me, Cruz shifted his body and got off the couch. He snatched his shirt from the floor and pulled it over his head while I got up and searched for my top. Once I found it, I picked it up and stood to find Cruz watching me. I held the shirt up to my chest to cover myself, but didn't put it on.

"You don't have to feel ashamed, warrior."

I gave him a small smile and confirmed, "I don't. Not with you. Never with you."

His face softened.

I explained, "I just thought it wouldn't be nice of me to torture you and stand here in my bra when I know you can't stay and continue what we started before you got that call."

"That's very kind of you," he praised. "But you should know

that seeing you standing there in your bra only makes me want to do what I've got to do as quickly as I can so I can get back to you. I enjoyed what this was tonight, Lex, and not just for the physical aspect of it. As amazing as that part was, I loved tonight for what it showed me about you and what you think about me. Thank you for trusting me to take this journey with you."

I dropped my shirt, stepped closer to him, and wrapped my arms around his neck. Pressing up on my toes, I brought my mouth to his, gave him a quick peck on the lips, and noted, "You make it easy."

Cruz brought his arms around me, nuzzled his face in my neck, and instructed, "Set the alarm after I leave. As much as I want to come back to you tonight, I don't think this is going to be quick. If it is, I'll come back. If it gets too late, I'm not going to disturb you in your sleep. Either way, don't doubt that this is exactly where I'd rather be."

"Did I ever tell you how much I'm really beginning to like you?" I teased.

Cruz chuckled. "You might have mentioned it once or twice."

"Go, Cruz. Be safe tonight."

"Always, Lexi. Good night, princess."

Cruz put his lips on my forehead, kissed me there, and left. After he walked out, I locked the door and set my alarm. Making my way through my apartment toward my bedroom, I turned off the lights along the way.

After removing my bra and throwing on pajamas, I sat in my cozy chair and wrote in my journal for a long time. I think I wrote so long because I was secretly hoping Cruz was wrong and he'd be back soon. Unfortunately, too much time passed and I was getting tired. I climbed into my bed and, despite my exhaustion, couldn't find sleep. Thoughts of my rendezvous with Cruz earlier in the evening played over and over in my mind and I found myself getting more and more turned on. I hadn't been this aroused in years. Heck, I hadn't been aroused at all in years. While there was a part of me that wanted that experience with Cruz, another part of me was screaming at me to take care of myself, to prove to me that I could be sexual again.

And that's when I knew I was going to give this to myself.

Slipping my hand underneath the waistband of my sweatpants, my fingers crept down to the top edge of my panties. I slid my hand under the fabric and my fingers moved through the wetness between my legs. My thoughts were on Cruz and how he used his lips and his tongue to excite me earlier. I continued to touch myself climbing higher and higher to a place I'd not seen in so many years. My free hand slid under my shirt up to my breasts, where it moved over one of my sensitive nipples.

It was a matter of minutes when I felt myself right on the edge. As much as I wanted to slip my finger inside, I held back. I was going to give myself this orgasm and I was going to thoroughly enjoy it, but I didn't want penetration until I could share that with someone who meant something to me. Visions of Cruz hovering over me earlier flashed before me and that's when it happened. I exploded, pure pleasure shooting through me to every inch of my body.

I moaned.

I whimpered.

Most of all, I gave myself something that nobody else could give me. Not an orgasm, but power over my sexuality. If I wanted to feel good, it was within me to give it to myself. And while I couldn't wait to share it with Cruz, because I knew deep down he was the man I wanted to share it with, it felt freeing to know I was finally in control. It would be my choice to give myself what I needed when I needed it.

Minutes later, I fell asleep.

CHAPTER 16

Cruz

"WHAT DO YOU HAVE FOR ME?"

I had just pulled up and was sitting in my truck outside The Rusty Spur. A minute after I parked, Dom was sitting in the passenger's seat next to me. Pierce and Lorenzo had gone inside.

"Jenkins called Reynolds not long before I called you," Dom started. "He's been here nearly all day, every day since the two of you stopped in. Poor guy's been torn up over the whole situation."

"This is his town," I put in. "He's a good guy; he feels the way we do. It's happening in our back yard. For him, it's happened several times at his local hangout."

"Well, apparently, he can spot these women as soon as they walk in. That's precisely what happened tonight. There's no guarantee, obviously, but he's convinced that she's going to be the next one targeted. She fits the profile, which doesn't necessarily mean anything, but it's the fact that Jenkins said there's also a guy in there that's not a regular. He said he just doesn't fit in. Instinct kicked in and he called us."

"Game plan?"

Dom shrugged and explained, "It depends on how it goes in there. If this does, in fact, turn out to be one of these cases, nothing is going to happen here. We let Reynolds and De Luca scope it out in there until she leaves. They call us when she walks out, we follow her. They will come behind us unless there's a reason for them to follow someone else. As much as I don't want this woman to be scared, I'm thinking we should try to see where they are going to try to take her. We know we aren't going to let anything happen to her and maybe we'll be able to save a few more girls in the process."

I dipped my chin in acknowledgment. "Fuck, I hope this gets us somewhere tonight. Not thrilled about the possibility of another woman being terrorized, but if we can get ourselves one step closer to finding the other women it'll be worth it."

"I hear you, brother," he agreed. "This case has been eating at me. My apologies, again, by the way."

I turned my head to the side and asked, "For what?"

"Interrupting your time with your girl. I know she's the first you've been serious with in a long time."

My girl.

Lexi.

Before Dom mentioned her, I was already struggling to stay focused. I spent the entire drive from her house to this parking lot replaying my evening with her, specifically the last part of the evening. Knowing what she'd been through a few years ago and seeing her find the courage to ask for what she wanted was a relief. More than that, I couldn't deny how good it felt to know she felt safe enough with me to trust she could ask me to give her what she needed and wanted.

I viewed each step she took toward giving herself what she deserved to have as a gift, especially when she took those steps with me. Now, I couldn't get the feel of her writhing underneath me or the sounds of her whimpering in desperation out of my mind.

"That look can only mean one thing," Dom interrupted my thoughts of Lexi. When I brought my attention to him, he grinned and continued, "You're in deep."

I chuckled. "A little."

I wasn't going to deny it. I was in deep and it was certainly more than a just a little.

"It's good to see. Happy for you, bro."

I didn't get a chance to respond because Dom's phone rang.

"Is it go time, De Luca?" he greeted. He paused and waited while Lorenzo answered. I watched as his eyes became fixed on the front door of the tavern and narrowed. Then, he continued, "Got her. You got a guy in there?" More silence. While he listened, I watched as the woman who walked out by herself made her way to her car. That's when I noticed a black SUV near where she was parked had just had its headlights turned on. It could have been coincidence, but I had a feeling it wasn't.

"Black SUV, headlights," I stated so Dom would know what I was thinking. He jerked his chin in acknowledgment.

Dom responded into the phone, "More than one then. If your guy in there is on the phone he's probably calling the guy in the SUV out here."

Silence.

"Headlights just went on. Parked close to her. She's in her car now and backing out. We're following. Stay on your man. I'll follow up if I can. You two get your situation sorted with him in there. If you haven't heard from me by the time you deal with him, call Michaels. Have him track the GPS and get a lock on our location."

Dom disconnected the call and updated me. "They've got a guy in there that's not a regular. As soon as she walked to the door, he was on the phone watching her. Jenkins recognized the guy because he's not a regular and he's definitely one that stands out. Reynolds and De Luca are going to stay on him. We've got her."

I nodded and the two of us watched as she drove to the entrance of the parking lot. Sure enough, the SUV followed behind her. We stayed back far enough that they wouldn't know we were trailing them.

Twenty minutes after she left the tavern, the woman turned into the parking lot of an apartment complex. I kept my truck parked pretty far back from the entrance where we saw the SUV turn in after her. We didn't want to give them any indication they were being followed and, thankfully, our view into the lot wasn't obscured by any walls, trees, or shrubs.

"She's going around the back side of the building," Dom noted. "If he follows, we go in."

The SUV was moving slowly, but followed her around the back. I pulled away from the curb and drove to the entrance of the parking lot. Taking the same route they did, we drove through the lot and toward the back, but never went completely around the back.

"I'm on foot from here," Dom declared. "I'll check it out, but I've got you in my ear."

We got ourselves connected so Dom could scope out the scene without alerting them to our presence and let me know when he needed me. Leaving the truck unmanned wouldn't bode well if they managed to get her in that vehicle and we needed to hightail it out of there.

I watched as Dom moved quickly around the back side of the building.

"She's parked about two hundred feet from where you are, Cruz," Dom said in my ear.

"The SUV?" I shot back.

"Two spots away from her. It's dark, but the lot is lit back here. She isn't going to notice them and they sure as fuck aren't going to know I'm here."

"How many guys?"

"Can't see yet," he said quietly. "She just got out of the car. I'm getting closer. About a hundred feet away."

I debated on whether or not to get out of the truck or to wait until we knew for sure how many guys we were dealing with.

"Interior light on the SUV just came on. One guy. He's getting out."

I heard Dom's breath hitch. This alarmed me.

"Talk to me," I instructed.

"Fuck," he whispered.

"Dom. What's happening?"

"She's so fucking beautiful, Cruz," he explained. "Get your ass down here. You get him; I'm getting her. She's not going anywhere with this guy."

He was letting this get personal.

"Keep your head on straight, brother. There are other women that we can locate if we follow him."

"He just walked up to her. She's terrified. You better be on your way down here."

"Stay focused on the bigger picture, Dom."

"Imagine if it were Lexi. He's got his hands on her and she's fighting back. I'm not playing. Get here now, Cr…fuck! The motherfucker just punched her in the stomach."

I came up behind him and ordered, "Get her; I've got him."

We took off in their direction and, as he hauled her toward his SUV with his hand over her mouth while she kicked her legs, he bellowed, "Lucky for you, you aren't worth much if your face is busted. You keep it up, though, and we're going to have problems."

She was struggling so much he never saw us coming. We approached him from behind. I got my hands on him and Dom went around the front to her. Being caught by surprise, his grip on her loosened enough that Dom was able to pull her away from him.

"I've got you," he said gently. "You're safe."

That was all I heard before I focused all my attention on the guy. As much as I wanted to beat him to a bloody pulp, I knew we needed to get some answers. I neutralized him just as Tyson and Holden appeared.

Noting my surprise, Tyson clarified, "Reynolds called Michaels and explained the situation. They're going after their guy and thought you could use backup. We were close by, so we figured we'd come down and see if you needed a hand. Looks like you've got it covered."

I rolled my eyes. "Can you hang with this motherfucker while I call Detective Baines?"

That got me a chin lift.

I took two steps away and shared, "Just so you know, he thought he was doing the girl some favors. Claiming her face pretty and not battered would be worth more, he decided to punch her in the stomach instead."

"Go call the detective," Holden urged, more than a hint of anger in his eyes. "We'll take care of this guy until Baines and his team arrive."

I walked away across the lot to where Dom was standing with his arm wrapped protectively around the girl's shoulders. Before I made an approach, I pulled my phone out of my pocket and called Detective Baines.

"Cruz Cunningham," he greeted me. "I hope you've got a good update for me."

"Just stopped an abduction. We've got the girl safe and the guy who attempted to take her here with us. Two of my other guys were following another accomplice from the tavern. I haven't heard anything yet on where they are with him."

"Where are you?"

"Highland Apartment complex. Back lot on the east side. Behind the building."

"Nice work. We're on the way."

He disconnected and I slid my phone back in my pocket. I walked over to Dom.

"Baines is on the way," I informed him as I got closer.

I could tell he was keeping a loose hold on his anger as he held the girl in his arms. She looked downright terrified.

"Are you alright?" I asked.

"It hurts to breathe," she responded quietly. Her eyes drifted from mine to Dom's. "Thank you for helping me."

His grip on her shoulders tightened. "What's your name, sugar?" he asked.

"Ekko," she responded.

"Echo?" he repeated.

"E-K-K-O," she clarified.

He gave her a look of understanding and asked, "Why were you at The Rusty Spur?"

Her eyes rounded in surprise before she dropped her gaze to the ground and nervously bit her lip. Aside from that, she made no move to answer his question.

"We're the good guys," I assured her. "We aren't here to judge you, darling. What we do need is any information you can give us because there were a few girls before you who were abducted and they've not been found yet. Anything you can tell us that can help us locate them is very much appreciated because they weren't as lucky as you."

Her voice was feeble when she answered, "I'm not sure I'd consider myself lucky." She paused a moment, fighting to stay strong when her face showed she was close to breaking down.

She took two slow, deep breaths before she continued, "I was desperate. I've hit a bit of a rough patch and I'm going to lose my apartment if I don't figure something out."

"So, what were you being offered? And by who?"

"A nice man in a suit. I'm a waitress at a diner and he came in a few times. I was having a particularly bad day earlier this week and he happened to be there. He asked me about it and I just couldn't shut up. When he heard about my troubles he told me he had a great opportunity for me. He said he was an executive at a modeling agency and that I could make a lot of money if I got into the business. It's not really my thing, but I'm desperate."

"And you just believed him?" Dom asked.

She shrugged her shoulders, but the disappointment was written all over her face. It was easy to see she now felt foolish. Even still, she explained, "I know I'm short and not typical model material, but he gave me his card. He was dressed nicely and he'd been to the diner a few times. I didn't think he was a bad guy."

"Do you have that card?" I questioned her.

She dipped her chin and replied, "In my purse in my car."

"We'll need that before we leave."

"Sure," she mumbled. "It's not like I'm going to be calling him again."

"Just to confirm, I'm guessing because you looked as panicked as you did when this guy approached you that he is not the same man who gave you his card."

She shook her head.

"Don't you have anyone that can help you out?" Dom pressed her.

She shook her head. "I've had an on-again, off-again boyfriend. He offered to allow me to move in with him, but I'd rather not. It's not...well, that doesn't matter."

"What about family? Friends?" I asked.

She didn't answer with words. She looked down to the ground and it was evident there wasn't anyone.

"How bad is your situation, Ekko?" Dom asked.

She let out a sarcastic laugh and answered, "They could write a book about me."

At that, she walked away from us toward her car. Dom and I stood there watching her. Or, I should say, I watched Dom as he watched her walk to her car.

"She's got a boyfriend," I reminded him.

His eyes cut to mine. "Yeah, one she doesn't want to move in with. You heard her hesitation. If that woman was in my bed, she'd not be hesitating. She's on my radar now."

"You sure that's a good idea?"

Dom turned his attention back to Ekko when he answered, "She won't know. I'm waiting it out, though. When she's had enough of this guy and he becomes the off-again boyfriend, he'll never have the chance to become on-again."

Now it was my turn to laugh.

Ekko walked back over to us and held the card out to me.

"Can I ask you a question, Ekko?" Dom wondered.

"Sure."

"How is it that you're surprisingly calm for someone who was just nearly abducted? Most other people would not be handling that this well."

"Most other people haven't lived my life," she answered. "Quite frankly, as terrifying as it was in the moment, the fact that you were here gives me a shred of hope that maybe my luck is turning around. Even if that hope is out of pure desperation."

Dom and I barely had a minute to process what she said before we heard the sirens.

Several hours later, I was in my truck headed home.

I had briefed Detective Baines on the events of the evening and the meeting Pierce and I had with Frank Jenkins a couple days ago. While I did that, Dom stayed with Ekko as she gave her version of the events that had transpired to one of the detectives. Tyson and Holden dealt with the officers who were there to cuff the suspect and take him to the station. Dom and I then took Ekko to the police station so she could give an official statement. As Dom waited with her, I took the time to reach out to Levi and let him know what had happened. He informed me that Pierce and Lorenzo had called into the office. They tailed the guy from the tavern, but decided against approaching him. They followed him to a townhouse, which they presumed was where he lived, but they decided to wait it out to see what his next move would be. They had given Trent the address and he would be looking into finding any information we could on the guy.

When we left the police station, we took Ekko back to her apartment. Dom saw her safely inside before I took him back to the office so he could get his truck.

It was late. It was much later than I had hoped it would be, but certainly not later than I had expected. Ultimately, it was undoubtedly well past the time that I would be willing to drop back in at Lexi's place. As much as I wanted to see her and continue what we had started earlier that evening, I wasn't going to do it at just after two in the morning.

So, I drove myself home.

And the entire way there I allowed myself the opportunity to put the case out of my head as thoughts of Lexi filtered in. It was a good place for my mind to be. Visions of her sweet little body underneath mine filled my brain. I replayed the sounds of her whimpers and moans.

As I pulled into the garage, I grew more and more turned on by thoughts of Lexi. I walked through the house, straight to my bedroom, and into the master bathroom where I turned on the shower. I needed to find some relief, so I stripped out of my clothes and got in. Then, I did what I had to do to alleviate some of the sexual tension.

When I finished in the shower, I found that my attempts to tamp down the desire for Lexi were mostly wasted. All I had to do was think of her and my cock was hard again. Exhausted and feeling little satisfaction, I collapsed on my bed and shoved my face into the pillow. Then, I groaned through my feelings of frustration hoping the slow course with Lexi was going to lead to everything I expected and hoped it would.

CHAPTER 17

Lexi

It was now Wednesday and had been one day shy of a full week since Cruz left my place to go save the world. He hadn't come back that night, but he did call me first thing the next morning. Considering he and Dom stopped an attempted abduction, saved a young girl, and made sure one of the bad guys was put behind bars, I didn't hold a grudge.

Monday arrived and with it came the official opening of the rape crisis center. WAAR opened as scheduled and everything had gone smoothly. Grant reached out to me late Monday afternoon and told me how well things had gone. While I was happy to know that there was a place for women to go for help, it saddened me at the same time to know that there was an overwhelming need for such an organization. I hadn't expected I'd ever step foot inside once it officially opened, but now three days later, I felt compelled to go.

It was partly out of curiosity and partly out of need. Something inside me was telling me to go, that I needed to be there.

So, after putting in several hours at the office today, here I was.

The second I walked through the doors, I found that I wanted to sit in on a group therapy session. That's precisely what I did since there was one just about to start. While I didn't share, there were several women I believed were much further along in their recovery who were sharing. Being further along didn't necessarily mean that their sexual assault experiences happened before mine did; it simply meant that they were healing differently than me. The one thing that I did learn from listening was that healing was an ongoing process. In addition to that, hearing their stories made me feel like I wasn't alone and I found myself wishing I had taken Dr. Lane's advice and sought the help of group therapy sessions long ago.

Now, I was beginning to consider the possibility of sharing my own story. It had taken me such a long time to get to a place where I could tell people I knew and trusted about what had happened. I didn't know if I'd be able to share so openly with strangers, but I admired the women who spoke today. Listening to them and seeing their strength made me realize that if I could bring myself to share my experience, I'd be able to show other women that there was a reason to hope and that their assault did not have to control them for the rest of their lives.

I got up and was headed toward the front door, excited to get home and call Cruz. He was going to be working later this evening on his case, but I knew he'd take some time to chat with me. I wanted to get home as quickly as I could so that I could tell him about my eye-opening experience today.

I never expected that I'd experience something that would have an even more profound effect on me than the meeting, but that's precisely what happened as I walked through the front door.

It was just before seven o'clock and I had opened the door to leave. As I stepped through the door, I was stopped in my tracks by what stood before me. Two young girls, one whose eyes were haunted. I took one look in them and I knew it wasn't good; though, the state of her clothes, hair, and exposed skin would have told the story if her eyes hadn't.

"My friend told me to come here," she mumbled.

The other girl spoke up. "I'm her friend. I saw some advertisements about this place, so when she called me just a little bit ago I picked her up and brought her here."

I gave her a gentle nod and said, "Okay. We can help you. Come inside."

Once inside, I got one of the volunteers who had been in the group therapy session. I planned to stay around to make sure she was alright, but when she was asked to go to one of the private rooms so that she could be evaluated, she pleaded with me to go with her and her friend.

"I..." I stammered, trailing off unsure of what to do. "I don't work here."

Her eyes filled with tears and she begged me, "I don't care. I don't want to be alone. Please come in there with me."

Getting a gentle nod from the volunteer, I agreed, "Okay. I'll come with you."

I knew how crucial it was to have support and while I rejected any help right after my rape, sometimes I now wished I hadn't. If this girl wanted to be surrounded by people she felt she could trust, I'd find a way to be that person for her.

Much to my dismay, but not a surprise at all, we learned that Riley had been brutally attacked by a man. Her friend, Paige, suggested she come to us because she'd heard about the center from part of the campaign work I'd done. Obviously, they didn't know anything about me or that I was the one responsible for them hearing about WAAR. Regardless, I was thrown. I never expected to be hit full force with just how crucial the work I had done was. I didn't have time to dwell on that, though, because not long after Riley was evaluated and checked out by one of the doctors on staff, she was surprisingly open about what happened and shared it with us.

"I guess this is what I get for trying to have a good time before it's over," she joked. "I'm a senior at Windsor College and I'm about to graduate. I was invited with some friends to go to a concert off campus. Paige couldn't go because she was far behind on a project for one of her classes. I decided to ride with my friends to the venue. Since it was early, we stopped for dinner and drinks first. I haven't let loose in a while and I don't have a class until later tomorrow afternoon, so I figured I'd enjoy myself. I had a lot to drink. We got to the venue, but it was outdoors. I ended up separated from my friends. I tried texting them, but they weren't responding. I figured I might have better luck calling, so I walked away from the crowd so I could hear."

Riley closed her eyes and sighed. "I was so stupid. My reception was terrible and I kept walking. By the time I realized how far away I'd gotten from the crowd, it was too late. He dragged me to the parking lot. I tried fighting him, but he was so much stronger."

The tears rolled down her cheeks and my heart broke for her.

She continued, "I was wearing this dress, so it was easy for him. He bent me over the hood of a car and held me down. I couldn't move. I couldn't fight. When he finished, he left me there alone. I called Paige and waited for her to come get me."

"Oh, Riley. I'm so sorry this happened to you," I said.

"If I had been there," Paige started. The guilt over what happened to her friend was clearly eating at her.

"Neither one of you is to blame for what happened," I insisted, cutting her off before she had the opportunity to condemn herself further.

Both girls were in tears at this point. The counselor

stepped in and we spent the next hour calming them down and reassuring them.

When they both settled down, the counselor talked to Riley about reporting the rape. She vehemently refused.

There was no pressure put on her and the staff got her and Paige set up with a place to stay for the evening. While they could go back to their dorm room, they ultimately decided it was best to stay where there'd be qualified staff on hand to help get her through the first night. After both girls were settled in one of the rooms, I pulled out my business card and handed one to each of them. I wanted Riley to know she had someone there for her if she needed to talk.

After that, approaching ten thirty, I left and went home. On the drive home, my day from the time I walked through the doors at WAAR until I left replayed in my head. Mostly, my thoughts were consumed by Riley.

Listening to her entire ordeal, not just what happened, but the manner in which she was handling it, was so familiar. Everything from the dead look in her eyes and the joking when she started telling the story, to the guilt, shame, and terror she expressed brought back so many memories. I didn't know how I was going to get through the rest of the evening. Riley's awful situation brought back so many horrible memories for me.

I walked through my front door, set my alarm, and walked to my bedroom. After taking a shower, I got myself ready for bed. Just as I was about to climb in, my phone rang. I fished it out of my purse and answered.

"Hey, Cruz. I was getting ready to call you."

"Are you alright? I hadn't heard from you and sent a text a while ago, but you never responded. I was just about to leave and come to check on you."

"Oh, I'm so sorry. I just got home. I had such a horrible night," I divulged.

"What happened?" he worried.

I told him about Riley. I didn't give him her name or all the details of what specifically happened to her because I wasn't sure I could relive it, but I needed to tell him how I was feeling about it. He listened to the story until he had to go. I was grateful I had the opportunity to talk with him about it, but even after I had I was still so unsettled.

It might have been roughly thirty minutes after Cruz and I disconnected and I was still no closer to finding sleep. I had tossed and turned, telling myself that I should have exercised when I got home even though it was late. But I knew that wasn't the reason I was having trouble sleeping. A minute later, I heard a knock at my door. I crawled out of bed, walked to the front door, and looked out the peephole.

Seeing who was on the other side, I couldn't open the door fast enough.

"Cruz," I called when I opened the door. "What are you doing here? I thought you were working."

He stepped inside and explained, "I got done what I needed to get done and have one of the other guys covering for me. I heard how upset you were on the phone and thought you might need someone here for you. I wanted to be that person."

I was going to cry.

Stepping into Cruz, I dropped my head to his chest and felt his arms engulf me. He held me tight while I took in a few deep breaths. When I had calmed myself enough, I looked up at him and asked, "Will you spend the night with me?"

He brushed a stray hair away from my face and admitted, "I actually planned for that. That's why I packed a bag. It's out in the truck, but I'll get it in the morning. Let's lock up and set the alarm."

After accomplishing that task, I asked, "Have you had dinner? Did you want me to make you something?"

"I'm good," he responded.

I watched as Cruz moved to the couch and it hurt my heart. He was here because he knew I needed him and he was going to sacrifice a decent night's sleep again by staying on the couch.

"Cruz?"

He turned around to look at me and wondered, "Yeah, Lex?"

I held out my hand and admitted, "I'd be alright with you staying in my bed with me tonight. It's bigger than the couch and probably a lot more comfortable."

He was surprised by my invitation.

"Are you sure? I don't mind the couch. I just want to make sure you've got someone here if you start feeling uneasy about what happened earlier tonight and it wakes you in the middle of the night."

"I couldn't even fall asleep," I confessed. "I'd really love having you next to me tonight."

With a grin on his face, he walked back to me, put his hand in mine, and instructed, "Lead the way."

I walked us down the hall to my bedroom. While Cruz sat on the edge of the bed and removed his shoes, I climbed under the blankets and put my head on the pillow. He turned back to look at me before he dropped to his back.

"Is that how you normally sleep?" I questioned him.

"What do you mean?"

I laughed. "I mean, in full clothing on top of the covers."

He dropped his head to the side and his expression was light. "It's not, but I'm also not looking to overstep any boundaries here."

"So, tell me how you normally sleep then," I urged.

"Usually just in a pair of boxer briefs," he divulged. "And always under the blankets."

"Then I'd like you to do that if you're comfortable that way."

Cruz turned toward me and brought his hand to the side of my neck. "I'm not going to make myself comfortable at the expense of causing you discomfort."

"Well," I started. "Then you should know that if you fall asleep on top of the blankets, that will cause me plenty of discomfort. This is because then I won't be able to steal the covers and make sure they're wrapped tight around me."

He held my eyes, but didn't respond.

I went on, "In all seriousness, Cruz, I want you to be comfortable. It's important to me because you are the reason I'm now comfortable doing things I've not been able to do in a long time."

And that was the truth. He'd proven to me so many times already that I could trust him. I didn't have doubts that he'd be respectful.

"You've got to make me a promise then," he stressed.

"What's that?"

"If I strip off the pants and the shirt, you've got to promise you're not going to fall in love with me."

I cocked an eyebrow at him. "Excuse me?"

Cruz laughed and clarified, "I want you to fall in love with me, princess, but I'm more than just a hot body. I've got a brilliant mind and it's much sexier, don't you think?"

"Are you trying to get me to admit that I think you've got a great body?" I accused him.

He sat up and pulled his shirt over his head.

I watched the muscles in his back and his arms flex with his movements. He stood, with his back to me, and worked at the waistband of his pants before he pushed them to the floor.

Wow.

He had a great ass.

I was admiring his ass when he turned around. That's when I swallowed hard and my lips parted. I was now looking at his...well, his front.

He cleared his throat and my eyes moved slowly up his body. The corners of his mouth had tipped up and I could tell he was trying to stifle the laughter threatening to take over.

There was no way I could speak, so I pulled the blankets back, indicating he could climb under.

And he did.

He rolled to his side so that he was facing me and took my hand in his. We stayed like that a long time. Cruz was offering me comfort and safety while I took the time to appreciate his sweet gestures. It filled me with such warmth to know he realized how taxing my evening had been on my mental state and he took the initiative to find a way to be here for me. Offering to sleep on the couch and then remaining dressed and uncomfortable in my bed, I couldn't help but fall a little harder for this man.

No matter how great my thoughts of Cruz were, I couldn't stop the events of the day from taking over.

"She was brutalized," I whispered.

Cruz's hand tightened around mine.

"I can't help thinking if I fought back the way she did, it could have been that much worse for me. Listening to her, I began wondering if I should feel grateful that what I experienced wasn't as violent."

"Lexi," Cruz's voice was firm. "No matter how awful someone else's experience may be, it does not diminish what happened to you. It doesn't make yours not as bad. *Nothing* about rape is good."

"I know," I sighed. "I just...I can't help it. She's been terrorized and it's devastating, but I think she's going to be okay. The strength she already shows is unbelievable. She called her friend right away and sought out help. She told me about it and she doesn't even know me. And one of the things I kept thinking was how I wish I had been strong enough to tell the people who would have been there for me."

"You did," he assured me.

I rolled my eyes and pointed out, "Yeah...four years later."

"It doesn't matter how long it took you. Everyone responds differently and everyone heals differently. Even if you didn't tell anyone, it wouldn't make you weak. You're still here; you're living and succeeding. You're just as strong as anyone else."

I let his words sink in a minute before I wondered, "How'd you get to be so smart?"

Cruz gave me his most handsome grin and responded, "I told you my mind was sexy."

I burst out laughing.

When I stopped laughing I noticed Cruz was just watching me.

"Thank you for being here for me tonight," I murmured. "You have no idea how much it means to me."

"I care about you, Lex. When you need me, I'm going to be here for you. Simple as that."

I closed my eyes and felt his words deep in my heart.

When I opened them, I challenged, "Since I've admitted that your mind is sexy, is there any way you'd be willing to allow me to get close to your body? I would love for you to hold me in your arms tonight; I feel safe there."

"Then you better get your ass over here."

I scooted over toward him. Cruz wrapped his arm around my waist and began turning me. I was so caught off guard, I squealed, "What are you doing?"

"Spooning you. I can't do that if you're facing me," he replied. "Are you alright with that?"

I thought for a moment before I agreed.

The next thing I knew I was wrapped in Cruz's arms and he was spooning me. A few minutes later, I felt myself drifting.

"Good night, Cruz," I said.

He pressed a kiss to my shoulder before he returned, "Good night, princess."

Then, he nuzzled his face in my neck, pulled my body tighter to his, and squeezed. I had to admit how good it felt to be there with him, feeling nothing but peace, safety, and a whole lot of good feelings. Cruz had gone well beyond the call of duty. While he took the time to listen to my fears and reservations about the situation, he spent most of the time successfully distracting me from what was causing me anxiety. I'd had a crappy evening and he made it better by bringing joy and laughter. He let me talk about what was upsetting me, but he didn't let me fall too deep into the hurt I was feeling. Most importantly, he made sure I was going to fall asleep feeling content. I couldn't get over how happy that made my heart feel.

On that thought, I cuddled further into Cruz and fell asleep.

CHAPTER 18

Lexi

Cruz's soft lips pressed to the skin at the side of my neck woke me the next morning. I didn't open my eyes, but I was awake. It was hard not to be. Somehow, it seemed as though I spent the entire night wrapped up in Cruz's arms and didn't move at all. I couldn't even begin to process how much I enjoyed waking with him there next to me.

Sadly, I couldn't stay in bed with him because I had things to get done and I'm sure he had a full day ahead of him as well.

But I was going to give myself a few more minutes to soak up all that I was feeling being tucked tight to his body. So, I took a few minutes.

When I had sufficiently soaked up all the Cruz I could, I slowly started to stretch out my body. Cruz's lips continued to kiss me. As I shifted my body and turned toward him, he didn't allow the movement to break the connection between his mouth and my skin. I loved it.

"Good morning, Cruz."

His mouth stopped moving and he pulled back to look at me. "I like your morning voice," he shared.

"You've heard it before," I noted.

"Yeah, but never in your bed before."

"Well, I like you in my bed," I declared.

Cruz grinned and insisted, "I'm cool with having regular sleepovers with you. Feel free to invite me over whenever you want."

"I'll have to keep that in mind," I shared as I leaned into him and pressed a kiss to his chest. "Thank you again for coming here for me last night. I know I keep saying that, but I really want to make sure you understand how much it helped me."

He leaned over and pressed a kiss to my forehead before I hugged him.

"Can I get your opinion on something?"

"Sure," he responded.

"Yesterday before I left WAAR, I gave the girl I told you about last night and her friend my business card. I wanted them to know they could reach out to me if either of them needed someone to talk to about what happened. From the moment I handed them those cards until now, I've been thinking and I am trying to decide whether or not I want to get some official volunteer training. They offer it at the center because I guess you really can't ever have enough help."

Cruz approved, "I think it's a great idea if you feel it's something you can handle. Obviously, I wouldn't want to see you do anything that's going to hurt you, but if you feel strongly about it, I'll support you one hundred percent."

His support meant everything to me, so I smiled up at him. "It might mean less time for us to spend together for a week or two while I get the necessary training. Plus, any time I spend there actually volunteering will be less time."

There was a gentle squeeze on my hip before Cruz maintained, "I'd never stand in your way of doing something like this. Obviously, I want to spend as much time as I can with you, but I'm not going to stop you from doing something that's going to possibly help you and will definitely help others."

"I'm going to call Dr. Lane this morning and see if she has any time this evening to meet with me. I want to talk to her about what happened last night and my thoughts about moving forward with volunteering. It was hard to see that girl show up yesterday, knowing what she'd been through. I just want to make sure I'm not setting myself up for failure in my own recovery."

He nodded and agreed, "That's probably a good idea. And just so you know, if you ever want me to go with you to a therapy session, I'm more than happy to do it. I don't know if that's something your doctor offers or if it's even something she'd encourage, but I want you to know that I am willing to do that for us."

For us.

"I think I'd like to kiss you, Cruz," I hinted, pressing my body into his.

He grinned at me and promised, "I'm not going to stand in your way of doing that, either."

The two of us spent the next few minutes in my bed kissing. It was a wonderful way to wake up and I found myself looking forward to more mornings doing that very same thing. I had a feeling it wouldn't be long before I invited Cruz for another sleepover.

Following my morning make-out session with Cruz, we both got ready for work. I made a quick call to Dr. Lane and found that she had some free time just after lunch where she could squeeze me in for a session. Cruz and I made a quick stop at Colvert's for breakfast before we went our separate ways. Cruz went to the Cunningham Security offices and, instead of heading to my office, I took a detour.

I stopped at WAAR because I wanted to check on Riley. I

didn't know if she'd still be there or even how she'd feel now that she had some time to process what had happened to her, but I figured if I could offer her a bit of encouragement it couldn't hurt.

I arrived and quickly got an answer. Paige was out in the common area, where she had a cup of coffee in her hand. She saw me and gave me a friendly smile and a wave, but one look at her told me it had been a rough night.

Approaching her, I guessed, "She didn't have a good night, did she?"

Paige's guilt was written all over her face. She shook her head. "Not at all."

I held up the bag of goodies I picked up at Colvert's and wondered, "Do you think she'll be up for some goodies and a visitor?"

"Yeah," she stated. "You seem to have made an impression last night. I think she'd like that."

Paige and I walked back to the room she and Riley stayed in last night. When we walked in, we found her sitting up in the bed, her back against the wall.

"Hey, Riley," I greeted her.

"Hi, Lexi," she replied, her voice void of emotion. "What are you doing here?"

She wasn't angry with me, merely curious.

"I hope it's alright that I stopped in. I was heading to work and thought I'd bring you both breakfast from the best place in town," I explained as I held out the bag to her.

Instead of jumping right in and asking her how she was feeling, I figured it was best to simply make my support known by being there. I didn't want to make assumptions based on how she reacted to me yesterday when she arrived at WAAR and then find out that she was no longer comfortable sharing. The truth was, when I was raped and chose not to tell anyone but my therapist, it was clear that I was uncomfortable with sharing my experience at that time. Riley had been the opposite of me in the first few hours after it happened in that she was open about it. Since I understood that everyone reacted differently to trauma, I wanted to let her be the one to lead the conversation wherever she wanted it to go.

Riley took the bag from my hands and opened it. I had purchased an assortment of croissants, bagels, muffins, and fruit.

"Thank you."

I gave her a nod.

"I'm confused," Paige cut in.

When Riley and I turned to look at her she went on, "Yesterday you said that you don't work here. If that's the case, why are you here?"

Hmm. I wasn't sure how to answer. I didn't know if I wanted to give them the full truth of why I was there.

"I gave you my card yesterday. I actually own a public relations firm. Those advertisements that you saw about the center were my work. I handled all of the marketing and promotion for WAAR."

"So, you're the reason I knew where to go," Riley stated. There was no question in her words. She was simply stating a fact. "Wow, I wish I could be you right now instead of being the one who needs to be here."

She had no idea that I'd been through the same thing as her. I wasn't offended by what she said and I completely understood her sentiments.

The girls pulled the food out of the bag and I was happy to see Riley was at least eating. After she'd gotten some food in her stomach, she looked at me and shared, "Last night was awful. I woke up crying uncontrollably and it took a long time for me to realize I wasn't in any danger."

"The staff here was amazing," Paige added. "I was panicked and unsure of how to best help her, but seeing them take care of her last night I now know I can help her after we leave here."

It felt good. As much as I hated that Riley was going through this, I was so proud to be part of something that was going to have a positive impact in the lives of so many women and girls.

Riley let out a sob and buried her face in her hands. Spontaneous crying. I knew all about it.

Paige immediately moved to her friend and wrapped her arms around her.

"I feel like I'm..." she hiccoughed. "It's like I'll never live a normal life again. I don't want to leave here."

I made a split-second decision.

I knelt down in front of her, held her hand in mine, and assured her, "It's ok, Riley. It is normal to feel fearful and to also want to feel normal again. But it takes time. And there's no deadline for getting yourself to a place that makes you feel like yourself again. The most important thing to remember is that it wasn't your fault and you're not alone. I look at you and can't even begin to tell you how strong you are."

"I'm not strong at all. I couldn't even fight him off."

"Riley, you are. And you're going to get through this. You've got an amazing best friend who is here for you, you've got the center, and you've got me here if you need me. We'll all make sure you get through this."

She sighed, clearly not believing that things would get better for her.

"I want to tell you something, sweetie," I started.

When her eyes came to mine, I let it out to the first person I didn't really know that well. But I did it because I knew she needed me to do that for her.

"I just told you I was here yesterday because I took part in making sure people knew that WAAR was here. What I didn't tell you is that four years ago I felt the same way you do now. I was raped by a guy I was dating during my freshman year in college. It took me just over two months to realize I needed to see a therapist. And then I never told anyone else up until three weeks ago. I came here yesterday to sit in on a group therapy session and I wish I would have sought help like that years ago. In my opinion, and having been there before, telling Paige and coming here is a huge first step toward healing yourself. It's going to take time, but trust me, you will get there."

"You were raped too?" she whispered her question.

I gave her a few slow nods and replied, "Yeah. And I hesitated when I was approached about doing the marketing for the center, but I came to realize that something this important needed to be handled properly. Giving up on something that would become vital to the recovery of sexual assault and rape survivors just wasn't an option for me."

"I'm so sorry that happened to you."

"Thank you. I've only told a handful of people about what happened to me. You and Paige are two on a very short list, but I want you to see that it does get better. You need to do what feels best for you, but if I can make any suggestion to you I'm going to tell you that getting help is so important. Talking with survivors can be tremendously helpful and I'm only just now learning that. If you decide you want that help, it's here for you."

Riley pulled her hand free from mine and shocked me by hugging me tight. I held on to her just as fiercely and ran my hand up and down her back.

"It gets better, I promise," I repeated.

"Thank you for sharing that with me. You've given me some hope."

"You're welcome," I started as I stepped out of her embrace. "I should get going because I need to talk with one of the workers here before I go to a meeting, but don't hesitate to call me if you need anything. And you can expect to see me around here on a regular basis now because I'm planning on becoming an official volunteer. I'm making it part of my own recovery and healing."

As I turned to walk out, she called out to me. "Lexi?"

"Yeah?"

"Would you mind being there with me for my first group therapy session? I think I'd like to go to the next one."

I gave her a bright smile and answered, "Absolutely."

At that, I turned and walked out.

I made my way out and spoke with one of the staff members. After expressing my desire to become an official volunteer, I was given a rundown on the specifics of the program. Essentially, I'd have to go through a seventy-hour counselor advocate training course in addition to consenting to a background check and child abuse clearances since it was possible children could end up coming in. I was truly looking forward to completing the training and not only healing myself, but also helping others on their road to recovery.

Just as I was about to head out to get to my appointment with Dr. Lane, Grant showed up. I hadn't expected to see him there.

"Hi, Grant," I greeted him.

He was caught off guard, his head jerking back when he saw me standing there. Blinking away his surprise, he replied, "Lexi, good to see you. What are you doing here?"

I wasn't going to bring up Riley, so I said, "I've been doing some thinking and I'm going to start volunteering here. I just got all of the information on the training course and I think I'm going to do the fast-track option this weekend. I think there's a lot of good I can do here."

His eyes rounded, evidently shocked by my admission. "Really? That's…well, that's great. We certainly can use all the help we can get. You've done so much for the center already, though."

"I appreciate that. While I'm hoping to help and have an impact on the lives of some of the women here, this is something I'm doing for myself, too."

"Your dedication is commendable, Lexi," he approved. "And thank you again for all that you've done to get the word out. This opening week has been a huge success. The donations still have not stopped and, from what I've gathered from the staff, we've been helping a lot of women. As sad as the last half of that is considering this is our first week open, it's good to know we're accomplishing what we hoped we would."

Before I could respond, my attention was directed to someone clearing their throat. When I turned my head to the side, there was a guy standing there.

"Um, hi," he started. "I heard that you guys help victims of sexual assault and rape. I was wondering if you could help me."

I looked to Grant who immediately answered, "I'm sorry, but this is a women's center. We can certainly give you a referral to another location."

This was horrible. I realized it was a women's center, but I couldn't imagine turning someone away who needed help.

"It's not for me specifically," the man clarified. "About a week ago my girlfriend was assaulted. I don't know how to best help her."

"Grant?" I called. "I don't mean to overstep, but when I came in yesterday and checked out the place I saw a few rooms in the back not being used. I don't want to traumatize the women any further, but there is plenty of staff here. And you're here occasionally. Maybe we could allow him to get some help just for today in one of those rooms?"

Grant gave me a nod and turned to the man. "What's your name?"

"Shaun."

"Follow me, Shaun," Grant said before turning to me. "Lexi, good to see you again. We'll touch base again soon about some community fundraising events we'd like to do."

"Sounds great. I'm looking forward to it. I'll see you later," I ended. Before I walked away I looked at Shaun. "It's admirable that you're looking for ways to help your girlfriend. I hope she gets the help she needs. If she's not comfortable in a setting like this, they can recommend therapists to help her in a one-on-one setting."

Shaun gave me a simple nod and thanked me. He and Grant took off toward one of the spare rooms at the back of the center and I left the building.

I made my way to Dr. Lane's office. The appointment with her went well and as expected. I was finding more and more that I already knew what Dr. Lane's responses to my questions would be. Even still, I found I still liked having that reassurance as added security. I didn't know if it was something I'd need forever. All I knew was that it was something I needed now and, even if she thought I didn't need to come any longer, Dr. Lane never told me I should stop visiting when I felt I needed her support.

After my appointment, I went to my office and got to work. I spent most of my afternoon and early into the evening working on things for Logan's garage and Leni's yoga studio. In addition, I started trying to do some planning for Elle. She had decided that she was going to do another mini-tour this coming summer. She didn't have any specific locations nailed down yet, but knew that she wanted to at least go back to Las Vegas since the last time she was there one of her shows was cut short. Other than giving me her timeline and telling me that she wanted to have enough time in between locations to drive and do some sightseeing, she was leaving the tour up to me.

After I shut everything down, I pulled out my phone and called Nikki.

"Hey, babe. What's going on?" she answered.

"Hi, sis. I was wondering if you've got any plans for tonight?"

"Nope," she replied. "I'm actually leaving the salon now and heading to Luke's."

Bummer. I didn't want to intrude on their evening.

"Oh," I started. "Never mind then. I thought if you were home and didn't have anything planned I could stop by and hang with you for a bit."

"So come to Luke's place," she insisted. "He's actually going to be working with my dad in the garage. Apparently, my dad's newfound freedom has resulted in him getting his own motorcycle. Of course, he bought one that needed work done to it, so Luke's offered to help him with it. I have no interest in that, so if you come over I'll have someone to keep me company."

"Are you sure?"

She laughed, "I'm begging you!"

"Okay. I'm leaving the office now. I'll see you soon."

I needed some girl time, even if it was only for a couple hours. Witnessing Riley and Paige earlier today had me feeling regretful that I'd lost so much of myself to my rape. One of those parts was my close connections with people. Friends. I wanted that again. Now that I was in a place where I was aware of what it took from me, I was determined to get it back. And Nikki was one who I'd be able to talk with about some of the other things I wanted to get back.

Things that involved Cruz.

CHAPTER 19

Lexi

"I'M SCARED."

My voice was muffled as I stood inside Cruz's arms with my face pressed to his chest.

"It's going to be okay, Lexi. I promise," he assured me.

I tightened my arms around his waist, attempting to find the security in his words. I wasn't sure I managed to accomplish that.

It was now Sunday afternoon, about three and a half weeks after Cruz and I had discussed my need to tell my parents about my rape. Cruz had just shown up at my apartment and we were going to be heading over to my parents' house for a late lunch. When Cruz and I talked about it a few weeks ago, I felt confident that the time was right and that I was ready to share the news with my parents. Despite feeling anxiety about telling them, I still knew I wanted to tell them. Not only did I know it would help me remove more bricks from my shoulders, but I also believed my parents deserved to know. They had always been supportive of me and, even though I knew they'd be shattered, I didn't want to keep it from them any longer.

"I know," I mumbled. "I'm just afraid of hurting them. They've been so good to me and my brothers."

"They're your parents. They love you. I imagine it's going to be difficult for them to hear, but I'm sure they'll find a way to show you that what's important to them is knowing that you're healing now."

I tipped my head back and looked up at Cruz. "Thank you for going with me. It means a lot that you're not only going to meet the parents today, but that you're willing to do that knowing what I'm going to deliver to them."

Cruz pressed a kiss to my cheek before he responded, "With every day that goes by, I'm finding that there isn't much I would say no to doing for you. Besides, in this situation, I'm thinking that it's not me that has the difficult job."

"I guess you've got a point there," I agreed before I let out a sigh. "I think we should head out now so I can finally do this."

"Kiss me first," Cruz requested.

Looking at his beautiful face as I stood wrapped inside his arms, I couldn't help myself from satisfying his wish. I pressed up on my toes while he lowered his mouth to mine. After I kissed him, Cruz took me to my parents' house.

On the way there, I found myself lost in my own thoughts. I was certain Cruz knew I needed the time to get my head together and he was more than happy to give that to me. My mind first took me to my phone call with Logan and those that followed when I set this up. I could tell immediately that he was surprised to hear from me since we had seen each other two days prior when I had my rescheduled meeting with him.

"Hey, sidekick, what's going on? Is everything okay?" he asked.

"Yes, I'm fine. I just wanted to see if you had any free weekends coming up? I think I'd like to tell Mom and Dad about what happened and I'd really like for you to be there."

He didn't hesitate. "We've got a big race this weekend, but I'm free for the next three afterward. As long as it's one of those, you tell me what time and I'm there."

"Thanks, Logan. I'm going to call Luke next, see when he and Nikki are available, and then I'll call Mom and Dad. I'll let you know a time once I talk to everyone else."

"Sounds good. How's everything else going?"

"Everything else?"

He huffed, "With Cruz, Lex. I was hoping you would have brought it up when we met on Wednesday, but you never did. I know you're grown up now and you've been through something terrible without my support, but I'm still your big brother and I care about you. I want to know that he's treating you right."

"It isn't your fault I didn't have your support, Logan. I know if I had told you years ago that you would have been there for me. And to answer your question about Cruz... yes, he's treating me right. He's precisely the kind of man I needed in my life."

"Happy to hear that, sidekick. If that changes, you better call me."

I laughed. "I don't think you'll need to worry about that happening."

We disconnected and I called Luke. Just like Logan, he immediately stepped up to the plate to support me, insisting that he and Nikki would be there for me. So, I called my parents and told them I wanted to have a family get-together. I told my mom that I started dating someone and I wanted them to meet him. Since I didn't want them panicking or upset from then until we got together, I figured it was best to leave it at them meeting Cruz. My mom was excited and said that she and my dad couldn't wait to meet him. Of course, they both knew Zane through Luke and snowboarding, so I had to guess that was why my dad wasn't completely freaking out.

We arrived at my childhood home and found that everyone had already arrived ahead of us. Cruz and I weren't late; I think my brothers just wanted to make sure they went above and beyond for me in this situation by arriving early.

After coming around to open my door, Cruz held my hand as we walked through the garage into the house. We stepped inside and followed the sound of voices to the kitchen. Sure enough, we found my parents, Logan, Luke, and Nikki were all there already. They turned their attention to us and I noticed my dad's gaze drop to where my hand was being held firmly in Cruz's grip. In an attempt to distract my father, I dove into introductions.

"Mom. Dad. This is Cruz. Cruz, these are my parents, Rick and Diane."

"It's so nice to finally meet you, Cruz. We've heard about you from your brother and Luke. Welcome to our home," my mom gushed. I had no doubts she'd be happy.

"The pleasure's all mine," he returned before holding his hand out to my father. "Mr. Townsend, it's nice to meet you."

My father's eyes narrowed, but he moved past it quickly and shook Cruz's hand. It was a bit tense, but thankfully, Logan came to the rescue.

"Cruz?" he called as he held out his hand to him. When Cruz's attention shifted to the side, Logan introduced himself. "Logan."

I jumped in. "And you obviously already know Luke and Nikki."

After he gave them both a nod, he stepped back beside me again.

"Ok, everyone into the dining room. The food is ready," my mom announced before it had a chance to get awkward.

Fortunately, it never got that way either. Once we were all seated at the table and eating, it was wonderful. Most of this was because, aside from Cruz, I had three people there who knew I had a huge task ahead of me and they did what they could to keep it relaxed.

We finished eating and that's when my father directed his attention to me.

"So, how has the business been going, sweetheart?"

"Really great," I started. "I've been keeping busy with Elle's stuff, obviously. Since snowboarding season is over, that's slowed down a bit. Wes is close to launching his surf board line, though, so I'm sure I'll be in demand for that soon enough. For the time being, I've had a few smaller campaigns I've been working on and one really big one that was a referral from Logan."

"Oh yeah?" Dad asked, glancing over proudly to Logan.

"What is it?" Mom wondered.

"They've just opened a rape crisis center in Windsor. It's called WAAR. It stands for Windsor Against Abuse and Rape. I've been doing all of the PR for it and talked with Grant the week before it opened. He's the one overseeing the center for his company and he told me that the donations started pouring in after I launched the campaign. I spent the week following that call working on getting the word out so that rape and sexual assault survivors would know that there's a place they can go for help."

My mother was beaming at me and there was nothing but pride in my dad's eyes. I hated knowing what I was about to do to them.

"I'm so proud of you, Lexi," Dad said.

"Thanks, Dad," I answered, dropping my eyes to my lap.

It grew silent in the room.

"Lexi?" my mom called.

I lifted my head and looked at my parents. I didn't notice until I felt Cruz's hand on my thigh that I'd been nervously shaking my leg. His touch offered comfort, but the feelings inside me were overwhelming.

"Sweetie, what's wrong?" Mom pressed.

"I don't... " I stopped myself, trying to get some control over my emotions. I took in a deep breath and blew it out. I felt Cruz's thumb stroking back and forth on my leg, just above my knee. My eyes moved from my parents around the table. There was nothing but loving looks coming from my brothers and Nikki.

"It's ok, Lex," Logan assured me.

When I looked back at my parents, I blurted, "I don't want you to be disappointed with me."

"Why would we ever be disappointed with you?"

"Because something happened a long time ago that I've never told you about."

"Lexi," my dad cautioned. "I swear, if you are playing another one of your pranks on us right now—"

"Dad," Luke interrupted, his tone low and foreboding. He shook his head at Dad.

My parents were both extremely concerned at this point. Instinctively, my hand sought out Cruz's. I squeezed tight.

"At the end of my freshman year in college, I was raped."

My mom gasped. My dad shot up out of his seat. He was breathing heavily. He looked to Luke and Logan and scolded them, "Did you know about this and keep it from me?"

They didn't respond.

Anger filled the space around him and the entire room. I glanced only briefly down at my mom to see her eyes filled with tears, but I couldn't process it because my dad roared, "*Answer me!*"

I jumped in my seat at the tone of his voice and lost hold on the last bit of control I had. Cruz pulled me into his arms.

"Rick, dear," my mother said.

I didn't see or hear anything she said. The next voice I heard was Cruz's.

"Mr. Townsend?" he called, his voice firm and strong.

I didn't see my father's reaction because my face was still planted in Cruz's shoulder as he moved his hand up and down my back.

Cruz continued, "With all due respect, sir, I'm asking that you try to get ahold of what you're feeling right now. I can't begin to imagine what you must feel as a father, but as someone who is falling hard for your daughter, I can tell you that I understand your anger at what happened to her. There's not a doubt in my mind that this entire family loves Lexi. I know that somewhere deep down you want to do what you've got to do to see her through this. Your reaction is not helping her right now."

Someone who is falling hard for your daughter.

Falling hard for your daughter.

"My little girl was raped," Dad hissed.

"There isn't a soul in this room that's happy about it either, but she's got more to share with you and you're not making it easy for her."

"Oh my goodness. There's more?" Mom repeated, her disbelief and shock evident.

After that, nothing but silence surrounded me for quite a while.

"Sweetheart?" Dad called after some time had passed.

Slowly, I pulled my face back from Cruz's shoulder. He brought his hand up and used the pad of his thumb to wipe away my tears.

When I turned back to face my parents, my father was seated next to my mother again and I could see the anguish on their faces. "I'm sorry," I apologized.

"Lexi, sweetie," Mom started. "You have nothing to be

sorry for and we're not even the least bit disappointed with you."

I shook my head slowly and shared, "I didn't fight."

They said nothing.

Tears began spilling down my cheeks as I cried, "I didn't fight, Dad. I didn't fight him."

My dad was up and moving. In a flash, he was at my side hauling me up in his arms, engulfing me, and comforting me.

"My sweet little girl," his tortured voice resounded in my ears. "You shouldn't have ever needed to fight. I'm so sorry, sweetheart."

I felt another hand at the small of my back before I heard my mom. "Lexi, you know this wasn't your fault, right?"

Turning toward her, I answered, "I know."

"It happened so long ago. I wish you would have told me, so I could have helped you. Have you gotten help? Are you okay?"

Nodding, I explained, "I started seeing a therapist shortly after it happened. I still see her, but not as frequently as I did in the beginning. She's really helped me a lot."

"Not to interrupt," Logan piped up. "But you should know that Luke and I just recently found out as well. Even if we had known the day it happened, I wouldn't have told you anything. It was Lexi's to share."

My eyes drifted back to my father's face. It was settling in and I knew how much he was hurting.

"I'm going to ask you to do the same thing I asked Luke and Logan to do for me."

"Anything, Lexi," Mom declared.

"Feel whatever you need to feel about it. I understand this hurts you and that you have a right to your feelings about it, but please don't hold on to it. As soon as you can, please let go of the hurt, anger, and guilt that you feel."

Dad's eyes drifted over my head toward Cruz. When they came back to me, he stated, "A real man doesn't take advantage of a woman to feel powerful. A real man is strong for a woman when she needs him to be. He will listen to you and be open with you. He'll trust you and have patience with you. And when you need it, he'll offer calm strength to protect you."

I gave him a nod of understanding.

"The person who did that to you was not a real man, Lexi."

"I know," I insisted.

His face softened. "I know you know. That's why you have that guy sitting beside you today," he noted, jerking his head toward Cruz.

Apparently, Dad wasn't finished. With his gaze focused on Cruz, he went on, "I wasn't exactly thrilled when her mom told me Lexi, her brothers, and Nikki were coming over today and that Lexi was going to be bringing her boyfriend. But with what happened today, having you call me out on my shit, I can't be angry about it anymore. You are giving my little girl that calm strength when she can't find the strength within herself. I know she's strong. She always has been. But, as her father, I want to know that she's got someone who's going to stand up and do what's best for her when she needs them to. Thank you for standing up to me and protecting her, Cruz."

"I appreciate that, Mr. Townsend. Lexi's very important to me, so I'm going to do whatever I can to see to it that she's never in any pain."

"Rick, son. Call me Rick."

Well, at least there was that. This wasn't exactly my idea of a fairy-tale meeting of the parents, but I had to admit I was relieved that my family could see how good Cruz was to me.

The seven of us spent the next two hours together. I told

my parents more of the details about what happened and I confessed that I hadn't reported the rape. Much to my surprise, there wasn't an ounce of disappointment. If anything, my dad felt tremendous guilt over the words he said to me so many years ago. He hated thinking that he'd told me to always fight and that because I didn't when the situation presented itself, I ended up keeping my rape a secret.

As the conversation shifted from the specific and horrible details of the rape, it moved to my relationship with Cruz. In any other situation, I think I would have felt nerves or anxiety, but I had reached a point in my life where I knew I was making choices that were healthy for me. I couldn't spend loads of energy worrying about how my decisions would be perceived by others. The truth was, that afternoon, my family proved to me that they had faith in me to do right by myself. And when the time came that I needed them, they'd offer me their unconditional support.

"Part of me believes that I need to tell you what you deserve," my dad started. "It's the part of me that wants to know that you know that what happened does not define any part of your life moving forward. But I don't think you need me to tell you that adult relationships are not filled with violence. I think you already know that love is something that will be beautiful and safe. What happened to you will not ruin your chances at having a healthy relationship. I want to repeat those words over and over until I know it's clear in your mind that rape does not define you. But I guess I don't have to repeat anything. It's evident to me that you've healed a lot since this happened to you. You've found a way to move forward and be successful. You've caught Cruz's attention and I believe he's a good man."

I didn't have an opportunity to respond because my father turned his attention to Cruz again. "I'm not going to try to intimidate you and push you to walk away from her. To be honest, I don't think any of it would work. You stood up to me in my own home for Lexi's sake. Her well-being was your concern and that's all I can ask of the person my daughter chooses to be with. But as her father, especially now, I need you to know that I expect you'll exercise every ounce of patience you have with her. No father wants to think of his daughter having intimate relationships, but I'm not an idiot. I just need your word that you're doing right by her knowing what she's been through."

Cruz didn't hesitate to reassure my father. He did that while simultaneously rocking my world. "From the moment I laid eyes on her nearly a year ago, I knew she was someone special. I've wanted Lexi for a long time, but unfortunately, she wasn't interested in pursuing a relationship. I didn't know the reason why at the time. When she finally got to a point where she decided she was ready to at least become friends, I still didn't know what was holding her back. Now I do. And it doesn't make me want her any less. I've got a shot at something good with your daughter. She's one of a kind in my eyes, so I'm not real keen on doing something stupid to destroy that or my chances with her. Lexi's happiness, safety, and comfort are what she needs. That comes well before what I want. I know if I give her what she needs, I'll eventually have a chance at getting what I want. And just to be clear, what I want is far more than just a physical relationship with her."

That was when it happened.

I fell.

I fell so hard for Cruz, I wasn't sure I'd ever get up.

I didn't know what to do with what I was feeling. My eyes landed on Nikki's. She was grinning at me and giving me a wink. She knew what just happened. She knew everything I was feeling and she was happy for me.

I scooted a little closer to Cruz.

His arm wrapped around my back as he tucked me into his side.

Not much later, we were walking to Cruz's truck alongside Logan, Luke, and Nikki after saying goodbye to my parents. We were parked behind everyone since we were the last to arrive. When my brothers stopped at their vehicles, they turned toward us.

Logan looked down at me and praised, "Proud of you, sidekick."

"Thanks, Logan."

When he looked to Cruz, he divulged, "I'm happy she's found you. Thank you for being someone she can trust and depend on."

Cruz gave Logan a nod before Luke added, "You know what I think of you. We're cool and always will be as long as you continue to be what she needs you to be."

"Appreciate it," Cruz responded.

"I'm happy for you, Lexi," Luke remarked, bringing his eyes to mine.

I grinned at him before he put his arm around my neck and pulled me in for a hug. Then, I was shuffled from him to Logan and, finally, Nikki. She whispered in my ear, "I'm happy for you, sis. Mostly because I know what I saw in there a little bit ago. He's good for you, babe. Most importantly, he's totally head over heels for you. Enjoy him and if you need anyone to talk to, you know you've got me."

"Thanks, Nik."

At that, Cruz and I walked to his truck, where he opened my door and let me in before rounding it and getting in on his side.

Once he was inside, he looked over at me and noted, "I'm proud of you, too."

"Thank you for being here with me today, Cruz. I'm not sure I would have gotten through it as easily without you."

Cruz didn't say anything. He simply smiled at me and put the truck in reverse. I sat there staring at him as he backed the truck out of the driveway. When he reached the end and pulled out, I called, "Cruz?"

He stopped and looked over at me. "Yeah, Lex?"

"I was wondering if you still wanted me to see where you lived?"

"Absolutely."

"Can we go there now?" I wondered, the intent clear in my voice.

He couldn't miss the suggestive tone and confirmed, "Are you sure?"

I nodded with a smile on my face.

Cruz reached over the center console, cupped my jaw, and stroked my cheek with the pad of his thumb as he searched my face. Then, he put the truck in drive and drove away.

CHAPTER 20

Lexi

WE ARRIVED AT CRUZ'S PLACE NOT LONG AFTER LEAVING MY parents' home. I wasn't sure what I expected going to his house, but it certainly hadn't been what I found. Knowing Cruz's brothers, I guess I thought his home would have matched theirs. I'd known Zane for most of my life because of his relationship with Luke and the two of them snowboarding together. His house was magnificent. Obviously, I'd been to Levi's house several times because of my meetings with Elle. Their home was stunning as well. While the style of each of their homes was completely different, there was one similarity. Both were huge.

Cruz's home was not.

It wasn't a shack, but it wasn't anything like Zane's or Levi's.

"Wow," I said absentmindedly as I took in the space. "This is not what I expected."

Cruz came up behind me and worried, "I'm not sure if that's a good thing or a bad thing."

I turned to look at him and explained, "It's not a bad thing. I guess I just assumed your house would be like your brothers' homes."

"They knew what they wanted," he responded through a

chuckle. "Zane and Levi had no issues buying homes they'd live in for the rest of their lives not knowing if the person they'd end up with would like the house. I'm not planning to stay here forever, but I think if I'm going to spend the kind of money Zane and Levi have on houses, I want to know that the woman I'm sharing it with likes it so we can make it ours together."

That was a really good answer.

Looking around at his space, I shared, "Well, this is a great place to call home in the meantime. It's super cozy."

"Thanks," he replied. "So, are we here so you can get the grand tour of my house?"

No way. Not at all. But I figured I'd tease him a bit.

"Well, yeah. What else did you think...oh, no. I'm sorry, Cruz. I didn't mean to lead you on."

His shoulders slumped and I could see the disappointment, but he so quickly recovered that I thought I made it up in my mind.

"You didn't lead me on, Lex," he began. "Come on, I'll show you around."

God, he was such a good man. I couldn't help myself. He was so good at making sure I was taken care of that he was doing precisely what he told my family he would. He was putting my needs ahead of anything he wanted. What he failed to realize was that I needed more.

I let out a laugh and he stopped in his tracks.

"What's so funny?" he asked.

"I love that you always take me at face value," I chortled. "While I'm interested to see your house, Cruz, that's not the real reason I wanted to come here."

A grin formed on his face as he stepped back toward me and snaked an arm around my waist. He pulled me into his body, buried his face in my neck, and kissed me. His lips moved up my neck to my ear. After pulling my ear lobe between his teeth and letting it go, his voice was low when he said, "You're such a smartass, Lexi. But you should know that it's one of the things I love most about you."

My breath hitched in my throat. I turned my head to the side and captured his mouth. Cruz's arm around my waist tightened as the other hand cupped the back of my head. We kissed. It was different than it had ever been.

Desperate.

Hungry.

I pulled back a bit and begged, "Show me your bedroom, Cruz. Please."

A deep growl escaped as he lifted me up, keeping one arm around my back and the other at my ass. I wrapped my legs around his waist and took his mouth again as he moved through his house. It was a matter of seconds before he lowered me to my back.

I was in Cruz's bed.

His mouth left mine and traveled down my throat. My hands were grabbing at the back of his shirt trying to slide it up so I could take it off his body. He lifted his torso just enough to pull the shirt over his head.

"You're beautiful," I breathed. "Everything about you is beautiful."

His face warmed as his hands went to the hem of my shirt. He didn't remove it, though. His eyes came to mine and they were silently questioning me.

"Take it off," I encouraged him.

Cruz took it off and lowered himself over me again. He pressed a kiss just off to the left of the center of my chest, right over my heart. He did this slow and deliberate. After taking his time kissing my heart, Cruz rolled to his back, taking me with him.

My legs fell over the sides of his hips and straddled him. Sitting up, I felt his arousal underneath me and moved my hands behind me to the clasp of my bra. After unhooking it, I slid the straps down my arms. Cruz couldn't peel his eyes from me.

I tossed my bra to the side and felt Cruz's hand cupping my breasts. His thumb swiped over my nipple, shooting a jolt of pleasure straight between my legs. As the wetness pooled there, my head dropped back and I rocked my hips over him. I gave in to the pleasure and just allowed myself to feel for a while.

Cruz moved, lifting his torso and scooting himself back against the headboard as he kept me firmly planted in his lap. His eyes held mine briefly before they dropped to my chest. Holding my breasts in his palms, he kissed between them before moving to one side and sucking my nipple into his mouth.

"Cruz," I moaned, not caring that I sounded overly eager.

My hands were at his shoulders, his neck, and his hair. I couldn't get enough. I wanted more.

No.

I needed more.

What he was doing was great, but I wanted so much more.

I moved my hands to his shoulders and pushed back. He felt it and immediately pulled his mouth from my body.

"Are you okay?" he worried.

I nodded and answered, "I'm perfect. But I want more, Cruz."

He froze, but I kept moving. I put my hand to the waistband of my jeans. Just as I was about to open the button, I changed my mind.

"No," I stated firmly, my hands now unmoving at my waist.

Cruz was no longer frozen. With his hands now on my thighs, he squeezed gently and insisted, "It's ok, Lexi. We can stop."

"I don't want to stop," I asserted.

Cruz gave me a confused look.

My hands went to his. As I lifted his hands from my thighs and moved them to the button at my jeans, I clarified, "I don't want to stop, but I don't want to do this on my own."

Something changed on his face before he confirmed, "Are you sure this is what you want?"

I shook my head.

"Then I can't do this, princess. As badly as I want to take that step with you, if you aren't sure it's what you want, we aren't going to rush it."

I brought my hands to either side of his neck and explained, "It's not what I want. It's what I need."

He tensed again.

"Earlier today, you said that making sure I got what I needed came before anything you wanted. What I need now is to know that I have the power to make decisions over what happens to my body. A few nights ago, you made me feel more turned on than I've ever been. After you left that night, I couldn't sleep thinking about how badly I wanted to feel good with you. But I gave myself something that night because I realized I wanted to be the first to give myself a good sexual experience after everything I've been through. So, I touched myself and I did it thinking of you. It was wonderful and beautiful."

The muscle in Cruz's jaw was working, but he stayed quiet.

"Now I want to share that experience with you. I need to know I can ask you to take the lead and guide me through this safely. I trust you to give me this, but I understand if the burden is too much."

He dropped his gaze briefly and took a deep sigh before he gave me his eyes again. "Lexi, there isn't much of anything I wouldn't do for you. I think you know that. But I really think you should be in control the first time we take this step."

"You don't understand, Cruz," I started. "I am in control. Because I've found a way to trust a man. A man who gave me a way to have the power. One word. I know I only need to say one word and you will stop. You'll know just hearing that word that I'm not okay and you'll do whatever you need to do to make sure that I feel safe. The only way I want to get this power back is by giving it up to someone I trust and knowing I can make it stop if I need it to. Beyond an emotional connection and physical attraction, I want a healthy, sexual relationship in my life. And I want that with you. Part of that means me knowing I'm sharing my body with you and trusting you to take care of it. It also means you trusting me to decide what I'm ready for. I'll never know if I don't try and I believe you'll see me through regardless of what happens."

Remaining silent, he held my eyes.

"You told my parents I was someone you were falling hard for," I went on. "I wouldn't take this step lightly. You should know, I've already fallen for you. And I like the way it feels in my heart and soul. Now I want to feel that love sharing my body with you."

That's when he moved.

Slowly, he rolled us in the bed until he was hovering over me. His fingers started at the side of my throat and worked their way down my body, caressing every inch of my skin. Every so often, he'd lower his head and press gentle kisses to my body. When his hands reached the waistband of my jeans, he didn't hesitate this time. He opened the button and, bit by bit, pulled the zipper down. He pulled my jeans down my legs and removed them after removing my shoes. Then, he stared down at my nearly naked body. There was no denying the heat in his eyes. It made me feel strong, sexy and desired.

"You're gorgeous, Lexi. So unbelievably beautiful," he rasped as he remained frozen on the spot.

I moved things along and brought my hands to the fabric resting at my hips. Sliding my fingers underneath, I began gliding my panties down my thighs. I got about halfway down before Cruz took over and removed them the rest of the way.

As his hand traced delicately over the skin on one of my thighs, I brushed one of my hands on the leg of his jeans.

"Will you take these off?" my voice was needy.

Cruz opened the fly of his pants before he stood and let them fall to the ground. He stood there in his boxer briefs, the evidence of his arousal straining against the black material. I reached my hand out to the side. Cruz took a step toward me. I put my hand on his solid thigh, slid my hand up, and stopped just before I got to his erection.

Looking up at him through hooded eyes, I shared, "I'd like to touch you."

"Please do," he urged.

So I did.

The moment my hand moved over the length of him, he groaned. It was low and deep and I loved hearing it. I continued for a bit, but eventually sat up in the bed and moved both hands to the waistband of his boxer briefs.

"Can I take them off?" I asked.

"Absolutely."

I pulled them down his legs, freeing him, and learned this part of him was just as beautiful as the rest.

"Lex?" he called.

"Yeah?"

"I'd love to have a taste of you. Do you think you'd be alright with me putting my mouth between your legs?"

My insides tingled, the spot he wanted to put his mouth on quivering.

"Yes."

He put a knee to the bed and bent at the waist to bring his head to mine. Cruz kissed my mouth, gently lowering my head to the pillow. His lips moved along my jaw, down my throat, across my breasts, and down my abdomen to my hip bones. He trailed kisses along the tops of my thighs and dipped toward the center, where my legs were pressed tight together.

His face was so close; I could barely contain my excitement.

He tenderly parted my thighs. As my knees fell to the sides and Cruz settled himself between them, his fingers trailed up my inner thighs. He never touched me there, though.

One second I was bursting with anticipation and the next I felt his mouth on me.

"Oh, God. Cruz," I cried.

His tongue swiped through my wetness causing my hands to ball into fists. Cruz's lips and tongue worked me relentlessly, each of my moans matched by growls and groans from him.

It didn't take long for Cruz to bring me to the brink of an orgasm. My breaths came quick and shallow.

He knew I was there.

His hands left my outer thighs, slid up to my hips, and finally reached out for my hands. The moment our fingers were interlaced, I squeezed tight and came apart. The feeling of pure satisfaction shooting through every square inch of my body, Cruz kept at me drawing it out.

And he held my hands throughout, refusing to let go of me.

When I came down, Cruz turned his head to the side and kissed my thigh. One hand remained clamped to mine, but the other disconnected and came to my hip. His fingertips trailed lightly from my hip down to the spot his mouth had just been. As his fingers circled my already sensitive clit, he looked up at me.

"Are you okay?"

I nodded, loving that he was checking on me.

"Do you want to keep going?" he asked, his fingers applying a bit more pressure.

Seeing the look in his eyes and feeling everything he was doing with his hand had only increased my desire to be with him.

"Yes, Cruz. I want more."

Keeping his eyes on mine, his fingers dropped lower. Slowly, he slid one finger inside. It was excruciatingly slow, but a glorious feeling. As much as I wanted to keep my focus on him, I couldn't. The pleasure was too intense and my head fell back to the pillow.

"Oh," I moaned loudly.

I felt him press a kiss to my thigh again before he ordered, "Look at me, princess."

It took a bit of effort, but I lifted my head and looked down at him again. That's when he pulled his finger back and pushed forward again. He was still moving slow.

"Does it feel good?" he wondered.

"Amazing," I breathed. There was no way I could form a coherent sentence with all that he was making me feel.

His smile grew and he picked up his pace. After working me with one finger for a few more strokes, he added a second. That was really nice. So nice, in fact, I was on the verge of another orgasm. He kept at me a bit before I called, "Cruz?"

"Yeah, Lex?"

"Will you stop?"

His eyes rounded in shock, but he immediately stopped and pulled his fingers from my body. I'm not sure how he did it so quickly, but his hand that had been connected to mine was no longer there. Instead, he'd moved up my body, settled himself next to me, and curled me into his arms.

He whispered through my hair into my ear, "I'm sorry, Lexi. Are you okay?"

Cruz had moved so quickly because his only concern was my well-being. Unfortunately, since he had done it so fast, he never gave me the opportunity to tell him why I wanted him to stop.

I pulled my head back from his body and looked up at him.

"Yes," I started. "I didn't want you to stop because something was wrong."

My hand that was resting on his side began moving down his body. As it moved closer and closer to his cock, I explained, "I wanted you to stop because I was going to come."

He looked confused.

"Isn't that the point?" he questioned me.

I nodded, but went on to clarify, "I want to come again, Cruz, but I don't want to do it with your fingers inside me."

My hand wrapped around his hardened length and stroked before I continued, "I want to do it with this part of you inside me."

"Are you sure?" he worried.

I continued to pump my fist around him as I nodded and answered, "Not a single doubt in my mind that it's precisely what I want."

He groaned.

"If that changes, you have to tell me."

"I know," I insisted.

Cruz dropped to his back and reached out to his bedside table. After rolling on the condom and turning back toward me, he informed me, "I'm nervous about this, Lexi."

I understood his anxiety, but I hated that he was feeling this way. Framing his face in my hands, I admitted, "I'd be lying if I said I didn't have any nerves. But I think it's a good thing we've both got them. My nerves aren't about uncertainty taking this step with you, though. And the fact that you feel some anxiety tells me that I've made the right choice with you. I know you want to make sure this is good for me. I don't mean physically, either. I'm sure you have no doubts that you'll make this good for my body, but you're worried that my mind might not be prepared to handle it. I can't make any promises, but knowing you care this much tells me it's going to be okay no matter what happens."

"I care about you, but it's not that."

My brows pulled together in confusion. "What is it?"

Bringing his hand up to the side of my face, he ran the backs of two of his fingers along my cheekbone. It was tender and sweet. "I remember your panic attack and the pure terror I felt seeing you like that. I don't want to cause you that kind of pain again. It hurt to see you that way. The reason I'm so worried isn't because I care about you. It's because I love you, Lexi."

My lips parted and my breath caught in my throat at his admission.

I love you, Lexi.

I heard his words over and over in my head at least a dozen times in a matter of seconds.

"Say it again," I begged him.

"I love you," he repeated.

"Then show me," I pleaded with him.

Cruz's mouth came down and caught mine. As our lips collided and our tongues tasted, my hands moved from his face to his hair and his neck. He shifted his body and settled in the space between my parted thighs.

He was positioned at my entrance with my legs wrapped around his waist. I felt Cruz's hands on either side of my head. He didn't move.

"Are you sure?"

"I want that part of me back. Please…make love to me," I whispered.

"You need to talk to me, Lexi," he instructed. "Don't continue if it's not right for you, okay?"

I nodded and tipped my hips slightly. Cruz pushed forward, filling me. Once inside, he didn't pull back. He kept his eyes on me, his fingertips pressing in a bit harder.

"You good?" he asked, his voice thick with emotion.

"Yes," I answered, my breath ragged.

Keeping his eyes focused on mine, he pulled back slowly and pushed forward again. Despite being overcome with sensations as Cruz moved himself in and out of me, I never dropped my gaze from him.

It was incredible.

Beautiful.

It was everything it should have been.

Tender.

Sweet.

Passionate.

Lovely.

We moved slowly together for a long time, but that soon gave way to an increased pace. My arms and legs were wrapped tight around him. I loved the feel of our bodies against one another. We fit perfectly together.

"Cruz," I whimpered as I felt the onset of my orgasm arrive.

It was beginning to take over.

"Take back what's yours, warrior."

It tore through me, shattering many demons inside. The

pleasure was ongoing and with each wave that rolled through, I felt it coming back. Me. I wasn't in pain. I was no longer empty. I was full and whole again. And Cruz helped me get that back.

Just as I came down from the onslaught of emotions and physical euphoria, Cruz thrust his hips three more times and buried himself deep inside me, groaning through his orgasm. I watched him and I loved every single second of it. He collapsed on top of me, burying his face in my neck being careful not to give me all of his weight.

We were covered in a sheen of sweat, our breathing labored. In spite of that, Cruz still saw to it that I was alright.

He turned his head to the side and kissed my cheek. "How do you feel?" he asked softly.

My emotions got the best of me and I croaked, "Beautiful."

"Lexi…" he trailed off.

We didn't say anything for a bit until Cruz said, "Unhook your legs, princess. I've got to get this condom off."

I did as he asked and watched as he left the bed and moved to the bathroom. Once he had disappeared behind the door, I pulled back the blankets and climbed underneath them. When Cruz returned and climbed in the bed next to me, he wrapped his arm around my waist and pulled me close.

"Thank you."

My voice was just barely a whisper.

"You can't possibly think you need to thank me for that, Lex. What you just gave me…I should be the one thanking you."

I pressed a soft kiss to his lips and shared, "I think I got a big piece of myself back just now. It feels really good."

"I'm honored that I got to play a part in that. It means a lot to me that you trusted me with your body. Are you sure you're feeling okay?"

I smiled at him and insisted, "Yes, Cruz. This is one thing I wouldn't joke about. I feel like a million bricks have been lifted off my shoulders. I don't have to be fearful of intimacy anymore. At least, not with you. And considering I love you, I'm guessing that's a really good thing."

I felt his body grow solid next to mine before he asked, "You love me?"

I nodded and responded, "I don't think I could have done this if I didn't."

"My warrior princess," he declared, snuggling further into me.

"Thank you for being there for me every step of the way through this, captain."

"Captain?"

I let out a little laugh before I clarified, "In my professional life, I'm always the one in charge of making sure things run smoothly. My clients are the talent and have the final say, but I'm the one guiding their ships. When it comes to my personal life, I've been steering my own vessel, especially through my recovery. But now I have someone I trust to maneuver through the water with me. It's nice to know I don't always have to hold that title and that I can depend on someone to hold my hand through the rough waters."

"I love you, Lexi."

His voice was deep and husky, emotion having clearly taken over.

"I love you, too."

Cruz and I stayed cuddled up in his bed for a while just holding onto each other. Holding led to touching. Touching led to kissing. And kissing led to another round of lovemaking. This round, though, was not nearly as slow as the first, but it was equally as satisfying.

After Cruz and I made and ate dinner at his place, he took

me home. Only this time, he didn't drop me off. Before we left his place, I asked him to spend the night with me at mine. That night, when I fell asleep I experienced the best night I'd had in my life and it had nothing to do with sex. It had everything to do with the man who was curled up behind me, tucking me close to his body and making me feel safer that I had in years. And he held me while, for the first time in just as many years, I fell asleep without having to wear pants.

CHAPTER 21

Lexi

Two and a half weeks had passed since I'd overcome what I had expected would be one of the biggest hurdles in my recovery.

Sex.

No, that wasn't right.

Making love.

Maybe I shouldn't have been surprised that it not only went well, but was also more than I could have ever hoped for. I mean, I'd had sex before the rape. Only with one person. It wasn't horrible; or at least, I didn't think it was horrible. We were young and neither of us had any prior experience. I think we were both more curious than anything else. It certainly wasn't true love that brought us to that point. More than anything, we were in a high school relationship and it seemed like that was what you were supposed to do. After that relationship ended, I put my focus into my schoolwork.

So, before I was with Cruz, I'd had two different experiences with sex. One was simply that, just sex. Not bad, but not over-the-top good, either. The other experience…well, that wasn't anything worth reliving. It was just all bad.

But with Cruz it was everything good. Better than good, actually. I knew we had only been together a short time and that sometimes messed with my head. I often wondered if I was clinging to Cruz because he was the first man I felt safe with following the rape. The moment we were at his house and in his bed, I knew that wasn't the case. The words we spoke to each other before, during, and after squashed any thoughts I had that it was anything but love between us. I was certain that this was the reason the experience had been filled with beautiful moments.

And over the last two and a half weeks, things between us had gotten even better. We spent several nights together, most of them at my place. I had to admit, though, that I enjoyed the nights at Cruz's home. It was bigger than my place and much cozier, but it didn't have all the things I needed there when I had to get ready for work.

Each day, I found myself looking forward to whatever the day would bring in my interactions with Cruz. Sometimes, it was the late-night phone calls when I was cuddled in my bed and he was working. Other times, it was heading home and making dinner for two, knowing that I'd be spending time with him. Tonight would be one of those nights and I found myself eager to spend the whole night with him.

Lovemaking had been an extraordinary experience over the last few weeks. It was always filled with such passion and desire, but what I found I loved the most was the excitement of trying new things with him…things I'd never had with anyone else. He was so good to me and made sure I enjoyed it every single time. I always did, but sometimes I felt like he was holding himself back for my sake. I didn't want to turn him off, but I knew I needed to talk to him soon about it. Until I worked up the courage to do that, I'd continue to enjoy what we had between us. And I planned to do that fully later tonight, but I still had to finish the remaining half of my day at work first.

The biggest thing on my work agenda for the day was a meeting with Elle. It was big only in the sense that it was the first time she and I were getting together since before Cruz and I had slept together. I knew that only a small portion of our meeting would be spent with the two of us discussing her upcoming tour and that most of our time would involve a discussion about my relationship with Cruz.

The only person other than Cruz who knew that we'd taken that step was Nikki. I think she knew things had changed for me the day we went to my parents' house. The next day she gave me a call on her lunch break to get the scoop.

"So, how was it?" she asked after I told her that Cruz and I had finally taken that step.

"Beautiful," I sighed. "Gosh, Nikki, he was so incredibly attentive and gentle. He was so concerned about my well-being. I never imagined it would be so wonderful."

"I'm so happy for you, sis," she started. "I knew Cruz would give you everything you deserved. And I'm thrilled that you now know just how breathtakingly perfect it is supposed to be when you willingly share your body with someone who deserves you and loves you back."

"Loves me back?" I questioned her. "How do you know?"

Of course Cruz and I had admitted our feelings to each other that night, but I didn't understand how she knew about it.

She laughed before she answered, "It was written all over your faces. And if I hadn't thought you were in love the moment he stood up to your dad when you told your parents about the rape, I would have known the instant he told them how much you meant to him just before we left."

It felt good to hear her say that. Not that I had any doubts about my feelings for Cruz or his for me, but knowing that it was apparent to outsiders how we felt about each other was nice.

I'd barely gotten through my recollection of my conversation with Nikki when there was a knock on my office door just before it opened. It was lunchtime and Elle came in early carrying food.

"Hey, El. You're early," I pointed out.

"I know, love, but we haven't really had much time to connect lately. I took a chance that you'd be free and figured we could catch up over lunch. We can deal with work stuff afterward."

"Works for me," I agreed. "What's for lunch?"

Elle beamed at me and brought the food over. Once we had gotten the food sorted, she hit me with some unexpected news.

"Levi proposed," she blurted.

My eyes nearly popped out of my head. "What?!" I exclaimed. "When did this happen?"

"This past weekend," she shared.

"I assume you accepted."

She held her left hand out to me. A beautiful ring sat on her finger, shining. "Oh, Elle. It's absolutely gorgeous."

I got up and moved toward her. Pulling her into a hug, I wished, "Congratulations. I'm so happy for you."

"Thanks, Lexi. I'm not sure I could be any happier than I am right now. I love him so much."

"You deserve it. After everything you went through," I trailed off.

She grew somber for a moment before she turned it around on me. "Yeah, but you know what? You're right. I do deserve it. It's the women like us that have gone through total crap that ought to have some good flow into our lives. We both come from incredible families, but somehow we've managed to find ourselves in situations with people who did us so wrong. Our happiness can now be a slap in the face to those who tried to bring us down."

Her words meant everything.

"I like the way you think, girl," I approved of her sentiments as I sat back down. "In fact, I've got my own news."

Elle leaned forward, curiously. "Oh?"

Nodding and trying to contain my excitement, I shared, "My relationship with Cruz has gotten a bit more serious."

"How serious?"

I bit my lip, thinking about the seriousness I was referring to and answered, "Very serious."

Elle couldn't contain her shock. "Oh, Lexi. That's incredible news! I imagine Cruz made sure you were handled with care."

"He was perfect, El. Absolutely perfect."

The two of us sat there in silence for a bit, soaking up the bliss of each of our current situations. I hadn't expected I'd ever feel normal enough again to even have friends, let alone be in a loving, committed relationship that I could actually talk to my girlfriends about. There was no denying how good that felt.

Elle and I finished eating lunch. After, we got to work on her summer mini-tour schedule. We spent the remainder of my day at work mapping out the dates for the tour so that she'd be able to not only drive from one location to the next, but also have time to spend at each one of those destinations.

When Elle left, I was ready to pack up and head home. I couldn't wait to see Cruz and spend the night with him. We hadn't been able to spend the night together the previous two nights, so I was really beginning to miss him.

Just before I left, my cell phone rang. Pulling it out of my purse, I looked at the display and saw my mom was calling. Ever since I'd shared the truth of my rape with my parents, my mother had been calling me more frequently. I knew it was part of the guilt she felt over what happened, so I tried my best to always take her calls. And while she hadn't brought up the rape at any point since she learned about it, I wanted to make sure she could see that I was doing well. I thought it might help ease the blame I assumed she placed on herself.

"Hi, Mom," I answered cheerfully.

"Hi, Lexi. How was your day today?"

"Great," I started. "Really productive. I not only had a meeting with Elle this afternoon, but she came over a little earlier and we got to catch up over lunch."

Telling her that wasn't necessarily something I would have done in the past, but I thought reassurances that I had friends around me would make her feel better.

"That's good to hear, sweetie," she began. I heard the nervousness in her tone and knew she had more to say.

"Is everything alright?" I asked.

She sighed, "I'm just so proud of you and everything you've accomplished. I still feel so much guilt over not being there for you, but hearing about your days and knowing you've made something of yourself despite what happened helps me. I've been doing a lot of reading and I learned that so many women end up dropping out of school because their assault takes so much away from them. You're such a strong, young woman."

As much as I appreciated the fact she wanted to learn as much as she could about what happened to me, it hurt my heart to know she was spending her days researching it. I didn't want that for her, so I made a split-second decision.

"It's your fault, you know," I informed her.

"What?" she asked, shock and confusion taking over.

"Actually, you and dad are both to blame."

"Lexi, what on earth are you saying?"

I laughed and clarified, "You and Dad are the reason I managed to overcome this. The two of you made me the person I am today, Mom. I blamed myself for a long time for not fighting back and for not doing something differently. I don't do that anymore. It doesn't mean I don't feel regret from time to time, but I've come to terms with it. And there's not a doubt in my mind that my strength comes from my parents. You taught me everything I know."

My mother was quiet for so long I began wondering if we got disconnected.

"Mom?" I called.

"You really are alright," she declared. "That's the first time in years you've joked with me about anything. I should have known when it stopped that something was wrong, but I just never imagined something so horrific had happened to you. It feels good to hear you teasing me and being playful again. I've missed that terribly."

"Can I ask you for a favor?"

"Absolutely, sweetie. Anything."

"I can appreciate your curiosity and the fact that you don't want to come to me with questions about what happened. If I wasn't ready to field the questions I'm certain you have, I wouldn't have told you about the rape. I think I'd like for the two of us to get together soon so that we can talk and you can ask me anything about it. I'm free this weekend if that works for you."

"But when I was reading, I saw several lists of all the different questions I shouldn't ask you," she debated. "I don't want to ask questions that bring up painful memories or set you back in any way."

"I know you would never do that," I assured her. "But I'm guessing you probably already know from reading that everyone's road to recovery is different. There are a multitude of reasons for that, but I know where I am in my own healing. So, if there's something you ask that I'm not comfortable with, I'll tell you that. One of the things I've learned over the last couple of years is that I have the power to say no to anything that doesn't feel right. That includes answering questions about my rape. If you ask something I'm not prepared to answer, I trust that you'll respect that."

"Oh, Lexi. Of course I will. And I'd love to get together with you this weekend. Your father will be outside doing yardwork all weekend anyway. How does lunch on Sunday sound?"

I laughed, "That's perfect. I've got to go now, though. Cruz is coming over for dinner tonight, so I need to lock up the office and get home."

At that, we disconnected and I locked up before I made my way home.

An hour and a half later, Cruz and I had just finished dinner and were cuddled up on the couch.

"I've missed you these last couple of days, captain," I announced, my head resting on his shoulder.

"Missed you, too," he returned. "I'm sorry I haven't had much time lately. This case is consuming so much of my life right now."

"I know," I declared. "I'm not trying to make you feel bad and I don't want you to apologize for working, especially on something so important. I just wanted you to know how much I like being around you."

Cruz's arm that was wrapped around me, curling me into his body, squeezed a little tighter. When I looked up at him, he pressed a kiss to my forehead.

I went on, "Nothing new on the case?"

"Nothing that makes me happy or helps us. Two more women are missing. Unfortunately, they weren't women that were seen at a place where we've got a contact helping us. It's beyond frustrating at this point."

"Whatever happened with the guy that you said went

back to his house after you saved that other girl from being taken? Still nothing?" I wondered.

He shook his head. "I think he's out of it now. Once whoever is running this found out that one of those guys had been taken in, the ringleader cut the other one loose to be sure."

With my arm wrapped around his waist, I returned the squeeze he gave me moments ago and lamented, "I'm sorry. I know how hard you're working to try and bring this case to a close and find those women. I'm proud of you. And I appreciate your willingness to share what you can with me."

He let out a laugh and noted, "I shouldn't be sharing anything with you regarding any of my cases. And the truth is that moving forward I probably won't. But this is something I let slip in the beginning because I was worried about your safety. Since you know about it and I now know everything you've been through, it's important for me to make sure you know the basics of what's happening. I'm not giving you names or places, but I want you being a little extra cautious until this is solved."

"I will be."

"But that's enough of that for now. You're safe tonight and I've missed you tremendously. I'd rather not spend our time with me having to live in the same frustration I feel while I'm working these days. We have the next two nights in a row to spend time together and I'd like to enjoy that. Don't forget that tomorrow night we're at my place."

"I'd never forget," I insisted. "But remember I'll be a little later than usual. Tomorrow is group therapy at WAAR."

That was the other thing that had become a regular part of my routine over the last few weeks. Aside from becoming an official volunteer at the rape crisis center, I regularly went to group therapy sessions. I went to my second session when I accompanied Riley to her first. Each session, we sat next to each other offering silent support. While I was finding those sessions to be very therapeutic for myself, I couldn't say they were having the same effect on Riley. I didn't imagine they were hurting her and truly believed they offered her some comfort, but I knew how raw she felt given how recently she'd been violated. There had been several occasions where she got up in the middle of the session and walked out. The first few times that happened, I walked out behind her to make sure she was doing alright. Some of those times were rough, but she was getting better now. If she got up in the middle of a session now, she would tap me on the shoulder or leg and let me know she needed some air and would return. I always asked if she wanted me to go with her because I didn't want to smother her. I completely understood her need to be alone sometimes. Either way, I knew the sessions were a place of refuge for her.

"I'd never forget," Cruz repeated my words.

I leaned forward and kissed Cruz. He slanted his head and deepened the kiss. I took that opportunity to make my move. Parting my lips and allowing his tongue to slip inside my mouth, I moved my hands to the hem of his shirt. I needed to have perfect timing with this, so I was careful not to touch him as I lifted the shirt. Thinking I was progressing things between us, Cruz took over and removed the shirt from his torso. Bringing a hand up to the side of my face, he brought his mouth back down to mine and started kissing me again. That's when I went in for the kill.

I pressed my ice-cold hands to his sides and immediately felt the muscles underneath my fingers tense.

"Christ, Lexi," he bit out, pulling his mouth back from mine. "Why the hell are your hands so cold?"

"My hands are always cold," I explained, as I began moving them across his heated skin. "And you are always so warm.

I've noticed that about you over the last few weeks. You are like a furnace."

As my hands moved from his sides, to his back, and around to his abdomen, his hand balled tightly into a fist and his head dropped back. The muscles contracted again under my fingers and his jaw was clenching.

"This is absolute torture, Lex."

My palms were a bit warmer from having touched his skin, so I flipped my hands over and began drifting them toward the waistband of his jeans. Just as I was about to slip my fingers in and under the elastic band of his boxer briefs, he captured my wrists.

"Not a chance," he warned. "That would kill me."

I leaned into him and begged, "Please? Your upper body is warm, but I get the feeling it's going to be much warmer down there. And you know how cold my hands are. How could you leave me freezing?"

He laughed at my lousy attempt to convince him and promised, "I'd never let you freeze. How about we find another way to warm you up?"

My shoulders sagged. "Alright, fine. But fair warning, my feet get cold from time to time as well."

"I'll consider myself warned," he confirmed.

Then, he slipped one arm behind my back and the other underneath my legs. He stood and carried me to my bedroom and through to the bathroom, where he proceeded to warm me up in the shower.

It was safe to say I didn't feel cold the rest of the night.

CHAPTER 22

Lexi

"I LOVE YOU."

My voice was soft as I delivered my sentiments with my cheek pressed to Cruz's chest, my body draped over his. Cruz woke me up this morning, made sweet love to me, and we were now basking in postorgasmic bliss.

I found that postorgasmic bliss typically resulted in me becoming chatty. Mostly, I became sappy and shared all of my feelings for Cruz with Cruz. He doesn't seem to be the least bit bothered by my need to share, so I continue to do it. I've often thought several times over the last few weeks why I did this. All I could come up with was that for so long I hadn't shared my feelings about anything with anyone other than my therapist and now that I had someone I wanted to share those feelings with, I couldn't seem to control myself.

"I love you, too," he said as he gently traced his fingers up and down my spine.

"I never thought I'd have this, captain. I dreamed of it when I was little, but that went out the window years ago. It never crossed my mind that it would become a reality because I didn't think I wanted it anymore."

Continuing to move his hands over the clammy skin on my back, he asked, "When did that change for you?"

"At Monroe's studio. The first time I saw you. I hadn't felt an attraction like that to anyone ever. I didn't even think it was possible for me to have feelings like that again. But as quickly as I felt them, I shut them down because the last time I had feelings for someone...well, you know how that ended. Then, months went by until I saw you at Luke's that day you came to give them an update on Nikki's dad. When you walked me to my car and asked me out I knew how badly I wanted things to change for me."

One of Cruz's hands was now in my hair, massaging my scalp.

"And, finally, when I saw you at Colvert's for the first time. That day was the day that I finally took steps to free myself. I knew I had to stop carrying the burden of my rape on my own. That's what it was going to take for me to heal, for me to get back to me. It's what I needed to do to find my way to you."

"My warrior, you're so brave. So beautiful, so smart, and so incredibly strong."

The two of us stayed like that a long time, Cruz tracing his fingertips over my skin while I listened to his heart beat under me. When I knew we'd taken too much time because we both had to get to work, I lifted my head and declared, "I'd really love to stay just like this, but we've got to get out of this bed if we're going to accomplish anything today."

"I don't mind changing our plans," he threw out. "I'll spend the day with you doing whatever you want to do, even if it's just staying here in bed holding you."

He was perfect. Completely perfect for me in every single way.

"We should plan a day like that soon, but not today. Besides, I'm looking forward to staying at your place tonight, which means I really have to get up now because I need to pack a few things I'll need for tomorrow morning."

Cruz's face softened and he gave me a gentle squeeze. "Alright. Can I please have a kiss before you get up?"

Since he asked so nicely I did as he asked. After kissing him, I got up and got ready for work.

An hour and a half later, I was pulling into the parking lot at my office. Before I got there, Cruz and I made our stop at Colvert's together for coffee and breakfast before we went our separate ways for the day. I loved how comfortable that small little routine became. It wasn't something we even discussed anymore; we always knew that mornings before work when we had spent the previous night together resulted in the two of us having breakfast at Colvert's. We had officially dubbed it our place.

As soon as I was inside, I got to work. I was so consumed in what I was doing that it wasn't until my phone rang that I realized it was already past lunchtime.

"Hello," I answered, smiling into the phone.

"Hey, sidekick. You busy?"

"Yes, but I've been working like a crazy person since I got in quite a few hours ago. I completely missed lunch. What's going on?"

"Nothing. I'm in the area; I figured I'd stop in and visit. I'll grab you something to eat real quick and be right there."

"Thanks, Logan. See you in a bit."

It wasn't much later when Logan came strolling through the front door of my office. He handed me a white paper bag. I looked up at him for an indication of what he got for me.

"California chicken sandwich," he divulged.

"Grilled or fried?" I asked, my voice hopeful.

"I had them substitute for fried and told them to hold the guacamole."

I grinned huge at him. "You are the best," I announced.

He chuckled and noted, "I've known you since the day

you were born, Lex. I'd like to think I know a thing or two about you by now."

He had a point.

I pulled out the sandwich and started eating while he sat in the chair across from my desk.

"No clients or appointments today?" he wondered.

I shook my head. "Nope. Just working on a few things."

He gave me a nod, but said nothing else. I got about halfway through my sandwich before I couldn't stand it anymore.

"So, what's really going on?" I asked with my mouth full of food.

He shook his head. "Nothing. I just wanted to stop in and see you."

This was unlike him and I didn't like the way it felt. I put my sandwich down, finished chewing, and swallowed hard.

"Logan?" I called gently.

His eyes came to mine and they were defeated. After holding my eyes for a beat, he let out, "I can't get over it, Lex. I know you want me to let go of it, but I can't. You're my baby sister and I didn't protect you."

I'd never heard such pain and emotion in his voice ever before.

"I'm sorry," I apologized. "This is why I never wanted to tell any of you. I knew you'd be overcome with guilt, even though there was nothing you could have done to protect me from it."

Logan leaned forward on his elbows and looked down at the ground. He took a few deep breaths. I hated seeing what this was doing to him.

"I'll find a way to get over it in time, but I guess I just have this need to reach out more often to check in on you."

"If it helps you to call or text me every day just to check in, I'm completely fine with that," I started. "But you've got to forgive yourself. There's nothing you could have done to prevent what happened. It wasn't your fault."

"I feel responsible," he croaked.

I needed to try something else. I couldn't stand to see him so torn up about this. "Do you blame me?"

"What?" he asked, shocked I had asked such a ridiculous question.

I repeated myself.

"Do you blame me for getting myself raped?"

"You don't *get yourself* raped, Lex. Of course I don't blame you. Why would you ever say that?"

I gave him a small smile and explained, "Because that's precisely what you're doing to yourself right now. Logan, you aren't responsible for me being raped any more than I am. There is one person at fault in this whole situation and, I'll give you a hint, that person is not sitting in this room."

"I don't want to burden you with this, Lexi," he began. "You've already been through enough. I'm just having a hard time not accepting responsibility for what happened to you and it consumes my mind every fucking minute of my day. I forgot to tighten lug nuts on one of my client's cars yesterday. Thankfully, I backed the car out of the garage and realized something wasn't right before anything bad could happen. But I was distracted."

"Come with me to a therapy session," I urged him. "Dr. Lane told me she'd be more than happy to help any of my family members who needed it. Come to one session and talk to her. She can help."

"You really think so?"

I nodded. "I have no doubts about it."

He let out a breath. In fact, it was more like a sigh of relief.

I stood and rounded my desk. When I made my way over to him, he stood and engulfed me in his arms. I held on tight to him and said, "It hurts my heart that you're carrying this around with you. I don't blame you and I wish you wouldn't blame yourself. Please know that I have no doubts that if you could have done something about it, you would have. I know if I'm ever in a situation where I need you to protect me, I know you'll do it."

"In a heartbeat, sidekick."

I closed my eyes and held on to Logan while he took the time he needed to collect himself. Since I had worked myself so hard earlier in the day, I took the remainder of the afternoon off and caught up with Logan. We stayed at my office because it was close to WAAR, but I didn't do any more work. I spent the time I had left before I needed to go to therapy bringing Logan up to speed on all of the things that were going on in my life. It was nice to have that time with him.

When I finally had to leave for my meeting, Logan saw me safely to my car. I couldn't say for sure, but I was pretty certain he felt better when he left than when he had arrived. I would call Dr. Lane tomorrow to set up a time for Logan and me to meet with her next week.

I arrived at WAAR with a few minutes to spare before the group session started, so I tapped out a quick text to Cruz.

Hey, captain. Hope your day is going well. Just got to WAAR, but I'm looking forward to seeing you later.

Cruz responded a minute later.

Same here, warrior. Call me when you are finished. I'll head home then.

Me: *Will do. Love you.*

Cruz: *Love you, too.*

I silenced my phone and slid it back in my bag before walking into the meeting. Two minutes after I'd gotten there, Riley walked in. Her eyes searched the room, looking for me. Once she found me, she walked over and sat in the empty seat next to me.

"Hey, Riley. How's it going?"

"I'm doing alright," she started. "I've got good days and bad days, but my nights are the worst."

I knew what she was experiencing all too well. "It'll get better," I promised. "You've just got to give yourself time."

"I hope you're right," she worried.

Offering a friendly smile, I pointed out, "You're doing everything you can to heal yourself in the way that feels right to you. You keep coming back here every week. Look around, girl. I've noticed over the last couple of sessions that some girls don't come back to them. I get it. This is hard. It's been four years for me and I still find it hard sometimes, so I understand that hearing other survivor stories might be difficult so soon after for some women. You have your moments, but you step out, take a breather, and come back. You keep showing up for yourself. It will get better."

"Thanks, Lexi. It means a lot coming from you. But it makes me wonder."

My brows furrowed. "What?"

"Well, it's been a long time for you and you feel like you still benefit from coming to these sessions. I can't say for sure, but I would think this might be a long-term thing for me as well. I think about some of these other girls when I leave here and I don't understand why they wouldn't come back. Girls like Violet. I thought she was doing extremely well. Her assault happened before mine and she even shared her story. But since that share, she hasn't come back. I thought she was doing well in her recovery, but not enough that I thought she wouldn't come back. It makes me worry that she's doing this alone."

Violet had been making great progress and I was proud that she was ready to share so quickly, but equally as surprised when she didn't show up to the last session. It also appeared she wasn't showing up to today's either.

I shook my head trying to dispel any fears she had. "It's different for everyone, Riley. While it saddens me to think Violet might be doing this alone, I can't say I don't understand her choice. I did it on my own for a long time. Of course, now I wish I hadn't. Regardless, there is no multi-step program that we can all follow to heal. It just isn't that easy."

Before Riley could respond, our attention was directed to the meeting. As I sat there listening to stories being shared and women either crying with or applauding other women, I knew what my next step was going to be.

I was going to share.

Not today, but at the next meeting.

Somewhere in the middle of the story being told by, Jocelyn, the last woman who was sharing, Riley had tapped me on the shoulder to let me know she needed to step out. I couldn't blame her. Jocelyn's story was heartbreaking. Like me, Jocelyn was a victim of acquaintance rape. That alone was a difficult pill to swallow, but what made it truly devastating for her was the fact that it was her boyfriend that didn't protect her. She'd been at a house party drinking, but her boyfriend was there. She never thought she couldn't trust him. She only remembered having two drinks before feeling extremely dizzy and drunk. Seeking out her boyfriend, she told him something wasn't right. He took her to one of the second-floor bedrooms so she could lie down. Not long after, she was fading in and out. She remembered hearing voices, then seeing one of her boyfriend's friends on top of her. She knew it was happening, but she had no control over her body. She remembered seeing her boyfriend in the room doing nothing while this other guy raped her.

I couldn't even imagine the pain she felt knowing that her own boyfriend could do something so cruel to her. The meeting ended and I found myself sitting there reeling from

Jocelyn's story. Many of us gave our trust so easily to people who did nothing to earn it; I had done that. And then I refused to trust anyone for years. I knew it wasn't healthy to believe that everyone was bad and I managed to find a way to trust people again, but they had to work for it. I truly hoped Jocelyn, who was feeling so beaten down and broken, would continue to come to meetings and get help because I wanted her to be able to trust people again.

Looking around the room, I realized Riley hadn't yet returned. She left her bag by her chair, so I picked it up and walked out to check on her. She wasn't in the common space out front and some women had walked outside, so I followed behind them to see if she had stepped out. I didn't think she would have come out alone and when I didn't see her I was relieved. I also noticed her car was still parked in the lot. Walking back inside, I went to the bathroom. She wasn't there either.

I started panicking. This just didn't feel right. Riley always came back to the meeting and, other than the first time she walked out of one when I followed her out, she was never gone more than ten minutes. It had now been easily twenty minutes since she walked out.

Hoping I missed her walking back into the group therapy session room when I went outside to look for her, I went back in. There were still a few women in the room, but no sign of Riley.

"Hey, girls," I interrupted one group. "Have any of you seen Riley?"

They shook their heads and one of them added, "I saw her get up during the meeting, but haven't seen her since."

I didn't want to worry women who were already so fragile, so I simply brushed it off and threw out, "Oh, she must be in the bathroom then."

Walking out of the room, I went back down the hall

toward the empty rooms at the back of the center. I needed to make a call and I didn't want to bring any undue stress on the rest of the women there.

First, I called Riley's phone. It was no surprise that her handbag I was holding started ringing.

Great.

I quickly disconnected and made the next call.

"Hey, Lex. All finished up?" Cruz answered.

"Captain, I need your help," my desperation evident, even with my hushed tone.

"Where are you? Are you alright?"

"I'm okay. The meeting just finished, but Riley is missing."

He listened carefully as I explained everything to him.

"I'm worried about her," I confessed. "She wouldn't just leave. Can you help?"

"I'm leaving the office now. Stay inside until I get there," he instructed.

"Okay. I'll see you shortly."

I disconnected the call and felt a hand grip my bicep. I tensed and heard a familiar voice fill my ears from behind me.

"I did not want to have to do this, but you've left me no choice."

I was in shock.

Frozen.

Again.

"The first thing you're going to do is call whoever that was and tell them you found your friend. Then, you'll need to come with me."

I was spun around and now face-to-face with him.

Oh God.

Oh no.

"Do you understand me?" his menacing voice asked.

I nodded and called Cruz back.

"Put the phone on speaker. You say one stupid thing and we'll have bigger problems," he ordered.

Putting the phone on speaker, we heard it ring once before Cruz answered, "Warrior, you okay?"

"I'm sorry for calling prematurely and bothering you at work. Grant just showed up and told me he saw Riley. Sure enough, she was in the bathroom."

"Lexi, you told me you checked the bathroom."

Grant's fingers squeezed my arm a little tighter, indicating I better think quick.

"Yeah, I know. I must have missed her when everyone was filing out of the room. I'm going to just finish up here and I'll see you at your place shortly, cupcake."

There was silence for a moment before he responded, "Ok, Lex. I'll see you there then."

I hoped he realized what I said and knew I needed him to help me.

Unfortunately, I couldn't begin to think about that because Grant took my phone out of my hand and began dragging me down the hall toward the back exit of the center.

There was a van parked behind the building. As he pulled me toward it, he barked, "I told them you were off-limits, but you had to go sticking your nose into things you shouldn't have. Now I can't do anything to save you. You'll end up wherever you end up and there's nothing I can do about it now."

"Grant, what are you doing?" I asked.

Maybe if I could keep him talking I'd buy myself enough time for Cruz to get here. I had to believe he knew I still needed him.

"Transporting you," he explained.

"Where? Where are you taking me?"

"To the place where you'll be prepped to be sold."

I shook my head, unable to speak. Grant was just about to open the back of the van, when I snapped out of it. I pulled my arm back, but he just tightened his hold on me. Even still, I struggled and tried to get away.

"Stop fighting me, Lexi."

No way. I didn't fight once before, but I wasn't going to let that happen again. I kept struggling until he backhanded me across the face. It was so hard; I saw stars and was disoriented.

That was enough time for Grant to open the back of the van, haul me up, and throw me in. When he slammed the door shut, I realized I wasn't alone.

Someone was curled up in a ball, shaking, crying, and terrified.

It was Riley.

CHAPTER 23

Cruz

CUPCAKE.

She used her safe word. Something was very wrong and I had no doubt Lexi knew what she was doing when she used that word.

I knew she was in trouble, but I couldn't tell her that I was going to come there anyway. I didn't know the situation, so I couldn't risk putting her in more danger.

The second she disconnected the call, I looked over at Lorenzo. He was sitting in the passenger's seat of my truck on our way to WAAR. After receiving the first call from Lexi when she stated she didn't know where her friend was, I had this gut feeling things were not good. Lorenzo happened to be standing nearby when I got the call and didn't hesitate to join me. As we walked out of the Cunningham Security office, we saw Dom and gave him a quick update.

"Go," he ordered. "I'm going to grab Pierce and we'll be coming right behind you."

No sooner did Lorenzo and I get into my truck and start pulling out of the parking lot when Lexi called back. I immediately answered her call through my truck's Bluetooth system. That's when she used her safe word and we were still just over five minutes away from her.

"Something tells me you don't believe her friend showed up," Lorenzo guessed after the call was disconnected.

"You'd be right," I confirmed.

"How do you know?" he pressed.

"She called me cupcake."

Lorenzo let out a sound and noted, "I'm not sure that explains much."

"I'm not sharing things that aren't mine to share," I started. "That said, Lexi needed a safe word when we got together. Cupcake is her word. This is the first time I've ever heard her use that word."

"Who's Grant?" Lorenzo changed the subject.

I was relieved to hear not an ounce of judgment in his tone after what I'd just told him. If I was being honest, I guess I never really believed I would have heard it, though.

As I drove faster to get to her, I answered, "The guy who facilitated the opening of the rape crisis center Lexi did the PR for, the same one she's now volunteering at."

"Got any other info on him? A last name at least?"

I shook my head. We never really discussed him to that extent. Then, it dawned on me. "He was a referral from her brother, Logan," I spat out. "Logan can probably give us more information."

We pulled up to WAAR. Lexi's car was parked in the lot, but there was no sign of her. Just as I was about to get out of the truck to go inside and look for her, my cell rang.

"Can't talk now, Levi" I answered, connected to the Bluetooth.

"She called here," he returned.

"Lexi?"

"She said she was thrown into the back of a white van. They're driving now, but she doesn't know where. There's a girl in the van with her. Riley. Apparently, when this guy, Grant, threw Lexi in the back of the van he took her phone. He didn't realize Lexi was carrying Riley's purse with her phone in it."

"Are you having Michaels track them?" Lorenzo cut in.

Trent Michaels was our resident tech guru. He could hang with the best of us in the field, but behind the computer is where he excelled.

"He is tracking the GPS on the phone, but the battery life was at less than ten percent. As much as I wanted to keep her on the phone and have her report what was happening, I didn't want to risk having the phone die."

"Did she tell you anything else?"

I was met with silence.

"Levi?" I warned. "What did she tell you?"

"Fuck, Cruz," he bit out. "After hearing the call she made to you, Grant said he could no longer protect her and that he was transporting her to where she'd be prepped to be sold."

Rage boiled up inside of me.

"Over my dead body," I seethed. "They aren't putting her through this again."

"Keep your cool, bro."

I couldn't.

"Levi, she was raped four years ago and she just now found a way to trust people again. If we don't get to her, I'm certain she's going to be damaged beyond repair."

"We're going to get her," he insisted. "I'm in Trent's office right now; he's going to tell you where they're headed. We've also got Dom, Pierce, and Holden on this call. They're two minutes behind you. I'm assembling the rest of the team that's available. If Grant is taking Lexi and her friend to wherever the rest of these women are, we're going to need the resources."

I maneuvered the truck back to the parking lot entrance. A second later, Trent told me where they were and the direction they were headed. They'd only gotten about ten minutes ahead of us. I pulled out of the lot, determined to get to Lexi.

We'd been driving a solid fifteen minutes, the last ten on the freeway.

"We don't think we're getting that cell signal anymore," Levi informed me. "Trent believes the battery died on the phone."

My warrior. The only connection we had to her was gone.

"What about Lexi's phone? Have you tried that?" I suggested.

"Already tried, Cruz," Trent assured me. "I'm guessing he turned her phone off. It's only showing me the last location, which is pinging off a tower near the place she was taken from. That signal hasn't moved since we started following them on her friend's phone."

"Get a number for Logan Townsend and bring him in on this call," I ordered. "He referred Grant to Lexi. Grant is one of Logan's clients from his shop. See if he can give us anything."

A few minutes later, Logan's voice filled the cabin of the truck.

"Hello?"

"Logan, it's Cruz," I announced. "I've got you on a multi-way call here. I'm in my truck with Lorenzo, and we've got Levi and Trent on the line back at the office. A couple of the guys are in the truck behind me."

"This already feels bad. Is Lexi okay?"

His voice was tense and alert.

"I'm on the freeway trailing a van she was thrown in the back of. I need you to tell me everything you know about this guy Grant she's been working with."

"Grant Chambers?" he asked. "He's one of my clients. What am I missing?"

"I'm thinking he's the ringleader of the case I've been working on," I shared.

"What does your case have to do with my sister?"

"I don't know enough yet to be certain or to give you details, but my case is the Windsor sex trafficking ring."

"You better be fucking kidding me, Cruz," he clipped.

"I wish I was," I shot back.

"Fuck!" he roared.

"Focus, Logan," I urged. "Any idea where I'm headed? Where would he be taking her?"

He was silent a moment before he responded with nothing but defeat in his voice, "He's the senior VP of Logistics and Distribution for Glazier's Supply. They've got tons of warehouses and they aren't just in the state of Wyoming."

This was not good. I understood Luke's downtrodden tone because Glazier's was a massive corporation. We needed to figure out a way to narrow down the possible locations that he could be taking Lexi.

"We were trailing him, Logan. There's another girl in the van with her and Grant doesn't know they have her phone. The battery on that phone had little power left and it just died, so we no longer have a way to track where they're headed.

"Which way are you going?"

"East on twenty-six," I began. "We're past Dubois, but still north of Willow Creek. I just pulled over because I don't want to keep going if they've gotten off at any of these exits."

"There's a new warehouse they're opening somewhere in that area," he blurted. "Grant told me about it in an email a while back when I reached out to him about some things on his car. Give me a second. I'll see if there's any information on that on their website."

I anxiously awaited any word from Logan. There was no guarantee that it would be where Grant would take them, but I was hoping for a miracle. As Lorenzo and I waited, my mind drifted to Lexi.

Normally, extreme cases like this didn't faze me. Years of working in the field and experiencing high-risk situations on occasion allowed me to have a sense of determination and focus. I never worried if I'd be able to get the job done, but now I was completely overcome with a feeling of dread and despair. I hated to think what would happen if we found her too late.

"I've got it, Cruz. The warehouse is in Crowheart, just a few minutes north of Willow Creek."

He went on to rattle off the address as Lorenzo punched it into the GPS. I only hoped our instincts were right and this is where he was taking her.

I wasted no time and got back on the road.

"You get that, Levi?" Lorenzo asked.

"We're on it," Levi responded. "Michaels and I are getting the location over to the rest of the team. You've got guys only a couple minutes behind you. I'll reach out to Detective Baines in the meantime."

"Thanks, Logan," I called out. "I'll let you know once I've got her safe."

"Bring her home, Cruz," he demanded.

"I won't come back to Windsor without her," I replied before disconnecting the call.

Keeping my foot on the gas, I drove to the location Logan gave us. The entire way there I hoped for a miracle.

Lexi

"Are they really going to sell us?"

Riley and I were still in the back of the moving van.

She was terrified. I was just as terrified, but I knew I needed to be strong for her, for myself.

"No," I assured her. "Cruz is going to get to us before that can happen."

The truth was that I had no idea if he'd know where to go. The battery on Riley's phone died, so there was no longer any way for Levi and his team to track where we were. Even still, I needed to stay positive. Riley was far too worked up. If I let my emotions get the best of me in this situation, we'd never stand a chance.

I was determined to fight.

"I'm scared, Lexi."

I moved close to Riley and put my arms around her. "I know," I tried to comfort her. "But we've got to stay positive."

I wasn't sure how long we'd been driving when the van finally stopped. Riley began trembling harder the moment she heard Grant's door open and shut. We sat in the van for a good five minutes before the back door opened.

I shouldn't have been surprised, but I was. Grant was standing there with Shaun, the guy who came into the center weeks ago looking for help to cope with his girlfriend's recent sexual assault. I couldn't understand what was going on.

Shaun grabbed Riley while Grant pulled me out of the back of the vehicle.

"Why are you doing this, Grant? My brother trusted you."

"It's nothing personal, Lexi. You weren't supposed to get caught up in this, but you sealed your fate when you made that phone call. Besides, we need to make up for the one that got away a few weeks ago. You're cute enough; you can take her place."

He had to have been referring to the attempted abduction of the girl Cruz and his team rescued.

"I don't understand," I pushed for more information to stall him, knowing I'd probably lose if I tried to physically fight. "I thought you were married and had daughters. How could you do this?"

"Shut up," he ordered.

I ignored his demand and continued, "I'm someone's daughter, too. I'm a sister, a friend, and a girlfriend. What if your wife were here? What about your daughters?"

"*Shut up,*" he roared, grabbing me by my hair and yanking.

As Grant and Shaun began dragging us across the lot, I took in my surroundings for the first time. We were in an industrial complex heading toward a huge warehouse. I remembered that Grant worked for Glazier's Supply. This had to be one of the company's warehouses.

Once inside, we were taken through an empty, but finished, office space down a hall through a set of double-wide steel doors. Beyond the doors, we stepped inside the massive warehouse. Rows upon rows of metal warehouse shelving lined the floors. There were a few shelves that had been used, but most were bare. Down the middle of the warehouse separating the shelves were shrink-wrapped pallets that lined more than half the length of the entire space.

Even with the things that were in the warehouse, it was evident that this was a relatively new space that wasn't officially being used. I started worrying that if Cruz and his team didn't find us, it would be a long time before anyone came here.

Grant walked over to the side of the warehouse, where I found that one of the empty shelves was not completely empty.

Duct tape.

Swiping the tape off the shelf he turned back toward me and pulled my wrists together.

No way.

I struggled against his hold, determined to get away somehow. His grip was strong, but I managed to get myself free. No sooner did I get away from him when I heard, "You move and she's dead."

I turned to see Shaun standing with his forearm draped across the front of Riley's chest and a gun pointed at her temple. The look of sheer panic and terror on her face was heartbreaking. I remained there, motionless. Grant seized that opportunity and began wrapping the tape around my ankles. I guess he figured it might be better if I couldn't run. I kept my eyes focused on Riley, until Grant was standing in front of me blocking my view. Even if he hadn't been, I'm not sure I could have held her gaze any longer. This was because he began wrapping the tape around one of my wrists.

The emotions came bubbling to the surface. I was terrified and panicking. I had tried to fight back, but I was frozen once again seeing the gun at Riley's head. My breathing grew quick and shallow as I was turned and my wrists were bound behind my back. The painful memories of the time when I was restrained at my wrists, unable to move, rushed back to haunt me. Suddenly, I was back in that dorm room. It took everything in me to keep breathing and not be overcome by the flood of dread threatening to consume me.

Once Grant finished binding my wrists, he turned me back around and moved to Riley. Thankfully, Shaun lowered the gun from her head and tucked it into the back of his pants.

"You're never going to get away with this," I warned. "People are going to be searching for us."

"By the time anyone realizes you're missing, you'll already be in Colorado with the rest of them. Nobody will even know I was involved."

"Why would you do this? I thought you set up the center

because you cared about survivors of sexual assault. Now you're facilitating a sex trafficking ring? What if this happened to one of your daughters?"

"I'm doing this for my daughters," he shot back, agitated with me. "I do what I've got to do and they stay safe."

This made no sense.

Unfortunately, I couldn't keep pushing for more information because Grant was tired of listening to me. He took duct tape and covered my mouth. Then, he did the same with Riley. As he lifted me up over his shoulder, Shaun got Riley. I couldn't see where we were going, but I listened as they spoke.

"You contacted Gomez and let him know we're ready for transport?" Grant asked.

"He's on his way. I expect he'll be here in less than ten. We've got to get the rig pulled around and the container loaded."

I tried to tell myself that being upside down over his shoulder is the reason I felt the bile creep up my throat, but I knew that wasn't the reason why.

Riley and I were running out of time.

We eventually stopped moving and I heard a door open.

The next thing I knew Riley and I were being tossed to the cold, cement floor. I looked up and saw Grant and Shaun's retreating backs go through the double doors we'd just walked through. I looked to my left at Riley. She was terrified, but she wasn't focused on me. Her wide eyes were directed at something behind me.

When I turned around, I saw that we weren't alone.

Sitting on the opposite side of the room, bound and silenced the same as Riley and me, were eight other women. One of those women was Violet.

It was then I realized why she never came back to another meeting. There were three other familiar faces from WAAR, but I couldn't recall their names.

I had to do something.

But there was nothing in that room, nothing but ten women who were petrified. That's when some of this suddenly began making sense. Taking women from a rape crisis center was perfect. These guys, whoever they were, preyed on women who were already beaten down and vulnerable. I remembered Cruz telling me about the woman he and Dom rescued. She had been down on her luck. Someone saw that and used it to their advantage. I had no doubt that the women in this room that weren't from WAAR were, in some way, already broken.

I wasn't going down.

I had already overcome too much to let my power be taken away again. I just needed to figure out how I could buy us more time.

There were ten of us and two of them. Perhaps it would soon be three of them considering Grant and Shaun were talking about someone named Gomez.

As I sat there trying to come up with an idea, the rumble of a vehicle outside interrupted my thoughts. It was then I noticed what was behind the group of women.

A garage door.

They were planning to load us into the rig Grant and Shaun were discussing.

It was only a matter of minutes before the sound of the engine was cut off. Sure enough, Grant and Shaun reentered the room. They walked over toward the garage door and opened it. Then, we were staring down the back of an empty trailer.

A few seconds passed before I realized that empty trailer was actually an empty shipping container.

CHAPTER 24

Cruz

WE WATCHED FROM THE PARKING LOT ACROSS THE STREET from the Glazier's warehouse as they moved an eighteen-wheeler around the building to one of the loading docks. The white van we assumed was the one Lexi told Levi she was thrown into was parked in the lot at the front of the warehouse.

"I'm not sitting here any longer," I announced. "She's in there and the only way she's leaving is with me."

"Dom, Pierce, and Holden are two minutes out," Lorenzo tried reasoning with me. "Tyson is another three minutes behind them. Our chances are better with the rest of the team. We don't know how many people we're up against."

"I don't care," I snapped. "I'm not waiting."

Getting out of the truck, I started moving toward the warehouse. I had no doubt that Lorenzo would follow behind me. No sooner did I cross the street when I glanced to my right and saw Dom's truck coming down the road.

He pulled up along the curb and the guys quickly filed out.

"What's the situation?" Dom asked.

"We know Lexi and her friend, Riley, are in there. At minimum, there's the guy who transported her and one other. We saw them moving the rig around the building. No idea what we'll find when we get inside," Lorenzo explained.

"My priority is Lexi," I declared as I turned my attention to Lorenzo. "De Luca, Riley is your priority. All I'm going to say is that she was at the rape crisis center for a reason. Be as sensitive to that as you can."

At that, I turned and made my way toward the building, doing my best to remain hidden behind the landscaping. When I was close to the building, I looked in through the windows. It was empty in the front office. Considering there were no other cars in the lot, I had expected as much, but didn't know if I'd find a fully furnished interior.

"The office is vacant," I called to the guys behind me.

"I've got the lock," Pierce declared, moving ahead of us to pick the lock.

Once he successfully opened the lock, we filed in. I had no doubt they had to be in the warehouse. Seeing the truck pulled up at the loading dock, I knew that's where I'd find my warrior. Unfortunately, the space was so big, we needed to check behind every door to find the one that led to the warehouse.

I finally made my way to a hallway, where I found a set of double-wide steel doors.

"That's it," Holden said from beside me.

The guys followed me down the hall.

"Lexi and Riley," I reminded them just before I pushed the door open.

We walked through, keeping ourselves as hidden as possible, but it was difficult considering the warehouse had a bunch of empty shelving. Other than the row of pallets down the center of the room, there was nothing.

We continued moving through the space toward the back of the building where the loading dock was.

"Cruz," Dom hissed.

I turned back and saw him pointing in the opposite direction.

He continued, "Open doors…over there."

When I looked in the direction he was indicating, I saw the open doors.

"Let's move," I ordered.

The closer we got, I heard the panicked whimpers. Dom and I stepped inside, while the rest of the guys stayed back out of view and assessed the situation.

There was only one guy. He was carrying a girl, who was not Lexi, over his shoulder out of the room to the shipping container. She was struggling against him when she looked up and saw us. Just as I put my finger to my mouth to tell her to stay quiet and not alert him to our presence, her whole body tensed. The guy felt it and turned around.

Pulling out my gun, I pointed it at him and ordered, "Put her down."

He wasted no time in reaching behind his back to pull out his own gun. Setting her down in front of him and putting the gun to her head, he countered, "No. You're going to put your weapon down and slide it over this way."

I lifted my hands and said, "Alright, just relax."

I lowered my gun to the ground and slid it toward him.

"You too!" he yelled at Dom.

Dom pulled his gun out and slid it across the floor.

"Shaun? What's going on?" we heard from inside the trailer.

At that moment, there was movement behind the guy I could only presume was Shaun. I looked behind him and just barely saw Grant climbing out the top of a shipping container.

"Who are you?" he asked us as he walked up beside Shaun.

"I believe you have something that doesn't belong to you," I responded.

He walked over to the guns Dom and I surrendered, picked them up, and instructed, "Shaun, put her in the container."

Keeping one of the guns pointed at us, Grant then continued, "Perhaps I should call the police and report trespassers."

"Something tells me that container you just put that girl in will be of interest to the police," Dom goaded as he crossed his arms over his chest. "I'll wait while you call them."

The truck started.

Grant smirked.

"Looks like my third guy is here," he started. "This truck is going to be long gone by the time the police get here."

Dom kept provoking Grant, but he was doing it on purpose because we saw Tyson hop up on the ledge of the loading dock. Lorenzo had hoisted himself up on the other side. Tyson moved quick and came up behind Grant as Lorenzo went toward the container where Shaun was climbing down the side of it.

I trusted my guys to do what they needed to do and didn't pay attention to another thing other than to shout out as Pierce and Holden came into the room to assist Tyson and Lorenzo, "We've got a guy in the cab!"

"Got him already," Tyson yelled back.

With Dom by my side, we took off toward the shipping container. I climbed up the side of it and looked in.

"Lexi," I shouted in the dark.

I heard whimpering, but no response.

I pulled my phone out of my pocket and turned on the flashlight. Shining it into the container, I realized there were a bunch of women inside. I moved the light over each of the women until finally I locked eyes with her. There was no response because every woman's mouth had been taped shut.

Passing my phone to Dom, I turned back and shouted, "I need hands!"

I climbed inside the container and the women all huddled together and shifted themselves away from me. It wasn't easy considering they all had their wrists and ankles bound together.

Fuck, they were all terrified.

"I'm one of the good guys," I assured them. "You're all safe. The police are on the way."

Muffled cries came from the group as more light filtered into the container. I walked over to Lexi and saw nothing but relief in her eyes.

"Princess," I said softly.

Tears filled her eyes.

"Are you okay?" I asked.

She nodded.

I put my hand up to the corner of the duct tape covering her mouth and gently started peeling it back. The moment I removed it she fell forward into me and quietly cried, "Cruz."

I wrapped her in my arms and insisted, "You're safe, Lexi. I've got you."

I held her a minute before I urged, "Let me free your hands and legs."

Reaching in my pocket, I pulled out my knife. I cut through the tape at her wrists before moving to her ankles.

"Come on, let's get you out of here," I suggested.

She shook her head and demanded, "No. Get the girls out first. I'm okay now."

"My warrior," I began. "You're the strongest woman I know."

I kissed her on her forehead. After, she looked around the container and said, "Ladies, this is my boyfriend, Cruz, and these are his friends. They work for a private investigations company and they are here to take us home. It's okay to let them help you. They won't hurt you and you're no longer in any danger"

I smiled down at Lexi. She jerked her head to the side and said, "Cruz, this is Riley."

My eyes moved to Riley. "It's nice to meet you, Riley. Are you alright with me taking the tape off your mouth?"

She jerked her head up and down furiously, indicating that she wanted the tape off. I removed the tape from her mouth the same as I did Lexi's. The second it was off, she let out a sob. Her knees buckled, but I caught her before she fell. I pulled Riley toward my chest and said, "You're alright, darling."

I gave her a minute to collect herself. "I'm going to free your wrists, okay?"

She pulled back and allowed me to cut through the tape at her wrists. I moved to her ankles and freed them next.

Over the next fifteen minutes, the guys and I worked to get all of the girls out of the container. Sadly, we had to carry them up and over the side of the container. In preparation for transporting the girls, Grant and Shaun had locked and chained the doors on the open-top container. Our options were to either keep the girls waiting in the container until we could locate something to open the chains or pick them up and hoist them out. Of course, we confirmed with all of them that they were okay with being carried out. For the most part, they all handled it well.

Not long after we had them all out and back in the warehouse, the Windsor Police Department showed up along with the local authorities. We spent the next several hours at the warehouse while the police questioned the women and took Shaun and Grant into custody.

Having Lexi in the well-lit space inside, I noticed some redness and bruising on her cheek. Lexi saw my inspection of her face and quickly lifted her hand to cover it.

"Did one of them hit you?" I asked, trying to control my budding rage.

"Grant," she answered with a nod. "When I tried to fight back."

I looked back in the direction of where I knew Grant and Shaun were and I knew instantly Lexi understood where my mind was. She placed her hand on my forearm and silently pleaded with me to let it go.

I gave in because as much satisfaction as I know I'd get from giving him what he deserved, I didn't want to do anything that would upset Lexi any more than she already was from this entire ordeal.

As soon as we could leave, I got Lexi in my truck and we made our way back to Windsor. Lorenzo, Riley, and another one of the girls named Violet rode back with Tyson. The remainder were split among the police officers.

Once we were on the road heading home, I handed my phone to Lexi.

"Here," I started. "Call Logan."

"Logan?" she asked.

"He's the reason we knew where to find you," I explained. "I hated having to do it and worry him, but we lost the signal on the cell phone we were using to track you. I had no choice but to call him."

"Oh, no. He's probably worried sick."

She tapped his number into the phone and held it to her ear.

"It's me, Logan," she said after he answered.

I glanced over as she waited while Logan responded. Tears streamed down her cheeks as she listened to him.

"I know," she started. "I'm ok, though. Cruz got there with his team and they not only saved me, but nine other women as well. There are still some women missing that were taken when this whole thing started weeks ago, but the police have a good idea of where to look now. There's going to be a search in Colorado."

More silence.

"I promise. I'm good. I'll call you tomorrow and we'll stop by the shop to see you. I'm taking the day off from work."

Lexi glanced over at me and gave me a hopeful smile. I was absolutely taking the day off tomorrow and spending it with her. I wasn't sure I'd ever want to go anywhere without her again.

"It's not your fault, Logan. You had no idea what he was planning. I don't think they know the full story yet anyway. Please don't blame yourself for this, too."

Too?

Lexi went back and forth with Logan a few more times before she finished her call with him and set my phone back in the center console.

"I have to call Dr. Lane," she whispered.

That was not what I wanted to hear. While I liked that she had a professional to confide in and help her deal with whatever she is feeling, I had noticed she was going less and less frequently. Hearing her now, I was concerned that what happened tonight was having a much greater effect on her than I thought. I'd support her, regardless.

"Are you alright?" I worried.

"Yeah, it's not for me," she started. "I need to call her for Logan. He blames himself for what happened to me in college and now he's blaming himself for this. He stopped by my office earlier this afternoon before I went to WAAR for the group therapy and he stayed for a couple hours. Logan's really having a hard time and feels awful about not being there for me years ago. Now, he feels responsible for what just happened since he was the one who not only introduced me to Grant, but also urged me to take on the job."

I reached over and wrapped my hand around hers and confessed, "I can't say that I wouldn't feel the same if I was in his shoes."

"I'll call first thing in the morning," she declared.

"I think that's a good idea," I agreed.

We drove for a while in silence. Once we were back within the city limits of Windsor, Lexi asked, "Can we still spend the night at your place?"

"Of course," I responded. "Since I have the stuff you packed this morning with me, are you alright with picking up your car tomorrow?"

"Yeah," she said softly. "I don't want to go back there tonight."

Just then, my cell rang and Lexi said, "It's Levi."

"Answer it," I urged her. "He'll be happy to hear your voice."

"Hello?" she answered.

I glanced over and saw the smile grow on her face.

"Thank you for everything," she replied to whatever he said to her.

Silence while he spoke to her.

"Well, I'm feeling a bit sad that I didn't know Cruz's number so I could call him, but when we used Riley's phone to look up Cunningham Security, I trusted you guys would do everything you could to get us back safely. Your team is responsible for saving so many girls tonight. You should be proud."

As Lexi listened to Levi's response, I couldn't help but wonder if she realized how it was her. I wondered if she understood that it was her quick thinking that saved those girls. I had every intention of seeing to it that she knew just how crucial her role was in all of this.

"Did you want to talk to Cruz?" she asked.

She waited.

She laughed. It wasn't until I heard it that I realized how much I missed it. We'd been running on adrenaline for the last several hours, with nothing but panic consuming our minds and bodies. Hearing the sweet sound of her laughter was a lot like coming home and it's a place I'm certain I'll never want to leave.

"Ok, then," she responded through her laughter. "Goodbye, Levi. And thank you, again."

Lexi ended the call and looked over at me. "He didn't want to talk to you, per se. He just wanted to make sure I was alright."

"Figured as much," I replied. "But I'd appreciate it if you could call him back for me because I need to talk to him."

I continued driving as Lexi tapped at the screen on my phone, pulling up Levi's number and calling him back. She handed the phone over to me just as Levi answered, "Yeah?"

"Just a heads up," I started. "I'm not going to be in tomorrow."

"I suspected," he returned. "Don't worry about it. Take care of Lexi; we'll see you next week."

At that, Levi and I disconnected. Not long after, Lexi and I were back at my place.

"I just want to shower," she announced as soon as I pulled the truck into the driveway. "Do you mind?"

I shook my head, parked, and answered, "Not at all. Go on up and hop in. I'll grab your stuff out of the truck and bring it up in a minute."

"Thanks, captain," she returned.

I watched as Lexi walked inside. Knowing she was here at my home and that she was safe filled me with such intense relief. Between the weeks I'd been putting in working on this case and the agony of not knowing if Lexi was okay for the last several hours, I felt like I was finally able to breathe a little easier. There was still work to be done on the case, but for tonight, I'd put it out of my mind and focus on my warrior.

On those thoughts, I grabbed her bag out of the truck and went inside.

CHAPTER 25

Lexi

"WE'VE GOT TO TALK."

I tensed a bit as I heard Cruz mutter those words. I'm not sure anyone on the face of the planet has ever heard those words and been able to remain calm.

Cruz and I got back to his place a little while ago. We had both showered and then made food since neither of us had any dinner. We'd just finished eating, cleaned up, and were now in his bed, my front to his.

"Ok," I responded.

Cruz pressed a kiss to my forehead before he alleviated my concerns. "There's nothing wrong, but I have two things I want to talk to you about."

I gave him a gentle nod.

"First, I need to apologize to you," he started. "I may have accidentally done something in the heat of the moment that I'm incredibly sorry for. If I had been thinking clearly, I never would have done it."

Cruz claimed nothing was wrong, but now I wasn't so sure. Why was he feeling the need to apologize to me?

"What happened, Cruz?" I worried.

"When I was on my way to WAAR after you called me

back and used your safe word, I knew something was really wrong. I drove as fast as I could to get there, but the traffic was horrendous. By the time I arrived, you weren't there. I only knew that, though, because Levi called me and told me you had called him and explained what happened."

He took a moment to pause and collect himself.

"I was boiling with anger and when Levi told me what Grant said he was planning to do with you, I lost it. I yelled at my brother that you'd been raped years ago and you just found a way to overcome so much of what that did to you. I didn't want to see your mind end up back in a terrible place."

"I can understand your frustration," I assured him. "I think it's normal and I'm sure I would have felt a mix of fear and anger if the roles were reversed. I'm still not sure why you think you need to apologize to me."

"Lexi, I screamed into the phone that you were raped," he remarked.

"Ok?"

He sighed. "I was yelling at Levi, but Lorenzo was in the truck with me and Pierce, Dom, and Holden were on the call as well, even though they were in a different vehicle. They heard and now they all know."

My brows pulled together and I had to ask the question that was on the tip of my tongue, regardless of whether I was prepared for the answer or not.

"Why does that bother you?" I asked, bracing for his response.

Cruz jerked his head back and explained, "Lexi, I'd never go around telling that to anyone who didn't need to know. It's not something I should be sharing with anyone. That's yours to share with whomever you choose. It was careless of me and I'm deeply sorry for it."

I felt myself relax at his answer. He noticed it and didn't let me off the hook. "Why else do you think that would bother me?" he questioned me.

I shrugged my shoulders and looked away from his face when I answered, "I wasn't sure if that was going to be your answer or if the reason you were upset about what you said had more to do with you being embarrassed about your co-workers knowing that I was raped."

"Princess, look at me," he demanded.

When I brought my eyes to his, he stated firmly, "I'm not, in any way, shape, or form, embarrassed about anyone knowing you were raped. I'm not embarrassed by you at all. But the information I shared is something *you* need to be comfortable with sharing, not me. To that end, you need to know that my co-workers, who are also very close friends of mine, would not pity or judge either one of us because of what happened to you. That's just who they are."

I felt the warmth spread through me, relieved to know he felt that way. As much as I wanted to believe he wasn't embarrassed by me being raped, it was hard to not let the thought cross my mind from time to time. I didn't want him worried that he'd done something that I couldn't forgive him for.

Leaning into him, I shared, "I'm not upset that you accidentally let it slip in front of Lorenzo and the other guys. I don't need an apology. Over the last couple of weeks, I've finally started realizing that I don't need to feel ashamed about what happened."

Cruz squeezed me a little tighter and continued, "You should know, though, that Lorenzo and the rest of them aren't the kind of people that will go around telling anybody your business."

"I know."

And that was the truth. I wholeheartedly believed that Cruz and the entire team he worked with were good guys. I saw the way they were with the girls only a few hours ago and it was evident they knew how delicate the situation was. They handled it professionally and treated the girls with the respect and care they all deserved.

After letting that settle between us for a minute, I wondered, "So, what's the second thing you wanted to talk to me about?"

"You."

"Me?" I asked, nervously.

Cruz nodded and explained, "I think you should know how lucky those girls were today that you were there. I hate that you were involved at all, but you deserve to know that it was because of your quick thinking that we could find you and them."

"It doesn't feel like it. I was terrified," I confessed. "Once Riley and I were in that warehouse and we saw how many other women were there, I panicked. I wanted to be strong and figure out a way to get us out of there, but between all of us being bound and so many of those girls being so emotionally battered and broken I didn't know what to do."

I felt myself getting choked up, but Cruz immediately eased my fears.

"You saved their lives, Lexi," he stressed. "I listened as you told the police what happened from the moment you were at WAAR and realized Riley had been taken. You stayed calm and acted fast by calling me. You used your safe word to tell me that something was wrong. Even when you were thrown into the back of that van, you didn't let fear take over. You called the office and you told Levi what was happening. I am so proud of you for everything you did tonight. There aren't a lot of people who would have been able to do that. And I'm not saying that's a bad thing; it's just the way it is sometimes. You know that. But in this situation, you found a way to overcome the awful circumstances and save yourself and those girls."

My lips parted in shock. All I could focus on was how we ended up in that shipping container and how I hadn't been able to stop that from happening. I never really thought about it the way Cruz had just delivered it.

Apparently, he wasn't finished because he went on, "You were a hero tonight. You've given those women a chance at healing because you were strong for them when they couldn't be strong for themselves. They owe you their lives, warrior."

I couldn't speak. I took a few minutes to process what Cruz had said and he happily gave me the time to do it.

"Thank you for saying all of that," I said softly. "There was a time where I used to worry about what I'd do if I was ever in a threatening situation again. Based off what happened in college, I've always worried that I would become a victim again to whatever the circumstances were. I no longer believe that I'm not strong enough. Maybe it was my age back then or maybe it was fear or maybe it was something else entirely, but regardless of the reason I froze then it wasn't my fault. Even if it happened again and I froze, it still wouldn't be my fault. But it feels good to know that I have what it takes to fight back, too. Thank you for allowing me to see that."

Cruz grinned at me and repeated, "I'm so proud of you."

I smiled back at him just as he lowered his mouth to mine. Cruz kissed me so sweet and tenderly. When he pulled back from me, I was desperate with need for him.

"Make love to me, captain," I pleaded.

Cruz brought his hand to my hip, where his fingers snuck underneath the hem of my shirt. They trailed up along the side of my body, taking the shirt I was wearing along for the ride. I lifted my body a bit to free the part of my top that was between me and the bed. Cruz used that opportunity to lift the shirt over my head and toss it aside.

I fell to my back as Cruz remained on his side next to me.

Lying next to him in his bed, in nothing but a pair of panties, I squirmed under his intense gaze. He brought his fingertips to my collar bone and traced along the skin there before moving them down. His touch was gentle as he brushed his fingers over my nipple. He gently squeezed my breast and used his thumb and forefinger to pinch my nipple. Finally, Cruz lowered his lips to my chest and captured my breast in his mouth. His hand left that breast and moved to the other one, where it teased me before moving down my body. Continuing to lick and suck on my breast, Cruz's hand reached the waistband of my panties and carefully slipped inside.

As soon as his fingers slid through my wetness, he lifted his head, brought his mouth to mine, kissed me and groaned into my mouth.

I brought my hands to my hips and pushed my panties down. Bringing my knees up so that my feet were flat on the mattress, I managed to get them down my legs and over my ankles before dropping my knees to the sides to give Cruz better access.

I wanted to feel him.

I needed to touch him.

His fingers continued to play at the sensitive spot between my legs while I kissed him and reached for his cock. Moving his boxer briefs out of the way, my hand stroked over the length of him. As I pumped my fist, gliding over it, I realized I wanted to taste him.

We'd explored each other and lots of positions over the last few weeks, but I hadn't yet had him in my mouth.

Pulling my mouth away from his, I struggled to catch my breath and admitted, "I want to taste you, captain."

His fingers didn't stop, but the look in his eyes and the grin on his face told me he was very much okay with me going after what I wanted.

It would have been so easy to give into what he was doing to me, but I fought against it and lifted my body. His hand was still between my legs, and I sat immobilized a moment allowing myself to feel the pleasure he was giving me. I wrapped my hand around his wrist and pulled his hand away before pushing him to his back.

Straddling one of his thighs, I leaned down and kissed his abdomen. I kept both of my hands on him, one on his shaft, the other massaging his balls. As I moved my lips down his abdomen and continued to work him with my hands, Cruz groaned. The sound was so sexy and only motivated me to move my mouth to its ultimate destination quicker.

I looked up at Cruz one last time and saw the look of pure need coming from him. The corners of my mouth tipped up and I kept my eyes on him as I wrapped my lips around the tip of his cock. My tongue swirled around the head and the heat in his eyes intensified. I took more of him in my mouth and watched as his hands clenched into fists. As much as I wanted to continue watching him, I wanted to please him even more.

So, I got down to business and moved my mouth down and sucked him in. I worked him as hard as I could, letting go of all inhibitions I'd had up to this point in our sexual relationship. The truth was that I didn't need to look up and see how he was reacting to know how he felt. I got it all in the rewards he gave me.

His approval was in the words he whispered.

It was in the groans he let out.

And I felt it in his body as it flexed underneath mine.

Suddenly, Cruz's hands were under my arms. He lifted me up his body and pressed his head against mine.

"That was amazing, Lexi," he praised me.

"Then why did you stop me?" I pushed back.

His face broke out into a grin before he responded, "You always come first."

"I don't mind taking care of you," I began.

"I mind it," he replied.

My face scrunched up.

"Wait. Are you saying you're never going to allow me to have you that way and see you through to the end?" I wondered.

"If you think I'm going to turn that down, you're crazy," he chuckled. "But I'm not alright with it happening before I've seen to it that you've been taken care of. The next time I eat you, I'll let you return the favor, but for now, I want to see you getting what you need while you ride me. Does that work for you?"

I nodded my head.

At that, Cruz leaned over to the nightstand and pulled out a condom. Once he rolled it on, I straddled his hips, positioned him at my entrance, and slid down over him.

"Cruz," I moaned.

He held my hips in his hands as I began riding him. My hands fell to his chest and I leaned into them as I worked myself over his hardened length, loving the feel of being filled by him. One of his hands would occasionally drift to my ass, where he'd squeeze before moving up to my breasts and doing the same. Sometimes, the way he'd squeeze me or the noises he'd make made me feel like he was the one who was keeping himself restrained.

I wasn't going to do it now, but I knew I needed to figure out what was holding him back and how to make him lose complete control.

Between all the touching Cruz did before I had taken him in my mouth and then the excitement I felt bringing him pleasure, it didn't take long before I was on the verge of coming apart. My hips began moving quickly as I sought to satisfy the pulsing and building pressure. Cruz knew it was coming.

"That's it, Lex," he approved, his voice thick with emotion.

"I'm going to come, Cruz," I cried just before it tore through me. Wave after wave of pure pleasure rolled through my entire body.

I barely had the opportunity to come down when Cruz flipped me to my back and drove himself in deep. It was glorious. I loved seeing this bit of unbridled passion in him. I knew it was just a small part of what he'd been holding back and I wanted more of it.

"More," I rasped feeling the pressure building again.

"Fuck," he growled as he powered his hips harder. "Worth the wait."

I gasped just before he lowered his mouth to mine and kissed me. He pulled back only a touch and quietly declared, "You're there."

"Yes."

"Come with me, princess."

So I did.

And he did.

It was magnificent.

A few minutes later, after he had disposed of the condom, Cruz had me curled into his body. He was on his back with his arm wrapped behind me, keeping me close to him.

"You okay?" he asked. I sensed nervousness in his tone.

I tilted my head back to look at him. It was now dark in the room, but I could tell he was looking down at me.

"I'm here with you," I noted the obvious. "Why wouldn't I be okay?"

"Just wanted to be sure," he said, but there was reservation in his tone.

I waited, hoping he'd give me more, but several minutes passed with not another sound from him.

"Talk to me, captain," I urged.

"About what?"

"Something is bothering you. You can talk to me about whatever it is."

He was quiet a minute before he finally revealed, "I've never felt so scared before in all my life. I've experienced things that have really affected me and the way I live my life, but some of that has always been stuff I've learned after it's happened. It's never been in the moment. With work, I've always been focused on my cases and doing what I need to do to get the job done, but I've never gotten emotionally involved. Sure, there were the situations with my brothers' women, but those were different for me. I wasn't prepared for what I felt tonight."

He paused, collecting himself. "Fear. I knew I'd stop at nothing to find you and bring you home, but the rage I felt was something I can't describe. What happened tonight proved to me just how deeply I feel for you. It was sheer terror I felt thinking I might not get to you in time or that I might not find you at all."

"You got me," I reassured him. "And I'm not going anywhere."

Cruz pressed a kiss to the top of my head before he gave me a gentle squeeze. "I wasn't too rough with you before, was I?" he questioned. "My emotions got the best of me and I lost control."

"I loved it," I announced. "It was actually kind of hot."

"What?"

"Cruz, a couple weeks ago you told me not to keep in how I felt. Whether it was sexy, scared, or anything in between, I could trust you with it. I want the same for you. I know you're holding yourself back with me when we're having sex. You don't have to."

His body tensed.

"What you do to my body when we are together is nothing short of amazing. I love it all, but I especially loved how you were tonight."

"I don't want to hurt you or scare you."

"I trust you and I know you'd never hurt me," I insisted. "But I also need to know that you are being yourself. I love when you're sweet and tender, but I think I could really enjoy it rough from time to time with you."

Cruz moved and turned toward me before shifting me in the bed so that he could spoon me. He hooked his arm around my waist and stayed silent. After too much silence, I called, "Captain?"

"Time for bed, princess."

"But what about our discussion?"

"It's been a long day," he noted. "We need to get some sleep."

"But," I managed to get out before he cut me off.

"Lexi, please," he pleaded. "Sleep now. We'll talk later. Can you give me that?"

It had been a long day and he had rescued me from an awfully scary situation for the both of us, so I acquiesced. "Ok, we'll sleep now."

He pressed a kiss to my bare shoulder. "Love you, Lexi. Good night."

"Love you, too. Good night, Cruz."

After I said the words, it didn't take long for me to feel the exhaustion and give in to it. I tried to wait until I felt Cruz fall asleep, but the events from the day had played their part on my body and I couldn't. If I had waited him out, I would have known that it wasn't until an hour later when Cruz finally drifted off.

CHAPTER 26

Lexi

IT WAS THE MORNING AFTER I'D BEEN KIDNAPPED AND NEARLY throw into the midst of a sex trafficking ring. Despite all of that, when I woke up I was in Cruz's bed alone. As someone who was normally up early, I was surprised to glance over at the clock and find that it was approaching ten o'clock. That explained why Cruz, who was also an early riser, was not there with me.

I rolled over, kicked back the covers, and walked to the bathroom. After finishing my morning business there and noting there was now officially a bruise on my cheek from Grant, I walked back out through the bedroom and went in search of Cruz. As I descended the stairs, I was hit by the delicious scents of breakfast.

Walking into the kitchen, I smiled when Cruz looked up from the frying pan where he was making breakfast potatoes and gave me a once-over.

"Morning, sleepyhead," he greeted me.

I walked over to him, put my hand to his chest, and pressed up on my toes to give him a kiss.

"Good morning," I replied.

"Coffee is ready," he informed me as he jerked his head toward the pot on the counter behind him.

After I poured myself a cup, I walked back over to where Cruz was standing and looked up at him. Given that I made no attempt to hide my assessment of him, it came as no surprise that he turned his head toward me and asked, "What?"

I shrugged my shoulders and answered, "I'm just surprised to see you awake and making breakfast. I thought we would have done the usual and gone to Colvert's."

Offering the same nonchalance, he returned, "I figured since neither one of us was going into work today, I'd make breakfast and we could take our time this morning."

"Well, it's not unappreciated. It smells fantastic and I'm seriously interested in trying those breakfast potatoes. What can I do to help?"

"I've got it. Everything is just about done anyway."

Cruz winked at me before he started removing the potatoes from the pan. At that moment, the timer on the microwave started beeping. Cruz finished putting the potatoes on the plate and moved to the microwave. He turned off the timer, bent at the waist, and opened the oven. He reached in and pulled out a tray of bacon.

After setting the bacon on a paper-towel-lined plate, he flipped the eggs he had put in the other pan while the potatoes had still been cooking. A few minutes later, we were sitting down at the table to eat breakfast.

"I'm worried," I confessed after we'd both gotten through a good portion of our food.

Cruz stopped moving and looked at me. "About what?"

"About what's going to happen with WAAR," I explained. "I haven't really had the opportunity to process the scope of the situation with Grant nor do we know what the reason for him doing this was, but the center is crucial. I'd hate to see it shut down because of what he did."

"Well, we have to go to the station today so you can make an official statement. By the time we get there, hopefully they will have learned something about his motives. I'm sure they're going to have to take a look into what was happening with the money that was being donated."

I gasped.

"What's wrong?" he worried.

"I never even thought of that," I declared. "What if the money that came in as a result of my campaigns to help keep the center free for sexual assault survivors was used to fund his illegal activities?"

"You're not to blame for what he did," Cruz began. "You went into this project for all the right reasons."

"I know," I admitted. "I just don't understand it. I don't understand why he did this. I keep thinking back to the meetings I had with him, even the very first one at Logan's shop. I hate to think that the signs were there and I missed them. He talked about his wife and daughters. I assumed one of them had been a sexual assault survivor, but yesterday when I was trying to fight him I asked him about them."

Cruz's brows pulled together. "What did he say?"

"He didn't really give me an answer. He just said that he was doing what he had to do to make sure they stayed safe."

"Someone was threatening him," Cruz declared.

"What?"

"That statement he gave you along with the fact that he was a long-standing client of your brother, who didn't hesitate to refer him to you, tells me that there's more to this story."

"What do you think it could be?" I wondered.

Cruz shook his head and answered, "I don't know. But we should get to the police station as soon as possible so you can give them this information. It's important."

"Ok," I agreed.

Forty-five minutes later, Cruz and I were walking into the Windsor Police Department. We were swiftly ushered to an office that was occupied by a Detective Jackson Baines. Cruz, who seemed to be well acquainted with him, made introductions.

"It's nice to meet you, Lexi," the detective started. "I'm sorry to have to make you relive what you went through yesterday, but I appreciate you coming in to make your statement."

I gave him a nod and was about to reply when Cruz interjected, "She's got new information about one of the suspects."

Detective Baines' brow lifted and his eyes shifted back to me, waiting for the news I had to deliver.

So, I gave it to him. I told him about the conversation I had with Cruz that morning and what I shared with him about my interactions with Grant. When I finished, his eyes went back to Cruz's.

"He's not talking," Detective Baines shared. "It all makes sense now if he's worried that someone's going to come after his family. What the hell did this guy do?"

"I'll get my guys on it if you want," Cruz offered. "Maybe we can figure out what's keeping him so tight-lipped."

"It's not going to hurt to have you guys doing some digging. We appreciate your willingness to help us out on cases like this."

Cruz shrugged his shoulders nonchalantly and shot back, "It goes both ways."

"What about his family?" I asked. "Have they been notified that he's here?"

"He called his attorney, who arrived not long after. Beyond that, nobody has been here to see him."

That was odd. If I were in the slammer, I'd like to think

the first people I'd call would be my family. Though, I guess if I were in the slammer, it might be for good reason...perhaps something I wouldn't want my family to know about.

At that, we moved on and I gave my official statement. Once I was finished, Cruz and I were back in his truck and he asked, "Do you want to go see Logan first?"

"First?"

"I don't plan on working today, but I'm thinking it might be wise to stop into the office for a minute and give an update to the team. The sooner they get started on looking into Grant, the sooner we might have some answers."

I didn't want to delay in seeing Logan, but I knew it was important for the guys to start investigating. To that end, Logan knew Grant. I wondered if he'd be able to offer some insight.

"Would you mind it if Logan came to the office?" I wondered.

Cruz shook his head and stated, "I don't mind."

"Since it's right around lunchtime, maybe I can talk him into taking a break at the shop and meeting us there. Who knows...maybe he'll be able to give you and your team something that'll help with the investigation."

"That's not a bad idea," he acknowledged. "Give him a call."

I called Logan and he agreed to meet us at the Cunningham Security office. Since he was coming from Rising Sun, I knew he'd get there after Cruz and I did.

We made it to the office and walked inside. Cruz held my hand as we stopped in front of the reception area.

"Hey, Deb," he greeted the woman at the desk. "This is Lexi. Lexi, this is Deb."

"It's nice to meet you," I offered.

She assessed me and looked back to Cruz before

announcing, "There's another one down and I can't tell you how happy that makes me."

Cruz didn't respond and confusion washed over my face.

"All three Cunningham brothers are officially spoken for," she explained. "While I loathe the fact that the three women who've stolen your hearts have endured such awful circumstances, it fills me with such joy to see you boys finally settling down, especially you. Lexi, dear, it's lovely to meet you, the woman responsible for making this guy have a life outside of work."

I gave her a smile.

"Thanks, Deb. We're not staying today. I just needed to stop in and see some of the guys about an update on the case," Cruz said.

"Check the conference room first. I saw them go in there before I left for lunch, but they might not be in there anymore."

He gave her a nod and told her my brother was coming by shortly before he guided me from the reception area to the conference room. Sure enough, when Cruz opened the door and ushered me in ahead of him, I saw that Deb was right. Most of the guys that had been present last night were in the room.

"Hey, Lexi," Levi greeted me. His eyes went to my cheek and his jaw clenched before he asked, "How are you doing?"

"I'm ok," I assured him. "Thank you again for what you did yesterday."

He shook his head and insisted, "Don't mention it. We're all just glad you're home safe and sound."

I gave him a small smile and felt Cruz tug me closer to his side.

"We didn't expect to see you here today," Levi directed his attention to Cruz.

"I'm not staying," Cruz started. "But Lexi and I were talking this morning and I learned a bit of news from her about Grant. We just left the WPD and Baines isn't against us doing a little digging to see what we can come up with."

"Ok, so what information do you have?" one of the guys I recognized from last night asked. I felt bad I couldn't remember his name.

"He was running scared," Cruz answered, but stopped when there was a knock at the door.

We turned around and Deb said, "Logan Townsend is here."

She moved out of the way and Logan filled the space in the doorway. The second he locked eyes with me his shoulders slumped and the breath rushed out of his lungs. No matter how hard I tried I couldn't stop the tears from welling in my eyes.

"Logan," I whispered.

He took the two steps inside the room, not looking at anyone else, and engulfed me in his embrace.

"Sidekick," he rasped.

He squeezed me tight.

"Shit, Lexi, I'm so fucking sorry. If I hadn't ever introduced you to him…" he got out before I cut him off by taking a step back out of his arms.

When I looked up at my brother's tortured face, I stressed, "If you hadn't introduced me, those girls would already be in Colorado joining the ones that went there already. What happened is not your fault."

Logan didn't respond and his eyes narrowed on my face.

Uh oh.

"Did he put his hands on you?"

I swallowed hard and remained silent.

"Lexi," he bit out. "Did he fucking hit you?"

I didn't want Logan freaking out, so I tried to do damage control. "Yeah, but it was only once when I tried to get away."

"Once is one time too many," he seethed, clearly not affected by my attempt to minimize the fallout.

He looked around the room and asked, "Where is he?"

"Logan," Cruz called. "Grant's in police custody. He's lawyered up and not talking, but we're hoping you might have something that can help us."

"What do you need to know?"

"Anything you've got," the guy I remembered as Dom chimed in. "There's enough evidence from last night that'll put him away for a long time. And even though we saved a lot of women last night, there are still some missing. We believe they're in Colorado. Do you have any idea who he might know in Colorado?"

Logan shook his head and confessed, "I've known him for years, but it's always been about cars. I know he's got a wife, two girls, and a high paying job. Beyond that, I don't know much else about him."

"Any idea who could possibly have a grudge against him or his family? Are there any shady people he's ever mentioned hanging around?" Cruz pushed for more.

"Wait," Levi chimed in. "Why do I feel like we're missing something, Cruz?"

Cruz turned back to Levi and explained, "That's what Lexi and I wanted to tell you about. She pressed him for information last night asking him why he was doing what he was doing."

"What did he say?" Logan wondered.

"He said he was doing what he had to do to keep them safe," I replied.

"Someone's hanging something over him," one of the guys whose name I didn't know announced. When he spoke, though, I took him in because he was the largest man in the room.

Tall.

Really tall.

And built like a tank.

"Let's get to work and see if we can find what this guy did for fun," Levi suggested.

When the guys rose from their seats, I looked up at Cruz and debated whether or not to ask what I wanted to ask him. As if reading my mind, Cruz asked, "What's the matter?"

"I was just wondering if you'd mind introducing me to your friends," I explained.

He smiled at me and stopped the guys before they walked out of the conference room. "Hey guys, can you hang tight a minute?"

They stopped and waited.

"Lexi wants to meet you all," he started. Their faces gentled as they turned their attention toward me.

Cruz held his hand out and pointed out, "I think you know Dom from the day you were here when I burned you."

I gave Dom a nod and corrected Cruz. "You mean when I burned myself."

He ignored my comment and moved to the next guy. Pointing to him, he said, "This is Pierce Reynolds."

"Hey, babe. Way to be quick on your feet yesterday," Pierce praised my actions.

"Thank you, Pierce. It's nice to meet you."

Cruz pointed to the massive guy who looked like he could crush you with just one hand and introduced him. "This is Lorenzo De Luca."

Lorenzo.

The one who was with Cruz last night. The one who sat in the truck and listened as Cruz shouted at Levi about me being raped.

Lorenzo's face got even softer, but I saw no judgment or disgust in his expression. Knowing Cruz and the type of guy he was, it was no surprise that he kept the company of people who wouldn't blame you for something that wasn't your fault.

"I'm happy you were there for Cruz last night," I said, offering him a friendly smile.

"No problem," he returned. "If the roles were reversed, he'd do the same. Mostly, all that matters is that we got there on time and you're home safe now."

"Thank you."

At that, the guys filed out of the room and went to work. Levi and Cruz chatted for a few minutes while I hung with Logan. He let me know that he didn't tell anyone else in the family about what happened to me last night. I told him I was going to be seeing our parents on Sunday, so I'd let them know then. In the meantime, I was going to go try to stop by Nikki and Luke's place sometime later in the evening after I knew she'd be home from work.

I'd kept something important from my family once before and I regretted it. I had no intention of doing it again. To top it off, surprisingly, it wasn't like I was feeling any major emotional distress over it.

Cruz finished up with Levi and the two of us decided, along with Logan, to go out for lunch together. I knew he was trying hard not to let it show, but Logan was really struggling with everything that had happened. After lunch, I hugged Logan goodbye and told him I was going to see to it that we got in with Dr. Lane early next week. Thankfully, he didn't argue. In fact, he agreed it was necessary.

Once Cruz and I were back in his truck, he confirmed, "Are you alright with going back to get your car now?"

"Yeah, I'd rather do that now before it gets too late," I started. "When you were talking with Levi, though, I told Logan that I was planning to go to Luke and Nikki's place tonight. Do you mind going with me?"

"Not at all," he responded as he turned out of the parking lot and started driving toward WAAR.

"Thanks. Where are we staying tonight?"

Cruz shrugged his shoulders. "Doesn't matter to me. I'm good as long as you're sleeping next to me."

"Your place," I decided as we pulled into the parking lot where my car sat. Before I got out of the truck, I asked, "Can we stop at my apartment so I can pick up a few things first though?"

"Sure. We can leave your car there, too. There's no sense in you driving to my place separately."

That worked for me. "Okay."

With our plans decided, I got out and hopped in my car. We drove to my place, where I packed up a few things before Cruz drove us to his place. On the way, I called Luke and confirmed that he and Nikki were going to be around later in the evening.

Since we had time before we'd need to leave his place, Cruz and I found a creative way to spend it.

A couple hours later, I told Luke and Nikki what happened roughly twenty-four hours before. They were shocked, but relieved I was sitting there.

When Cruz and I got back to his place relatively late that night, we were both exhausted. Climbing into bed, Cruz tucked me close to his side, kissed the bare skin at my shoulder, and whispered, "Love you, princess."

"Love you, too, captain."

CHAPTER 27

Cruz

"DO YOU WANT THE GOOD NEWS OR THE BAD NEWS?"

I looked up from my desk and saw Trent standing in the doorway.

It was late Wednesday afternoon. Monday was my first full day back after taking off last Friday, Saturday, and Sunday. I spent those days mostly with Lexi. After spending most of the day running around on Friday visiting the station, stopping into the office, picking up her car, and visiting with both of her brothers, we spent a quiet day together on Saturday. On Sunday, Lexi had plans to meet up with her mom, so I dropped her off at her parents' place for a few hours while I came to the office to get some work done. She called me when she was ready to leave and I went back to pick her up.

She'd been staying at my house since Thursday night and her car was back at her apartment. I didn't mind driving her around and she seemed content with it. The truth was that I was still very unsettled about the whole situation. The WPD had three guys in custody, but were no further along in solving the case.

While it seemed that money would be the reason behind what was happening, it didn't make sense that Grant got involved for that reason. He was the senior vice president of a major corporation and he made a ton of money. Given what we learned about him over the last few days from Logan and by doing some further research into him, he was a devoted husband and a loving father.

I couldn't deny that I'd been feeling particularly frustrated over the course of the last several weeks. Once this situation escalated to the point that Lexi was targeted, frustrated was no longer the word to described how I felt. I was angry. Lexi seemed to be handling the situation remarkably well, but I waited each day for her to break down. I began wondering if the time was going to come where she would suddenly realize how lucky she was that we were able to get to her in time. And, if I was being honest, it had me acting particularly cautious around her. I simply didn't want to bring that pain on her.

Of course, there was the possibility that I was waiting around for something that wasn't going to happen. On Monday, Lexi did go to visit with Dr. Lane. Logan met her there. He had already been consumed with so much guilt over her rape. With this new situation thrown into the mix, he was feeling particularly responsible for it. It was my hope that the meeting was not only going to help Logan, but also Lexi if there was anything mentally harmful lingering there for her.

With everything happening in my head, I wasn't sure I wanted the bad news that Trent had to deliver.

"Give me something good," I answered.

"They got them."

"What?"

His arms were folded over his chest as he leaned into the door jamb with one ankle crossed in front of the other. Aside from that, he had a smug look plastered on his face. He explained, "I'm guessing you're going to be receiving a call from Detective Baines sometime soon."

"They found the women?" I pushed for more information.

Trent nodded and clarified, "I've been following the updates that are coming through the system I rigged up to monitor what was happening out in Colorado. All of the women were rescued."

"All of them. Are you telling me that every missing woman associated with this case has been recovered?"

"Every single one of them."

Good news.

I needed that.

Unfortunately, I guess I needed to know the bad.

"So, what don't I want to hear?"

He sighed. "They've got the women, but there were no suspects recovered."

I sat back in my chair and exhaled. "We're back at square one then."

"Looks like it," Trent maintained. "There was enough information to lead them there, but I'm guessing they had an idea the authorities were on to them. They left quick. And the women are so terrified, they're not saying much."

"Anything else?"

He shook his head, a wave of disappointment washing over his face.

Just then, my cell phone rang. I assumed it was Detective Baines, but looked at the display and saw Pierce's number.

"Reynolds?" I started. "What's up?"

"I need backup. Grant Chambers' residence. His daughters got home from school twenty minutes ago. His wife left shortly after lunch, but hasn't returned home yet. Two black SUVs just pulled up, four men got out."

"On it," I returned, already moving to the door. "You got anyone with you?"

"Negative. I called Locke before you; I knew he was close. He's five minutes out."

"We're five minutes behind him. Be smart," I instructed before disconnecting the call.

Looking at Trent, I declared, "Trouble just drove up to the Chambers' home."

I gave him the details as quickly as I could as Levi walked up.

"Let's move," Levi ordered.

At that point, Dom and Lorenzo were already moving to the front door. I called out to them and Dom yelled back, "Locke called and briefed us."

Dom and Lorenzo pulled out of the lot ahead of me; Levi was behind me. No sooner did we pull out when Trent called all of us and informed us that the GPS tracker on Pierce's vehicle was on the move.

Trent got Pierce in on the call.

"They walked up to the door, one of the girls opened and was immediately hauled out. Two of the men barged inside, found the other girl, and carried her out."

"Any witnesses that you noticed?"

"That neighborhood is quiet. Everyone is at work."

We stayed connected throughout the drive until Pierce finally informed us, "We're outside Mile High Motorsports."

"What?" I asked, utterly confused. "What the hell are they doing there?"

Noting I was still five minutes out from the destination, I ordered, "Michaels, bring Logan Townsend in on this call."

Not even a minute later, I heard, "Hello?"

"Logan, it's Cruz."

"Is Lexi okay?" he instantly worried.

"She's fine. Do you know anything about Mile High Motorsports?"

"I don't know what shady shit they're into, but they sell stuff ridiculously cheap and do awful work. The legitimate businesses in the industry wouldn't be able to sustain themselves at the prices those guys sell at. My guess is they do it all as a cover for something illegal."

"Do you have a name for the owner?"

"They call him Slick; I have no idea what his real name is."

"I'll see what I can find out," Trent chimed in.

Pulling up behind where Pierce and Holden were parked, I announced "I've got to go, Logan. Thanks for your help."

"No problem," he responded before disconnecting.

The guys and I were all out of the car, keeping ourselves hidden, getting an update from Pierce.

"It looks like it's normal business hours right now, so there have been customers going in and out through the front door. They pulled around the back side of the building. Nobody here would know they had those girls."

We quickly came up with a plan and put it into action. First, Dom and Holden were going to go in through the front door and check out the place. They were both interested in motorsports, so they'd be able to pull off playing the part of potential clients. Once we got confirmation from them from inside, we'd figure out how to implement our plan for going in through the back to get the girls.

A few minutes after they were inside, Holden sent us text updates and let us know that there was still one other customer inside who was paying for some parts. Thankfully, there were only two guys working in the front showroom, though. We had no clue how many people were working in the garage and who, if anyone, was in the warehouse.

While we waited for more news from our guys inside, Levi grabbed our attention. "Back of the building. Three guys walking to the black SUVs. Are they the ones from the Chambers' residence, Reynolds?"

"Yeah," he confirmed. "Looks like one guy is hanging back with the girls."

"De Luca," Levi called. "You're with me. We'll follow them."

Levi and Lorenzo took off behind the SUVs just as Holden came outside.

With a grin on his face, he shared, "Dom's getting a tour."

"How'd he manage to pull that off?" Pierce asked.

Holden shrugged his shoulders and threw out, "You know him. He can bullshit with the best of them."

"Why are you out here?"

"I told them I needed to step out and call my wife before I made any purchases."

"You don't have a wife," I pointed out.

"Yeah, but they don't know that and it's a perfectly plausible excuse. These guys hear it all the time."

Pierce put his phone to his ear and waited a minute before he said, "Three of our four guys in the SUVs just came out the back. Holden's with us. If you're good in there, we're heading in through the back."

We waited a moment while Pierce listened.

Pulling the phone away from the side of his head, he looked at us and confirmed, "Dom's good."

The three of us moved to the back of the building and found the door had been left propped open. This led us to believe that someone would be returning.

Looking in, I could see Grant's daughters bound to chairs, crying and terrified. There was nobody else around; however, I couldn't see the rest of the space.

Just as I was about to cautiously open the door and look around, a guy in a suit walked over to where the girls were sitting.

"That's one of the guys that picked them up," Pierce hissed.

Suddenly, he started speaking and, thankfully, he was doing it loud enough for us to hear.

"There's no need to cry," he taunted them. "I expect Mommy is going to do what she needs to do to see to it that you get home safe tonight."

"Who are you? What do you want from our mom?" one of the girls asked.

He laughed and clarified, "I don't want anything from her. My boss wants what your father owes him."

"Our dad is away on business," the other girl cried. "Who is your boss?"

He walked over closer to her, pressed his fingers to her forehead, and pushed her hair back from her face. "Darling, your father is not away on business. He's been in prison since last weekend."

"What?" she whispered.

He nodded at the girls and explained, "Yeah, he was about to deliver something for my boss that would have helped to repay his debt, but the delivery was foiled. My boss is done waiting for his payment, and since dear old Daddy is unavailable now, we're just going to have to get your mom to pay up."

"What debt? I…I don't understand."

"Your dad loves to gamble," he started. "And it just so happens he's lost a lot of money that he needs to pay back."

Gambling debt. That explained it.

Moving his hand to the other sister's cheek, he wondered, "So, how much do you think you're worth? Will Mommy pay the four million two hundred and sixty-three thousand dollars owed for the two of you? Or are we going to have to auction you off?"

The girls' eyes rounded and I'd had enough.

"Tell Michaels to call it in," I ordered.

Once the call was made, I wasted no time. I moved in quickly and quietly, doing my best to remain focused on him, but also wanting to take in my surroundings. I knew my guys would cover me, though. I was only a few steps away when I caught the attention of the guy. He tried to pull out his weapon, but he wasn't fast enough. I managed to take him down and neutralize him. There was nobody else in the warehouse.

By the time I looked up, Pierce and Holden already had the girls free and were moving them out. I decided to collect more information.

"Who's your boss?"

No response.

"I hate to break it to you, but protecting him at this point isn't going to do you any good. The police are on their way. If you give me a name, I might be willing to talk them into taking it easy on you for cooperating."

Still nothing.

"Is it Slick?"

He reacted. It was quick, but it was enough.

"Where can I find him?"

Just then, I heard the sirens in the distance.

"Looks like your time is just about up," I goaded him. "This is your last chance to help yourself."

"Fuck you!"

Realizing I wasn't going to get anywhere with him, I shrugged my shoulders and stood. "Suit yourself."

Minutes later, the place was swarming with cops, questioning the girls, cuffing the guy I'd taken down who still refused to talk, and talking with the sales guys in the showroom. Detective Baines arrived on the scene and sought me out.

"Mrs. Chambers was at the station when she got a text showing her daughters bound to chairs," he informed me.

"Wait," I started. "She was there *before* the text came in?"

He nodded and explained, "Apparently, she got home and realized her daughters weren't there. Her eldest daughter's car was there, but neither of the girls were. She was alarmed, but called them first. When their phones started ringing inside the house and they were nowhere to be found, she knew something wasn't right."

"Are we sure we believe her story?"

"Yeah," he began. "This woman was distraught. I was just as skeptical, but when she said that the phones were home, I knew. Teenagers rarely go anywhere willingly without their phones. Add to that the fact that we have Grant Chambers in custody and he's apparently pissed someone off, I believe her."

"It's gambling debt," I blurted.

"What?"

"He owes over four and a quarter million dollars to someone named Slick, who apparently owns this shop. My guess is that, based on the name, he's got another operation in Colorado."

"The guy makes *really* good money at his legitimate job," Detective Baines noted. "Enough that it'd hurt, but he could have paid this debt. It makes no sense that he'd want to get involved in setting up a sex trafficking ring and bring this kind of trouble down on himself and his family."

"Did she know?" I asked.

"Who?"

"His wife," I clarified. "Did she know he was locked up? Because his daughters believed he was away on business. My guess is that if they had that kind of money to part with, even if Mrs. Chambers wasn't involved in the day-to-day finances, she'd notice more than four million dollars missing."

Detective Baines rolled his eyes. "So, his pride got the better of him and instead of admitting he had a gambling addiction that they could have possibly worked through, he put them at risk."

"Classic case, I'm guessing?"

Baines let out a chuckle, "Yep. Good guy thinks he can fix his mistake caused by bad decisions by simply making more really bad decisions. Deep down, he was probably a good guy trying to protect his family. Unfortunately, especially for his daughters, I don't see him walking free any time soon."

I sighed. It was a shame.

"Listen, if you're good, I've got to make a call to Michaels to see where Levi and Lorenzo are. They were here and took off a bit ago to follow the three other suspects. I want to make sure they're good."

He shook his head, "They're good. They apprehended those guys and I have units there already."

"Not a bad day's work," I joked.

"Thanks, Cruz," he returned. "You know we've got a small force, so we'd have been scrambling on this case and been stretched way too thin."

I offered him a chin lift and expressed, "You know we'll always do what we can to help overcome the bad. Besides, sometimes I need a little action like this. Real estate and insurance fraud cases can become a bit mundane."

He laughed and instructed, "Get out of here. We'll talk soon."

"See you later."

I met up with the rest of my team, talked for a few minutes with them, and got in my truck to head home. It had been a long few days and while the case wasn't completely closed, it was certainly getting closer. At least now the WPD knew where to start looking for the ringleader of the operation.

They'd have to call in other police departments in Colorado and hopefully they'd be able to collectively bring down this guy Slick.

In the meantime, I knew my team and I would stay alert. Keeping our locals, like Frank Jenkins, informed would only help to keep Windsor safe. For me personally, I'd stay extra vigilant in making sure those I loved stayed safe, especially my warrior.

As thoughts of her filled my mind, I found myself eager to get back home. It was late, much later than I had been getting home recently. Pulling my phone out, I called Lexi.

"Hey captain," she answered cheerfully. "Is everything okay?"

"All good, warrior. I'm on my way home now. Are we at my place or yours tonight?" I asked.

"Mine," she answered.

"See you in about fifteen," I returned.

"Ok, be careful. Love you."

"Love you, too."

At that, I started my truck and drove to Lexi's place. Fourteen minutes later, I had her in my arms.

CHAPTER 28

Lexi

"I THINK I'M GOING TO HEAD OUT EARLY, CAPTAIN."

"You're going to my place, right?" he confirmed.

"Yeah," I responded. "Does that still work for you?"

He chuckled before he answered with his own question, "Do you really think you even need to ask me that?"

I didn't, but I still liked asking because he always laughed when I did. And lately, I found that I was craving more and more of carefree Cruz. Of course I loved his overprotective nature and the fact that he always put my needs before his own, but seeing him relaxed sometimes was nice.

"I'll see you soon then?" I confirmed.

"I'm just finishing up a few loose ends and then I'm leaving," he stated. "I should be there maybe forty-five minutes or so after you get there."

"Ok," I started. "Love you."

"Love you, Lexi."

Cruz and I disconnected and I immediately gathered my things and left my office. I had a plan and I didn't have much time to prepare.

It had been four weeks since I was kidnapped and nearly tossed into a sex trafficking ring. It was also roughly three and a half weeks since Cruz and the rest of his team managed to rescue Grant Chambers' daughters, who may have been facing the same fate. The day the Chambers girls were rescued, Cruz learned the real reason Grant got caught up in the sex trafficking ring. Since then, all I knew was that Grant's wife set things up so that she and her daughters would have private, personal security to keep them safe until the man Grant owed from his gambling debt was caught.

My life over the last couple of weeks had settled down a bit. Work was steady—Elle was getting ready to go out on her mini-tour soon, Wes had contacted me about the promotion of the surfboard line he was planning to launch in the next few weeks, Leni was finally set up in her yoga studio, and I was getting referrals for new clients on a weekly basis.

I had been worried that after the situation with Grant and the fact that he'd taken women from WAAR that the center was going to be shut down. Thankfully, the owner of Glazier's Supply refused to allow that to happen. Not only did he terminate Grant, but he also saw to it that every penny that had been donated to WAAR was, in fact, used for legitimate means. Learning that two hundred and fifty thousand dollars had been taken from those donations and used for Grant's illegal activities, Mr. Glazier put that money back into the center out of his own personal funds. He hated what Grant did, but knew, with a little convincing from me, that WAAR was fundamental in helping so many women heal from such horrific situations.

So, to ensure the safety of the women at WAAR, Mr. Glazier hired Cunningham Security to install security and surveillance. Cruz and a few of the guys came in to get everything set up and extreme care was taken to see to it that none of the women were left alone or in a room where the guys were working. Of course, I knew that every single one of those men would have taken a bullet to protect any one of the women inside, but those women didn't know that. We could have shouted it from the rooftops and it wouldn't have made any difference to them since so many of them were there so soon after their sexual assault. When all was said and done, though, WAAR had twenty-four-hour surveillance that was monitored back at the Cunningham Security offices.

Then there was my personal life.

For the most part, things were going extremely well. My relationship with my parents was out of the awkward stage. I knew they never intentionally tried to make it awkward, but part of that was my own insecurity about how they'd handle the news of learning their daughter had been raped. I guess it was par for the course, but treading lightly was something I could no longer do. The weekend following the kidnapping, Cruz dropped me off at my parents' house and I had several hours to talk with both of them, but mostly my mom. It was incredibly beneficial and they were both finding a way to move quickly past the guilt.

While Luke was managing his feelings about everything I'd been through over the last few years rather well, Logan had been having a particularly difficult time. Once he learned what Grant did, the burden of guilt Logan felt grew exponentially. I immediately got the both of us in to see Dr. Lane and we'd been visiting her regularly. I knew it would take time for him to completely let go of the blame, but we found those sessions were tremendously helpful.

And finally, there was Cruz.

Things between the two of us were great. He was, as always, charming and sweet while being protective and nurturing. Best of all, he loved me. Everything about me. He loved me when I was worried or scared. He loved me when I was playful or teasing. And he loved me as ferociously as I did him.

But there was that one thing.

One little thing that was still wedged between us.

And today I was going to do something about it.

It had been gone for me the moment I gave myself to him, but I needed it gone for him, too. Permanently.

So, I pulled up in the driveway outside his house, parked, shut off my car, dug out the key he'd given me several weeks ago, grabbed my bag filled with the items necessarily to pull off my plan, and went inside.

Then, I hightailed it to the bedroom. I dumped my bag and my purse on the bed and moved to the bathroom. Unable to waste a shred of time, I started stripping out of my clothes before I could walk across the room and turn on the shower. I quickly made it there and turned the water on. As it warmed up, I threw off the last of my clothing and took one of my makeup remover wipes to my face.

Over the last few weeks I'd been slowly leaving little things at Cruz's place. Things like makeup wipes, lotions, extra clothes, and a few accessories. He didn't seem to mind and, because I enjoyed being here with him more than at my own place, I took advantage of that. In fact, Cruz not only didn't mind, but every time I saw his face when he realized I'd brought over something new, his lips would twitch and he'd fight to not break out into a full-blown grin.

With my makeup off and the temperature of the water perfect, I hopped in and got down to business. I did what I had to do as quickly as I could and got out. Once I had dried myself off, I ran out into the bedroom and looked at my phone. I had twenty minutes until Cruz was going to be home.

I darted back into the bathroom, where I dried my hair and slathered on my lotion. When I finished, I went back out into the bedroom and pulled the sexy nightie from my bag. After putting it on with three minutes to spare, I settled myself in the middle of the bed and waited.

While I waited, I did my best to control my breathing. I knew what was ahead and I only hoped it wouldn't blow up in my face.

I'm certain it wasn't more than two or three minutes later when I heard the garage door open, though it felt like hours had passed. It took a bit longer than I expected it would for the door to chime indicating that Cruz had finally come inside. I listened to the sound of his footsteps as he moved through the house.

"Lexi," I heard him call from the bottom of the stairs.

Clearing my throat, I called back, "I'm in the bedroom."

"Where are your keys?" he retorted.

Seriously?

This could not be happening right now.

When Cruz gave me a key for his place several weeks ago, he also gave me one of his garage door openers. He insisted that I pull my car into the garage, but I couldn't bring myself to do it. He had a single-car garage and I didn't think it was fair for me to take the space that was his.

Most days, he'd eventually end up going outside and moving my car in, but of course today he felt the need to do it immediately.

"They're up here," I answered.

Then I heard his footfalls as he climbed the stairs. With each step he took, my heart started pounding a little faster. There was such nervousness running through my body.

Cruz started talking before he made it to the room. "I keep telling you to pull your car into the garage and somehow I end up being the one..." he trailed off as he stepped inside his bedroom.

He swallowed hard as he remained frozen on the spot and took me in.

I smiled sweetly at him.

His brows pulled together and he asked, "Did I forget something?"

Letting out a little laugh, I shook my head.

"You look so pretty, Lexi," he said softly.

Flashing a coy smile, I teased, "I think I've heard that once or twice from you before."

Cruz chuckled, unstuck himself from the spot where he was standing, and walked toward me. He sat on the edge of the bed, leaned forward putting one hand behind my head, and pulled me in for a kiss.

It was delightful.

When he pulled back, he held my eyes briefly before letting his eyes wander down my body. He did not attempt to hide the fact that he appreciated what he saw.

As his eyes met mine again, I shared, "I was hoping to do something with you today."

Cruz gave me a disbelieving look and insisted, "You don't need to hope for that. I'm always a willing participant."

I shook my head and clarified, "Let me rephrase that. I was hoping to do something a little different with you today."

His eyes narrowed a bit as his head tilted to the side. "I'm curious as to what you have in mind, but I'm guessing if you being in this is part of it, I'm not going to have a problem with it."

"I hope that's true," I wished. Clearing my throat, I held out the long piece of satin fabric and rasped, "I want you to tie my wrists above my head and have your way with me, Cruz."

"Warrior," he whispered.

He was silent for a long time, his eyes moving from the fabric in my hands, to my eyes, back to the fabric, down to my body, and back to my face.

"Lexi, you don't have to do this," he reassured me.

"I want to do this," I stated, firm and strong. "I don't want him between us when we're with each other this way. I let go of that the first time we were together and it's been beautifully perfect every single time with you since then. But I know you're holding yourself back. Sometimes, you lose control for just a few seconds and it's magical. You are always quick to reign it back in and I truly appreciate your reasons for doing that. But I don't want that anymore. I want you wild and uninhibited with me."

"I'm not going to do something that will hurt you," he replied, his voice thick with emotion.

"If I didn't know that, I wouldn't be sitting here asking you to do this. You've always made me feel like a princess. I love it. I love that you're sweet and gentle. But I also love that you see me as a warrior, as someone who is strong and completely capable of being able to conquer anything that stands to knock me down. I know I want this, but I can't force you. That doesn't mean I won't give it everything I've got to convince you otherwise."

He remained silent, the muscle in his jaw working.

"Overcome this last battle with me, captain. Don't allow this to stand between us any longer. I've given you all there is of me to give and you are holding on to that piece of you that I've only gotten a small glimpse of before now. I want all of you, Cruz. Sweet, tender, loving, wild, and most of all, uninhibited. Please bind my wrists above my head and give me that last piece of you."

I had nothing left to say, so I waited.

After several long, agonizing moments, Cruz lifted the satin from my hands and urged, "Lie down and put your arms over your head."

The nerves I'd been feeling left me and all that was left was pure excitement. Cruz was going to give this to us. My heart was no longer just beating fast. It was fast and loud and I loved everything about it.

I did as Cruz wished and fell to my back. Once my arms were over my head, he took the time to carefully wrap the soft fabric around my wrists and through the thin opening in the wood frame of his headboard. Every so often, his glittering eyes looked into mine, confirming I was not in any distress. There was such a look of awe and approval on his face. It was easily a mix of him wondering how it was possible we were at this point knowing my past and how proud he was that we were here.

"Comfortable?" he asked when he finished securing my wrists.

I nodded, feeling a few lingering nerves in my belly.

"You don't feel any pain, right?"

I shook my head.

Leaning over the side of the bed, he removed his shoes and socks before sitting up and lifting his shirt over his head.

Cruz brought his finger to the side of my head and tapped. "And everything feels okay here, too, right?"

I hesitated.

Did it?

"Yes, I think so," I finally breathed with a bit of caution.

"One word, Lex. You still have that," he reassured me. "You *always* have that."

"I know," I confirmed. "Will you hold my hand a minute?"

Cruz's hand came up and his fingers interlocked with mine. I closed my eyes and took a few deep breaths. I didn't want to say that word and I had felt so confident going into this. Being here now had me a bit on edge and I needed a minute to collect myself.

"Princess?" he called softly.

"You're here with me, captain. It's just you and me," I said, knowing I was doing it for the both of us.

"I'm always here with you, Lexi," he returned.

"Can you do one more thing for me before I give you complete control?" I asked.

"Anything."

"Kiss me while you hold my hands like this," I urged.

So he did. And that's when those last few nerves I felt vanished.

After kissing me, Cruz pulled back and took me in.

He gave me a gentle smile.

When I returned the gesture, his gaze turned wickedly sexy. One of his hands left mine and a single finger began tracing a path down along my hairline, the side of my throat, and over my collarbone. That finger traced over the swell of my breast before his whole hand cupped and squeezed it.

I let out a ragged moan, so beyond turned on in just the few seconds he'd had one hand on my body. And once that sound escaped from the back of my throat, Cruz acted. He took teasing to a level I didn't know was possible nor had I anticipated. Other than the one time he squeezed my breast, he didn't touch either one again. And he never went near the spot between my legs.

Actually, he did.

He went near it.

Very close to it.

With his hands, his lips, and his tongue.

But he never touched me there.

My hips were writhing, my body on fire, and Cruz was content to take his time teasing. He opened the fabric of the nightie that was tied behind my neck and removed it from my body. Up to that point I thought all of the kissing and touching was erotic. It was, but it didn't even come close to being nearly as stimulating as it was to be there in his bed, unable to get up, watching him as he looked at me.

Like I was meant to be treasured yet devoured.

Like I could grant his every wish just by allowing him to claim me this way.

Like I was not only a princess, but also a warrior.

When he finally stood up beside the bed and removed his jeans and boxer briefs, I thought I was going to explode.

"Tell me what you want, Lexi," he ordered as he began rolling a condom on.

"You," I replied, my voice full of desperation.

"You already have me. I want to know what you want *from* me."

I moistened my lips with my tongue as Cruz's eyes drifted to my mouth. Then, I answered, "I want you to hold my hips in your hands while you power your cock into me, hard and fast without any inhibitions, until I come."

He cocked an eyebrow at me and asked, "What if I didn't want to do that?"

I pouted.

And I didn't care one bit.

Cruz laughed and wondered, "What's wrong, princess?"

I squeezed my legs together, frantically trying to relieve some of the sexual tension. Cruz saw it and wrapped his hands around the backs of my thighs. He separated them and settled himself between them.

When I whimpered at the aching pulse, he questioned, "Is that how you really want this to go? With you delivering your own orgasm?"

I shook my head, wiggled my hips, arched my back, and begged, "Please, Cruz."

Cruz brought his hand to my core, found I was more than ready for him, and finally, gave in.

And he did it exactly like I had asked.

Hard.

Fast.

Without any inhibitions.

I was so worked up it only took a matter of seconds for me to come and it was one of the most powerful orgasms I'd ever had.

Cruz didn't relent as I came down.

"Did you like that?"

"Yes."

Continuing to power into me, he went on, "You're going to do it again, Lexi, okay? You want that again?"

"Yes," I panted. "Please, yes."

From there, Cruz worked me hard and it built. He moved with such abandoned power. With no ability to use my own hands to get us there, I relished the feel of his hands cradling my hips, his fingertips digging in as he worked to help us both climb higher and higher.

And I knew in this moment that I never had to be afraid of anything with Cruz. I knew he'd always be that support not just for me, but for the two of us together, doing whatever was necessary to take us where we needed to go. And because I trusted him, I'd allow him to continue to steer my ship.

The physical sensations coupled with my emotional state had me on the verge again. I cried out, "Oh, Cruz."

My body trembled in his hands as his pace grew quicker. Suddenly, one of his hands left my hip as he fell forward and reached for my hand. He planted himself to the root and claimed my mouth. Cruz groaned through his orgasm, while I committed the sound to memory. He pulled his mouth from mine, as the pleasure moved through him, and buried his face in my neck. I felt his body still above me, fighting to regain his breath, and I knew, for as long as I lived, I'd never forget what this experience did for me.

What Cruz did for me.

I was so overwhelmed with joy and happiness that I never dreamed I'd have again, that a sob escaped.

Cruz immediately lifted his head and worried, "Are you okay?"

I nodded through my tears and barely got out, "Perfect."

His hand left my hip and came up to wipe away my tears while he pressed tender kisses to my cheek.

"Love you, warrior," he whispered in between two of them.

"Love you, captain."

Cruz pulled himself from my body and immediately moved to release my wrists. Once they were free, he brought them to his mouth, where he delicately kissed my palms and my wrists.

"Be right back," he promised before he got up from the bed and moved to the bathroom to dispose of the condom.

When he came back into the room, he fell to his back in the bed and I instantly curled my body into his. I needed to touch him. He left me to it for a long while.

"This meant everything to me, Lexi," he divulged.

"Me too."

"If all we had was what we had before this, I would have been a very happy man. Having this, knowing you trust me with your mind and your body like this, means something I can't even begin to describe," he added.

The arm I had draped over his abdomen gave him a gentle squeeze and I shared, "You earned it. You were patient and helped me get back so much of myself that was missing, so much that I couldn't get back on my own."

"I know you think that I did something incredible, but it pales in comparison to what you gave me. Other than your love, there's no greater gift."

"Cruz," I rasped.

He just squeezed me a little tighter in response.

For the next half hour, we stayed there with our naked

bodies pressed against one another. I broke the silence and called, "Hey, captain?"

"Yeah?"

I lifted my cheek from his chest and looked at him when I asked, "Can we do that again some time?"

A smile formed on his face. "I prefer when your hands are free to touch me, but if you want to be restrained again, we can do that on occasion. That said, you can expect wild and uninhibited on a regular basis, princess."

Now it was my turn to smile.

With that, Cruz instigated round two. It was soft, gentle, but filled with just as much passion.

It was after when I realized just how lucky I was to have met him. A few months ago, I knew I would have gotten nearly every part of myself I'd lost four years ago back. But there was that one missing piece, that one thing that I wasn't sure I'd ever have again. And while I knew that Cruz believed I gave it to myself, I could diminish the role he played in it. Not just anyone would have been up to the task. I felt truly fortunate that he chose to walk down a difficult road believing I was worth it.

In the end, I gave him not just my body, but also my trust. And in doing that, I couldn't help but to give him my heart. Luckily for me, I knew that Cruz would stand beside me no matter what was ahead and together we'd overcome any obstacle that came our way.

EPILOGUE

Cruz

One Year Later

"It never fails," I muttered under my breath to myself as I pulled into the driveway at my house.

I'd been trying, and failing, for more than a year now to get Lexi to pull her car into the garage whenever she was at my place. There were many occasions when she'd arrive here after work ahead of me; however, she refused to pull her car in. And every single day she refused, I would get home and do it for her.

At first, it pissed me off. This was mostly because there was so much happening around us when we first got together that I didn't want her safety at risk. Of course, I didn't expect there would be any trouble at my house, but I also knew you couldn't ever be too careful. As the months went by and she continued to park outside, I was no longer pissed off about it. I'd grown to love that stubbornness.

I parked my truck, got out, and went inside.

Finding her where I always did, sitting in the oversized chair in the family room after having finished a workout and showered, I bent down and kissed her. She was always sitting there. Sometimes, she was hard at work on her laptop focusing on last-minute details for a client's upcoming project. Other times, like today, she'd just be watching television.

"Keys?" I asked when I pulled my mouth from hers.

"On the island," she answered.

"You really need to start pulling your car in, you know?" I repeated the same thing I'd said to her every other time before that.

Just as she always did, she looked up at me with her almond-shaped, brown eyes and pointed out, "No, I don't. I have you."

At that, I stood up and moved back to the kitchen to get her keys. After pulling her car into the garage, I closed the door and came back inside.

I went back to the family room, picked her up, and settled her in my lap in the chair. She cuddled into me and we watched the rest of whatever show she was watching. I wasn't really paying attention, though, because I was considering what I was preparing to talk to her about.

When the show ended, she pulled her head back and looked at me. "How was work?" she asked.

"Nothing exciting to report," I remarked.

She gave me a nod and continued, "Are you ready for dinner?"

I dipped my chin in acknowledgment and said, "Yeah, but first, I need to talk to you about something."

I felt her body tense.

"Nothing is wrong," I started. "But I really need to discuss this situation regarding the car in the garage."

She rolled her eyes at me.

"It's not a big deal, Cruz."

"It is to me," I maintained. "All winter long you refused to do it and then had to trudge through the snow whenever you got here just to get inside. I don't like that."

Her shoulders slumped. "I love how chivalrous you are, captain, but I'm not taking *your* spot."

"Princess, in case you hadn't noticed, I haven't been parking in the garage for more than a year now because *I* keep pulling your car into *your* spot."

"This isn't my house," she returned softly.

"Why the fuck not?" I pushed. "You're here practically all the time as it is."

She jerked back and murmured, "Oh. I just…I like being here with you."

Damn it.

"Lexi, I didn't mean it the way you took it. I just meant that this house is just as much yours as it is mine. I love having you here."

"But it's not mine and I'm not going to park there. If you put my car there, that's different," she reasoned.

I sighed. "Then I guess that leaves us only one option."

"Which is?"

"We're going to have to move," I stated.

"Move?" she questioned.

"Move," I repeated.

She stared at me, a bit shell-shocked. "You want us to not only officially move in together, but you want us to do that while buying a house that we'll own together?"

I looked at her a bit suspiciously and wondered, "Are you thinking there's someone else out there with whom you'd rather buy a house and live?"

"What? No," she rebutted.

"So why are you even the least bit surprised right now?"

Her head moved slowly back and forth before she answered, "I just didn't realize we were at that point in our relationship."

"You love me and you want to be with me, right?"

She nodded.

"I love you and want to be with you," I noted. "I'm not

sure if you think there's some appropriate amount of time that needs to pass before we can get serious about our future. I'm happy to discuss it now, though."

Her face got soft and her voice was sweet when she asked, "You want a future with me?"

"Lexi, I bought you a ring two months ago," I blurted. "I was going to wait until we went on vacation to propose, but I'm just as happy to put it on your finger right this minute if that helps you realize how serious I am about spending the rest of my life with you in a house that you don't constantly refer to as just mine."

Lexi stared at me a minute before she dropped her face to my chest and clutched the side of my shirt in her hands. I wrapped my arms tight around her back. It was quiet for so long, I started worrying that maybe I shouldn't have thrown so much at her at once.

"Where's your head right now?"

She pulled her head back and I saw the tears that were spilling down her cheeks. I brushed them away and asked, "Why are you crying?"

"You've given me everything I never knew I wanted anymore."

"Is that a 'yes'?" I asked.

Her head dropped to one side as she countered, "Well, I'm not sure there was ever a question asked."

I immediately shot back, "Will you marry me?"

"Yes."

I framed her face in my hands and added, "You are my whole world, Lex. I'll love you forever."

"You better," she threatened. "Or there will be consequences."

I grinned at her before I kissed her, long and hard. It got hot between us pretty quick and Lexi moved to lift my shirt over my head. Sitting in my lap, it was easy for her to remove it completely. She had just barely gotten my shirt off when I sprang from the couch, with her in my arms, and yelled, "Lexi, are you crazy?!"

She burst out laughing. "I'm sorry," she giggled. "My feet were cold."

This was an ongoing thing with her. If it wasn't her hands, it was her feet. They were always ice cold and she insisted on warming them up by putting them on me when I least expected it.

I shook my head at her and wondered, "What am I going to do with you?"

She shrugged her shoulders and reminded me, "Apparently, you're just as crazy. You just asked me to marry you."

I held her in my arms and returned, "Yeah, I did."

This time, she leaned in to kiss me.

"Come on, princess" I urged when I pulled my mouth from hers. "Let's go upstairs, get my ring on your finger, and celebrate."

"Ok, captain."

With that, I carried my fiancée up the stairs, where I put my ring on her finger and followed it up with a celebration.

The next day, we started looking for our home.

Did you love this story? If so, I'd be so appreciative if you would share your thoughts in a review on Amazon or Goodreads.

Also, be sure to flip ahead to read the prologue from *Desperate*, the next installment in the Cunningham Security series.

Beyond that, find all the ways to connect with me on social media. Happy reading!!

LOVE GIVEAWAYS? Be sure to sign up for my monthly newsletter. There's something given away every month!!!

PROLOGUE

Ekko

THE CLOCK ON THE MICROWAVE INDICATED IT WAS JUST AFTER eleven-thirty at night. I had just crept down the hall to the kitchen to find something to eat. There was one can of chicken noodle soup left in my backpack, but I wouldn't be able to cook it without running the risk of waking my mom. I prayed I'd find something else in the house.

Opening the refrigerator, I saw it had nothing but beer and two-week-old leftover Chinese food inside of it. That food wasn't mine. It probably belonged to one of her men. I knew better than to take the food that didn't belong to me. The cabinets were bare, other than a few canned goods. My mother didn't keep the house stocked with food. Any money she had was spent on keeping her drunk and drugged up, which she apparently preferred over making sure she and her daughter were fed. When a man came over and they got their fix, sometimes he'd bring food. If there was enough, she'd eat.

I couldn't remember the last time she went to an actual grocery store. She might occasionally take a trip to the corner store to pick up a few things, but even those were rare.

So rare that I was in this predicament again.

Hungry.

No food in the house.

A mother who didn't care.

Sadly, I had grown used to the growling and the empty feeling I always felt in my belly these days and it looked like tonight would be another one of those nights I'd go to bed with nothing in my stomach. I hadn't had anything since lunchtime yesterday at school, which was mostly my own fault.

On that thought, I quietly made my way down the dark hallway back to my bedroom. If I hadn't spent the last two days after school at the library, I would have had enough time to come home and make the soup before my mom got home. I hated being here, so I stayed at the one place I had that gave me just a shred of peace and happiness.

The local library.

I guessed that most parents would have been worried sick if their child hadn't come home after school, but I learned quickly that the less my mother and I were around each other, the better. Wanting to avoid her after the encounter we had two nights ago, I figured it was best to just wait until I knew it was safe to come home. Thankfully, being able to sit down in a clean, comfortable chair at the library and spend hours reading never felt like a chore.

As soon as I arrived there, I quickly got any homework I had to do completed and then I spent the rest of my time reading. I consume books of nearly every genre, but my favorite is romance. I dream that one day I'll find a love like I read about in those books. That there will be a good man with whom to spend my days. That he'll stick around, unlike my own father, who walked out before I was even born. That he won't leer at young fifteen-year-old girls like the men who come around to see my mother do to me. That he'll love me, respect me, and protect me. I hope he'll make me feel like I am special. Most of all, I hope to be able to have a home with him that'll be unlike what I've lived in to this point.

That thought settled in me as I closed my bedroom door. Bedroom doesn't quite seem like the right word for it, though. There isn't even a real bed. Instead, I've got a small mattress thrown on the floor in the tiny room. There's a thin sheet covering the old mattress and a tattered, torn blanket for me to cover up with. Aside from that, I've got my backpack, a small dresser with some clothes, and a pair of worn-out sneakers.

With no other options and unable to ignore the rumbling in my stomach, I pulled the can of soup out of my backpack. I opened the front pouch that I put a plastic spoon in yesterday at school and lifted the tab on the soup can to remove the lid.

Cold soup.

It was better than nothing.

I sat in the middle of the mattress, struggling to eat slowly. It was difficult to control the urge to satisfy the hunger quickly. I forced myself not to hurry through it, though, realizing that if I could feel full on just half the can, I could save the rest for tomorrow.

As I sat there eating, my thoughts drifted to Ms. Grace. It was on nights like this when I missed her the most. Ms. Grace used to be our neighbor at the apartment building where we lived. She was an elderly, black woman who wore pretty dresses, gave incredible hugs, and treated me better than my own mother did. She didn't spend her days drunk or high on drugs. She was the kindest, most gentle soul I'd ever known. Sometimes, when my mother had one of her men over, I'd sneak out and knock on Ms. Grace's door.

"Oh, dear child," she said when she opened the door and saw me standing there for the first time. "Come inside."

I suspected she knew what was happening inside my own apartment, but she never made me feel bad about my situation. I was only seven years old the first time I knocked on her door. She allowed me to come inside, where we watched television together. We watched Jeopardy and Wheel of Fortune regularly from that point forward. And every night I managed to sneak out, she'd make sure I was fed. The first night, with me being an unexpected visitor, she made me a peanut butter and jelly sandwich. Every night after that, there was always a warm meal waiting to fill me up.

But she died six months ago.

And now I was eating cold soup, alone and in the dark.

I think she knew it was coming because two months before she passed away, she started giving me extra food to take with me.

"A snack for later," she'd insist, watching me intently until I put the food in my backpack.

Given that I was older, I didn't need to sneak out like I did when I was little. As the years went on, my mother became more and more dependent on her alcohol and drugs. She spent more time passed out than awake, so it was easy for me to make daily visits to Ms. Grace. I knew that she was the kind of person I aspired to be. She taught me what a real mother does, and it saddened me that she never had the opportunity to have children of her own.

"Wallace and I tried to have children, but it just wasn't in the cards for us," she admitted to me two years ago. "But we had each other and that was enough for us."

"Was he nice?" I asked.

She smiled, and it lit up her whole face. "He was the best man I'd ever known. In the fifty-five years we were married, there was never a single negative exchange. At least, not on his part. I had moments where I was moody as does happen to us women sometimes, and he always saw me through those times with love and tenderness. We had the occasional debate about things, but even in those discussions, he never denied me the right to my feelings. And he always made me laugh. That was the most important thing for me because what's life about if you can't laugh and be happy?"

I sighed, "I hope I can meet a man like Mr. Wallace one day."

"You will, my child. You just keep yourself focused on finishing up school and taking care of yourself. Don't get distracted by the things surrounding you. If you do what you've got to do to become the woman you want to be, he'll find you."

From that day forward, I knew I'd never forget the many lessons she imparted on me or the way she made me feel.

Now, as I sat here alone with the last can of soup I had from her, I fought the urge to break down. I missed her.

I missed her hugs.

Her kindness.

Her words.

Her company.

As much as I wanted to give in to that sadness, I didn't. I needed to stay strong and focused on what I had to do because I made a vow to myself and to her. The day I turned eighteen, I would walk away and never look back.

I wouldn't become my mother. I wouldn't choose drugs and alcohol and men over my child.

I was only a month away from turning sixteen. Then, I'd be able to get a job at the library and start saving. I'd only use what I had to just to feed myself and the rest of it would be saved. I had my plan. I only needed to wait a month to put it into action.

On that thought, halfway through my can of soup, I put the resealable top back on and laid down to sleep.

Three days later, my plan was blown to smithereens.

The police barged in and arrested my mother along with her guy of the week.

I was put into foster care.

ACKNOWLEDGEMENTS

With every book I publish, I become more aware of who is in my corner. And it never fails. My husband and my two beautiful boys. Thank you for supporting me in this journey. There are never enough words to tell you all how much you mean to me. I love you.

To Megan—I appreciate all that you do. Your input on the story was invaluable. And thank you for sneaking into buildings just to send me your thoughts on the story! I can't wait to see what's next.

To N, KP, JC, and the rest of the Inkslinger team—Thank you for allowing me to be part of such a wonderful family of authors. I'm truly honored to be in such good company. The appreciation I feel regarding your loyalty, hard work, and dedication to your clients goes beyond what words could ever express. Thank you.

To my ARC Team Members—You are rock stars! Thank you for believing in me and my work enough to want to be part of my team. I appreciate all of you.

To the book bloggers—There are too many to list, but I see each and every one of you. Thank you for taking your valuable time to recommend and share my work. It does not go unnoticed.

And to my loyal readers—Thank you for continuing to support me in my dream. It means everything to me.

OTHER BOOKS BY A.K. EVANS

The Everything Series

Everything I Need
Everything I Have
Everything I Want
Everything I Love
Everything I Give

The Cunningham Security Series

Obsessed
Overcome
Desperate
Solitude
Burned
Unworthy
Surrender
Betrayed
Revived

Road Trip Romance

Tip the Scales
Play the Part
One Wrong Turn
Just a Fling
Meant to Be
Take the Plunge
Miss the Shot
In the Cards (Coming April 6, 2021)

CONNECT WITH A.K. EVANS

To stay connected with A.K. Evans and receive all the first looks at upcoming releases, latest news, or to simply follow along on her journey, be sure to add or follow her on social media. You can also get the scoop by signing up for the website newsletter.

The newsletter is delivered once a month, sometimes twice, and includes a monthly giveaway. Be sure to sign up:on my website.

Website: www.authorakevans.com

Facebook: www.facebook.com/authorAKEvans

Facebook Reader Group: www.facebook.com/groups/1285069088272037

Instagram: www.instagram.com/authorakevans

Twitter: twitter.com/AuthorAKEvans

Goodreads Author Page: www.goodreads.com/user/show/64525877-a-k-evans

Subscribe on YouTube: bit.ly2w01yb7

ABOUT A.K. EVANS

A.K. Evans is a married mother of two boys residing in a small town in northeastern Pennsylvania. After gradfuating from Lafayette College in 2004 with two degrees (one in English and one in Economics & Business), she pursued a career in the insurance and financial services industry. Not long after, Evans realized the career was not for her. She went on to manage her husband's performance automotive business and drive the shop race cars for the next thirteen years. While the business afforded her freedoms she wouldn't necessarily have had in a typical 9-5 job, after eleven years she was no longer receiving personal fulfillment from her chosen career path. Following many discussions, lots of thought, and tons of encouragement, Andrea decided to pursue her dream of becoming a writer.

Between her day job, writing, and homeschooling her two boys, Evans is left with very little free time. When she finds scraps of spare time, Evans enjoys reading, doing yoga, watching NY Rangers hockey, dancing, and vacationing with her family. Andrea, her husband, and her children are currently working on taking road trips to visit all 50 states (though, Alaska and Hawaii might require flights).0 states (though, Alaska and Hawaii might require flights).

Printed in the USA
CPSIA information can be obtained
at www.ICGtesting.com
CBHW021923111223
2574CB00005B/41